No man had a right to look that good . . .

Chelsea closed her eyes, lulled by the sound of Nicolas's voice. There was *something* going on between them, even if she didn't know what it was. An incredible feeling of peace suffused her body, relaxing her. . . .

"I don't understand what's happening to me. . . ."

"You will, in time." His voice was low and soothing. "But you'll have to look into the past. Into your heart."

Chelsea shook her head. "What am I supposed to remember?"

"Perhaps this will help bring it back."

She gasped, feeling the searing heat of his mouth against her skin. But what shocked her even more was the sharp stab of desire that arced through her body. Only moments before, she'd been talking to him like a stranger. Now, all she wanted was to get close to him, as close as it was possible to be. . . .

Praise for

The Dream Spinner

"A magical tale of love in which two people were meant to be together, with a little help from the powers beyond. A true love story, which will leave you breathless and begging for more."
—*Rendezvous*

"A totally delightful story . . . a page-turning plot and a colorful setting. Gail Crease has delivered a unique tale that will leave readers smiling as they turn the last page."
—*Old Book Barn Gazette*

"*The Dream Spinner* is a beautiful contemporary updating of Rumplestiltskin. The story line is entertaining as it grips the audience with a compulsion to read it in one sitting. . . . Gail Crease modernizes the fairy tale into a wonderful adult romance."
—*Midwest Book Review*

Poseidon's Kiss

Gail Crease

JOVE BOOKS, NEW YORK

MAGICAL LOVE is a trademark of the Berkley Publishing Corporation

POSEIDON'S KISS

A Jove Book / published by arrangement with
the author

PRINTING HISTORY
Jove edition / December 2002

Copyright © 2002 by Gail Crease
Cover art by Leslie Peck
Cover design by George Long

Visit our website at
www.penguinputnam.com

ISBN: 0-515-13416-3

A JOVE BOOK®
Jove Books are published by The Berkley Publishing Group,
a division of Penguin Putnam Inc.,
375 Hudson Street, New York, New York 10014.
JOVE and the "J" design
are trademarks belonging to Penguin Putnam Inc.

PRINTED IN THE UNITED STATES OF AMERICA

10 9 8 7 6 5 4 3 2 1

My sincere thanks to Kelly Sinanis, for giving me the opportunity to write this very special love story.

Also to the Ladies of the Red Door, who, despite the ups and downs, have learned to smile, shrug, and tug elbows with the best of them. Your friendship and support have been invaluable.

Prologue

The Irish Sea, 1863

I am going to drown.

That thought came to Rebecca Lynn Mallory as clearly as though the Devil himself had whispered it in her ear. Even now, she heard his evil laughter echoed in the winds as the storm raged and the seas boiled like a cauldron of witches' brew.

Off in the distance, the great ship loomed like a shadow on the windswept waves. Only moments before, it had been her safe transport back to England. Now, it was a haven beyond reach, pushed ever farther into the night by the violence of the winds.

She was going to die. And she would never see her beloved Jeremiah again.

A jagged fork of lightning ripped open the night sky, and as thunder exploded above her head, Rebecca screamed, "I am afraid, God. Help me! Save me from this terrible night!"

But even as she prayed for a miracle, Rebecca knew there would not be one, for she had lingered too long on deck, spellbound by the power of the storm; held there as if by some mystical force, so that when the huge wave had broken over the ship, there had been no time to take shelter. Like some great black monster rising from the depths, it had unfurled its mighty arm and plucked her from the deck, and now she and the child she carried inside her were at its mercy, helpless in the grip of the demon.

In one last desperate attempt to save herself, Rebecca kicked out, fighting to keep her head above water, but her legs only became entangled in the fabric of her skirt. The weight of it dragged her down, sucking the energy from her limbs and the spirit from her soul. She felt the chilling languor of death, and knew her time was running out. But with the realization came anger. Anger that her unborn child would be made to suffer for her carelessness.

Surely a loving God will not allow such a tragedy to take place, Rebecca cried inwardly. Surely a benevolent Father would permit a mother to sacrifice her *own* life, rather than take the life of an innocent babe. For had such a sacrifice been possible, she would gladly have made it. But knowing that such things were not possible, Rebecca merely placed a hand upon her stomach and whispered a prayer for her unborn son or daughter.

Then, resolved to her fate, she closed her eyes and slipped quietly beneath the surface of the sea.

Instantly, the high keening of the winds ceased. Silence engulfed her; silence more terrifying than anything Rebecca had ever known. Awareness loomed and then receded, and in those last moments, she saw them: faint, evanescent shadows hovering at the very edge of the darkness. The angels were coming for her. She could see their brilliant robes as they floated toward her, and though she could see no wings, she knew they were coming to take her to heaven.

As a result, she felt no fear when the Radiant One swam up to her and placed gentle hands upon her arms. She had no need of eyes to see his face, nor of ears to hear his words. In her mind's eye, she saw him plainly: the deep blue eyes and perfectly sculpted mouth, the jet-black hair floating like a misty halo around his head. Indeed, so beautiful was he that even Jeremiah's mortal handsomeness could not compare, for this creature's was a magnificence that would surely cause the stars in the night sky to dim by comparison.

He spoke to her in a mellifluous voice, whispering that she need not be afraid. His words calmed her, and when Rebecca closed her eyes again, she truly *was* no longer afraid. She gazed once more into the face of the angel, offered him a prayer for forgiveness, and then gave herself up to the will of the Almighty.

Suddenly, a tremendous shudder shook the waters all around her. A deafening roar arose from the depths, and the angels fled back into the darkness until only the Radiant One remained, steadfast as he gazed at her.

When he spoke again, Rebecca was beyond understanding. She was in a different place; neither alive nor dead, neither awake nor sleeping. She thought she heard him say something about another time. Another place. A promise.

Then, as bone-chilling numbness gripped her body, she felt the touch of a hand on her left shoulder, the brush of a mouth against hers—and then nothing more, as she passed into the peaceful oblivion beyond darkness.

Part One

THE RETURN

One

The man stood on the glistening white balcony, admiring the vast expanse of water that stretched out before him like a rippling sheet of sapphire silk. Overhead, deepening shades of turquoise and rose heralded the oncoming night, and the sun dimmed as it sank toward the dark line of the horizon. A few minutes more and it would vanish completely, setting the sea on fire and turning the sky above it a deep, burnished gold.

Nikodemus's mouth curved in an unconscious smile as he watched the spectacle unfold. Was it just his imagination, or were sunsets in the Caribbean more glorious than anywhere else in the world? He knew there were those who claimed that the movements of the sun and the stars over Delphi were the equal of this, and perhaps they were, but he had always found the wonders of nature to be more breathtaking here than in the old country. The foliage was more lush, the magnificent flowers more sweetly perfumed. Even the ocean seemed more vibrant, its colors of a richer and deeper hue. Indeed, it was the verdure of this tropical atoll that had drawn him to it in the first place, though he would have been hard-pressed to say how long ago that was.

Years slipped into decades when one had no need to chart the passage of time.

"Nikodemus?"

Her gentle voice startled him, as did her sudden appearance. But then, he never knew when to expect Lysianassa. She was like the wind, drifting in when the spirit moved her, drifting out again when she grew restless or bored. She spent little time on land, which made her visits to him all the more special. Her beauty and vivacity never failed to lift his spirits, and in a world where he had to hide so much of what he was, any time spent with her was precious.

"Lysianassa!" He turned to greet her with unconcealed pleasure. "I wondered how long it would be before your wandering spirit brought you back."

She smiled as she walked toward him, a tall, slender woman with hair that fell like a ribbon of silver down her back. She wore a coral-colored tunic in the one-shouldered style of the ancient Romans, the hem of it falling to just above her ankles. Her complexion was milky, her high, exotic cheekbones hinting at Polynesian or Asian origin. But it was her eyes, thickly lashed and shimmering with the pale, iridescent light of opals, that gave her lineage away—if one knew enough to recognize the signs.

"Forgive me for startling you, Nikodemus, but in truth I did not think it was possible to," she said, her voice lightly teasing.

His smiled widened. "It is possible to startle *anyone* when they are not expecting it, and I admit I was somewhat lost in my thoughts." He raised her hands to his lips and kissed them with deep affection. "But it is good to see you back, Lysia. I have missed you these past ten months."

"Ten months? Surely it has not been so long."

"Well, perhaps not so long," he admitted sheepishly. "Perhaps I have just grown tired of my own company. But I *was* beginning to worry about you."

Her lovely eyes widened in pleasure. "You were?"

"Of course. Who else argues with me the way you do, or challenges my opinions until I am tempted to call down the wrath of the gods upon your head?"

"And here I thought you were just concerned that I had

fallen in love and run away to the other side of the world."
Lysia pouted. "I should have known you would not have
missed me for any of my more endearing qualities."

"Ah, but I do." Nikodemus tucked her hand into the crook
of his arm and led her across the wide balcony. "I miss everything about you. The sound of your laughter, the sweet sight
of your face. Even your tempestuous nature."

"Tempestuous?" Her lips twitched. "Do you truly think of
me in such a way?"

"Yes, but only in that you have a spirited, passionate out-
look on life."

She laughed openly. "Dear Nikodemus. You would have
made an excellent statesman. But I'm sure my *passionate*
nature must come as a welcome change from the blandness
of the mortals with whom you surround yourself."

"They are hardly bland, my dear." Reaching a small table
upon which a decanter and glasses were set out, Nikodemus
poured her a small glass of wine. "You would be surprised
at what strong-willed beings they have become. You might
even find yourself liking them if you were to give them a
chance."

Lysia shrugged, the gesture as graceful as it was dismis-
sive. "You have always preferred to see their noble qualities.
I see only their arrogance and greed."

"Aristotle was not a greedy man, nor Shakespeare an arrogant one," he said, handing her the glass. "Nor were Tchai-
kovsky, Beethoven, Monet, and da Vinci. They were mortals
all, and creators of some of the greatest works the world has
ever seen."

"Yes, but only think how much greater their contribution
could have been had they enjoyed the life span of a god!"
Lysia said, her bright eyes sparkling. "Think of the wonders
they could have created had they possessed the ability to
transcend generations, rather than shrivel up and die like all
things made of flesh and bone!"

"Nevertheless, you cannot belittle what contributions they
made during their brief time on earth."

"Why not? Would you trade such temporary brilliance for
the gift of immortality?"

Nikodemus closed his eyes, pinching the bridge of his nose

between thumb and forefinger. "There are times when I wonder why I have these conversations with you, Lysianassa."

"You have them because you need to be reminded of who you are!" she said vehemently. "You are so much more than these mortals, Niko, yet you choose to live among them as though you *were* one. Why? Does it fulfill something within you? Something that being the son of a god does not?"

He shook his head, wishing he could make her understand. "I cannot spend my days pursuing idle amusements, as do so many of our kind. I need to engage in activities that stimulate my mind and bring meaning to my life."

"But you do! Your art is a testament to your genius. Everyone who sees it is humbled by your brilliance. Even I, who shun the mortal world, know of your reputation. Yet why do I feel it does not make you happy?" Lysia asked, searching his face. "Why do I sense this uncertainty? This . . . restlessness within your soul?"

"Perhaps because for the first time in my life I *am* uncertain." He stood very still, gazing out across the waters that stretched as far as the eye could see. "The time has come for me to fulfill my obligation, Lysianassa. The day approaches when I must claim my bride."

She went pale, her hand trembling as she set the glass back on the table. "Mother of Zeus, so soon?"

Nikodemus sighed. "It is hardly soon. The promise I gave my father is an old one. It is not surprising that he would wish to know when I intend to honor it."

"I don't know why he bothers," Lysia muttered. "His own example as a husband and father is hardly one to be admired."

"No, but my father is a law unto himself. It is not my place to question him nor to pass judgment on his morals." Nikodemus turned from his study of the water to look at her. "But I do not think your reluctance to see me marry stems from the fact that you think *I* will make an unworthy husband."

"No, because I know you will not. Nor am I . . . reluctant to see you wed." Lysia stepped away from him and crossed her arms over her chest, hugging herself. "I will be glad to see your solitude come to an end, for I know how lonely you

have been. But I will not say I am happy about your choice."
She turned and gazed into his face, her concern for him evident. "She will not bring you happiness, Nikodemus. How can she, when she has no concept of who or what you are? She cannot live in our world. She cannot reach out her hand and command the winds to blow, or the sea to rise up in anger."

A smile tugged at his lips. "Neither can you."

"No, but *you* can. You're the son of a god!" Lysia whispered, walking back to him. "Perhaps not an Immortal like your father, but almost as powerful. What can you have in common with a mortal whose life span is but a hundred years, and whose existence is so fragile that a moment's carelessness could wipe it out?"

Nikodemus sighed. What could he say to make her understand? She knew what he had done. Just as she knew there was nothing he could do to alter the course of his destiny. "You know as well as I do that the choice is not mine to make," he said quietly. "Even if I wished to, I could not relinquish her. From the moment of her birth, her fate and mine became one."

"But she is not the one you pulled from the sea!"

"No, but she is the first female of her issue, and as such, the one who will allow me to fulfill the promise I gave my father."

"Oh, *why* did you not let that woman drown all those years ago?" Lysia cried, turning from him in frustration. "It was written that she should. The Fates had ordained it!"

He sighed. "Because I could not let it happen."

"But why? You let it happen before." Lysia's eyes searched his face, looking for answers. "It is not our place to save those who die at sea, Niko. It never has been. You must have sensed your father's anger when you intervened."

"Of course, which is why I cannot turn from my obligation now. I gave my father my word, Lysia, and I will not go back on that. As to why I saved her . . ." Nikodemus paused. How could he explain his feelings to her? How could he justify a yearning so deep it felt as though it was rooted in his soul?

He walked back to the edge of the balcony and stood there

for a long time, gazing out to sea. When he spoke again, his voice was hushed, as though he feared to say the words too loud. "What will she think of me? What will she think of a being whose existence is so totally unlike her own? I am beyond all she knows. All that she can comprehend. Yet, by virtue of who she is, she will be closer to me than any woman, mortal or goddess."

Sighing, Lysia shook her head. "I do not know, Nikodemus. How can I say what she will think, when I have no knowledge of her? But mortal or not, I have no doubt you will make her love you."

"But will love be enough?" Nikodemus's voice was strained. "When I try to reach out to her now, it is the Darkness she sees first, and that from which she recoils."

"Of course, because it is the darkness of death," Lysia said softly. "All mortals fear it. They accept it because they must, but they do not embrace it as we do. They see it not as a gateway to what lies beyond, but as an end to all they know. However, if you are to have any chance at happiness with her, you must teach her to love you, for once she does, there will be no room in her heart for fear."

Her voice broke, and Nikodemus, turning swiftly, caught the shimmer of tears in her eyes. But they were not tears of regret. They were tears of disappointment and pain, and instinctively he took a step toward her. "Lysia?"

She held up her hand, stopping him even as he would have reached for her. "No. I should not have said anything. It is not my place. I overstepped the bounds. I—"

He heard the catch in her voice again, and saw the softness in her eyes. Only then did he realize what had happened. "Lysia, forgive me," he whispered. "I didn't know—"

"Of course not," she said, gently forestalling him. "You weren't meant to know." A smile trembled over her lips. "My feelings for you are more than they should be, Niko, and that is no one's fault but my own. You did nothing to encourage me. It is simply a truth that our hearts sometimes lead us places our minds would never go. That is what mine has done, and I must accept the consequences. You owe me no apologies."

"Nevertheless, I would offer you apologies from here until

forever if I thought it would take away the pain," he said, his voice infinitely gentle. "I wouldn't hurt you for the world. You know that, don't you?"

Her expression softened. "Of course I do, just as I know how foolish it was to let my emotions become involved. I knew you were destined to be with this mortal, and if it is truly time for you to take this step, Nikodemus, then I wish you joy of it." She stood on her tiptoes and pressed a tender kiss to his mouth. "Just know that you will always have a special place in my heart, dearest, and if you ever have need of me, I will always be there."

Nikodemus heard the sadness in her voice and wished he could find the words to comfort her. She didn't deserve this. Not from him. If he'd realized what her feelings were, he would have done all he could to discourage them, for it had never been his wish to hurt her.

"One day, you will find the one who is meant for you, Lysianassa," he said in a voice husky with emotion. "Then you will understand this restless burning of the soul."

"I understand it now." Her smile held more than a fleeting trace of sadness. "But do not be concerned; all will be well. I have already learned that my father is planning my marriage, and while I do not expect it to be a love match, I shall make the best of it." She lifted her shoulders in a gesture of resignation. "I am not even sure I wish to fall in love again. The pain of losing it is too great. But you are still my best friend, and I will console myself with that. Besides—" her eyes took on a mischievous gleam—"I can always hope your mortal does not find favor with you."

Nikodemus shot her a twisted smile. "It is far more likely I will not find favor with *her.*"

"Then she is a fool, and all the Kingdom shall know it," said Lysia quietly. "But I have vowed to say no more, so I shall not." She walked toward the steps leading to the ocean far below, her carriage proud, her movements imbued with a grace that was entirely unconscious. "Come, Nikodemus. Join me in the sea we both love, for once your mortal comes, there will be precious little time for us to enjoy such pastimes."

Wishing to banish the shadows from her eyes, Nikodemus said, "Shall we race to the equator?"

She hesitated, turned, and a smile appeared. "Only if you give me a mile's grace."

"A mile! You swim faster than the dolphins as it is."

"Ah, but no one is faster than you, great prince. Surely a mile's grace is not so much to ask."

"Very well," Nikodemus relented, against his better judgment. "A mile, but no more."

Satisfied, Lysia raised her hand to the clasp of her tunic and released it with a gentle flick of her fingers.

Nikodemus caught his breath as the silken garment slid to the ground. By Jupiter, she was magnificent! He had always believed Lysianassa to be the most endearing of the Nereids, but as he gazed at her now, all soft shadows and naked curves, he realized she had also become one of the most beautiful. Her figure had ripened, the curves becoming lush and womanly, and though his feelings toward her were that of a friend, it was hard not to be stirred by such physical perfection.

No wonder her father was thinking to settle her in marriage. Given the way she looked, Nereus should have done so long ago.

Seemingly unaware of the thoughts running through his head, Lysia walked toward the far side of the balcony, where the cliff dropped down to the sea, and climbed onto the rail. Raising her arms above her head, she cast one flirtatious look at him, smiled, and then executed a spectacular dive into the glittering depths far below.

"Show-off," Nikodemus muttered, walking toward the long flight of stairs that led down to the water. His house, like most of the others he'd built around the world, was designed to be accessible from the sea. This one was set into the side of a hill, in such a way as to allow for sweeping views over the surrounding ocean. The luxuriant gardens that grew close to the walls kept him safe from prying eyes, and the island's distance from the mainland assured him of privacy.

When one kept secrets like his, it was necessary to live in isolation.

At the bottom of the stairs, Nikodemus slipped off the brief garment that encircled his hips, and sank into the warm, tropical waters.

As always, it was like coming home. He felt the waters of the ocean swirling around him, welcoming him. His body shimmered as though bathed in iridescent light, and when he opened his eyes, he knew the pupils had dilated until no vestige of blue remained.

With barely a movement, he started into the depths.

At a thousand feet he leveled out. The pressure here would have killed a mortal man, but Nikodemus was impervious to it. He drifted on the current, letting the water cradle him as he floated in the indigo silence, giving Lysia the head start she craved.

Until her voice, taunting and defiant, drifted into his head. *You won't catch me now.*

It was a battle cry to a warrior, and smiling, Nikodemus opened his eyes. *Just watch me, little nymph. Just watch me.*

With no more effort than it took to raise his hand, Nikodemus formed his arms into a V and launched himself into the depths; hurtling toward the center of the world at speeds no equipment on earth would have been able to track, intent on teaching a mischievous sea sprite the perils of offering challenges to the son of the god of the sea.

Milford-by-the-Bay, Massachusetts

It had been the day from hell.

Chelsea Porter unlocked the side door to her beachfront house and listlessly pushed it open. Why was it that some days just started out bad and only got worse? The critical artwork she'd sent to the graphic artist first thing this morning had been delivered four hours late, effectively killing any chance of its being ready for the meeting with the client Monday afternoon. Then the product samples that were being shipped to her from a supplier in London had somehow turned up at a design firm in British Columbia. On top of that, the pre-gala meeting with Jonathan Blaire, the one that was supposed to have lasted only thirty minutes, had dragged on for three and a half hours. It would have gone on even longer if the dapper art director hadn't suddenly received an urgent page about a dinner commitment he'd apparently forgotten.

Thank God the man leads an active social life, Chelsea thought as she wearily dropped her keys on the table. The sophisticated ex-Bostonian might be a wonderful managing director for the new art gallery, but his constant harping on every detail drove her to distraction. And to think people accused *her* of being a perfectionist!

Trying to ignore the hammers pounding in her brain, Chelsea shut the door and let the blissful sounds of silence envelop her. She'd almost forgotten what peace and quiet was like. Ever since Turner and Parsons had been awarded the prestigious contract for the design and construction of the new art gallery north of Boston, and she'd been put in charge of the project, she hadn't had a moment to herself. There had been endless meetings with town planners and organizing committees, lengthy consultations with architects and designers, and a never-ending stream of letters and official documents that seemed to be an integral part of the process when one undertook the building of anything bigger than a doghouse.

Once construction had gotten under way, there'd been a whole new set of problems to deal with, like the ongoing battles with the painters' union, the carpenters' union, the electricians' union, and just about any other union Chelsea cared to think of. It was no wonder she was tired all the time. There just weren't enough hours in the day anymore.

And it didn't help that her sleep was being fractured by these strange, unsettling dreams.

Ignoring the sink full of dirty dishes and the overflowing laundry basket, Chelsea headed for her bedroom. Her once pristine home was starting to look like a derelict's hangout, but she couldn't be Martha Stewart *and* businesswoman of the year. And right now, work took priority over everything else. There'd be plenty of time to get caught up on the domestic goddess stuff once Saturday night's gala reception was safely out of the way.

Leaving the chaos of the kitchen behind, Chelsea moved toward the stairs. She loved this house. She had ever since she'd seen it advertised in the window of the local real estate office. And thanks to having lived the kind of existence that would have made a nun proud, she'd been able to save enough money to put a reasonable down payment on the house and to call the beachfront two-story her own.

Martha be damned! She hadn't done badly for a single woman in her mid-thirties.

A quick glance at the answering machine in the living room showed no messages, and Chelsea sighed in relief. Good. No messages meant no problems at the site, and right now, that ranked up there with unexpected tax refunds and a clean bill of health from the dentist. It also meant that nobody was calling to ask her to take a walk along the beach or go for a drink at The Latte Café. But she certainly didn't have time for a social life, and she sure didn't have the energy for one.

Still, she never stopped wondering if Duncan might change his mind and call. . . .

Yeah, right, and one day elephants might fly, the nagging voice of her conscience said. *You had your chance, and you blew it. When are you going to accept that and move on?*

Chelsea snapped on the bedroom light and kicked off her navy blue pumps. Honestly, there were times when she could have strangled that exasperating voice. But as much as she hated to admit it, she knew it was right. She *had* blown it with Duncan Rycroft. Why else would he be living in a swanky condo in Boston while she was up here in the bucolic tranquillity of Milford-by-the-Bay?

At least, Chelsea *assumed* Duncan was still in Boston. He might already be living the good life in Mexico for all she knew. That's where he'd said he was going the day he'd packed his bags and walked out.

Chelsea slipped off her suit and blouse and hung them in the crowded closet. Yeah, she'd blown it all right. One day Duncan had been painting romantic pictures of the two of them living in a quaint little casa on a rose-covered hillside— the next, he'd been taking the fast lane out of her life. The sad part was, Chelsea knew she could have stopped him. If she had just let her emotional side prevail over her practical one, she could have sailed off into the sunset with him and spent the rest of her days sipping margaritas and sporting a permanent tan.

But no, *she* had to start asking questions. Big questions, like where they were going, and what the relationship meant to him—which was really stupid, since she'd known Duncan wasn't looking to settle down. He'd told her on their first date that he'd just come through an ugly divorce and he didn't know if he'd ever be able to commit to a permanent relationship again.

Chelsea thought she'd understood that. Thought she'd understood how a bitter divorce could sour someone on marriage. And she'd convinced herself that as long as they were together, it didn't matter that Duncan didn't want to get married. Right?

Wrong. In the end, it had mattered, because Chelsea had *needed* some kind of commitment from the man she loved. She'd wanted to talk about the future and make plans, but with Duncan it was always live for today and let tomorrow take care of itself. Well that was fine to a point, but what if tomorrow didn't take care of itself?

Yet, Chelsea *had* loved him, despite his reckless, devil-may-care ways. And it was *because* she'd loved him that she hadn't been willing to settle for the transient, no-commitment kind of relationship he'd been offering. Fly away to Mexico with her? Sure. Live together in a cozy hacienda on the cliffs? No problem. But give her an idea as to when, or if, he'd ever be willing to commit?

Not in this lifetime.

Give it up, lady, the voice said more gently. *You're not doing yourself any good thinking about something you can't change.*

Chelsea sat down on the bed and wearily shook her head. No, she wasn't. Dwelling on Duncan was like committing emotional suicide. Every time she thought about him, she died all over again, and she *couldn't* let herself get sucked into that emotional morass again. She'd done it once, and the *only* way she'd been able to drag herself out was by burying her head in work. She'd put in sixteen-hour days, seven days a week. It hadn't had anything to do with climbing the corporate ladder or lusting after a key to the executive washroom. It had been desperation, plain and simple.

She'd worked to forget the pain. Suppressing her unhappiness by pretending it didn't exist. Eventually, she'd become so good at it, it became a way of life.

Chelsea Porter. Certified workaholic.

Making a sound of irritation, Chelsea grabbed a brightly colored towel from the back of the door and headed for the beach. She needed a vacation, that's all. She hadn't had one in nearly three years, and the long hours and sleepless nights were finally beginning to take their toll. *That's* why she was having these weird dreams. She was mentally exhausted; stressed out from living on caffeine and nerves. Hell, *anybody* would have nightmares trying to keep up the pace she did.

There was something incredibly liberating about swimming at night, Chelsea thought as she cut smoothly through the darkened waters of the bay. Maybe because there were no boundaries. You could swim for miles with your eyes wide open and never see a thing.

That would have terrified most people, but Chelsea had never been afraid of the water. The mysterious depths didn't frighten her. They beckoned to her, weaving their own kind of mystical spell around her. She still remembered the first time she'd really experienced the underwater world. Right after her twentieth birthday, she had gone on vacation with friends for the first time in her life, and she'd fallen in love. Not with a man, but with the magnificent Caribbean Sea.

Chelsea was sure she'd never seen anything so breathtaking before. That vast expanse of turquoise-colored water fringed with long stretches of pure white sand had left her breathless. And when she'd borrowed a friend's mask and dived into the crystal-clear waters, a whole new world had opened up before her. A world bursting with color and life; a magical place filled with hidden delights and secret treasures.

It hadn't surprised anybody that she had signed up for scuba lessons and earned her certification before she'd left the island. It had probably helped that Chelsea had been such a strong swimmer. She'd had to teach herself, of course, given her mother's obsessive fear of the water, but that was okay. She'd had to do a lot of things on her own. Having a father who spent three-quarters of the year on the road hadn't exactly made for a close-knit family.

After graduating from college, Chelsea continued to dive, mostly in the crystal-clear waters around the Bahamas and the islands of St. Lucia and St. Barts. She still tried to get away for a diving vacation whenever she could, but it seemed that lately, there hadn't been time for anything but work. Even now, she found her thoughts drifting back to the events of the day, lingering on the argument she'd had with the graphic artist. She was going to have to apologize for that. Not because she'd asked the guy to do his job, but because of the *way* she'd asked him to do it. She'd snapped at him like an irate terrier going for the mailman.

Maybe it's the onset of age, Chelsea thought as she closed her eyes and floated over onto her back. In two months, she'd be thirty-six. Maybe her hormones were kicking in early. Either that, or the pressures of the gallery opening and the reception Saturday night were weighing heavier on her mind than she thought.

Whatever it was, Chelsea knew she couldn't keep pushing herself like this. It wasn't healthy. She couldn't keep coming home exhausted every night and then get up at 4 A.M. and start all over again. Especially when what little sleep she *did* get was being rocked by these strange and rather frightening dreams. . . .

The splash was so faint that Chelsea thought she'd imagined it. But she didn't imagine the surge in the water that followed. She knew a pressure wave when she felt one, and this one was big. Something was in the water below her. Something large enough, or moving fast enough, to displace a huge amount of water.

Mouth dry, Chelsea opened her eyes and glanced toward shore. She was in about forty feet of water and roughly fifty yards out. Not far as distances went, but far enough to put her in a lot of trouble if something *was* in the water with her.

The cloud that had been blocking the moon slowly moved past, allowing milky light to bathe the silver crescent of sandy beach and the placid waters of the bay. But when it did, Chelsea's eyes only widened more, because the sea wasn't just placid. *It wasn't moving.* There wasn't a ripple or a swell or even the slightest indication of a wave as far as her eye could see. Apart from the flutters she was creating with the back-and-forth movements of her hands, the surface of the bay was absolutely still.

And there was no sound. Almost as though there was . . . no life.

Chelsea stared in disbelief. What was going on? The sea couldn't stop moving. It contradicted the laws of nature. It defied the rules of gravity, for crying out loud! But her eyes weren't playing tricks on her. The water *wasn't* moving.

No, wait! *Something* started to move. A line of silver-capped ripples drifted slowly across the surface of the bay. Ripples caused by something large moving just below the surface.

Something that was moving slowly and inexorably toward her!

Fear slammed into Chelsea's gut, holding her like an animal trapped in the headlights of an oncoming car. *What kind of creature generated that kind of wake?* She hadn't seen any signs of a fin, but that didn't mean anything. Sharks usually circled their prey from below and then attacked. So what did that leave? A whale?

Suddenly, Chelsea felt it again. A surge, like a door opening and closing in the depths below. But it was stronger this time, closer, the force of it lifting her half a body length out of the water.

The creature was on the move—and whatever it was, it was massive.

That was enough for Chelsea. Kicking into high gear, she struck out for shore, praying her agitated movements wouldn't draw the creature closer.

She didn't get far. Something moved in the darkness off to her right, hurtling toward shore, then doubling back, creating a huge black wall of water that rose like a nightmare before her eyes, blotting out all sight of land.

It happened so fast Chelsea didn't have time to scream. The wave exploded around her, the incredible force pushing her down into the depths. She felt the current tugging at her body, and began to panic in earnest. She had to break free before it grabbed her and swept her out to sea.

Suddenly, Chelsea was being thrust toward the surface again, powerless against the incredible impetus of the water. She sculled her arms in a desperate attempt to right herself, but in the frightening black void, she had no idea which way was up. She was hopelessly disoriented and running out of air fast.

She was going to die!

No, you're not! the voice of sanity shouted. *Hold your breath and keep your wits about you.*

Desperate, Chelsea struggled to listen. She *couldn't* be any more than ten, maybe fifteen, feet down, and the creature hadn't attacked. It was still there, silent, unseen, but whatever it was, it hadn't killed her yet.

With renewed determination, Chelsea kicked out, praying her body was pointed in the right direction. The turbulence around her was easing, but that didn't mean anything. The creature might have moved off, but she wasn't naïve enough to believe it was gone.

Suddenly, Chelsea felt a pain in her left shoulder, as though she'd been stung. She turned her head—then froze in terror and disbelief.

Something huge and white was floating in the water beside her.

Whatever fragile threads of logic remained, snapped—and Chelsea reacted.

Survival. That was the only thought in her mind now. The desperate, human need to stay alive. And mindless of everything *but* that need, she grit her teeth and kicked hard. She had to get away. That *thing* had come within a few feet of her. She had to get away before it came back and finished her off.

Finally breaking the surface, Chelsea threw back her head and gulped great mouthfuls of air into her lungs. Then, adrenaline surging, she struck out at a fast crawl, arms pumping like well-oiled pistons.

It was the longest swim of Chelsea's life. She swam without thinking, arm over arm, breath after breath, half expecting to be caught and dragged down into the depths, torn apart by the razor-sharp teeth of a monster.

Please don't let me die like that, Lord, she prayed fervently. *Anything but that!*

It was the desire to survive that drove Chelsea home, but it was sheer determination that kept her body going. Stroke after stroke, she swam like a machine until finally, only moments away from sheer exhaustion, she flung out her arm and hit beach.

Safety lay within reach!

Calling on reserves she didn't know she had, Chelsea dug her fingers into the sand and pulled her body out. Stumbling to her feet, she ran toward the house. Her head was pounding and her chest felt like it was locked in the grip of a steadily closing vise, but she didn't stop running. She finally collapsed at the foot of her deck stairs, and risked a quick glance back over her shoulder—only to gasp in disbelief. "What the—?"

There was nothing there. No monstrous creature rising from the depths, no unholy calm flattening the surface of the bay. Everything was exactly as it should have been, exactly as it *had* been, before she'd heard that splash in the water and her nightmare had begun.

Chelsea shivered. Beads of perspiration sprang out on her forehead, and she heard a high-pitched whine. She was seconds away from fainting.

Dropping her head between her legs, Chelsea forced herself to breathe. She took slow, steady breaths, focusing on the rhythm of her inhalations until eventually the feeling passed. Her stomach was still queasy, but at least she wasn't in fear of fainting—until she opened her eyes and saw a blotch of red smeared across her left thigh. *Blood?*

She turned her head and glanced at her left shoulder.

The birthmark was bleeding. There weren't any cuts around it, nor was the skin near the shell-shaped mark bruised, but the mark itself was definitely bleeding.

On jellylike legs, Chelsea headed for the bathroom. Flicking on the light, she reached for a tissue and carefully blotted the spot dry. That's when she saw it. A sliver-fine cut, right in the center of the birthmark, no more than a quarter of an inch long. But the fact that it was so small did nothing to lessen Chelsea's horror, because for the first time, she actually had *proof* that something had been out there in the water with her. Proof that something huge and evil had risen from the depths and swum to within a few feet of her.

Something that had come close enough to kill.

Two

Chelsea wasn't in the best of moods when she got to the gallery Saturday night. Probably because she hadn't been able to *think* straight for the last two days. She'd done nothing but worry about the terrifying encounter in the water, racking her brain until she'd given herself a headache trying to figure it out. But she'd kept coming up blank, unable to think of one logical explanation for what had happened to her.

She knew that the waters of Massachusetts Bay were home to all manner of aquatic life. Schools of white-sided dolphins and finback whales—some as large as sixty-five feet in length—were known to frequent the waters along the New England coast, but she also knew it was rare for them to come that close to shore.

As to the likelihood of it being a shark, Chelsea had already ruled that one out. Sharks weren't generally known for being playful.

A call to the police station Friday morning, and to the Oceanographic Institute at Woods Hole hadn't shed any light on the problem either. According to their records, there hadn't been any shark or other unusual marine life sightings during the past week.

Then what *had* been in the water with her?

The question had kept her awake the last two nights—which likely explained why she'd fallen asleep on the couch this afternoon. Unfortunately, the nap had put her way behind schedule in getting ready for the reception, as had finding a tear in the black satin gown she'd planned on wearing. She'd had to settle for her midnight blue cocktail dress, only to find she didn't have the right color of pantyhose to go with it.

Honestly, some days it just doesn't pay to get out of bed, Chelsea thought as she ran, bare-legged and panting, up the floodlit steps and into the gallery proper.

Thankfully, once inside the magnificent glass and marble lobby designed to resemble the huge open prow of a ship, Chelsea felt some degree of normality return. She was back in the land of the living. Back where structure and logic mattered, and where she could see, touch, and smell everything around her.

She took a flute of champagne from the tray of a passing waiter and moved into the elegantly dressed crowd. The formal ribbon-cutting ceremony and press reception were already over, but with any luck she hadn't missed too much else. She gulped down two mouthfuls of the ice-cold champagne, then took a quick look around.

Yes, there was her partner in the business, Joe Turner, and his wife, Patty, along with a few of the firm's architects and interior designers, talking to a group of local businessmen. As usual, Patty looked bored out of her mind. She hated functions like these and resented the time that Joe gave to the company he'd built from a one-man operation into the thriving success it was now. Though she certainly didn't seem to mind the wonderful holidays it allowed her to take, Chelsea thought narrowly. According to Joe, that was about all she enjoyed.

As for the architects, they all looked stiff and uncomfortable in their tuxedos, which wasn't surprising, given that most of the time they lived in Top-Siders and jeans. Even Joe, who wore a suit three days out of five, looked ill at ease in the formal black jacket and ruffled shirt.

Feeling a little sorry for him, Chelsea caught his eye and waved.

Joe waved back, his raised eyebrow indicating surprise that she'd turned up late, and relief that she'd turned up at all. He gestured for her to join them, but Chelsea shook her head, mouthing the word "later." She still needed a few minutes to compose herself. Rumor had it that several bigwigs were coming up from Boston to give the gallery the once-over, and if she wanted to help the company get more business, she needed to project a cool, professional image—something she wasn't likely to do if she looked like she'd been running around like an idiot for the last hour and a half. Unfortunately, looking cool and composed was a bit of a stretch when she jumped a foot every time somebody came up behind her.

Was she getting a little close to the edge?

Chelsea gulped down another mouthful of champagne. Joe seemed to think so. He'd mentioned a few times that she'd been brusque with people on the phone, and God knew, the terrifying encounter in the water hadn't helped. But did she really look like someone who was trembling on the brink of a stress-induced meltdown?

Stopping to check her reflection in one of the long mirrored panels, Chelsea tried to be as objective as possible. Okay, so she'd lost a few pounds over the last few months. She still didn't look as gaunt as half the supermodels flaunting their bodies on the runways of the fashion capitals these days. And her face?

Chelsea tilted her head to one side. It wasn't a bad-looking face, she decided. Somewhere between oval and round, it had a small, narrow nose, cheeks that were high-boned and smooth, and a mouth that was a little too wide to be called sexy. Her eyes were probably her best feature. Round and heavily lashed, they were an unusual shade of green that seemed to change with the light. A skillful application of makeup had done wonders to hide the violet shadows rimming them, but Chelsea didn't think she saw any signs of dysfunction in their depths.

As for her hair, she'd left her thick, honey-colored waves loose about her shoulders. Putting it up would have been entirely too much of an effort tonight.

Somewhat reassured, Chelsea moved away from the mirror

and into the Egyptian Gallery, where paintings of Cleopatra and Nefertiti shared wall space with magnificent busts of Ramses the Great and Tutankhamen. If nothing else, at least she *looked* like she was in control. Still, it probably wouldn't hurt to talk to Joe on Monday about taking a few days off, Chelsea thought, allowing a passing waiter to refill her glass. Better that than be forced to sit with an overpriced professional who'd take her money and listen to her rattle on about her problems, then send her home with a prescription for happy pills.

The Meridian wing was devoted to works of art that drew their inspiration from the sea. The walls of the room were hung with colorful seascapes and large oil paintings of old sailing ships, and the blue and white marbled floor offered whimsical statues of bronzed dolphins leaping from the waves and graceful mantas soaring through the sea foliage.

It was there Chelsea first saw the man. She couldn't say exactly what it was about him that made her stop. Maybe the way the light from the overhead bulbs shone down on him, accentuating the glossy blue-black highlights in his hair and casting intriguing shadows over his face. Or maybe it was the way he stood, confident but perhaps a little reserved, as he watched the steady flow of people through the room.

Or it might just have been the fact that he was so damned beautiful, Chelsea couldn't help but stop and stare.

He was tall, and though he was turned slightly away from her, she could still see the perfection of his features. His cheekbones were prominent, his eyebrows a dark slash of color against radiantly healthy skin. Chelsea wondered if he might be some kind of New Age health and fitness guru. She'd run into her fair share of them at the trendy ski resorts of Aspen and Smugglers Ridge.

He was dressed more casually than most of the men at the gala. His tailored black pants bore no gleaming strip of satin down the side, and his white shirt, French-cuffed and open at the neck, held only the slightest trace of a shine. He wasn't even wearing a tie.

And yet, for all that, he made more of an impression on Chelsea than any man she'd ever seen. The same lines she'd once seen in a drawing of a Greek god were evident in this man's face. In fact, the resemblance was uncanny.

But who was he? Not one of the gallery employees, that was for sure. A corporate executive up from Boston? A millionaire art lover looking to pick up some new pieces for his collection? Or just your average, run-of-the-mill hunk who routinely showed up at functions like this where money and taste were prominently on display?

When a young woman drifted over to him, and he gestured to the painting on the wall behind him, Chelsea's eyes widened in surprise. An *artist*? Good Lord, she hadn't pegged him as the artistic type, but he certainly could have been one, given the authoritative way he was talking to the young woman, and the faintly dazzled way she was smiling and nodding in response.

Suddenly, as if becoming aware of Chelsea's stare, the man turned his head and looked right at her. The gaze was sharp and focused, and completely unexpected. But as his eyes locked with hers, Chelsea felt everything fade into insignificance as she discovered, in those few brief moments, what it was like to be completely exposed.

As she stood there, unsure of what to do, her soul was laid open and bare to his gaze. His expression was so intense that Chelsea could hardly breathe. In fact, she had to remind herself to breathe. She felt impaled on eyes so intensely blue it was like being pierced with slivers of cobalt light. But it was more than just a visual exchange.

Something was happening to her. It was almost as though he was reaching out to her with his mind. Chelsea knew that didn't make any sense, but that's exactly what was happening. For the first time in months, she felt a glorious stillness suffusing her soul. Worries vanished, and she was filled with profound sense of tranquillity. She closed her eyes and felt herself relax. Her mind was floating in a place filled with shadows and dreams; a place where she felt protected, cared for. *Loved.*

Yes, the feelings of love were tangible and strong. They rolled toward her in great, sweeping waves, reaching out to her and drawing her closer. . . .

Yes, come, beloved, whispered a beautiful masculine voice.

It is time. I have waited so long for you. So very, very long. . . .

"Hey, kiddo. Having a good time?"

The interruption was unwelcome. A harsh intrusion into her peace. Chelsea jumped, and looked up to see Joe Turner smiling down at her.

She shook her head, struggling to free herself from the invisible bonds. "Joe, h-hi. How . . . are you?"

"I'm fine, but you look a bit out of it." He leaned in closer and winked. "Dazzled by all the hoopla or just had a little too much champagne?"

Champagne? Chelsea's eyes dropped to the empty glass in her hand. The last time she'd looked at it, it had been half full. Had she really been drinking that much?

"Probably just nerves," she said, setting the glass down. "We've worked so hard on this one, it's nice to see it all come together."

"Amen to that," Joe murmured, nodding at a passing couple. "Though there were times when I wondered if it would."

Chelsea smiled, knowing there was never any doubt the company would pull it off. Joe Turner was one of the finest architects in the state. When he took on a project, there was no question it would be done, and done right. Chelsea had learned so much working as his right-hand person. She'd grown, both as a designer and as a businesswoman, and she had been honored when Joe had asked her to become a minority partner in the business.

But Joe Turner wasn't just a savvy businessman. He was a man well known and well liked in the community, a man who, at fifty-six, was in better shape than most forty-year-olds. His hair was still dark, showing only smudges of silver at the temples, and his eyes were a clear, light blue. He was on his second marriage, had no children from either, and spent most of his time at work.

Chelsea had liked him from day one. He'd seen her through some tough times, including Duncan's defection, and she'd worked hard to earn his respect and approval. Respect she didn't intend to jeopardize by appearing unprofessional now.

"Do you think any of the city papers will cover it?"

Joe shrugged. "Who knows? The Boston rags usually aren't too interested in anything going on north of the city. Salem, maybe, or Gloucester, but hardly Milford-by-the-Bay." He took another glance around the room, but this time his attention was focused on the guests. "Sure is interesting to see so many prominent people in town, though. Have you had a chance to talk to any of the artists yet?"

Chelsea's eyes flashed back to the spot where she'd first seen her mystery man, but the corner was empty.

"Chelsea, you okay?"

She swiveled her gaze back to his face. "Sure. Why?"

"You seem preoccupied, and it's not like you to be anything but one hundred percent on at events like this." Joe dropped his voice. "Are you sure you haven't had too much to drink? I know what a cheap drunk you are."

Chelsea laughed, not in the least offended by the remark. She *was* a cheap drunk, and usually allowed herself no more than one glass of wine at functions like these. The fact that she'd had two tonight said a lot. But how could she tell Joe it had nothing to do with the champagne, but with an incredibly handsome man who'd stared at her across a room, and with a mysterious voice that had called her *beloved*?

"I'm fine. Really," Chelsea said, determined to make him believe it. "The evening just got off to a bad start, but I'm fine now."

"Are you sure? I wondered when you didn't show up for the ribbon cutting," Joe admitted. "Not that you missed much. Mayor Blackman gave his usual see-what-we-can-do-when-we-all-work-together speech, cut the ribbon, and was on his fourth drink by the time he reached the press gallery."

"You're becoming a cynic, Joe."

His mouth twisted. "Hazard of being in business too long, I suppose. Speaking of which, I'd better get back to work. The president and CFO from Beckley Fitch are here. They're looking for somebody to handle their Dallas expansion. Figured it might be a good fit for us."

"It would be," Chelsea agreed, trying to sound enthusiastic. "Beckley Fitch is a huge corporation. If you need me, just give me a wave."

"I will. And listen, a bunch of us are going over to Delmaggio's for lobster and beer after this. Why don't you come along? It might be good for you to let your hair down for a change."

Chelsea knew where Joe was coming from, and though she blessed him for his concern, she shook her head. "Thanks, but I think I'll head straight home. It's been a pretty intense week."

"Tell me about it. Patty's been threatening to change the locks."

She glanced at him sharply. "Is she serious?"

He shrugged again. "Who knows? She's been quiet lately. But never mind, you don't need to listen to me pour out my troubles. Patty and I will sort it out. We always do. Anyway, if you change your mind and decide to join us for a beer, you know where we are. If not, I'll see you Monday. And do *not* go in to the office tomorrow, you hear?"

Chelsea laughed. "Yeah, I hear, but I'd better not find out that you did either!"

Joe gave her an affectionate pat on the shoulder. "I'm the senior partner. Stuff like that doesn't apply to me." Then, with a wink and a smile, he moved off, disappearing into the crowd of elegant movers and upscale shakers.

Chelsea sighed. She really was lucky to have teamed up with Joe Turner. When she'd moved here from Colorado, she sure hadn't expected to end up a partner, even a minority one, in a successful firm like Turner and Parsons.

Of course, moving to Milford-by-the-Bay and working with an architectural and design firm had taken some getting used to. It was a far cry from living in Denver and visiting clients who routinely hired her to design or remodel their lavish mountainside ski chalets. But Chelsea had no regrets. She'd always wanted to live by the sea. Now, at any time of the day or night, she could look out her bedroom window and see the sun or the moon kissing the waves with silver and gold.

Intent on her thoughts, Chelsea didn't notice that she'd walked into the corner where her mystery man had been standing—until she looked up and saw the painting on the wall straight ahead of her.

What if he saw her standing here and came back?

As she started to back away, Chelsea realized how stupid she was being. What was the matter with her? There wasn't anything alarming or unusual about the man she'd seen earlier, and there certainly hadn't been any kind of *emotional* connection between them. Okay, so she'd experienced *something* she couldn't explain. It didn't mean it had anything to do with him. More than likely, it *was* just the champagne. She was imagining things.

Yes, he was better-looking than just about anybody she'd ever seen, but was that any reason to avoid him? As to the voice, she'd probably just overheard a conversation in one of the adjoining rooms. Gallery acoustics were funny that way.

Chelsea closed her eyes and took a deep breath. She was letting her imagination get the best of her again. She'd wanted to see his painting, hadn't she? And what better time to see it than right now, when the artist was nowhere in sight?

Giving her head a shake, Chelsea deliberately moved forward. She glanced at the brass plate tacked to the wall before looking at the work itself.

Poseidon's Sorrow
Artist, Nicolas Demitry

Interesting title, Chelsea thought. And the artist's name certainly sounded Greek, which explained the dark features and smoldering good looks. But when Chelsea turned to look at the canvas itself, she could only stare at it in disbelief—because it was, without question, the most incredible depiction of mythical undersea life she had ever seen.

Caught in the velvety darkness of a fathomless depth, the sea god sat on a huge white rock, staring at the ghostly outline of an old sailing ship that lay like a drunken sailor upon the ocean floor. On his face was a look of such sadness that it tore at Chelsea's heart.

The ship itself was a lifeless hull; the tall, center mast split like a rotten branch lying broken and useless on the sea floor. Torn sails hung like ghostly veils on the rigging, and snakelike lengths of rope trailed away into the sand.

Balanced against the bleak gray tones of the death ship

were the rich, vibrant colors of the sea god and his splendid raiment. The golden trident in his hand seemed to flash with a brilliance all its own, and his stately crown, encrusted with emeralds, rubies, and sapphires, sparkled and danced from the surface of the canvas.

His long, shimmering hair floated like a halo of silver around his head, but it was the face of Poseidon to which the eye was drawn. It was a powerful face; fearless and bold, yet graced with an ageless wisdom that somehow tempered the steel and made his great sorrow believable. As he looked out over the ghost ship in the huge, dark ocean that was his world, Chelsea could almost feel his sorrow at the passing of all those lives; his compassion for the men who had once walked proud on the decks of that mighty vessel. The sea had become their tomb. And the mighty king, the keeper of their souls.

It was a picture of desolation; a once proud ship that lay silent and impotent beneath the majestic waves it had once ruled.

As Chelsea stood there, an intense feeling of despair reached out to envelop her. The painting was so perfectly detailed, so exquisitely rendered, that she could almost *feel* the cold fingers of loneliness wrapping around her.

"It's pretty amazing, isn't it?" a woman said quietly behind her.

For the third time that night, Chelsea jumped. Honestly, if this kept up, she was going to *have* to get something to calm her nerves.

She turned around to find herself in the company of an attractive woman who looked to be in her early fifties, and whose warm smile and expressive brown eyes immediately made her feel comfortable. Her short, ash-blond hair was worn in a stylish bob, and she looked stunning in an off-white, silk shantung gown. She certainly seemed to be relaxed and at ease in the gallery.

"Yes, it is," Chelsea said finally. "I don't think I've seen anything like it before."

"It's having that effect on everyone. Mr. Demitry is an incredibly gifted artist, and most people seem a little taken aback by the realism of his work, but we're delighted he

agreed to participate. And lucky." The woman smiled and
held out her hand. "I'm Grace Thornton. Public relations
representative for the gallery."

Chelsea returned the handshake. "Chelsea Porter, Turner
and Parsons."

"Well, I certainly know *that* name." Grace's dark eyes
glowed. "Your firm has done an incredible job here, Miss
Porter."

"It's Chelsea, and thank you." Chelsea's attention slid
back to the painting. "You said you were lucky to have this
artist's work here tonight. Why? Is he particularly well
known?"

"Not to the general public, but he has something of a cult
following in the art world."

Cult. Chelsea tried to ignore the shadowy images the word
conjured up. "I don't think I've ever heard of him. But then,
I'm not much of an authority when it comes to artists and
their works."

"It wouldn't matter if you were. Nicolas Demitry is an
extremely private man. He seldom displays his works at galleries."

"Then why did he agree to have this one here?"

"Likely because he and Jonathan have a personal friendship," Grace told her. "Nicolas called about two weeks ago
and offered to send along his newest work. Naturally, Jonathan was thrilled. He's been a fan of Nicolas's for years,
and he's something of an expert when it comes to the realm
of the strange and unusual."

Chelsea nodded. The painting certainly qualified in that
area. But what bothered her more was the degree to which
it unsettled her. "And what's Mr. Demitry like?"

"Incredibly handsome and extremely charismatic," Grace
said without hesitation. "He was talking to an associate of
mine earlier and left her feeling somewhat dazed, to use her
own words."

Chelsea glanced at her quickly. "Dazed?"

"It seems he's a very spiritual man," Grace explained.
"Not in terms of God and the church exactly, but on a more
metaphysical plane, if that makes any sense. It didn't to me,
but then my associate is more into this New Age thing than

I am. She said he was absolutely fascinating. Unworldly, somehow."

Unworldly? Chelsea decided to ignore that one, too. "Yes, well, I'm sure anybody who can dream up stuff like this would have to be different." *Different, unique, and maybe not quite normal.* "Still, whatever his background, he's certainly making a name for himself tonight."

"Oh, he's already made his name," Grace told her. "Nicolas's works command incredibly high prices in the private sector. In fact, if he could have donated the painting anonymously, I think he would have, which is surprising when you consider how most artists clamor for publicity. But Nicolas avoids it at all costs. I was hoping to get some background information on him for the handouts, but apart from a telephone number I had to pry out of him, he wouldn't tell me a thing about himself."

Chelsea's smile grew tight. "A mystery man, then."

"He's a mystery, all right, but a thoroughly charming one. I wish they were all that easy to get along with," Grace said with a sigh. "Well, I'd better start circulating again. It was nice meeting you, Chelsea. Enjoy the rest of the show."

"Thanks, I will."

Chelsea watched Grace walk toward another group of visitors, and then turned back to study the painting by Nicolas Demitry.

A mystery man, Grace had said. One who by virtue of his brilliance was recognized by dedicated collectors all over the world, yet who disclosed next to nothing about himself.

Why? What was it about Nicolas Demitry's paintings that affected people so deeply? More to the point, what was it about *this* painting that left *her* wishing she'd never laid eyes on it?

By eleven-thirty, Chelsea was more than ready to call it quits. She'd done her bit for the company. She'd put in her mandatory appearance and hobnobbed with the beautiful people. She'd even talked to Patty Turner and a few of the artists in attendance.

But not to Nicolas Demitry. Chelsea hadn't even seen the famous artist since she'd spoken to Grace Thornton, and she wasn't sure she wanted to. She didn't like the idea of talking to someone whose work inspired a cult following, and who wasn't willing to volunteer so much as a scrap of information about himself. That suggested either a man who was supremely arrogant—or one who had something to hide.

And yet, she kept returning to his work. Staring at the majestic figure of Poseidon sitting all alone in his watery kingdom, keeping watch over the souls that had so recently become his. How could a person paint something like that? Where did Nicolas Demitry get his ideas? Was he a dedicated historian who specialized in Greek mythology, or just a lover of marine biology?

And how did he manage to convey such incredible depth of emotion? It was only paint on canvas, yet looking at it now, Chelsea could almost believe she was sitting beside Poseidon on his lonely rock, watching the majestic ship sink through the depths until at last it came to rest on the ocean floor. She could almost hear the cries of the sailors as they clung to their vessel.

How could a mortal know that kind of sorrow?

He can't—and you should know better than to ask, the familiar voice scolded.

Chelsea bit back a sigh. Boy, she was getting tired of that voice. But it was right. This wasn't *The Twilight Zone,* and *Poseidon's Sorrow* wasn't a faithful depiction of life under the sea. It was a product of Demitry's imagination. If she analyzed it any further, she would need a vacation *and* therapy!

Intent on her own thoughts, Chelsea didn't look up when a man suddenly stepped into her path. She mumbled a polite "excuse me" and tried to walk around him, but when he moved again and was still standing in her way, Chelsea began to get annoyed. "Look, if you don't mind, I'd like to get—" She looked up and gasped. *"You!"*

The mouth of the darkly handsome man curved upward in a smile. "Hello, Miss Porter. I was hoping for an opportunity to speak with you before you left. I'm Nicolas Demitry."

His voice was like fine cognac: deep, rich, and incredibly smooth. Definitely a voice you remembered. But there wasn't any trace of an accent. If Nicolas Demitry had been born in

Greece, he'd left the country a long time ago.

"How did you know my name?" she asked, unconsciously taking a step backward.

"Grace Thornton told me. She also said you were intrigued by my painting."

Wishing Grace hadn't been quite so forthcoming with information, Chelsea inclined her head. "Yes, I am."

"Do you like it?

The bluntness of the question took her by surprise. "If you knew I was intrigued by the painting, why would you ask if I liked it?"

"Because liking something and being intrigued by it aren't the same thing," he said, sounding faintly amused, "which I think you already know."

Chelsea flushed. "Mr. Demitry—"

"Please, I really would like to hear what you think," the artist said quietly. "Even if it's only to tell me that *Poseidon's Sorrow* is the worst thing you've ever seen."

"But it isn't! The painting's extraordinary."

"But?"

"No buts."

His glance was indulgent, much like that of a teacher catching a pupil in a lie. "It's all right to say what you think, Miss Porter. I've been painting for a very long time, and I doubt there's anything you can say that I haven't heard before. And believe me, there's nothing you can say that will offend me."

There was more than a hint of amusement in Nicolas Demitry's voice, and it was a few seconds before Chelsea realized that she was smiling, too. She was also staring at his mouth. It was an incredibly attractive mouth: the bottom lip full, the top one beautifully curved. "T-that may be so, but I'm really not the person to ask." Funny. She'd never focused on a man's lips so much before. Other than Duncan's, of course, but even his hadn't struck her as being this sexy. "I'm hardly a connoisseur of fine art."

"Then it's a good thing I don't paint solely for aficionados." His gaze traveled over her face, touching on her mouth, lingering on her eyes. "But I'd still like to hear what you think."

Chelsea knew he was trying to put her at ease. Unfortunately, the way he was looking at her was doing anything *but*. "Well, since you asked, the painting—" How did she phrase this tactfully? "—the painting disturbs me."

He raised one eyebrow. "Disturbs you?"

"Yes. Look, please don't misunderstand. It's an extremely powerful painting and it's totally unlike anything I've ever seen before, but . . ."

"It disturbs you."

"Yes."

"Why?"

"I'm not sure." Chelsea bit her lip. "Maybe because it makes me feel sorry for Poseidon." She glanced at the canvas again and laughed. "Crazy, huh?"

He watched her for a moment, his own eyes shuttered. "Not at all," he said quietly. "In fact, that's exactly the emotion I was hoping to convey. I wanted people to feel Poseidon's sadness. To understand his sense of isolation, and to empathize with his despair."

"Well, you certainly succeeded in doing that," Chelsea murmured, aware that it wasn't only the artist's mouth that was throwing her thoughts into disarray. As a package, Nicolas Demitry was nothing short of breathtaking. Tall, dark, and with a beautifully proportioned body that even tailored pants and an expensive shirt couldn't disguise, he would have reduced even the most hardened female activist to a puddle of panting femininity. There was just something about him. Something mysterious.

Something not quite attainable. . . .

"I understand that participating in gallery shows is a departure for you, Mr. Demitry," Chelsea said, struggling to sound like the cool professional she was—and failing miserably. *What was that incredible aftershave he was wearing?*

"Yes, but only because I find doing shows like this somewhat difficult."

The scent reminded her of spring rain and the breeze blowing in from the sea. "Difficult?"

"Perhaps 'unfulfilling' would be a better word," he said.

Needing to concentrate on what he was saying, Chelsea jerked her attention back to the conversation. "But I don't understand. Everyone thinks your work is fantastic. How can praise like that be unfulfilling for an artist?"

"I'll let you in on a little secret, Miss Porter," Nicolas said, lowering his voice: "Most of the people in this room haven't the faintest idea of what they like, and they have even less intention of admitting it."

"Excuse me?"

"People tend to go with the popular opinion. If the consensus is that a piece of work is good, you'll generally hear nothing but praise. If the opinion is that it's bad, you'll probably hear nothing at all. Art is a very subjective thing, and most people, in their heart of hearts, acknowledge their own ignorance."

"Isn't that a somewhat elitist way of putting it?"

"In this case, I refer to ignorance as being a lack of knowledge rather than an absence of taste," Nicolas said without a hint of condescension in his voice. "Everyone's entitled to his or her own opinion, but if, for example, a wine connoisseur told you that the wine you were drinking was of the finest vintage, and you thought it tasted like vinegar, would you be likely to express an opinion to the contrary?"

Chelsea couldn't fault his logic. "Point taken."

"That's why I say that for me, gallery shows are seldom rewarding. People say what they *think* they should rather than what they'd like to, and usually for no better reason than to avoid offending the artist."

"Maybe so, but even given my limited experience, it's obvious that people like your work," Chelsea said. "Grace told me your paintings command incredibly high prices in the private sector."

"Yes, but more than likely because they're out of the ordinary."

Just like the painter, Chelsea found herself thinking. Because there definitely wasn't anything ordinary about Nicolas Demitry. He had charm and intelligence to go along with those model looks, yet it was obvious he didn't take himself or his talent too seriously. And he *was* beautiful. But it was a kind of strong, masculine beauty that seemed strangely out of place in this contemporary setting. Maybe that's why he was having such a bewildering effect on her.

After all, when was the last time she'd come face-to-face with a man who looked like he'd stepped off the pages of Greek mythology?

"Well, it was nice meeting you, Mr. Demitry." *Greek mythology?* God, she was pathetic. "Good luck with your painting."

"Thank you, Miss Porter." Nicolas stretched out his hand to enclose hers in a warm grip. "But the pleasure was all mine. I look forward to seeing you again."

Chelsea didn't know why the casual touch of his hand should suddenly push her pulse into the stratosphere. "I don't imagine there'll b-be a next time, Mr. Demitry. I'm not much of an art enthusiast. In fact, I'm one of those people who doesn't make a habit of checking out galleries and museums when I visit a new city."

"Neither do I. Unless it's a marine exhibit, of course." Nicolas's remarkable blue eyes glowed. "Nevertheless, you'd be amazed at what a small world it is." With that, he roguishly winked at her, then turned and walked away.

Chelsea watched him leave. She'd never met a man like Nicolas Demitry. Even now, as he wound his way through the crowded gallery, he didn't look or act like one of the hottest artists on display tonight. He paid no attention to the blatant come-hither looks he was getting from almost every woman in the room. If anything, he seemed blissfully unaware of the turmoil his presence was creating. And yet, when he did stop to talk to someone, Chelsea saw the genuine interest and sincere warmth reflected in his smile. What was it Grace had said? That he was a spiritual man?

Yes, Chelsea could understand that now, although she wasn't sure "spiritual" was the right word. There *was* something about Nicolas Demitry; something that went far beyond the norm. It was more than the impact he made with his physical appearance.

He was one of the few men she'd met who had presence.

He was also incredibly sexy, and that wasn't something she liked being aware of so forcefully. She wasn't used to being thrown off balance by a handsome face. Life in a popular ski center had taught her to take good-looking men in stride, but there was no doubt she'd been thrown off-kilter

tonight. Why else would the thought of seeing Nicolas Demitry again, as unlikely as that was, cause the breath to catch
in her throat? Why could she still feel the warmth of his
fingers on hers, and still smell the wonderful fragrance he
wore?

Why did she have a sneaking suspicion it was going to be
a very long time before she forgot the night she met the
brilliant but reclusive artist Nicolas Demitry?

Three

Nicolas Demitry stepped out of the gallery and into the balmy summer night. Several people were standing on the steps, smoking cigarettes and sipping champagne, and though he nodded to them, he didn't stop to talk. He was anxious to get home. Anxious to be alone with his thoughts.

The limousine he'd hired for the evening was parked exactly where it was supposed to be, and Nicolas quickly made his way toward it. He seldom resorted to such elaborate measures, but he'd felt it a good idea for tonight's high-profile event. Better to be seen taking an accepted form of transportation to and from the gallery than to risk his normal mode.

Nicolas smiled to himself as the uniformed chauffeur opened his door. Emerging from the water and changing into formal clothes on the beach would certainly have raised a few eyebrows.

"Evening, Mr. Demitry," the driver said deferentially. "Have a good time?"

"Yes, thank you, Tom. I did." Nicolas slid into the welcoming darkness of the spacious interior. "Straight home, please."

As soon as they were under way, Nicolas breathed a sigh

of relief, happy that the evening was over. Functions like this
were all part of a successful artist's life, but to him, they
were just a trial to be endured. There were always so many
people and so much noise, and the chance of exposure was
intense. But, he would have risked far more than that for the
chance to finally meet and talk with Chelsea Porter.

He hadn't expected her to be so beautiful. She had high
cheekbones set in a delicate face, sweetly curved lips, and a
wide, intelligent brow. The radiance of her complexion had
reminded Nicolas of the rose-tinted perfection of a pearl, and
her eyes were an unusual shade of green, a color that made
him think of the sea when she was at peace.

Chelsea was wary of him, of course, but that was only to
be expected. His inexcusable behavior when he'd glanced at
her across the room was entirely to blame. He'd been so
caught up in the prospect of finally meeting her that he'd
forgotten to sheathe his telepathic abilities. He'd done so
within seconds, but it hadn't been soon enough to prevent
Chelsea from hearing his thoughts. It was only natural that
she was startled, and perhaps a little frightened, when he'd
approached her.

But he couldn't have let her leave without meeting her,
not after all these years. And what he'd discovered about her
had made everything he'd risked worthwhile. She had both
passion and humor in her soul, and a bright, inquisitive mind.
She was also aware of him as a man, though Nicolas doubted
she was ready to admit that, even to herself. But that was all
right. They would have plenty of time to get to know one
another. For now, it was enough that the introduction had
been made, and in a way Chelsea would find entirely believable. He had taken pains to ensure that nothing in their introduction should seem forced or inappropriate. He was an
artist whose work was on display in the gallery. She was the
interior designer in charge of the project. What could have
been more natural than that?

It was only as Chelsea was leaving that he'd touched her;
a brief handshake; carefully impersonal, a courtesy ex-
changed between two strangers meeting for the first time.
Even so, Nicolas knew it had shaken her. He was too good
a student of human nature to miss the signs. The quickly

indrawn breath, the widening of the eyes, the subtle increase in body temperature. Oh, yes, she was aware of him, and even that small sign had given him hope.

The drive to his house took less than an hour, and once there, Nicolas paid the chauffeur. As he watched the car pull away, he felt the night air flow around him, warm and heavy, sweet with the scent of the sea. Above him, the moon hung like a great silver ball, making the water seem black and the shore ghostly pale. A dark swell rolled in and broke on the shore before slipping back, humbled, into the depths. Moments later, he heard her song, sweet and melodious, like music plucked from a mermaid's harp.

Nicolas's mouth curved in a smile as he searched the shallows for her. "Yes, I know. I am late."

In his bedroom on the second floor, he quickly undressed. Then, wrapping a towel around his waist, he walked through the darkened house, his strides sure and steady. He had no need of lights. His eyes were accustomed to seeing in a darkness much more intense than this.

Opening the back door, Nicolas stepped out onto the wooden deck that circled the house, then headed for the beach. As he approached the water, he felt the wind begin to rise, and saw the waters of the bay roll as though fanned by an unseen hand. Farther out, he saw ripples form on the water, evidence of something floating just below the surface, its great body hidden in the liquid folds of darkness.

Without hesitation, Nicolas Demitry walked into the waters of Massachusetts Bay.

In the space of seconds, she was beside him; rising from the waves, droplets of water sparkling like diamonds on her naked breasts and smooth white shoulders. Her silver hair glistened in the moonlight and her eyes shimmered like opals. "Well, did you see her?"

Expecting the question, Nicolas inclined his head. "Yes."

"And?"

"And what?"

"Is she what you expected?"

"She is all I hoped she would be, yes."

"You don't sound very enthusiastic," Lysia complained.

"I am merely trying to make this as painless for you as possible," Nicolas said. "I know you're trying to make good on your promise, but I have no wish to cause you more grief by talking about Chelsea more than is necessary."

Lysianassa's smile turned wistful. "The pain was in coming to terms with the fact that you did not love me, Nikodemus, not that you had chosen another. But come," she said, turning toward the bay. "They are all waiting for you. Anxious to hear your news."

He stayed her with the gentle pressure of his hand. "You would like her, Lysia. If you were to meet her—"

She shook her head, stopping his words. "Do not ask this of me, Niko. I know what she means to you, and I *am* trying to be happy for your sake. But she is still a mortal, and you know how I feel about that."

Nicolas sighed. He wanted to remind her that Chelsea would not be mortal once she crossed over, but in deference to Lysia's feelings, he let it go.

A cloud drifted in front of the moon, deepening the shadows, and Lysia sank soundlessly beneath the waves. Nicolas remained a moment longer, senses alert as he peered into the darkness. Time and experience had taught him the need for caution. He could never be absolutely sure of his privacy. He knew the power of long-distance cameras, of zoom lenses and telescopes. It was part of the price he paid. But most of the time, there was little need for concern. The remoteness of his homes made it difficult for even the most ardent fan to reach him, and his senses were developed to such an extent that there was little chance of discovery.

Seeing no signs of trespassers or curiosity seekers this night, Nicolas dropped down into the water.

There was a brief flash of silver, the shadow of a great wing fanning the surface of the water, then stillness as the moon slowly emerged from the clouds and quiet descended once more.

The official opening of the new art gallery garnered rave reviews, and when Chelsea arrived at her office first thing Monday morning—bleary-eyed from having suffered through yet another nightmare-plagued sleep—it was to find copies of both the weekend papers and the Boston daily on her desk.

She gave her secretary an amused glance as she tucked her briefcase under the desk. "Do I have you to thank for these?"

"Nope. Joe brought them in." Phyllis put a steaming cup of cappuccino from The Latte Café on her desk. "Pretty good write-up, eh?"

"Don't know, I haven't read them yet. Mmm, that coffee smells wonderful," Chelsea said, inhaling the aroma. "Thanks for the treat."

Phyllis stared at her in disbelief. "Are you serious?"

"About the coffee? You bet."

"Chelsea! I'm talking about the write-ups in the paper. Are you honestly telling me you didn't rush out Sunday morning to see what the critics had to say?"

"No." Chelsea picked up her coffee and took a sip. "Why? Was I supposed to?"

"Well, I guess. It's only the biggest project we've ever had. So how was the party anyway?"

"Same as usual." Chelsea picked up one of the papers. "Too many people, not enough ice. . . ." But she smiled as she opened it to the marked page and quickly skimmed the article.

> . . . the creative use of space, the skillful utilization of natural light, and the highly unusual design of the structure all deserve lavish praise, as do Turner and Parsons for being the designers of this impressive and highly original structure. . . .

"Not bad," she commented.

"Did you see your name?" Phyllis asked.

"Where?"

"Down toward the bottom of page 2. Definitely a piece for your scrapbook."

Chelsea found and read the glowing report of her own involvement in the project, and grinned. "I recognize Marketing's hand in that. I'll stop by Jim's office later and thank him."

"Better do it before noon," Phyllis warned as she headed back to her desk. "He's booked on a three o'clock flight to Maui."

"Some people have all the luck," Chelsea muttered. About to close the paper, she hesitated, her attention suddenly caught and held by one name that seemed to jump out at her.

One of the more striking pictures at the opening was "POSEIDON'S SORROW," by artist Nicolas Demitry. Mr. Demitry, who owns a summerhouse on Oyster Point, is an extremely talented artist whose fantastical paintings of sea creatures and the underwater world have sparked a definite cult following. His works command exceptionally high prices on the private market, but this is the first time Mr. Demitry has been known to display one of his works at a gallery opening. Unfortunately, Mr. Demitry was not available for comment. . . .

Chelsea read the brief piece over twice. Well, wasn't that interesting. Oyster Point was a small spit of land that jutted out into the bay. It was surrounded on three sides by water, and when the tide was in, it was accessible only by boat. There weren't any public beaches on it, affording those who *did* live there—absentee millionaires, for the most part—the luxury of complete privacy. Only one road ran the length of the spit. It ended at the bay.

The Point itself was about an hour's drive north of where Chelsea lived, and she had to admit it was an ideal location for an artist who painted bizarre pictures of the sea. When she'd first moved to the area, she'd driven there herself, struck by the wild, untamed beauty of the place.

Was it possible she'd seen Nicolas Demitry's house and not even realized it?

Acting on impulse, Chelsea pulled out the telephone directory and flipped to the listings for Oyster Point, but he wasn't there. No Demitry, Nicolas, or anything resembling it.

Chelsea closed the book. He must have an unlisted number, which made sense. Any celebrity who went to the trouble of moving to an out-of-the-way place like Oyster Point was hardly going to advertise his whereabouts by putting his address and phone number in the local directory. And Nicolas Demitry must have fans. He probably had to get away for part of the year so he could paint his amazing pictures in undisturbed isolation.

Unbidden, the memory of Nicolas's face returned, and Chelsea felt a strange, fluttery feeling in the pit of her stomach. She didn't usually go for guys with long hair, but it suited Nicolas perfectly. He also had the darkest brows, the longest lashes, and the most gorgeous eyes she'd ever seen. But that color—

"Phyllis, do you know many men with black hair and *really* blue eyes?" Chelsea asked when her secretary came back into her office.

"Sure. Why not?"

"I don't know. I saw a guy who looked like that over the weekend, and he turned quite a few female heads."

Phyllis's face lit up. " 'Saw' as in 'dated'?"

"No. 'Saw' as in 'saw.' "

"Too bad. You had me going there for a minute. Black hair and blue eyes, huh? Was he handsome?"

Handsome. Why did the word suddenly seem so inadequate? "Yes."

"And tall?"

Tall enough that she had to tilt her head back to look at him. "Uh-huh."

"Bingo. Tall, dark, handsome, and with blue eyes to die for. So did you get his number?"

"Of course not!"

"Chelsea! You let a gorgeous man like that get away without even trying? Honestly, how do you ever expect to find a husband if you don't go out looking! Did you at least talk to him? Find out who he was?"

Chelsea shifted uncomfortably in her chair. Phyllis had been married for three months, and was at the stage where she thought everybody else should be married, too. She'd never understand why a successful, unattached woman like Chelsea wouldn't *leap* at the chance to get to know a successful, unattached, and wildly handsome man better. "I knew who he was, but I didn't get much time to talk to him.

At least, not about anything other than his work," Chelsea added, knowing that Phyllis would grill her over everything that *wasn't* work-related. "Anyway, it doesn't matter. I'm sure there are far more important things to worry about first thing Monday morning than handsome, blue-eyed men."

"You got that right. Olivia Wainwright's holding on line 2. She wants to know if you're still going to be able to help out at Crab Fest on the twenty-first."

Crab Fest! Chelsea swore softly under her breath. Damn it, she'd completely forgotten about the charity auction and crab dinner the Milford-by-the-Bay Women's Society organized every year. When she'd volunteered her services back in December, there hadn't been any critical deadlines looming on the horizon. But December was eight months ago. Eight months that might as well have been eight *years,* given everything that had happened in between.

Still, it *was* dear, sweet Olivia. Pillar of the community, and one of the hardest-working seventy-seven-year-olds Chelsea had ever met.

"Take a message for me, will you, Phyll? I can't talk to her right now."

"Sure. Need some time to shuffle your schedule around?"

"You know me too well," Chelsea said ruefully, making a note of it on her calendar. "Anything else?"

" 'Fraid so." Phyllis plunked two thick files on Chelsea's desk. "Obstinate electricians or itinerant painters. Take your pick."

Joe called Chelsea into his office shortly after four o'clock.

It was a bit of a joke around the company that Joe's office looked more like a living room than an architect's working space, but considering the horrendous hours he put in, Chelsea figured he was entitled to a few comforts. After all, there had to be some perks to owning a company that had already cost him one wife and might be on its way to costing him a second.

"Sorry I couldn't see you earlier, kiddo." He waved her into one of the leather armchairs in front of his desk. "I've been having problems with the specs for the new Horizon Oil headquarters. I'd like you take a look."

"Sure. And don't worry about the delay, I've had my own hands kind of full this morning."

"Problems?"

"Nothing I can't handle," she assured him. "I'll make a few more calls and let you know where things stand."

Joe grunted, and Chelsea sat down in the chair closest to the door. She could always tell what kind of a day he was having. His clothes said it best, and today obviously wasn't going well. His expensive silk tie was flung over the back of his chair, his jacket was nowhere in sight, and his shirt-sleeves were rolled up past his elbows. There was a large blue stain on his thumb and right forefinger where one of his trusty fountain pens had leaked again.

"So, what were your impressions of Saturday night?" Joe asked, his attention still fixed on the blueprints. "Did you enjoy hobnobbing with the rich and famous?"

"Not really, but from a professional standpoint, the evening was a success. How did it go with Beckley Fitch?"

"Good. I spoke with Peter Fitch, and it sounds like we're going to get a chance to bid on the work. By the way, who was that guy I saw you talking to just before you left?"

Chelsea's face burned. "You saw that?"

"You bet. Patty did, too, and I thought her mouth was going to hit the floor. So, who was he? An old flame?"

Chelsea snorted. "Hardly. He was one of the artists."

"Really? I didn't think you were into art."

"I'm not."

Joe shrugged. "I'll take your word for it. So, what did you want to see me about?"

Glad to be off the subject of Nicolas Demitry, Chelsea took a breath. There was no point in beating around the bush, so she didn't. "I need some time off."

He looked up. "Time off?"

"Yeah. I haven't had a break in nearly three years, and it's starting to show. I can't concentrate, I'm losing my temper, and I'm afraid that if I don't get away soon, things are going to start falling through the cracks."

"That bad, eh?"

" 'Fraid so." She gave him a forced smile. "It started with the strip mall from hell in Vegas and went downhill from there. The gallery was just the icing on the cake."

Joe sat down and rubbed his thumb across his chin, leaving a wide blue streak in its wake. "Where do things stand with your other projects?"

"Everything's under control. The Baker deal's a go, but there's nothing we can do right now. The management team's still having in-house meetings regarding the final colors for the boardroom and reception areas." Chelsea pulled a clean tissue from her pocket and handed it to him. "Chin."

"What about the preliminary layouts for the shopping center?" Joe dipped one corner of the tissue into his water glass and dabbed at the stain. "Are they any good?"

"They're fabulous, but we knew they would be. As for Kelton Insurance, I'll have the rest of the information I need to prepare a quote by the end of the week. Borden Industries and the medical building are still reviewing our proposals."

"You're one organized lady," Joe commented as he wiped the last of the ink from his face.

"I should be, considering who taught me. Seriously, Joe, can you carry on without me for three or four days?"

"Sure, but you're taking more time than that." He dropped the tissue in the wastebasket sat back in his chair. "In fact, I want you to take a month."

"A month!" Chelsea stared at him in disbelief. "Are you crazy? I can't take a month off. I've got meetings scheduled with clients, bids to work out, and with all the new projects we've got lined up—"

"You can't afford to be anything but on the ball," Joe agreed, "and frankly, you're not even close right now. You just said you were having trouble concentrating, and I know for a fact that you've been having a hard time keeping a lid on your temper. I heard you light into Vince about the blueprints the other day, and then there was that argument with the graphic designer—"

"That wasn't an argument," Chelsea muttered. "Mitch was just being unreasonable. He knew how important the drawings for the shopping center were, but because the courier was late, and for reasons entirely beyond our control, he dug in his heels and said he couldn't get them done before the weekend. *I* was just trying to get him to put his business life before his personal one."

"And I understand that, but you've always been able to deal with crap like that without going ballistic," Joe said. "This time when he pushed your buttons, you went off like rockets on the Fourth of July. The fact is you're working too hard, Chels, and the strain's beginning to show. Trust me, I know the signs. You're not burned out yet, but you're getting there."

Embarrassed heat flooded Chelsea's cheeks. She liked and respected Joe Turner, and given that his praise meant so much, it was hard to hear this kind of feedback from him—especially when she knew it was justified. "Sorry, Joe. You know I usually handle myself better than that."

"Yes, I do, and that's why I want you out of here. I know how hard you've been pushing yourself, and I know you love your work, but there are limits to a person's endurance, Chelsea, and you've reached yours. Stress builds up," Joe said quietly. "It becomes mentally *and* physically destructive. Trust me, I've been there. And I've seen it happen to people stronger than you. One day they're fine, the next they're taking Prozac just to get them through the day without screaming."

Chelsea sighed in exasperation. "I'm not a candidate for burnout yet. I'm just trying to keep a lot of balls in the air, like everybody else around here."

"No, not like everybody else. The rest of the people have lives. You and I are the ones who don't, because we're too much alike. My first wife left me because of my work habits."

"I know, but you were building a company," Chelsea said, automatically defending him. "And that takes time."

"So does building a marriage. Unfortunately, I gave one too much time and the other not enough. Anyway, that's my life. But the fact is, things are only going to get crazier from here on in, and I need you on my team, Chels. But you're not going to be much help if I have to run around after you doing damage control."

That one stung. "You really know how to stick it to a person."

"Only the ones I care about," Joe said in a gruffly affectionate tone. "So consider yourself on vacation as of five o'clock Friday. I don't want to see you in here until the old sparkle is back in your eyes. By the way, you did a helluva job on the gallery." He leaned forward and handed her an envelope. "Use this to buy yourself a first-class vacation. I've heard cruises are a great way to meet men."

"Okay, that's it for me," Chelsea said, getting up. "It's bad enough when my secretary gives me the gears about marriage. I sure don't need them from my partner as well!"

She purposely ignored the sound of his laughter as it followed her down the hall.

Chelsea told herself she *had* to go back to the art gallery first thing Tuesday morning. She had to check that the wallpaper the guys had substituted at the last minute in the downstairs ladies' washroom blended with the rest of the decor, and that the bare spot on the staircase leading to the upper gallery was gone.

But the upper gallery and the ladies' washroom were nowhere near *Poseidon's Sorrow*—which Chelsea found herself standing in front of a short while later.

Why did she keep coming back here? What was it about this damn painting that kept tugging at her heart? Why did she get this feeling of sadness and desolation every time she looked at it? One thing she knew for sure: Nicolas Demitry couldn't have picked a better title for his work. If ever a man was suffering, it was Poseidon.

Not for any particular reason, Chelsea glanced down at Demitry's signature. Unlike most artists, he'd signed the painting in the bottom left corner of his work, rather than the right. As she bent closer to examine the fine black lettering, Chelsea wasn't at all surprised to see that he had worked it into the background of a shell.

A shell that was exactly the same shape and color as the birthmark on her left shoulder.

She jumped back so fast she nearly knocked over the woman standing behind her.

"Grace!" Chelsea cried, blushing when she saw who it was. "I'm so sorry! I didn't know you were there."

"That's okay. I wasn't a moment ago," Grace said in a calm, unruffled voice. "I had an appointment with Jonathan and saw you walk in, so I came over to say hello. But are you all right? You look a bit shaken."

Chelsea wasn't about to admit that shaken didn't even begin to describe the way she was feeling. "No, I'm fine. Really." *How could Nicolas Demitry have duplicated her birthmark so closely? It had to be a coincidence.* "Actually, I just stopped by to see if one of Dan Gallagher's guys had been in. Jonathan's been on my case about a light that keeps shorting, and Dan said he'd send somebody down to fix it."

"I think he did. I seem to recall seeing an electrician wandering through here about an hour ago."

"Oh, good, that's what I wanted to hear," Chelsea said, even as her thoughts drifted back to the shell. *Was it the same shape?* Maybe she was just being stupid, or forgetful. Maybe it didn't look like the birthmark on her shoulder at all. Maybe she just *thought* it looked like it.

"Chelsea, are you sure you're all right?"

She looked up—and was embarrassed to see Grace staring at her again. "I'm fine. I've just had a lot on my mind lately." Chelsea quickly marshaled her thoughts. "Anyway, I probably won't see you for a while. I'm on vacation as of Friday."

"Lucky you! How long? A week?"

"Closer to a month," Chelsea said, hoping she didn't sound as guilty as she felt.

"What I wouldn't give to have a month all to myself! I'd actually get caught up on my reading. Still, you've probably earned it after all the work you did to get this place ready on time. Speaking of which, do you remember the conversation we had about Nicolas Demitry Saturday night?"

Unconsciously, Chelsea tensed. "Yes?"

"Well, I had a chance to talk to him before he left, and he was every bit as charming as my girlfriend led me to believe. Despite all the excitement his picture was generating, he was as calm and as unassuming as he'd been when I spoke to him on the phone."

Chelsea slowly let out the breath she'd been holding. "Yeah, he struck me as being pretty down-to-earth, too." At Grace's look of surprise, she added, "I spoke to him myself

just before I left. He said he'd noticed my interest in the
painting, and came over to ask me what I thought."

"Oh, Chelsea, how flattering. What did you tell him?"

Chelsea felt her cheeks grow warm at the memory. "That
it disturbed me."

"You *told* him that?" Grace's eyes widened in astonishment. "What did he say?"

"To be honest, he didn't seem all that surprised. I got the
feeling he was used to hearing comments like that." Chelsea
hesitated for a moment. "I read Laura Hopkins's article about
him in *The Liberal Arts*. Did you know he kept a summerhouse on Oyster Point?"

"I'd heard rumors to that effect, but I didn't read the article. What else did it say?"

Chelsea wasn't sure if Grace was asking for details about
Nicolas Demitry or about the gallery opening as a whole, so
she opted for the latter and purposely avoided any further
reference to the artist. But as she walked back to her car, the
image of the shell in the corner of Nicolas's painting came
back to haunt her. It *had* to be a coincidence. There were
only so many shapes a shell could come in, and Nicolas
Demitry had obviously chosen the one that most closely re-
sembled the birthmark on her shoulder. That really wasn't so
hard to believe.

Was it?

Four

Late that afternoon, Chelsea got a call from Jonathan Blaire. He was calling from the gallery, and it was clear that he was extremely upset. "Chelsea, would you mind coming down here? We're still having problems with that damned light in the Meridian wing."

Chelsea gripped the phone tighter. "That's impossible. I was there this morning and it was working just fine."

"Well, it's gone again now, and and the electrician's refusing to take responsibility. I told him you'd come down and meet with him."

Chelsea swallowed a groan. The *last* thing she wanted to do was go anywhere near the gallery. Unfortunately, Jonathan was still her client, and if he said something needed fixing, she didn't have a choice.

Consequently, less than an hour later, she found herself standing in the managing director's office, with Jonathan on one side of her and Dan Gallagher, the chief electrician, on the other.

As usual, Jonathan was at his nattiest. He was wearing one of his stylish Armani suits teamed with a silk shirt and a pair of expensive, handmade-in-London shoes. His blond hair looked like it had been freshly styled, and he was wearing a new pair of designer glasses.

Chelsea wondered if anything he owned wasn't stamped with somebody else's name.

By comparison, Dan was wearing faded blue jeans and a New York Knicks sweatshirt. His hair looked like it hadn't seen a brush in days, and a piece of black electrical tape was all that held the two sides of his glasses together. But there was one thing the two men *did* have in common. Neither of them looked particularly happy.

"Look, I don't like coming down here any more than you like calling me to come," Dan said tersely, "but the truth is, I don't *know* why that damned light keeps going out. I've had my guys look at it, and they say the wiring's fine."

"Then you're obviously using too powerful a bulb." Jonathan glanced impatiently at his watch. "Why don't you try using a lower wattage?"

"Because it's not that kind of bulb," Dan drawled. "Besides, they're not burned out."

Chelsea glanced at him in surprise. "They're not?"

"Nope. They're just dead."

Jonathan sent him a pained glance. "What do you mean, dead?"

"Dead. No juice. Like they were sapped. When we try them somewhere else, they work fine."

"Sapped, my ass!" Jonathan said testily. "There's got to be a reason why one light in the gallery keeps going out, and I want it found! An artist like Nicolas Demitry is not going to appreciate having his work hanging in darkness fifty percent of the time!"

Nicolas Demitry? A warning bell sounded in Chelsea's head. "What does this have to do with Mr. Demitry?"

"Everything! The bulb that keeps going out is the one over *his* painting," Jonathan said. "Thankfully, it's never been out when Nicolas was here, but I'm beginning to think that's only because we've been lucky. I've been trying to get that man's work into the public eye for years. I want to carry more of it, but that's not going to happen if he knows his work isn't being properly displayed. I want this fixed, Gallagher, and I want it fixed now!"

"I told you, it's not the lighting," Dan snapped. "The line and the socket both check out. There's absolutely nothing wrong with the equipment or with the wiring!"

Chelsea subsided into an uneasy silence as the two men argued around her. One problem. One problem in the entire gallery, and it had to be centered on *Poseidon's Sorrow*. Why? If the circuitry and the sockets were in good working order, why did *that* bulb keep going out when bulbs weren't going out anywhere else in the gallery?

"I'll get back to you, Chelsea," Dan said, his deep voice breaking into her thoughts. "And just to make you happy, I'll check out the wiring myself!" He glared briefly at Jonathan, then stalked out.

"Neanderthal," Jonathan muttered. "I tell him there's a problem, he gives me a song and dance." He looked at Chelsea in exasperation. "Why can't they just get it right the first time?"

"I don't think it's written into their contracts," Chelsea mumbled, rousing herself from the tangle of her thoughts. "But to be fair, the wiring for the gallery was a huge job, Jonathan. If this is the only light that keeps shorting, I think we're doing all right."

Jonathan didn't seem to hear her. "The man can't understand that correct lighting is *essential* to an art gallery. I *have* to have those lights on all the time, especially over *that* painting. It has to have the proper illumination to set it off."

"I'm sure Dan understands that, but if he can't find a problem—"

"Of course he can find the problem. He's just not looking hard enough." The director's mouth set in a hard line. "I never thought I'd hear myself say this, but I'm almost glad Nicolas is taking it away. I'd hate to have him think we run a shoddy operation."

Chelsea had opened her mouth to speak when one of the gallery assistants appeared at the door. "Excuse me, Mr. Blaire, but we've taken security off that painting. Do you want me to lock it in the vault?"

"No, leave it where it is, Steve. It won't come to any harm now that the gallery's closed." Jonathan looked at his watch again. "Besides, Nicolas said he'd pick it up shortly after six, and it's nearly that time now."

As soon as the assistant left, Chelsea said, "Mr. Demitry is taking the painting away already?"

"Yes. We had it on loan for only a week. I don't usually accept work for such a short period, but those were Nicolas's terms, and I was more than happy to make an exception in his case."

"I understand you're something of a fan of his," Chelsea said carefully.

"You bet I am, and I think this is the finest thing he's ever done. Come with me, Chelsea."

Chelsea blanched. "I really should be getting back—"

"Don't worry, this won't take long."

Harboring a definite feeling of dread, Chelsea got up and followed Jonathan into the gallery. She knew where they were going, which explained why she felt about as optimistic as a condemned man being led to the electric chair.

Sure enough, moments later, she found herself standing in front of *Poseidon's Sorrow* again.

"Look at this." Jonathan leaned closer to the painting and used his pen to indicate the figure of Poseidon. "Have you ever seen such incredible detail? Look at the way Nicolas has painted the scales on Poseidon's tail. The infinitesimally fine brush strokes and the perfect blending of these opalescent colors. See how, even without benefit of proper lighting, it seems to glow. And here, on the ship, look at the detail on the rigging. The torn sails, the lengths of broken and frayed rope disappearing into the sand. You can almost feel the texture of them. Remarkable, don't you think?"

Chelsea shuddered. "Very."

Jonathan glanced at her as if seeing her for the first time. "You feel it, don't you?"

"Excuse me?"

"The emotion. The power of the painting. You understand what Nicolas is trying to say."

"I do?"

"Of course, I can hear it in your voice. Oh, there's no need to be embarrassed," Jonathan assured her. "I felt the same way the first time I saw one of Nicolas's paintings. It was years ago now. I was working in a small gallery down the coast. Nothing fancy like this, but we had some good pieces. Anyway, one of the directors tipped me off that a painting by Nicolas Demitry was going to be shown to a select group of buyers, and he asked me if I wanted to sit in. Naturally, I agreed, and thank God I did. It was the first time I'd ever seen one of Demitry's paintings, and as soon as I did, I was hooked. It was called *The Guardian,* and it was the most incredible painting I'd ever seen."

"What was it?" Chelsea whispered, almost afraid to ask.

"A manta ray. A giant one, floating just below the surface of the water. Nicolas said he'd seen one like it near the Socorros."

"The Socorros?"

"They're a chain of islands about 220 miles south of Cabo San Lucas," Jonathan explained. "Apparently, it's an incredible area for diving because the islands are largely untouched by man. Nicolas told me he'd spent months in the water down there. Obviously that's where he got his inspiration for the painting." Jonathan shook his head in wonder. "Even now, it's hard to come up with just the right words to describe it, except to say that it was absolutely breathtaking. The sunlight was filtering down through the water, running along the back of this magnificent creature. It was amazing how Nicolas managed to convey the impression of size. There was nothing else in the water, yet you knew the creature was huge. Almost as if—" Jonathan broke off as he heard his name called over the paging system. "That better not be Gallagher. Excuse me a minute, Chelsea."

Chelsea nodded, and watched Jonathan walk back down the hall toward his office. As soon as he reached it, she turned back to the painting.

He was right. Even without the benefit of proper lighting, the painting seemed to glow with a strange iridescence all its own. The blue of the water required no outward illumination to intensify its incredible hue, nor did the rubies and emeralds studding Poseidon's crown look any the less dazzling for the want of a bulb. They sparkled and flashed as though touched by brilliant beams of sunlight. Even his hair and beard seemed to shimmer with a faint, silvery light.

Chelsea glanced up at the track lighting overhead. Sure enough, the bulb was out. Without adequate lighting the colors in the painting should have been muted and the details lost. Yet the colors were bright, and the details as distinct as ever.

"I knew I shouldn't have come back here," Chelsea muttered. "This painting definitely gives me the creeps."

"I hope not too many people share your opinion, Miss Porter. Otherwise I'd soon find myself out of a job."

The familiar voice, deep and incredibly sensual, sent a ripple of awareness through Chelsea's body. It also had her wishing she could curl up in a ball and roll out the door. Anything to avoid having to turn around and face the artist after what she'd just said.

"Mr. Demitry, I am *so* sorry," she apologized. "I had no idea you were standing right behind me."

"I know. And please don't apologize for being honest, Chelsea. I remember you telling me how much the painting disturbed you."

Chelsea wasn't sure what surprised her more—the fact that he'd called her by name or that he genuinely seemed to care about what she thought. And right now, she wasn't sure she wanted to know. "And I remember telling you that my opinion really wasn't worth considering."

"On the contrary, every opinion is worth considering." His smile widened. "Tell me, what is it about *Poseidon's Sorrow* that troubles you the most?"

Chelsea sighed. "I don't know. Maybe it's something to do with the fact that it's such a graphic depiction of death. Everybody on that ship is dead, and Poseidon's just sitting there taking it all in. It's . . . depressing. Couldn't you have painted him doing something more fun, like chasing mermaids or playing water volleyball?"

It was a poor attempt at humor that had Chelsea wishing she could drag the words back. Unfortunately, life wasn't that kind.

"It was meant to be a realistic depiction of Poseidon's life," Nicolas said quietly.

"Realistic? How can *anyone* know what's realistic when

it comes to something like that?" Chelsea gave a nervous laugh. "Poseidon doesn't even exist except in mythology."

"And perhaps in our dreams."

"Then you must have some pretty strange dreams."

"No stranger than yours, I shouldn't imagine."

Chelsea was *very* glad to see Jonathan return.

"Nicolas, so good to see you again," the director said, enthusiastically extending his hand. "I'm terribly sorry to have kept you waiting."

"No need to apologize, Jonathan. Miss Porter and I were having a most enjoyable conversation about *Poseidon's Sorrow,* and about the individuality of our dreams."

"Ah, dreams. *'We should show life neither as it is or as it ought to be, but only as we see it in our dreams,'* " Jonathan quoted softly.

"Tolstoy put it very well," Nicolas commented.

"He did, but then I've always felt that comparisons to dreams are particularly appropriate to *your* work, Nicolas. Your paintings have such an ethereal feel to them. Especially *Poseidon's Sorrow.*" Jonathan turned back to study the canvas. "It's one of the most powerful depictions of grief I've ever seen, which is interesting, when you consider that Poseidon wasn't known for being particularly compassionate."

"He wasn't?" Chelsea said, suddenly wishing she'd paid more attention to Greek mythology in school.

"Oh, no. Poseidon was a difficult god," Jonathan said. "Changeable and demanding. Quarrelsome. And, like his brother, Zeus, hopelessly unfaithful. He sired over a hundred children by several different wives."

"Yet he could stretch out his hand and calm the sea, or cause new lands to rise where only ocean existed before," Nicolas said quietly.

Jonathan smiled. "I see you prefer to see the virtuous side of the god."

"I wouldn't want Miss Porter to think he didn't have one."

"She's hardly likely to do that. You've succeeded in making Poseidon look like both a caring *and* a compassionate being in *Poseidon's Sorrow.* And if you don't mind my saying, Nicolas, I think it's the best thing you've ever done. Are you sure I can't convince you to leave it with us for another week? The reviews have been astonishing."

Nicolas shook his head. "Thank you, Jonathan, but you know that's not how I work."

The director shrugged his shoulders in a gesture of good-natured defeat. "No, but I thought it was worth asking. Well, we've removed security, so you can take it anytime you like. I'll have one of my assistants give you a hand carrying it out to your car."

"No, that's fine. I can manage."

"If you don't need me anymore, I'll be running along, too," Chelsea said.

"Hmm? Oh, yes, Chelsea, of course. Thanks for coming down. I'm sure I'll be hearing from Gallagher very soon over this other matter."

Nicolas glanced from one to the other. "Problem?"

"Nothing to be concerned about," Jonathan was quick to assure him. "Just a small electrical issue we're checking out."

"Actually, it's something of a mystery," Chelsea said, not sure what manner of alien creature had suddenly taken control of her mouth. "It seems the light above your painting has a mind of its own."

"Chelsea, I really don't think Nicolas needs to hear—"

"For some reason, it keeps going out."

Jonathan uttered a sound halfway between a gasp and a cough, but Nicolas didn't bat an eye. "I shouldn't worry about it. It's likely just a case of faulty wiring."

Chelsea shook her head. "The electrician said the wiring was fine."

"Maybe it's the bulb. It's been known to happen."

"No, Dan said the bulbs were fine, too. He also said they don't burn out. They just lose energy." She watched his face for the slightest change in expression. "He said when he tries them in another socket, they work just fine."

"Personally, I think it's all a huge conspiracy," Jonathan declared, completely ignoring Chelsea in what was obviously an attempt to deflect conversation away from the light. "And they're all in it together. The electricians, the lighting companies, the wire manufacturers."

"You may have something there," Nicolas agreed with an easygoing smile.

Chelsea smiled too, but the gesture felt anything but easy. *Was she crazy?* The artist didn't need to know they were having problems with the lights over his painting, and she sure hadn't scored any brownie points with Jonathan by telling him they were.

"I'll give you a call when I hear from Dan," she said, deciding to cut her losses and run.

"If you don't hear from me first," Jonathan replied through clenched teeth.

Muffling a sigh, Chelsea turned toward the man standing silently beside her. She was definitely in hot water over this one. "Good-bye, Mr. Demitry."

Nicolas held out his hand, and Chelsea could have sworn she saw amusement lurking in the depths of his eyes. "Good afternoon, Miss Porter."

As she drove back to the office, Chelsea could only shake her head. Well, that certainly hadn't been one of the brightest moments of her career. She had embarrassed herself in front of Nicolas again, and she'd ticked off a client. She made a mental note to warn Joe he'd be getting an irate call from Jonathan before the day was out.

She thought about Nicolas as she drove. As far as she could see, the man was perfect. There wasn't an actor in Hollywood who could touch him for looks, and for a world-renowned artist, he was endearingly humble. He even had a sense of humor.

So what was it about Nicolas Demitry that kept alarm bells going off in her head?

The long-awaited Friday finally arrived. Unfortunately, it was after ten o'clock by the time Chelsea finally got out of the office. Last-minute problems had sprung up, and of course, she'd felt obligated to stay and see to them.

Good thing Joe hadn't stuck around to see her out, Chelsea mused as she walked toward her car. But at least she could go home with a clear conscience, knowing that all the loose ends had been tied up.

It was nearly eleven by the time Chelsea turned off the

highway. She'd have to pass through Milford-by-the-Bay, a
fishing village-cum-tourist resort nestled close to the shore
that gazed out across the waters of Massachusetts Bay. It
reminded her of Nantucket with its cobblestone streets and
quaint shops, though it didn't have the same air of genteel
perfection. The population, six thousand at last count, dou-
bled during the summer, but unlike most residents, Chelsea
didn't mind the influx of vacationers. Tourists meant laughing faces and money pouring into the coffers of the local
merchants. Besides, the tourists eventually left, and the place
became her own sleepy little village again.

She turned on the radio and rolled down the window, taking
a deep breath of air fragrant with wildflowers and the fresh,
salty tang of the ocean. The sea always had a profoundly
soothing effect on Chelsea's nerves. She often sat on her deck
and watched the tide roll in, or lay in bed and listened to the
music of the waves, letting them lull her to sleep with their
own mysterious, magical song. In many ways, it was surprising that she would feel such an affinity for the sea. Her mother
was terrified of it, and her great-great-grandmother had nearly
drowned in it back in the mid-1800s.

It was her grandfather who'd told Chelsea the remarkable
story of Rebecca Lynn Mallory and of her amazing deliv-
erance from the sea. She used to sit in his lap and listen to
him tell of how her great-great-grandmother had been swept
overboard during a violent storm, and then been found
washed up on shore close to her home the next morning. Her
grandfather had also told her about the strange shell-shaped
birthmark they'd found on her shoulder. A mark that hadn't
been there when Rebecca had left on her ill-fated voyage to
Ireland.

Her grandfather called it Poseidon's Kiss, a mark put there
by the sea to signify that it had claimed Rebecca for its own.
But how or why the sea had marked her, he'd never been
willing to say. All he'd said was that if Chelsea wanted to
learn the truth, she'd have to read the diaries her great-great-
grandmother had kept from the day she'd married Jeremiah
Mallory until the night she'd died.

Chelsea hadn't read them, of course. Nor had she given
much thought to the shell-shaped birthmark on her own

shoulder. Until a few days ago, she'd taken it for granted, like a mole or freckle. She'd certainly never put it down to a psychic link between herself and her ancestor. But then, until recently she'd never had frightening dreams about water either.

Strangely enough, the dreams started just after she and Duncan split up, and they hadn't been all that bad to begin with. Just a random collection of scattered thoughts and unrelated images, not unlike the dreams Chelsea had been having most of her life. It wasn't until the weeks went on and the dreams had become darker and more disturbing that she'd realized the images weren't random anymore. It was one of the reasons she'd given serious thought to seeing a psychiatrist. After all, she had to talk to *somebody* about what was going on in her head. Somebody who might be able to tell her why she was being tormented by frightening images of storms at sea, and of dark water closing over her head.

Had Nicolas Demitry ever been afraid?

The question startled her. Chelsea wasn't even aware she'd been thinking about him again. And yet, why wouldn't she? She couldn't shake the memory of him or of his vivid painting.

He probably had a healthy respect for the water, as would any trained diver, but Chelsea couldn't imagine him being *afraid* of it. Not when he spent so much time in places that were known to be havens for sharks and devilfish and God only knew what other manner of strange, underwater creatures. Or maybe his sources of inspiration didn't come solely from the sea. The last time they'd talked, he'd mentioned something about dreams. Was it possible he suffered from dreams even more bizarre than hers?

He had claimed that *Poseidon's Sorrow* was a realistic depiction of the sea god's life. Was that what *he* saw when he went to sleep? Poseidon holding court over his ancient kingdom, raising his golden trident as mighty seahorses drew his chariot through the depths and beautiful, blond mermaids swam by his side?

If he did, she could only envy him. It was sure a hell of a lot nicer than anything she'd been seeing lately!

• • •

Chelsea was about ten minutes from home when she caught
a flash of silver on the beach. She glanced at the dashboard
clock. It wasn't all that late for teenagers to be out swimming, but it was strange she hadn't seen a car or a truck
parked anywhere along the road. She eased back on the accelerator and peered out over the water.

There was nothing there. Just the gently rolling waves lapping smoothly against the shore.

She started to speed up when she saw it again. Yes,
there—by the tide marker. A figure standing in the shallows.

Chelsea flicked on the high beams and peered into the
darkness. It looked like a man, given the broad shoulders and
narrow-waisted build, but it was hard to tell at this distance.
His skin glistened, indicating he must have just come out of
the water. Strange that she hadn't seen so much as a bike
parked anywhere along the beach.

Curious, Chelsea swung the car around and pulled over to
the side of the road. Aiming her high beams out toward the
marker, she got out of the car.

But the man was gone. And the beach was deserted.

"What the—?" Confusion furrowed a deep groove in Chelsea's forehead. He'd disappeared. Where? There weren't any
trees or small bushes he could hide behind. There was only
the sky and the beach and the—

Oh, no, you don't! Chelsea scolded herself. *Do not start
weaving fantasies about make-believe worlds. If you saw
somebody in the water and don't see him now, it's only because he's back in the water and swimming toward whatever
land-based place he came from.*

People did *not* just appear from and disappear into the
waters of Massachusetts Bay.

"Good thing you're thinking about seeing a psychiatrist,
Porter," Chelsea mumbled as she got back into her car. "Because if you're starting to *believe* there's anything more to it
than that, you really do need a whole lot more help than you
thought!"

A persistent breeze blew in from the northeast, pebbling the
inky surface of the water and ruffling the strands of sea grass
edging the line of beach. Sand dunes tufted with clumps of

grass, brown and brittle from the salt in the air, bristled and chafed in the gentle night breeze.

In the shallows close to shore, Nicolas stood very still, gazing up at the beachfront house. His body glistened like polished marble, his head lifted on the breeze, his senses alert for sounds undetectable to the human ear. He knew that Chelsea was home. He'd heard her car pull into the driveway about ten minutes ago and had seen the lights go on throughout the house. He'd watched as she'd drifted back and forth in front of the windows, occasionally stopping to look out before she moved into another room, and even from this distance he'd been able to see the apprehension on her face, and to sense the turmoil of her thoughts.

As much as it saddened Nicolas to know that he was the cause of her fear, he knew there was nothing he could do to ease her suffering. Chelsea didn't know who he was or what he would eventually be to her. Until she did, she would find no solace in her nights, or peace within her dreams.

A faint splash in the water made him turn around to peer into the darkness. He saw something move beneath the surface, then sighed as he turned back toward the house—just in time to see the lights go off and the house settle into darkness again. Chelsea would not be swimming tonight.

"So, she is still afraid," Lysia said, materializing out of the darkness beside him.

Nicolas slid her a sideways glance. "I thought you had no interest in my courtship."

She shrugged in the manner he'd come to know so well. "I cannot change anything, so I thought perhaps I would try to help you."

"Help me?"

"Yes. By giving you the benefit of my female intuition."

"Regarding Chelsea?" Nicolas chuckled, though it wasn't meant unkindly. "I doubt anything you can tell me would be of help in understanding a mortal, Lysia."

"Why not? We're both female. And though we may not think alike in *all* matters, I cannot believe our sentiments would be all that different when it comes to matters of the heart. But if you wish it, I shall leave."

Nicolas shook his head, surprised yet pleased by her offer.

"No, I'd like you to stay, if only so you can learn a little more about these irritating mortals, as you call them."

"If I stay, Nikodemus, it will only be to help you." Lysia glanced toward the darkened house. "Is that where your mortal resides?"

"Her name is Chelsea. And yes, that is where she lives."

"It seems a rather curious structure. Very rigid."

"It has to be, to withstand the climactic conditions along the coast. The winds blow in hard from the ocean. A fragile structure would soon be swept away."

Lysia nodded her understanding. "How long do you think it will be before your mort—before *Chelsea* comes back to the sea?"

Nicolas sighed, his mind returning to his problem. "I have no idea. She was badly frightened by her encounter with the Guardian, and I fear it may be some time before she finds the courage to venture into the water again."

"If the Guardian is the cause of her concern, why don't you just tell her about him?" Lysia suggested. "If she is of an inquiring mind, she will be fascinated to learn that such a creature exists. After all, no mortal has ever seen his like, and if she is to be your bride, she will see stranger things than this."

"True, but most mortals harbor a deep-rooted fear of large sea creatures," Nicolas said. "A noted author once set a futuristic story in the depths of the sea, and children had nightmares about the giant squid that came to life on its pages."

Lysia's laughter was like the tinkling of silver bells. "Foolish creatures. Do they not know he is timid by nature?"

"How would they? Few mortals have ever seen one alive, and popular fiction has turned them into nightmarish creatures with grasping tentacles and a beak meant to tear them apart."

Lysia shrugged again, causing the tiny droplets of water on her skin to twinkle like stars. "If your mortal shares that opinion, she will make you a poor wife, Niko. But, if such is the case, and her fear is as great as you say, you may have to wait a considerable time before her memory of the event fades."

"I know, but it is not easy to wait when there are so many

things I wish to tell her and share with her." Nicolas tilted his head back and gazed at the night sky. "Oh, that I had been blessed with gentle Hestia's nature, rather than cursed with the impulsive one of my father and uncles."

"I'm not sure patience is all you need now, Nikodemus," Lysia said in a soft voice. "You asked me what she would think of you, and how she would look at a creature so far beyond her level of comprehension. Given that, you may have to face the fact that Chelsea will never be willing, or able, to give you the love you need. She may never be able to conquer her fear."

He slid her a sideways glance. "You know as well as I do that it is not a question of *if.* Chelsea has no choice. A life in exchange for a life, remember? That was the promise I gave my father. Besides, why should she wish to linger here? She is not happy. She fills her life with work so she doesn't have time to remember how lonely she is."

"Perhaps, but does running away from failure in one life guarantee happiness in another?"

His dark brows drew together. "She would not be running away. She would be coming to something."

"Only if you succeed in making her fall in love with you. Otherwise, she would be exchanging unhappiness in one life for confusion and perhaps fear in another. It would be wrong to mistake a cry for help as a declaration of love, Nikodemus. You know what will be required of her. You know what will happen if there is even a shadow of doubt in her mind when she tries to pass through the Darkness."

Nicolas drew a long, deep breath. There were times when Lysia's insight astonished him, but he had to remember that prophecy was one of her gifts, and surely being able to see the future taught one a great deal about wisdom.

Was he making a mistake in approaching Chelsea so soon? Maybe she wasn't ready for this. Perhaps he was mistaken in his belief that her desire to escape the loneliness of her life was reason enough for him to take her into another one. If that was the case, where did he go from here?

He heard Lysia slip back into the water and, glancing over his shoulder, saw the water surge as the Guardian—the great creature that had so terrified Chelsea—drifted silently into the depths. Disheartened, Nicolas turned to follow.

Ah, Chelsea. If only you could have known. You would have been fascinated by him, not terrified, for he would never have harmed you. He was only being playful in trying to welcome you to my world.

Unfortunately, Chelsea'd had no way of knowing that, and it was only natural that her first reaction had been one of fear. Given the creature's great size, his *playfulness* would have appeared terrifying.

Sadly, there was nothing Nicolas could do about it now. All he could do was keep coming back until Chelsea moved beyond her fears and embraced the sea once more, because there was no question in his mind that she *would* embrace it. A yearning she could not possibly understand would draw her to it, much in the way instinct drew all God's creatures back to the place of their birth. It was in her blood.

Besides, she bore the mark of Poseidon. The right to choose had been taken from her over a century ago when her great-great-grandmother had given him her promise. A promise that could not be broken, for it had been given in death and sealed by life. But it was a promise Chelsea had no knowledge of, and for that reason Nicolas would be patient. He would not force her to join him, for taking her by force went against everything he believed in. The sacrifice Chelsea would be called upon to make was too great to be contemplated without the existence of a love so deep, so unshakable, that the very thought of living without it was untenable.

No, he would wait for her to make her decision for the right reasons. And if that meant coming back tomorrow night, and the night after that, and every night until her need finally overcame her fear, that's what he would do. As a son of Poseidon, Nicolas Demitry had all the time in the world.

It was Chelsea Porter who did not.

Five

Through sheer force of habit Chelsea sprang out of bed at five-thirty Saturday morning. But the belated awareness that it was Saturday and that she didn't have to go into work today had her falling back into it. In fact, she didn't have to go in at all; she was on vacation.

As she snuggled back under the soft covers, Chelsea wondered how long it was going to take *that* little bit of reality to sink in.

Unfortunately, old habits died hard, and when she still hadn't been able to get back to sleep twenty minutes later, Chelsea gave up trying. The body might be willing, but the mind was definitely weak. Obviously she was going to have to ease into this new relaxation mode a bit at a time.

With that in mind, she got up and took her first leisurely shower in months. She indulged herself with a variety of bath products she didn't even know she had, lathering her hair with raspberry shampoo and moisturizing her body with lily-of-the-valley lotion. But as she stared at her reflection in the mirror, she realized it was going to take a lot more than a long shower and a bunch of sweet-smelling creams to spruce her up. There wasn't a trace of color in her cheeks, and the circles under her eyes were darker than ever. No wonder Joe said she'd needed a vacation.

Unbidden, Chelsea's eyes dropped to the birthmark on her left shoulder. The bright pink color had faded since the night of the attack, but there was still a tiny scab marking the spot where the cut had been. Gingerly, she touched her finger to it, wondering why the skin around it hadn't been bruised.

Refusing to dwell on it—or the attack—Chelsea donned a pair of shorts and a tank top, and headed down to the kitchen.

The coffee was already made, thanks to the wonders of preprogrammable appliances, and while she would have loved a toasted bagel slathered with honey, she had to settle for a bowl of slightly stale cornflakes. She was out of just about everything else. Definitely time to hit the grocery store. If she planned on being home for the next four weeks, she was going to start eating like a real person again.

For that reason, two hours later, Chelsea found herself standing at a checkout counter at the Bayside Market, holding her breath as Winifred Morrison rang up the bill.

"That's quite a load of groceries you have there, Chelsea," Mrs. Morrison commented, gazing at Chelsea over the top of her glasses. "Having company in for the weekend?"

Winifred Morrison was a retired English teacher who'd moved to Milford-by-the-Bay eleven years ago. Her retirement had lasted exactly nineteen days. On the twentieth, she'd marched into the Bayside Market and applied for a job. She'd worked there ever since.

Most people called her Mrs. Morrison rather than Winifred. Chelsea figured it had something to do with the woman's being a schoolteacher most of her life.

"No, just filling up empty shelves, Mrs. Morrison," she said, smiling.

Mrs. Morrison smiled, too. "Well, I always say a well-stocked kitchen is a happy one, and it's good to have things on hand in case company does drop in. You have a nice day, Chelsea."

Assuring Mrs. Morrison that she would, Chelsea put her groceries in the cart and headed for the door. She had no doubt that by the end of the day, everyone in Milford-by-the-Bay would know she'd spent nearly five hundred dollars on groceries and that speculation would be rampant as to who she might be entertaining.

Life was just like that in a small town.

The automatic doors of the store swung open, and Chelsea was greeted by a blast of hot, steamy air. The coast had been basking under an unusually intense heat wave for the past few weeks, and the temperature was already well into the eighties. By the time she reached her car, little rivers of perspiration were rolling down the cleft between her breasts.

Chelsea had just about finished loading her groceries into the car when she looked up and saw a man walk out of the craft store two doors down from the market. She didn't have to look twice to know it was Nicolas Demitry. He stood out like a New York model at a high school reunion.

Dressed all in white, he wore close-fitting cotton trousers belted with a tan leather strap that seemed to accentuate the slimness of his waist, while the white cotton shirt, oversize and filmy as gauze, gave him a decidedly swashbuckling appearance. His black hair was brushed back from his face, exposing a strong forehead and the beautiful curve of gleaming black brows. High cheekbones graced a face that had been bronzed by sun and wind, but his skin certainly didn't look leathery or dry. He wore soft, moccasin-type shoes, and around his throat, a thick gold chain. He wore no watch, and there were no rings on any of his fingers.

Resisting a childish impulse to duck behind her car, Chelsea stayed right where she was. She really didn't care if he saw her dressed in denim shorts and a pink tank top, but she didn't want him thinking she was staring at him again— which was exactly what she *was* doing, since it was virtually impossible not to. He'd obviously been shopping for art supplies. He held a small bag with what looked to be the tip of a paintbrush protruding from the top in one hand, and a large square of something wrapped in brown paper in the other hand.

Chelsea wondered what kind of car a famous artist drove. A gleaming black BMW or elegant silver Jaguar? Or maybe a big, brawny SUV. But when he left the parking lot and kept on walking, Chelsea lifted her brows in surprise. No car? Surely he hadn't *walked* all the way from Oyster Point on such a blistering hot morning.

Quickly stashing the rest of the groceries, Chelsea got into her car and backed out of the lot. She didn't spend a lot of time thinking about what she was doing. If she did, she wouldn't do it. But there was no doubt in her mind that Nicolas was at serious risk of getting sunstroke if he walked all the way to Oyster Point. Surely she owed it to the artistic community to step in and do the neighborly thing.

"Mr. Demitry?" Chelsea slowed the car as she pulled up beside him. "Hi, remember me? Chelsea Porter."

He stopped and turned toward her, his beautiful blue eyes narrowing against the glare of the sun. "Chelsea, of course. How are you?"

"I'm fine, but you're not going to be if you stay out here much longer. Do you have a hat stashed anywhere in that bag?"

"I'm afraid not."

"Then you'd better get in. I'll give you a lift wherever you're going."

Nicolas bent down and gazed at her through the open passenger window. "I'm on my way home, but it's not exactly around the corner."

"That's okay. I can swing by Oyster Point on the way."

"You know where I live?"

Chelsea cursed the hormones that had her blushing like a teenager. "There was an article in one of the papers. It said you kept a summerhouse there."

He hesitated a moment. "You're sure it's no trouble?"

"Not in the least. Hop in."

Regardless of whether he saw the wisdom in her suggestion or not, Nicolas did as she advised. He set his bags on the backseat and got in beside her. "Thank you. I don't usually come out when it's this hot, but I ran short of supplies this morning."

"No problem." Chelsea checked the rearview mirror as she pulled back into traffic. "The sun can be ferocious this time of day. I'm surprised you didn't drive."

"That would be difficult, since I don't own a car."

She flicked him a look of disbelief. "Are you kidding? How do you get around?"

"I make other arrangements. It's really not all that difficult."

"It may not be difficult, but it must be inconvenient. I'd be lost without my car."

"Obviously, since you've got enough groceries back there to feed an army."

In spite of herself, Chelsea laughed. "Well, the current state of my cupboards isn't exactly an advertisement for healthy eating. Work's turned me into a processed-food junkie. There isn't a brand of frozen dinner or microwave popcorn I'm not familiar with."

"So why the sudden switch to real food?"

Chelsea shrugged. "Guess it's time for a change. Besides, I'm on vacation now, so I really don't have an excuse."

"You do if you don't like to cook."

"But I do. Or I did." Chelsea grimaced. "I'm not sure I remember how to boil an egg anymore, but I'll figure it out."

Nicolas smiled. "How long are you on vacation?"

"A few weeks. It's been years since I've taken any time off, so my partner told me I could take it all at once if I wanted."

"Is that what you're going to do?"

"I don't know. Depends on how much fun I'm having."

It sounded good, but Chelsea knew she was evading the issue. She didn't want Nicolas knowing she was on leave, because being on leave said more about a person's state of mind than being on vacation did. A person *took* a vacation, but they were *given* a leave. At least, that's the way she'd always looked at it, and she had no reason to think Nicolas Demitry would look at it any differently.

Not that it mattered what he thought, Chelsea reminded herself. Just like it didn't matter what she thought about his not owning a car. She'd offered him a lift home, not a psychiatric examination.

A forlorn country-and-western lament drifted out of the radio, filling the air with steel guitars and a woman crying over her hard-loving man. Chelsea abruptly changed the station.

"Jonathan told me you were the driving force behind the

design of the gallery interior," Nicolas said in a casual tone. "You must be proud of how well it all turned out."

Relieved that the conversation was taking a more professional turn, Chelsea nodded. "I am, but I had a great bunch of people working with me. Everybody went above and beyond the call of duty. Projects like that don't come together otherwise."

"There always has to be a leader."

"True, but a leader can't do much without a good team."

Again Nicolas smiled, but he didn't say anything. He just turned his attention toward the gently rolling waters of the bay. Chelsea took advantage of the opportunity to turn and look at *him*.

In the casual white shirt and pants, he looked every bit as breathtaking as he had the night of the gala. Chelsea wondered again how old he was. There wasn't a hint of gray in the glistening black hair, and the skin around his mouth and eyes was remarkably smooth and unlined. She wished she could have said the same for her own. She might be only thirty-six, but there were already crow's-feet and tiny fissures starting to form.

Was it possible that Nicolas Demitry employed the talents of a good plastic surgeon?

"Is that mainly what you do?" he asked, turning suddenly and trapping her in that brilliant cobalt gaze.

Chelsea gulped. "D-do?"

"Yes. Gallery interiors. Is that your speciality?"

"Ah, no, not really." Chelsea was amazed he didn't ask if staring at handsome men was what she did best. "This is the first art gallery I've ever done. I usually work with large corporations, designing their executive offices and that kind of thing. I've also done some government installations and several retail locations up and down the coast."

"No residential work?"

"Not if I can help it. I decided when I moved here that decorating other people's homes wasn't for me anymore. It's way too personal."

Nicolas lifted one dark eyebrow in amusement. "Personal?"

"Yeah, you know, as in trying to design a room around Aunt Matilda's favorite chair, or listening to the owner describe his or her personal life so I can get a better *feel* for what they'd like done in the room."

"And you don't like getting involved in other people's lives?"

Chelsea shook her head. "Not to that extent. Sometimes you get *way* more information than you need. Like why a seventy-year-old man needs the conversation pit in his six thousand-square-foot chalet lined with rubber and outfitted with a drain."

"Problems with incontinence?"

She slanted him a meaningful gaze. "*That* would have been preferable to what he *did* tell me. I had no idea senior citizens indulged in that kind of stuff."

Nicolas's eyes sparkled. "Sex isn't only for the young, Chelsea."

"No, but I always thought the kinky stuff was," she admitted ruefully. "Anyway, after that, I decided to make the switch to commercial interiors. Corporations give me the guidelines, set out the budgets, then leave me alone to do the work."

"So you've no regrets about making the move?"

"None. Careerwise, it was a good one."

"What about the personal side of your life? Has that fared as well?"

Chelsea's grip tightened on the steering wheel. "I'm not married, if that's what you mean, but I don't have time for a relationship. I'm what you might call married to my job."

Nicolas's eyes flicked upward as a large gray-and-white seagull swooped low over the hood of the car. "A person should always make time for the things that are important in life. I learned that a long time ago."

"I suppose that depends on what you call important," Chelsea said, striving for a casual tone as she watched the big bird head out to sea. "Personally, I'm not sure love's all it's cracked up to be."

"You sound cynical for one so young."

"Young?" Chelsea slid him a sardonic glance. "Have you seen the latest batch of prepubescent pop singers out there,

Mr. Demitry? Thirty-six isn't exactly young anymore."

"Nicolas. And it's not so terribly old either." A glint of humor appeared in his eyes. "At least, not to me."

"It's old enough to know I'm better off spending my Saturday nights with a good book and a bowl of popcorn than wasting it on an unfulfilling date," Chelsea muttered.

But does settling for mediocrity really make you happy?

She glanced at him in surprise. "Excuse me?"

Nicolas slowly turned back to look at her. "I'm sorry, did you say something?"

"No, but I thought *you* did." At his blank stare, Chelsea returned her attention to the road. She was sure he'd said something. Or had it just been the voice of her conscience again? Lord knew, she'd been hearing enough of *that* for the last six months.

"So what about you?" she said, deciding to turn the tables on him. "What does a successful artist do when he's not painting? Spend time with his wife? Play with his four kids? Wash the dog?"

Nicolas's lips twitched. "I'm not married, I don't have children, and I've never owned a dog."

"You're kidding! Not even a mutt?"

"Not even. I'm too much of a nomad. I've spent most of my life traveling."

"So where do you call home?"

He looked at her with quiet intensity. "Wherever I am at the time."

Chelsea looked back to the road again. Whoa, definitely some issues going on there. She took a deep breath and tried again. "What about your social life? You're not married, but I can't imagine a famous artist like you not having *somebody* in his life."

His expression grew openly amused, though whether as a result of the boldness of her question or her preconceived notions of what a famous artist did or didn't do, Chelsea wasn't sure.

"There is someone," he said after a brief pause, "but the relationship is in its early stages. I don't get to see her as often as I'd like."

"Because of what you do?"

"Partly."

"So your work doesn't allow *you* much time for a personal life either."

It was meant to be a dig, but Nicolas deftly turned it around. "On the contrary, I fit my work *around* my personal life. I enjoy what I do, but I don't use it as a way of shutting out the rest of the world." He paused. "If you didn't have your career, what else would bring the same degree of fulfillment and satisfaction to your life?"

Chelsea felt the intensity of Nicolas's eyes on her and quickly glanced away. "What are you, some kind of amateur psychiatrist on top of being a famous artist?"

His smile deepened into laughter. "Some things are obvious even to the untrained eye. I sense the blinds around your heart as surely as I see the shadows under your eyes."

"Yeah, well, sleep and I haven't exactly been seeing a lot of each other lately," Chelsea admitted. "Guess it's all the coffee I'm drinking."

It wasn't the coffee at all, but Chelsea wasn't about to tell him what was *really* going on. Nicolas had already touched on a few sore spots in her life. She didn't need him delving into her twisted psyche as well.

"Maybe it's not so much that you can't sleep, as that when you do, your dreams give you no peace," Nicolas said unexpectedly. He leaned his head back against the seat and closed his eyes. "Perhaps the vacation will help that, too."

Chelsea stared straight ahead, speechless. *Who was this guy?* And where did he get off making comments like that? She'd told him she couldn't sleep—*not* that she was having bad dreams that kept her awake half the night. How could he possibly have known something like that?

At first glance, Nicolas's house looked like most of the others dotting the New England coastline. It was only on closer examination that one realized other decorating styles had been incorporated into the design as well. The ornate cornices and dormers gave the large, three-story house a decidedly Victorian look, while the brass portholes that flanked the door lent it a certain nautical charm. Chelsea wasn't familiar with the history of the house, but she thought an old sea captain had lived here once, and she suspected he was the one responsible for the seafaring touches.

The house was located at the very end of the spit, and was definitely the most isolated. The front faced directly onto the bay, and a line of scrubby trees protected the back. Because of the way the land curved, however, the house was almost totally hidden from the mainland. A man could live here for months and never see—or be seen by—anybody.

"Well, here we are," Chelsea said, purposely keeping her voice brisk as she brought the car to a halt. "One famous artist, delivered safe and sound." She left the engine running so Nicolas wouldn't think she was asking for an invitation inside. "No charge."

To her relief, he didn't offer. "Thanks for the ride, Chelsea." He got out of the car and collected his packages from the back. "I hope you have a great vacation."

"Thanks, I will. And good luck with . . . whatever you're working on."

It sounded a little lame, but Nicolas was obviously used to hearing things like that. He turned and walked toward the house, waving once before opening the door and disappearing inside.

Chelsea didn't even wait for the screen door to close before throwing the car into reverse and backing out of the driveway. *Was she crazy?* She should *never* have stopped to pick Nicolas up. What did she care if he got sunstroke? It might have been better than sitting in the close confines of a car with him and listening to him analyze her life!

". . . I fit my work around my personal life. . . . I don't use it as a way of shutting out the rest of the world."

"Yeah, well, maybe you don't have a *reason* for shutting out the rest of the world, Mr. Rich and Famous Artist," Chelsea mumbled under her breath. After all, what would Nicolas know about disappointment and heartache? The only thing successful men like him ever regretted was not getting rich sooner. And she was willing to bet no woman had ever dumped him the way Duncan Rycroft had dumped her.

Well, she wasn't going to get caught under his psychiatric microscope again, Chelsea decided. The next time she bumped into Nicolas Demitry, she was going to turn and walk the other way. She had no intention of getting up close and personal with a man who had the ability to read her life like an open book!

The heat remained steady throughout the next few days. Thankfully, the offshore breezes kept it from becoming oppressive, but by five o'clock Monday, Chelsea decided she'd done enough work. She'd put a huge dent in her list of domestic chores, but there was no point wearing herself out. She still had three weeks and four days to go.

With that in mind, she grabbed one of the paperback novels she'd picked up at the market and curled up on the sofa, intending to get lost in the pages.

She was about two chapters in when she heard a knock on the back door. Surprised, she got up to answer it. She was even more surprised when she saw Joe Turner standing in the doorway. "Joe, what are you doing here?"

He looked awkward and a bit uncomfortable. His hands were thrust deep into his pockets, and there was something in his face that told Chelsea this wasn't just a social visit. "What's wrong?"

He tried for a smile. "Does something have to be wrong for me to drop by?"

"No, but you don't look like a man who just won the lottery either. Coffee?"

He sighed. "Thanks. Actually, I was in the neighborhood and thought I'd stop by to see how you were enjoying your first few days of rest and relaxation."

Thinking of the laundry she'd washed, the dust she'd vacuumed, and the windows she'd cleaned, Chelsea wasn't sure that rest was exactly the right term. But she also didn't believe that Joe's concern for her was the reason for the visit, so she decided not to quibble. She filled the kettle with water and plugged it in. "Not bad. I found out that the grocery store carries food that doesn't have to be thawed out or reconstituted, and that I *do* remember how to operate a washing machine. But I have to admit, it's going to take some getting used to this I-don't-have-to-go-to-work-today thing."

"Perfectly normal." Joe crossed his arms and leaned back against the counter. "Think of it as withdrawal symptoms for the workaholic. I suppose you've already cleaned the house from top to bottom?"

"Not quite, but I figure I'll be ready for the crew from *Better Homes and Gardens* by the end of the week. So," she said, turning to face him, "enough with the polite social chit-chat, what's really going on?"

Joe looked ready to argue, then sighed, as though realizing there wasn't any point. "You always could see through me."

"Not always, but I've learned to read the signs. Is it Patty?"

Chelsea wasn't sure what made her ask. It had just been a hunch. But if he hadn't said a word, the look on his face would have given her the answer.

"She walked out," Joe admitted heavily. "Packed her bags and left."

Chelsea sighed. She wasn't going to lie and say she was surprised, but she did feel bad for him. "Did she say why?"

"She didn't have to." Joe ran a hand through his hair. "I can't say I didn't see it coming. We haven't exactly been getting along the last few months. But I have to admit, she sucker punched me with the news that there was . . . another man."

Chelsea's mouth hit the floor. "What?"

"Yeah." He looked at her then, and Chelsea caught a glimpse of the pain he was really suffering. "She's been having an affair since March, and I didn't even know it."

Chelsea abruptly sat down. She didn't know what to say. What *could* you say to a guy whose wife had just run off with somebody else?

"Maybe it's not too late," she said. "Maybe if the two of you talked, you could straighten things out."

"I don't think her new boyfriend would like that," Joe said in a wry tone.

"Never mind him, this is about you and Patty. Maybe the two of you just need to get away for a while. You know, take a vacation so you can talk and get things straightened out."

"You know I can't take time off right now."

"You could if I came back," Chelsea said promptly. "And I can be in first thing in the morning. You could get Phyllis to book you and Patty on a fabulous getaway somewhere—"

"Whoa, stop right there!" Joe said abruptly. "I didn't come here to ask you to come back to work. Besides, there's nothing to talk about. Patty's gone, and she's not coming back. I just wanted to let you know where things stood. Bad news travels fast, and I didn't want you hearing it from somebody else."

"But—"

"No buts, Chelsea. I said I'll get through this, and I will," Joe said, his voice rough. "It might have been different if she'd come to me. I knew she was angry, and she had a right to be. She wanted a husband, and what she got was a workaholic who was never home."

"She knew that when she married you," Chelsea said quietly. "And a leopard doesn't change its spots."

"No, but I guess she hoped it would. And I did try in the early days," Joe admitted. "But when it's your own business, you have to be there. Nobody else is going to nurse it through the bad times, because nobody else cares as much." He stopped, ran a hand over his face, and suddenly looked his age. "But I can't forgive the betrayal, Chelsea. I can't forgive her for that."

Chelsea pressed her lips together and nodded. She wasn't going to try to change his mind. Instead, she just got up and put her arms around him, holding him close. He was her friend, and he was in pain, and Chelsea knew all too well what it was to hurt, to feel empty. "Call me if you need me," she said gently. "If I'm not here when you call, I'll get back to you before the end of the day."

"You're not going away?" he said in surprise.

"Afraid not. The singles cruise was sold out."

"Too bad for the guys." Joe held her for a minute, then let her go. "Thanks, Chels. By the way, we got the Beckley Fitch job, so you don't have to worry about me sitting at my desk twiddling my thumbs while you're gone."

Chelsea found a laugh and dug it out. "Like there was any chance of *that* happening. But that's great news, Joe, congratulations." She walked him to the door. "Are you sure you won't need my help? You could E-mail me the files. I could work from here—"

"Damn it, lady, you're on vacation. That means *no* work, not reduced hours." He bent and kissed her affectionately on the cheek. "I've trained you too well. But I will keep in touch, if that's all right. I figure I'll need to hear a friendly voice now and then."

"You got it, Joe," Chelsea said. "Like I said, I'm not going anywhere."

Six

In the spacious studio on the third floor of the old Victorian house, Nicolas sat on a stool and stared at the canvas. The depressingly *blank* white canvas.

He had created nothing since finishing *Poseidon's Sorrow,* a failing that would have given any artist cause for concern. But it was one that came as an entirely new experience for Nicolas; he'd never had to wait for inspiration to strike. Why would he, when all of the creatures and situations he painted were taken from real life?

No one knew that, of course, and Nicolas certainly couldn't admit that such was the case. He shuddered to think what people would have said if they'd known that the detailed and somewhat frightening rendition of *Architeuthis dux* he'd done for a private buyer in San Francisco last year *hadn't* been based on photographs he'd found in scientific journals, but on firsthand observation of the giant squid at nearly half a mile down.

No, Nicolas was well aware that his current inactivity had nothing to do with a lack of inspiration, but with his inability to channel his creativity and focus his thoughts on his work. And *that* was as a direct result of Chelsea Porter and the questionable state of their relationship.

Nicolas knew Chelsea was wary of him. He'd seen the uncertainty in her eyes the first time they'd met at the gallery. He'd seen it again today when she'd stopped to give him a ride home. Despite her good intentions, she'd been on edge the whole time, and he wasn't vain enough to believe that his status as a famous artist had anything to do with it.

Chelsea simply didn't know what to make of him. She didn't understand how he could know what was going on inside her head, and she certainly hadn't appreciated his rather pointed comments about the state of her dreams. Why would she? She didn't know who or what he was, and if he told her, he could just imagine what she would say.

After all, how easy was it for any mortal to grasp the concept of gods and immortality?

But there were a lot of other things Chelsea didn't understand, Nicolas admitted sadly. Like why *Poseidon's Sorrow* had fascinated her so much. Or why, on some deeper level, she'd needed to keep coming back to it when all she'd felt on a conscious level was revulsion for the images it portrayed.

Suddenly restless, Nicolas got to his feet and walked toward the window. There were so many things he wanted to tell her. So many things she needed to know. But how was he to tell her without awakening in her a horror so deep that it might scar her for the rest of her life?

Perhaps it would have been better if he *had* adopted some of his father's high-handed methods and just abducted her. At least then the decision would have been taken out of Chelsea's hands. Unfortunately, the ways of the other gods were not his ways, Nicolas admitted. Chelsea deserved better than that. When she came to him, it would have to be *because* she loved him.

But *if* that happened, how long would that take? Could he even guarantee that she *would* come to him within the brief time frame of her mortal existence? And how would she feel when she found out what he was? Astonished? Entranced? Repulsed?

The wind began to blow, and in it Nicolas heard the song of the deep; the gentle whisper that called to him every night, drawing him back to the place of his birth. He was a creature of the sea, yet he was not irrevocably bound to it. Nor did he need it to sustain his life, but it was a part of him. Not for him the soaring mountain peaks or lush rolling hills from which poets and philosophers drew their inspiration. It was the sea from which Nicolas drew his life, just as it was the waves, ever moving, ever changing in a timeless rhythm as old as life itself, that soothed his restless spirit and gave him comfort.

Sighing, Nicolas turned back toward the easel and stared again at the blank canvas. He wondered if he would find comfort anywhere tonight. He *should* be working. Two new commissions had come in, and he had yet to make a start on either of them. His mind kept slipping back to Chelsea, and to the fact that after all these years, she was finally in his life.

But those thoughts were destructive to all others, and knowing he would create nothing worthwhile tonight, Nicolas stopped trying. He might as well go down to the sea. There would be no bursts of creative energy tonight. His ponderings on his future with Chelsea had effectively put an end to that.

As always, Lysianassa was in the shallows, waiting for him.

"I had almost given up hopes of seeing you," she said, greeting him with her usual warm smile. "I thought perhaps you were going to shock us all and sleep in your land house tonight."

Nicolas sighed. "I was in my studio, searching for inspiration."

"Do you usually find inspiration in your studio?"

"Sometimes. Unfortunately, all I found tonight were reasons *not* to paint."

Lysia gently cupped a starfish in her hand. "Because you saw her again today?"

"Yes." Nicolas smiled as he remembered the concern in Chelsea's voice when she had pulled over to the side of the road. "She gave me a ride home. She feared I would suffer damage from the heat of the sun if I walked all the way here."

Lysia's smooth brow furrowed. "Why would she think that? You are not affected by such things."

"No, but all mortals are, and Chelsea has no reason to think I'm any different."

Lysia started to say something, then thought better of it. "They are fragile creatures, are they not?"

"In some ways. In others, they are incredibly strong. When you come to know them better, you will find that to be one of their most endearing traits."

Nicolas stepped into the bay and immediately felt the water rush forward to greet him. Whispers of foam curled around his ankles, caressing his feet and washing the sand from his toes. Tiny fish gathered in the shallows, their bodies gleaming silver in the moonlight as they hovered close but not touching, while spiderlike crabs emerged from the sand and lined up like watchful sentinels. As the moon slipped behind a cloud, he turned to take one last glance toward shore, his eyes scanning the shadows for any kind of movement.

"Do you ever tire of the need for caution, Nikodemus?" Lysia asked softly. "Is it truly worth spending so much of your life away from the sea, to live among mortals?"

"It is to me." Nicolas heard her sigh, and turned to look at her. "You should make use of the gift you have been given, Lysia, if only for a short time. You might be surprised at the pleasures you find on land."

But Lysia shook her head, dislodging a small shell from her temple. "If what I see you going through are the pleasures of living on land, I would just as soon do without them. My world is peaceful, Niko. Uncomplicated. Can you say the same of yours?" Not waiting for his answer, she sank beneath the waves.

Breathing a sigh of mingled frustration and regret, Nicolas followed, wondering if, for once, Lysia might just be right.

The water was unbelievably cold. It paralyzed her limbs and made her body feel heavy and lethargic. She struggled to keep her head above water, but her legs only grew more hopelessly entangled in the fabric of her skirts, until at last she had no strength left at all.

Please don't let me die, *she cried to the heavens. I don't want to die like this.*

But even as her heart whispered the prayer, her mind knew there was no chance of it being heard. Soon the dark waters would close over her head, and she would begin her long descent into the depths. Even now, she felt the dreadful lassitude of encroaching death. . . .

Suddenly, a jagged fork of lightning ripped open the night sky. Thunder rolled, and there was a tremendous crash—

A crash that jolted Chelsea awake. She sat up in bed, eyes wide as she fought to catch her breath, fighting to rid her mind of the terrifying images.

It was only a dream. You're not in the sea. You're safe, at home, in bed. Safe. It was only a dream. . . .

She repeated the words over and over until her feelings of panic began to subside and her eyes gradually adjusted to the dim light. She began to recognize shapes of things in her room: her dresser against the wall, the wicker chair in the corner, safe, familiar shapes that drew her back into the land of the living and kept her safe from the terrors of the night.

Chelsea flicked on the lamp and light flooded the room, chasing the shadows from the corners and vanquishing the ghosts. Yes, she was all right now. Her frenzied pulse was slowing and her breathing was returning to normal. But it was no wonder she'd dreamed that long skirts were hampering her. Looking down the bed, she saw that the sheets were twisted around her legs like the wrappings of a mummy. And there, on the floor, shards of broken glass floated in a pool of water. The remains of the glass of water she'd brought to bed with her.

That must have been the noise she'd heard, the crash that had jerked her awake. She'd obviously sent the glass flying when she'd been flinging her arms like the woman struggling in her dream.

Struggling not to drown.

There was something therapeutic about cooking. It was safe. Normal. Exactly what she needed, Chelsea decided, as she sliced, diced, and chopped vegetables for an omelette at lunchtime the next day. She needed to feel like her life was on an even keel, because when it was, she could forget about the weird things that were happening to her. Forget about the nightmares and the whispering voices, and pretend they didn't exist.

Too bad she couldn't pretend Nicolas Demitry didn't exist.

Chelsea sighed as she grated cheese into a bowl and set it aside. No, that wasn't fair; she didn't want him *not* to exist. She just didn't want him taking up such a huge chunk of her thoughts. She didn't even know why he was. What was it about the man that kept tying her in knots? Okay, so he was drop-dead gorgeous. So were half the actors on TV, but she didn't spend her days lusting over them.

Lust. Oh, God, was that what all this was about? She thought she'd moved beyond all that. But what other reason did she have for thinking about Nicolas all the time? It wasn't like they had anything in common. She was an interior designer, he was an artist. One who earned half a million dollars for every painting he did. When was the last time somebody had paid *her* that kind of money for specifying blue paint over green in their boardroom?

Chelsea broke three egg whites into a bowl and whisked them until they stood in soft peaks. Okay, if it *was* just physical, what was she looking for, specifically? Sexual gratification? Emotional fulfillment? Or just the intimacy of being close to a man? She'd never considered herself a sexual creature before. Sure, she and Duncan had enjoyed some good times in bed, but there'd been nobody in her life since he'd left.

Frustrated with her inability to figure things out, Chelsea gave up and went back to her preparations. Cooking was so much easier than relationships or men. You just opened the book, followed the instructions, and things generally turned out the way they were supposed to.

Why couldn't it work that way in real life?

Chelsea was pleasantly surprised to find that she could still whip up a half decent omelette, and for the next hour she devoted herself to the pleasures of enjoying it. She lingered over tastes, savoring the combination of flavors and textures, and for the first time in months actually began to relax. She didn't feel the need, or the desire, to rush back to her computer and check her E-mail or find out what was happening in the world.

Instead, she poured herself another glass of wine and sat staring at the bay. She listened to the music playing quietly in the background and let herself drift away on the melody— which was likely why it was a few minutes before she realized that a man was standing on the beach, directly in her line of vision.

Chelsea slowly got to her feet. There was something familiar about him. His golden body was beaded with droplets of water and his dark hair lay sleek against his head, indicating that he'd just come out of the water. He was standing in about a foot and a half of water, his hands on his waist and his face turned toward the bay. A brief bathing suit sat low on his hips, displaying to perfection the beautifully sculpted lines of his . . .

Chelsea was out the door and on the beach before she could stop herself. "Hello?"

He didn't turn around. He just kept staring toward the water.

Heart pounding, and swaying a little from the effects of two glasses of wine, Chelsea cleared her throat and tried again. "Excuse me."

This time the man turned. When he did, Chelsea could only gasp and stare at him like an awestruck schoolgirl. It *was* Nicolas Demitry, but looking so incredibly, devastatingly *male* that he literally took her breath away. Genetics or a rigorous exercise program had blessed him with a perfectly developed body. His shoulders and upper arms were powerfully muscled, his pecs and abdominal muscles were exquisitely toned, and his stomach was hard and flat. He stood tall and straight, exuding vitality and, to Chelsea's dismay, an alarming amount of raw sex appeal. Long, firm legs, beautifully shaped, rooted him in the water like a mighty oak.

In a bathing suit the size of a spandex bandage Nicolas had to be the fantasy of every woman over eighteen. But where had he come from? And why was he standing on the strip of beach right outside her house?

"What are you doing here?" she finally blurted out.

Nicolas looked at her, seeming neither surprised nor embarrassed by the unexpected meeting. "Hello, Chelsea. You look a little surprised to see me."

A *little* surprised? "You're a long way from Oyster Point."

"By road, maybe, but it's not all that far by water."

Chelsea blanched. "You *swam* across Oyster Point Narrows? You didn't tell me you were a decathlete, Mr. Demitry."

"Nicolas," he reminded her. "And it's not such a huge undertaking for a long-distance swimmer. I've been training since I was a child."

Well, that certainly explained the build, Chelsea thought, letting her eyes drift back over that amazing physique. But not even a marathon swimmer could swim twelve miles in cold water and not be breathing hard. Could he?

Chelsea dragged her thoughts—and her eyes—back to his face. "It's not the type of swim a person usually undertakes alone. What if you get a cramp?"

"I wouldn't."

"That's impossible. Anyone could get a cramp."

"Not me."

"You mean you never have."

His smile widened. "All right, I never have."

She stared at him in bewilderment. Why didn't she feel like she was making any headway here? "There's always the danger from the current. And sea life."

"Sea life?"

"Yes. I saw something in the water myself just a few weeks ago."

"Interesting. Did you see what it was?"

Chelsea stiffened at the gently mocking tone. "No. It was too dark. But I know it was big. Huge, in fact."

"I'm sure it wouldn't have harmed you."

"You don't know that."

"Did it attack you?"

Even through her wine-induced haze, Chelsea recognized logic when she heard it. "Okay, so it didn't attack. It did give me a nasty sting."

For the first time, Nicolas's eyes dropped to her smooth shoulder, and to the skin left bare by the formfitting halter top. "So I see. You bear a most unusual birthmark."

His voice was composed, but Chelsea could have sworn she saw something flash in the depths of his eyes. Had he just made the connection that her birthmark was the same shape as the shell he'd painted in the corner of *Poseidon's Sorrow*?

"I've been told it's a family trait," she said, wondering if there was some way she could ask without sounding like she was curious. "Apparently my great-great-grandmother had one just like it."

"That's not unusual." Nicolas's gaze remained fixed on the mark. "I've known entire families to share a common birthmark. Most believe it to be a fluke of nature. Others give it a far more significant meaning."

"Like what?"

"Some say it's a symbol put there by a higher power. In my family, it indicates a sharing of souls." To her surprise, he raised his right hand and with the tip of his index finger, slowly traced a circle around the birthmark. "A gift given by one generation to another."

Chelsea felt it at once. Heat. A pinpoint of warmth that started in the center of the birthmark and radiated outward until it eventually encompassed her entire shoulder, draining the tension from her muscles and making them feel wonderfully relaxed and supple. "How did you do that?"

"What?"

"Whatever you just did." Chelsea rotated her shoulder in a series of slow circles. "The last time my muscles felt this good was after an hour and a half's massage. What was that? Some kind of therapeutic touch?"

"Something like that." Nicolas's hand dropped back to his side. "Although it could just be a result of your skin being overly sensitive from the sting."

"Oh, right. The sting I got when *something* I couldn't see, and that wasn't dangerous, attacked me," Chelsea couldn't resist pointing out.

His smile returned, a gentle ruffling of his mouth. "Exactly." He stared at her for a long time, his expression unreadable. "Well, I should be heading back. I didn't mean to take you away from your meal."

"You didn't. I was just lingering over some wine. None

of that fine vintage stuff you were talking about at the gallery, of course," Chelsea said, wondering why she was still talking. "Strictly a domestic Chardonnay."

"There's no embarrassment in drinking the wines you like, Chelsea." His lips parted in amusement. "Did I sound like a snob?"

"No, just somebody who knew what he was talking about. You've probably sampled a lot of wines on your travels."

"I have. Maybe one day I'll take you to a restaurant on Santorini where you can sample some of the finest wines in the world."

Say no! shouted the voice. *Make it clear you don't want to have anything to do with him!*

"I'd like that," Chelsea said.

"Good." Nicolas glanced up at the house. "You have a lovely home. You must like the water, living as close to it as you do."

Chelsea's face clouded, her feelings of compatibility vanishing. "I did, but I'm not so sure anymore. I haven't gone swimming since the night of the attack."

"Have you tried?"

Chelsea had, but she didn't want to admit it. What was the point? She hadn't been able to overcome the fear. She'd stopped at the edge, unable to take another step, afraid that the monster might still be out there, waiting for her. It had let her go once, but that didn't mean it would let her go again. Maybe it was hiding, hoping she'd be lulled into thinking it wasn't there. With thoughts like those, was it any wonder she'd turned around and gone back inside?

As if sensing her answer, Nicolas said, "Sometimes it's easier to overcome fears when you're not alone. Why don't you come for a swim with me now?"

Chelsea glanced up. It was such a simple request; an invitation, nothing more, yet she couldn't do it. Even knowing she wouldn't be alone, she couldn't find the courage to go into the water. "I'm sorry, Nicolas. I know this doesn't make any sense to you, but the truth is, I can't." She glanced at the water, hating the weakness that made her shudder. "I haven't got over what happened to me."

"Nothing's going to harm you, Chelsea." His voice was

quietly reassuring. "Not while I'm with you."

"Oh, right, and who are you? The Man from Atlantis?"

Nicolas didn't move. In fact, Chelsea could have sworn he stopped breathing.

"Hey, I was only kidding," she said quickly. "It's just that you sound so at ease when you talk about being in the water. You know. You don't get cramps, you don't get tired, and now you're saying that as long as I'm with you, I'm safe. Nobody's *that* comfortable in the water."

"I am." Nicolas's voice was calm, his gaze steady on hers. "I've always swum in the sea, Chelsea. I've dived in the waters off the Great Barrier Reef, and in the waters of the Sea of Cortez. Nothing's ever harmed me, and I've seen some pretty amazing things."

Chelsea bit her lip, filled with anger, regret, and something uncomfortably like envy. "I'm sure you have. And I used to feel that way, but I don't anymore. I want to, but I can't."

"If you loved the water once, you can learn to love it again. Let me show you there's nothing to be afraid of." Nicolas held out his hand. "Come into the water with me, Chelsea, just for a little while. Give the sea another chance. I'll show you there's nothing to be afraid of."

He made it sound so inviting that just for a moment, Chelsea was tempted to say the heck with it and just follow him in. She almost *wanted* to return to the water, to embrace it as she always had. But then the images returned. The memory of *something* huge and white floating in the water beside her, like some giant, bloated corpse—

"I can't," Chelsea cried, shutting out the image. "I saw something! It wasn't my imagination. Something *was* in the water!"

Nicolas drew his hand back, his eyes filled with compassion. "I'm not saying there wasn't, but it's probably moved off by now. Large creatures don't usually stay in one place for any length of time. They're nomadic by nature."

"Yeah, well, I guess I'm afraid this one might want to become a homebody." A wave crashed on the shore, making Chelsea jump. "I'm sorry, Nicolas. Thanks for the offer. I know it was well meant."

When he didn't say anything, Chelsea turned and started

back to the house. A headache was coming on, a consequence, she supposed, of two glasses of wine on a hot afternoon, but that was a minor embarrassment compared to the humiliation of having to tell him she was afraid to go into the water. She'd wanted him to think she was strong, capable, and independent. Instead, she'd proved the opposite. She was still an unwilling victim of her own fears and obsessions.

"Chelsea?" Nicolas called softly. "Did you ever stop to wonder what it was about *Poseidon's Sorrow* that *really* bothered you?"

The question stopped her in her tracks. "I told you what bothered me." She turned around and faced him. "The painting's about death. About all those poor sailors drowning in the sea. What could be more depressing than that?"

"So it's the thought of dying that frightens you?"

Chelsea looked at him as if he were crazy. "Of course it frightens me. What kind of question is that? Doesn't it frighten you?"

"No, because I don't allow myself to think about it the way you do. Every time you step into the water, you wonder if it's going to happen. Even your dreams reflect your feelings about it."

Chelsea blanched. "That's ridiculous!"

"Is it?" Nicolas looked her straight in the eyes. "You keep on saying that *Poseidon's Sorrow* is about death and about all those poor sailors drowning, yet the only person you actually see in the painting is Poseidon. You see the wreck of a ship and an ancient god. But you don't see death, Chelsea. Unless that's the only thing you're looking for."

With that cryptic remark, he turned and walked back into the bay.

Chelsea turned on her heel and marched back to the house. Damn him! Why did he keep on doing this to her? More important, *how* did he do it? How did he keep on reaching into her psyche and pulling up handfuls of neuroses?

Yes, she'd been terrified as a result of her ordeal in the water. How was she *supposed* to feel after something huge played cat and mouse with her in forty feet of black water? Was she supposed to take that lightly? Pretend it hadn't scared the daylights out of her? She wasn't that good an actress.

And then to calmly suggest that *she* was the weird one because she was afraid of dying. Boy, this guy had missed his calling. He should have hung out his shingle in L.A. or New York, and been raking in three hundred dollars an hour seeing patients who routinely poured out their deepest, darkest secrets in the hopes he'd miraculously be able to cure their sickness.

Chelsea pressed her fingers to her temples. The fuzziness in her head had ripened to a full-blown headache. Irrationally, she blamed Nicolas for that, too. Why couldn't he have left things alone? Had it been necessary to bring up the subject of that damn painting again? Hadn't he figured out it was something she didn't like to talk about?

Just like she'd never consciously questioned life *or* death until she'd started having these bizarre dreams about drowning. Dreams that were so incredibly disturbing, because they left her wondering if she'd ever find the courage to go back into the water again.

Seven

By the sixth day of her vacation, Chelsea was in desperate need of a diversion. She'd cleaned everything that could be cleaned, she'd organized her closets from top to bottom, and she'd put on three pounds from eating all the desserts she and Emeril were preparing together. Yet she was still having nightmares.

That was the worst part of the whole thing. More than anything else, Chelsea had hoped the vacation would stop the dreams. She'd hoped it would shut down the part of her brain that was being overstimulated and let her sleep in peace. But if anything, the images were only getting worse, the meanings darker and more difficult to interpret. Last night, Chelsea had dreamed that *she'd* been the one drowning.

She'd been standing against the rail of a ship, peering down into the sea, when a huge black wave had suddenly risen from the depths and pulled her over the side. She remembered screaming as she fell, then gasping as her body had hit the icy green water. She remembered feeling the terror of watching the ship go down, realizing, as it did, that her last chance of survival went down with it. The last thing she remembered was sinking into the abyss and feeling a terrible pain in her chest as her lungs had filled with water.

Why was her mind doing this to her? She'd never had a near-death experience in the water. She didn't even know anybody who had. And other than the bizarre incident in the water a few weeks ago, she'd never come close to drowning. So why was she having dreams about it now? What was so deeply buried in her subconscious that she had no recollection of it except through the hazy mists of her dream world?

Escape came in the form of a telephone call from her best friend, Elaine Edwards. Owner of her own successful advertising agency in New York, Elaine called to say that she had to be in Boston on business, and that while she'd be tied up with meetings during the day, she wanted to spend the evening with Chelsea.

Chelsea couldn't have been happier. She'd missed Elaine. The two had met at a luxury ski resort in Colorado, striking up a conversation in the lodge and forming a surprisingly strong friendship, even though they were as different as two women could be. At the end of the week, Elaine had gone back to New York, but she'd made a point of keeping in touch and Chelsea had done the same. Now, the thought of spending an entire evening in her bright, irreverent company was enough to put the spring back into Chelsea's step. She'd been rusticating on the coast too long. She needed to do something that didn't involve cleaning, cooking, organizing— or the water.

She needed a jolt of city craziness.

The night before she left, Chelsea spent over an hour on the Internet trying to find out more about Nicolas. But the longer she searched, the greater the mystery became.

Nicolas Demitry was an enigma. People were familiar with his work, but not with him. Apart from a handful of articles dedicated to his paintings, there was nothing in the public domain about him at all. No record of where he'd been born, no history of where he'd grown up, no details as to how he'd spent the early years of his life.

The first reference Chelsea had found to him was in an art magazine dated ten years earlier. It had referred to Nicolas as a renowned artist who painted startlingly lifelike, though

highly imaginative, portraits of the undersea world. It hadn't
made any personal mention of him at all. Nothing about his
nationality, his marital status, or his family.

A second article, dated approximately one year later, had
detailed the sale of one of his paintings to a wealthy California businessman. The proceeds of the sale had gone to the
newly established wildlife rescue center on the coast.

Two years later, a different magazine had chronicled Nicolas Demitry's donation of another original work to the
newly opened Waterside Gallery in San Diego, where he had
elected to donate funds to a sea life reserve. Again, there
hadn't been a single thing written about the artist. Why?
Even the most low-profile celebrities had *something* out there
about them, but there was nothing about Nicolas Demitry.

Chelsea tried to tell herself that everyone was entitled to
his or her privacy, and that Nicolas didn't *have* to be like
every other famous personality. But why was she suddenly
having such a hard time believing it?

Boston on a warm summer day never failed to delight. It was
a wonderful mixture of old and new, a striking combination
of glass and steel towers juxtaposed against ornate Victorian
mansions and charming Old World architecture. It was exactly what Chelsea needed to blow the cobwebs away and
breathe new life into her soul. She spent a few hours brows-
ing through the magnificent Isabella Stewart Gardner Museum, and then paid a visit to Newbury Street, where she
browsed at some of her favorite boutiques. After that, she
treated herself to lunch at a bistro on Fairfield before leisurely
making her way back to the Public Gardens. There, she sat
on a bench close to the pond and watched the steady parade
of people pass by.

All these people, Chelsea marveled. All these accents and
languages. People from all over the world came to spend time
in Boston. Some of them even changed their lives and moved
there. Maybe it was time she did, too.

The thought brought her up short. Was she seriously thinking about moving to Boston? She'd spent most of her adult
life trying to get *out* of cities. And yet, the more Chelsea
thought about it, the more sense it made. Why shouldn't she

move to the city? After all, what was the point of living *on* the water if she was afraid to go *into* the water? Surely it was better to get away from it altogether than be forced to sit and stare at it like a conscientious dieter staring at a box of chocolates.

"Chelsea?"

Startled by the voice, Chelsea looked up—and felt her stomach do a back flip. "Nicolas? W-what are you doing here?"

His compelling blue eyes smiled down at her. "I had an appointment at the Museum of Fine Arts. When it was over, I decided to stroll around the city for a while. But I didn't expect to see you here on such a beautiful day."

Chelsea tried to ignore the way her pulse was hammering. She had no trouble believing that Nicolas had come into the city on business. He looked every bit the success he was in a pair of dark blue trousers topped with a cream-colored shirt, and a beautifully tailored sports jacket.

"I'm . . . meeting my girlfriend for dinner," she said quickly. "But I'm surprised you didn't head straight back to the coast after your appointment. You don't strike me as the type of person who enjoys spending time in big cities."

Chelsea hated the breathlessness in her voice—and her sudden inability to converse like a woman who was well over the legal drinking age. Yes, his cobalt-blue eyes seemed deeper than ever, and the shaft of sunlight striking his hair reminded her all too forcibly of the first time she'd seen him at the gallery, but that hardly excused this embarrassing bout of teenage stammering.

In contrast to her own state, Nicolas appeared relaxed and completely at ease. "As a matter of fact, you're right, I'm not much of a city person. Skyscrapers and narrow streets always tend to make me feel claustrophobic. But I haven't spent much time in them recently, so it gets a little easier to take. And Boston isn't as congested as Rome or Athens or some of the other major European centers I've visited."

The offhand comment gave Chelsea a brief, tantalizing glimpse into his life. "Have you traveled much through Europe?" she asked, wanting to know more.

"When I was younger. May I?" he asked, indicating the bench beside her.

"Yes, of course." Chelsea moved over to leave him room.

"I did travel quite a lot in my youth," Nicolas continued. "As a young man, I was always interested in learning about other cultures and how people lived. I soon realized that the only way of doing that was by living among them. So I embarked on my own version of the Grand Tour, and just kept going."

Chelsea smiled. "Do you have a favorite city or place?"

Sunlight played across his face, bringing out the flecks of gold in his eyes. "I have several, all of them near water. A small island in the Caribbean, another in the South Pacific, still another off the coast of Greece."

"You were lucky your parents could afford to send you all those places," Chelsea said enviously. "My parents didn't like traveling. At least not for pleasure. Dad was a salesman with a flooring company and spent most of his life on the road. The last thing he wanted to do when it came time for vacation was get in his car and drive anywhere. Fortunately, we lived in southern California, so it wasn't like we had to get away."

"You grew up near the sea?"

"Yes. My dad always liked the water." Chelsea sighed. "My mother was the one who hated it. That's why we ended up moving to Colorado when she and Dad split up. He got a transfer to Miami; I went to Denver with her and finished college. After I graduated, I got an apartment, a job, and pretty much started leading my own life."

"Do you see your parents often?"

"No. Dad's remarried and I don't like his new wife much. My mother and I were never close."

Nicolas was silent for a moment, staring down at the pavement. "Did she ever tell you why she hated the water?"

"No. I used to ask her, but she wouldn't tell me." Chelsea watched one of the little swan boats float by, thinking how much she would have loved to ride in one when she was young. "Maybe she didn't know. She just kept saying it was dangerous. All I know is that I was one of the few kids who didn't get to spend their weekends on the beach."

Nicolas sat forward and rested his elbows on his knees. "Sometimes it's hard for people to communicate their fears to others, especially if they don't fully understand them themselves. But it's fortunate she didn't pass her fear onto you. That often happens."

"I suppose," Chelsea agreed, "though until recently I'd never found anything in the water to be afraid of." She stared down at her feet, wishing she'd stopped to get a pedicure. She was wearing sandals, and though her toenails were neatly trimmed, a coat of polish would have made them look better.

She hastily tucked them under the bench. "So what about your appointment at the Museum of Fine Arts? Are they interested in buying one of your paintings?"

"Actually, they want me to create something new."

"Oh, Nicolas, that's so exciting! Imagine having your work hanging in such a prestigious venue. Your family must be incredibly proud."

It was the first time she'd mentioned his family, and Chelsea realized she was curious to know who they were and where they lived. But again, Nicolas's answers were disappointingly vague.

"I imagine they are. We don't see much of each other. We all have our own lives."

"Are your parents still living?"

"My father is. He's old but in remarkably good health. My mother died when I was very young."

"What about brothers and sisters?"

Nicolas fixed his attention on the top of a nearby building, watching the large silk flag fluttering in the afternoon breeze. "I have brothers, but we're not close. I suppose you could say we're all rather nomadic by nature."

Chelsea nodded. "I know what that's like. I still have family in England and Ireland, but I never hear from them."

"Would you have liked to have brothers and sisters?" he asked.

She looked into his eyes and saw something that warmed her all over. *He really is interested,* she thought. *He's not just making conversation.*

"I would have liked a sister," she said, hesitant at the admission. "I always thought it would be great to have somebody to share things with and talk to."

"I take it your parents didn't want a large family?"

"My mother didn't want any children at all. I was the unwelcome result of one night of unbridled passion." Chelsea grimaced. "The only reason she had me was because she was afraid of having an abortion."

Nicolas's eyes darkened. "I'm sure that wasn't the case."

"Yes, it was. My mother's never been maternal. Hey, it's okay, you don't have to feel sorry for me," Chelsea said, seeing the expression in his eyes. "Not everybody's cut out to be earth mother. Sure it bothered me when I first found out, but I'm okay with it now. Actually, it's kind of funny when I think about it. None of the women in my family had strong maternal instincts. My great-great-grandmother had only one child, and the tradition carried on down."

"What about you?" Nicolas asked. "Do you want children?"

Did she? "I suppose I would if I met the right person. I've never really thought about it." She slid him a sideways, uncertain glance. "What about you?"

Nicolas watched a towheaded little boy run by with a small black-and-white spaniel yipping at his heels. "I'd like a son. A man should always have someone to follow in his footsteps. But I'd like a daughter, too." He turned to look at her, and his eyes were quietly assessing. "One who took after her mother and reminded me, every time I looked at her, of the woman I loved."

Chelsea opened her mouth—then shut it again, aware of a strange, shivery feeling at the way he'd said *the woman I loved.* What would it be like, she wondered, to have him say that about her?

Nicolas stood up. "I suppose I should be heading back. What time are you meeting your friend?"

"Six." Chelsea rose, too, still wondering about his last comment, and her reaction to it. "Elaine's tied up with meetings until then, but we'll have the evening to get caught up." Standing so close to him wasn't helping. The man positively exuded sexual magnetism. "But it was . . . nice bumping into you, Nicolas. It seems like the first time we've really had a chance to talk."

"Yes, and I fear the fault is definitely mine." His glance surrounded her like a warm embrace. "I never meant to frighten you, Chelsea. You know that, don't you?"

Chelsea blushed all the way down to her unpolished toes. "I . . . don't know what you're talking about."

"I think you do." There was no recrimination in his voice. Just a sad acceptance of the way things stood. "But I hope I don't frighten you anymore. I'd like us to be friends. I think we got off to a bad start that night at the gallery, and I upset you again the day you drove me home. But if you're willing, I'd like to put that behind us. I'd like us to start again." Nicolas held out his hand. "Friends?"

After a moment, Chelsea took it. "Friends." She felt the warmth of his fingers close around hers, felt the strangest shiver, and suddenly, it was as though the sun had emerged after a rain. The grass looked greener; the flowers seemed brighter, and even the sky appeared a deeper, more brilliant blue. She could smell the sweetness in the air and hear the rustle of the leaves in the trees.

All because Nicolas was holding her hand—

"Chelsea?"

She looked into his eyes and realized she was being totally absurd. *Get a grip, Porter. You don't suddenly see lights and colors because a man's holding your hand.* Maybe Nicolas did have some kind of ability to channel energy, but it didn't make sense that all it took was a touch of his hand to make her feel this good.

"Yes, I'd . . . like that, too," Chelsea said finally. A nice thought, but irrational. "And I suppose I'd better get going, too. I still have some exploring to do. By the way, what *arrangements* did you make to get here today?"

Nicolas's one-sided smile indicated his recollection of her comment about the inconvenience of not having a car. "The museum curator sent a limousine to pick me up."

Chelsea was impressed. "He sent a limo all the .way to Oyster Point?"

"No. *She* did."

Ah, so the curator was a woman. That figured. "I suppose

she's sending you home in one, too?" Chelsea drawled.

"Actually, she offered to drive me back herself, but I told her I'd made other plans."

"And have you?"

"Of course." He said it with a straight face, but the glint in his eye made Chelsea wonder. But she forgot about that, too, when he suddenly reached for her hand and raised it to his lips. "Have a wonderful time tonight, Chelsea." He kissed the back of her hand, the touch of his mouth soft but profoundly moving. "I look forward to seeing you again soon."

Chelsea tried for a lighthearted answer. Some bright, witty comment, or even a bad joke about chivalry being dead, but her memory banks were empty and she came up blank.

Good thing she had four hours between now and six o'clock to get her mind back in gear, Chelsea thought as she walked away. Because if the last twenty minutes was anything to go by, it was going to take at least that before she was capable of rational thought, never mind scintillating conversation!

Elaine Edwards hadn't changed a bit. If anything, she was even more flamboyant and irreverent than she'd been the last time Chelsea had seen her. She turned up at the French restaurant in three-inch heels, diamonds flashing from all but two of her fingers, and wearing a bright fuchsia dress that looked fabulous against her blond hair and tanned complexion. "So, sweetie, are you tired of living in sandals and shorts yet?" she asked, enveloping Chelsea in a warm, Chloe-laced embrace. "I expected to find you looking like a tie-dyed beach bum."

"You make it sound like I live and work *on* the beach."

"Well, don't you?"

Chelsea laughed as they followed the hostess to a table by the window. "You're so rude, Elaine. No, I'm not tired of the laid-back lifestyle yet. In fact, *you* should try it. It might save you a fortune on that overpriced shrink I assume you're still seeing."

"Kevin is not overpriced." Elaine sat down and put her tiny jeweled clutch bag on the table. "His rates are very competitive for Manhattan. Besides, he's drop-dead gorgeous, and if I have to pour my guts out to somebody, it may as well be to a man who's easy on the eyes."

"So you are still seeing him."

"Yes, but not on a doctor–patient basis. He told me sleeping with his patient was a violation of his ethics, so I resolved the problem by switching to another doctor. Frankly, sex with Kevin is better therapy anyway. Scotch on the rocks," she told the waiter. "Easy on the rocks."

Chelsea sighed. "Gin and tonic." Elaine never changed. "Easy on the gin."

"Boring."

"I have to drive home."

"Spoilsport. So, never mind who I'm sleeping with, what's happening in *your* life? I know you're not married, unless my invitation to the wedding got lost in the mail."

Chelsea reached for a slice of oven-warm focaccia. "As if I'd be brave enough to get married without telling you. You'd likely show up at the church and put a halt to the ceremony. No, I'm not married, but work's been great." She dipped the bread into a heady mix of fresh garlic, extra virgin olive oil, and imported balsamic vinegar. "The gallery was a huge success, Joe gave me a raise, and—"

"Never mind all that, what's going on with *you*? Are you in love?"

"Yeah, right."

"Are you seeing anybody?"

"Try again."

"Are you having sex?"

"Strike three. That pretty much does it for the intrusive questions."

"Not in my ballgame. Chelsea, you're almost forty years old. Don't you think it's about time you *started* indulging in some extracurricular activities?"

"I'm thirty-six, and I'm too busy keeping up with my job to get out there and meet men," Chelsea replied. "Besides, you're forty-six, and I don't see you rushing up the aisle."

"Of course not." Elaine smiled, revealing a row of beautifully straight and very expensively capped teeth. "I'm not cut out for monogamy. But my God, Chelsea, you *work* at an architectural firm. There must be all kinds of gorgeous men running around. I remember the tech boys at college. I used to love watching them bending over their drafting tables. Talk about tight ends . . ."

"Elaine, I swear you get worse as you get older," Chelsea scolded mildly. "And I hate to disappoint you, but architects don't spend as much time bending over their drafting tables these days. AutoCAD's done away with a lot of that."

"Damn! Yet another area where technology has conspired against us. Well, what about other men? You must come across some in the course of your life. I meet them every day."

"Of course. You live in Manhattan. Milford-by-the-Bay isn't exactly the cosmopolitan center of Massachusetts."

"Tell me about it! The last time I was there, it took me three weeks to get the sand out of my Guccis. But you've got to give me *something* to work with."

Chelsea bit her lip, wondering how much she should tell Elaine about her relationship with Nicolas. She didn't want her reading anything into it, because there wasn't enough of a relationship to read anything into. But she had to admit it would be fun to tell Elaine that she at least knew a famous artist. And as long as there *wasn't* anything going on, where was the harm?

"All right, I do occasionally meet handsome men," Chelsea said. "For instance, a few weeks ago, I met this gorgeous artist—"

"An artist! Oh God, Chelsea, *please* don't tell me you'd get involved with one of those!" Elaine sounded horrified by the very idea. "They're unbelievably neurotic, hopelessly narcissistic—and talk about mood swings! They make menopausal women look positively rational. Misha was an artist, you know."

"Misha?"

"Misha Petroukashe. The Russian fellow I was seeing. I told you about him."

Chelsea thought for a moment. "Oh, right. The one who kept you locked in his bedroom for a week."

"Well, he didn't exactly have to *lock* me in, sweetie. It wasn't like I was *going* anywhere," Elaine purred. "However, ignoring the fact that he was one of the most incredible lovers

I've ever had, his mood swings were horrendous. When he was starting a new project, I couldn't go *near* him. I couldn't speak to him, couldn't touch him, couldn't even *breathe* around him. Said it disturbed his *creative urges*." Elaine tipped back her scotch. "Didn't do a hell of a lot for *my* creative urges either, let me tell you."

"I'm sure," Chelsea said, knowing how much Elaine enjoyed the physical aspect of her relationships. "But I'm not talking about anything like that."

"Why? Haven't you slept with him yet?"

"Of course not! I hardly even know him."

"So? What better way to *get* to know him than to sleep with him?"

Chelsea's cheeks burned. "You're not listening. I said I *met* a man, not that I was having a relationship with him. Nicolas Demitry is way out of my—"

"Nicolas Demitry? Oh my God! You *know* Nicolas Demitry?"

"Well, yes. Why? Have you slept with him, too?"

Chelsea said it as a joke, but she could see that Elaine was looking decidedly envious. "Don't I wish! I saw a picture of him in one of those rag magazines once. It was hazy, of course. The photographer was actually shooting a picture of some reclusive European actress who happened to be standing next to Demitry, but I definitely remember seeing his name and thinking he was the most gorgeous man I'd ever seen."

"He also happens to be an incredibly gifted painter."

"Really? I wouldn't know one of his paintings if I fell over it. But if he walked into this room, you'd have to tear me off him. My God, Chelsea, how can you even *talk* about the man without breaking into a sweat? Have you ever seen such an incredible body? And that mouth." Elaine tossed back the rest of her drink and signaled for another. "When I think what I'd like him to do with that mouth . . ."

Chelsea hastily reached for her glass. She'd made a mistake bringing up Nicolas's name. How could she talk to Elaine when, by her own admission, just *thinking* about the man made her sweat?

"Never mind. I can see we're not going to have any kind

of *intelligent* conversation about this," she muttered. "I only told you so you wouldn't think I didn't meet any men at all."

"Well, if that's the kind of men you're meeting, the situation's not as desperate as I thought," Elaine said, clearly relieved. "But you're on the level here, right? You honestly don't have a thing going on with him?"

"I honestly do not."

"And you honestly don't have the hots *for* him."

Chelsea opened her mouth to say not a chance. To her horror, nothing came out.

"I knew it!" Elaine said triumphantly. "Something *is* going on! You poor child, you never could lie to me."

"There is nothing going on!" Chelsea cried, trying to do damage control. "Nicolas and I chatted at the opening of the new gallery, but there weren't any sparks—"

"Have you seen him since?"

"A few times, but strictly casual."

"How many times? Once means a chance encounter, twice means there's a plot afoot, three times or more means he's definitely got you in his sights."

Chelsea started counting, then reached for her glass. "You're way off base."

"Then why are you red from the roots down?"

"Premenopausal flush."

"I don't think so. So where does the hunk live? Here in Boston?"

Chelsea had a sinking feeling she wasn't going to be able to pull this off. "Oyster Point."

"Good. With a fishy name like that, it has to be somewhere close to where you live," Elaine said, reaching for her drink. "And I'm delighted to hear that you've got something going in your life, even if it is with a rich but reclusive artist who's probably as self-absorbed as all the rest. You know how I worry about you. I have ever since that jerk Rycroft walked out."

"Duncan wasn't a jerk, and I'm fine."

"Oh, yeah? What about the nightmares? Do you still get them?"

"Not as often as I used to," Chelsea fibbed. "I think it was giving up the tequila shooters before bed."

"Don't make jokes. There's nothing funny about night-mares."

"No, but there's no point in worrying about them either. Everything's fine, Elaine, honest," Chelsea said when she saw the doubt lingering in her friend's eyes. "I'm over Duncan, I've got a great job, and I'm not unhappy."

"But you're not happy either, and you're alone," Elaine insisted. "And the older you get, the harder it's going to be to find a meaningful relationship. Trust me. I've seen the stats."

"I've seen them, too," Chelsea said, laughing, "and if I'm not worried about them, why should you be? One day a nice guy's going to sweep me off my feet, and then I won't be alone anymore. In the meantime, I'm not going to waste my time wondering where he is. When Mr. Right knocks at my door, I'll answer it. Trust me, I'll know the right man when I see him."

Eight

Nicolas stood on the small wooden balcony and stared at the waters of the bay. At the edge of the surf, a speckled sand-piper dashed in and out, searching the waves for tiny crus-taceans, while overhead, sharp-eyed seagulls dipped and soared, looking for unwary fish that strayed too close to the surface.

Dusk was falling, and though it would soon be time to leave, Nicolas knew there was no urgency. As much as he loved the sea, he treasured his time on land. It was the greatest gift his father could have given him. A gift he'd nearly lost as a result of a momentary weakness on his part so many years ago. But now, as he and Chelsea grew closer, Nicolas held on to the hope that it was a mistake he'd soon be able to put behind him. Certainly his running into Chelsea today had been a good start.

He'd felt a little guilty about letting her believe the meet-ing had been a coincidence, but given the outcome, he wasn't going to worry. They had achieved something of a break-through. Chelsea had been far more relaxed in his company than at any time in the past. They'd chatted like friends, and even the brief silences between them hadn't seemed awk-ward. Was it any wonder he actually felt a glimmer of hope?

Leaving his view of the bay, Nicolas walked back into his studio. Something else good had come from his improved state of mind. He'd finally started work on a new painting. Not on any of his commissioned works, but on a painting of Chelsea; one that would capture her beauty and immortalize it on canvas. If all went well, it would be his wedding gift to her.

Poseidon's Sorrow was once again hanging on the wall opposite the window, where it could bask in the light of both the sun and the moon. It was necessary that the sea paints be exposed to either one or the other so that the marvelous iridescence wouldn't fade.

Nicolas chuckled as he remembered Chelsea's confusion over the little "problem" she and Jonathan Blaire were discussing at the gallery that afternoon. Of course the bulb over his painting would keep going out. When not exposed to the direct light of the sun or the moon, the paints would draw energy from whatever source they could. It was the reason he didn't use the sea paints on any of the works he sold to the public. It would have been difficult to convince a serious collector to keep a painting in a sunny room rather than in a sheltered alcove. It was also the reason Nicolas had decided to do all of his future works with conventional materials. While he would miss the iridescence of the sea paints, it would be safer using the others. After a while, even a dedicated fan like Jonathan Blaire would start looking for explanations *beyond* the electrical setup of his gallery.

Looking at *Poseidon's Sorrow* now, Nicolas felt a rush of pride. He seldom studied his own work, but he was particularly pleased with this painting. Perhaps because he truly believed he had captured his father in one of his few compassionate moments. He'd been able to depict the bleakness of his expression as he'd sat alone in the great depths.

Jonathan was right, it probably was the most evocative painting he'd done, and he wasn't surprised that Chelsea had been so moved by it. If only she could look at it without fear in her eyes.

He stared at the painting for a long time. If only . . .

•   •   •

Chelsea didn't make it back from Boston that night. Elaine, being her usual impulsive self, had decided not to fly back to New York first thing the next morning, but to delay her flight until later in the day so that she and Chelsea could have a longer visit. Chelsea had been anxious to get back, and maybe to see Nicolas again, but she also enjoyed Elaine's company, and knowing it would be some time before they got together again, she agreed to stay over. As a result, the two of them went back to Elaine's hotel and stayed up until nearly three in the morning, laughing and gossiping like teenagers at a sleepover.

Chelsea drove Elaine to the airport, and with a promise that she'd get to Manhattan before Christmas, had bid her a fond farewell. Then she'd picked up the highway and headed back up the coast. She had to make a few stops on the way, and as a result, it was nearly nine-thirty by the time she finally got home. She grabbed her overnight bag from the backseat, and humming softly under her breath, unlocked the kitchen door and went in.

Chelsea felt better than she had in ages. She'd had a wonderful two-day escape, a fabulous dose of city life, and a delightful catch-up with her best friend. She'd also bumped into Nicolas, and for the first time since she'd met him, hadn't made a complete fool of herself. She'd actually enjoyed talking to him, and hadn't once felt like he'd been analyzing her. She hadn't been suspicious of him either. Instead, she'd just enjoyed their conversation and the time they'd had together. She'd liked hearing him talk about his family and his travels, and she was surprised at some of the things she'd told him about herself.

Yes, something had definitely changed between them yesterday. It was almost as though they *had* started over, as Nicolas said. Whatever it was, it left her feeling hopeful that they would be seeing more of each other in the future.

Deciding to catch a few hours of television before calling it a night, Chelsea poured herself a glass of milk and then headed for the den. She walked through the living room, starting slightly when a shimmer of silver caught her eye.

She reached for the lamp on the table and switched it on—only to freeze in shock and disbelief.

Poseidon's Sorrow was hanging in the middle of her living room wall.

Chelsea wasn't sure how long she stood rooted to the floor. It was probably only seconds, but it felt like days. *It had to be a hoax.* It couldn't possibly be Nicolas Demitry's original painting. She'd been at the gallery when he'd taken it away. She'd seen him pick it up and carry it outside.

How could it be hanging on her living room wall now?

Eventually regaining the use of her legs, Chelsea stiffly approached the canvas. In the confines of the room, it seemed to dominate the wall, the figure of Poseidon virtually leaping off the canvas at her.

It had to be a fake.

Unfortunately, the closer Chelsea drew, the more she *knew* it was the real thing. There could be no mistaking the brilliance of Nicolas's work. The tiny brush strokes Jonathan had taken such pains to point out; the beautiful, opalescent colors no one but Nicolas used. And there, in the left-hand corner, the tiny shell into which he'd painted his signature.

But . . . how on earth had the painting come to be hanging on her wall? And more important, why?

Chelsea's hand was already on the phone when she remembered that Nicolas's number was unlisted. She tried calling Jonathan Blaire at home, but all she got was his answering machine. Even Grace Thornton was out, and it was too late to call the gallery.

Chelsea thought for a minute. She didn't want to drive all the way out to Oyster Point, but what choice did she have? She had to know why the painting was here, and Nicolas was the only one who was going to be able to tell her that!

As she was heading for the door, she saw the envelope on the kitchen table. Surprised she hadn't noticed it when she'd come in, Chelsea picked it up and saw her name scrawled across the front in black script.

She turned the envelope over and drew out a single sheet of paper.

Dear Chelsea;

*I hope you'll forgive my boldness. I came to see you
and found you weren't at home. I noted, however, that
the back door was open . . .*

Chelsea glanced up in surprise. *The door was open?* She
could have sworn she'd locked it before setting off yesterday
morning. Resolving to check it later, she returned her attention to the letter:

*. . . so I decided to leave the painting for you. It would
give me great pleasure if you would allow Poseidon's
Sorrow to hang in your home for a few days. I expect
you'll find my request strange, but knowing how intrigued you were by it, I'm hoping that with further
study, you'll come to see it in an entirely new light. I
hope you won't mind that I also took the liberty of
locking the door behind me.*

> *Yours respectfully,*
> *Nicolas Demitry*

Chelsea let the letter slip from her fingers. He wanted to
leave the painting with her? *Was he out of his mind?* She
couldn't possibly keep a half-million-dollar painting in her
house. What if someone stole it? What if a . . . a fire broke
out, and the picture was damaged?

How would she explain *that* to Nicolas Demitry?

Chelsea started to pace. It didn't make sense. Why would
any artist, let alone one of Nicolas Demitry's reputation, decide to just *loan* out one of his paintings? And why to her?
Jonathan Blaire would have killed to have one of Nicolas's
paintings hanging in his house. Why had he chosen *her* to
be the beneficiary of his big-heartedness? Because she'd
shown such an interest in it at the gallery?

Or because he, too, had sensed that something had
changed between them yesterday?

Setting the letter down, Chelsea headed for the back door.
She carefully examined the area around the lock. Sure

enough, there weren't any signs of a forced entry, which either meant Nicolas was as good at breaking and entering as he was at painting, or that she really *had* left the door unlocked—neither of which struck her as being particularly believable.

Chelsea glanced at her watch. Ten o'clock. Too late to go to Nicolas's house? She had no idea what kind of hours artists kept, and his house was an hour's drive away. But if she didn't go now, he might think she *intended* to keep the painting. After all, he'd probably left it here after he'd returned from Boston yesterday, which meant it had actually been here *two* days.

No, she really didn't have a choice. The painting would have to go back tonight!

A heavy rain was falling by the time Chelsea turned onto the Oyster Point road. There weren't any streetlights on the spit, and except for her headlights, nothing alleviated the gloom all around her.

She glanced in the rearview mirror at the painting propped carefully against the backseat, and frowned. Even in the dimly lit interior of the car, it seemed to glow.

"I sure would like to know what's in those paints, Nicolas," Chelsea muttered, returning her eyes to the road. "Because they aren't like any I've ever seen before."

Nicolas's house was located about a mile and a half in from the main road. Usually the distance made for a pleasant drive, but tonight the dark stretch of road seemed dismally long. Finally, she drove past the thin line of trees and the artist's house came into view.

Chelsea swung her car into the spot beside the garage and turned off the lights, plunging her into darkness. The wind moaned like a lost soul, and the waves lapping against the shore had a decidedly bleak sound. Worse, there were no lights on in the house, making the place look dismally dark and unwelcoming.

Chelsea rapped her fingers against the steering wheel. She didn't like the thought of wandering around the property alone, but after driving all the way out here, it only made sense to see if Nicolas was home. She couldn't assume that he wasn't. Perhaps he was sleeping.

It was only a twenty-yard dash to the door, but by the time Chelsea reached it, her hair was plastered flat against her head, and her thin nylon jacket clung to her body like soggy tissue. She shivered as she searched for a doorbell. Not finding one, she opened the screen door and knocked.

When she didn't get an answer, Chelsea chewed on her lip. What now? As tempting as it was, she couldn't just leave a half-million-dollar painting on the porch and run.

Pulling her windbreaker close, she followed the deck around to the front of the house. Maybe Nicolas was watching television and hadn't heard her knock. Unfortunately, the front of the house was as dark as the back. Nicolas obviously wasn't home, which meant she had no choice but to come back again tomorrow.

It was as she was leaving that Chelsea saw the footprints. They started at the base of the stairs and went right down to the water. But as far as she could tell, there was only one set going in and none coming out. She peered across the black, choppy water of the bay. Surely Nicolas hadn't gone swimming in weather like this. He might be a long-distance swimmer, but nobody trained in conditions like this.

Oblivious to the storm raging above, Lysianassa drifted effortlessly through the depths. Nicolas swam beside her, but even if he hadn't, she would have felt completely safe. Because the sea was her home; the only place she had ever truly *wanted* to call home.

It was true, she had been gifted with the same duality of life as Nikodemus, but unlike him, she had never felt the urge to explore the land. She had no desire to live in the world above, or to take her place among the mortals who inhabited it. She'd meant what she'd said about having seen too much of their violence and greed to ever feel comfortable around them. Nikodemus had tried to give her an appreciation for the beauty of the land, of course, and had brought her some of its most fragrant flowers. He had shown her, in the Great Pool, many of the wonders that waited to be discovered, and sometimes, just for a moment, Lysianassa would experience a stirring of curiosity, and a desire to learn more about the creatures with whom she and her kind had shared an existence for so many eons.

But then she would take a brief excursion onto land, and listen to them talk, and once again realize that the gap between them was too wide to bridge. She was a Nereid, a spirit of the sea. She had nothing in common with the fragile mortals who ventured into the depths with their heavy plastic fins and clumsy diving apparatus. Creatures who, from the moment of their birth, were disadvantaged in a liquid environment.

And yet, Nikodemus had adapted surprisingly well to his dual life. He had embraced the air world and made his life in it a success, creating a place for himself and earning the respect and admiration of the mortals with whom he came in contact. But when fate had compelled him to take a bride from among them, Lysianassa had wept, not only for the loss of her own dreams but also for the passing of his. She feared that Nikodemus would never find true contentment with such an earthbound creature. Even if she became more when she passed through the Darkness, she would never truly be able to appreciate his greatness, for her mind was incapable of grasping such concepts.

Unfortunately, as the day of reckoning drew closer, Lysianassa was besieged by far greater worries than that, for she knew things Nikodemus did not. Hers was the gift of prophecy, and today she had looked into the Window of the Oracle, and seen what was to come.

What she had seen had caused her to recoil in horror.

How could she tell Nikodemus what he faced? How could she prepare him for what was to come? There was nothing she could do to change it. The Fates had long since written how the events would unfold. She had merely been given a glimpse into what would be. She doubted even Nikodemus himself could have affected the outcome, had he known what to expect.

Nicolas was aware that Lysianassa was being unusually quiet beside him, and wondered what lay at the root of her discontent. It wasn't like her to be moody. Her good humor and vivaciousness were two of the qualities he admired about her most, but something was definitely troubling her tonight. He wished she would confide in him, as she had done in the past. Sadly, he had a feeling that part of their relationship was over.

Lysia had changed considerably over the last few weeks. She'd always been a curious mixture of wisdom and naïveté, but ever since he'd told her about Chelsea, she seemed to have pulled away from him, perhaps in an attempt to protect her own feelings. He didn't blame her. Losing love was never easy.

He only wished she might find something else with which to occupy her mind. He had tried to interest her in the world above, but she had never shown an inclination toward venturing into it. Unmoved by his appeals, she had remained in the depths. Had she been afraid of what she might find in the world beyond? Afraid, perhaps, of what she might learn about herself? Lysianassa was far worldlier than most of her Nereid sisters. She had a gift for expression and an intellect that went far beyond theirs. Indeed, if anyone had the ability to exist in the two worlds, it was she. And yet, she shunned the air world, steadfastly resisting all of Nikodemus's attempts to have her join him there, preferring to spend months away at a time exploring the farthest reaches of the Kingdom.

He wondered if she ever got lonely. She professed not to want a husband, but her nature was the kind that would naturally reach out for love. Perhaps it was that loneliness that was weighing so heavily on her now.

A movement off to one side drew Nicolas's attention to the great black creature beside him. The giant manta had been his companion for decades, traveling with him and offering its own silent companionship as they crossed the mighty oceans together. The largest of its kind, it soared like an eagle on the invisible currents of the sea, its movements graceful, the slightest turn of one wing propelling it in any direction, the effortless circles reminding Nicolas of a beautiful underwater ballet.

In earlier days, sailors had likened the huge cephalic fins of the manta to horns; hence the nickname devilfish. But the moniker was a false one, for the creature was docile by nature and used its fins to scoop vast quantities of plankton and small fish into its mouth. It had few predators, but Nicolas knew that if the need ever arose, the gentle giant would swiftly become his guardian. Thankfully, such an occasion was unlikely to occur, for as a prince of the sea Nicolas was assured of safe passage through even the darkest reaches of the Kingdom. Not even Sephonia would dare oppose him, for Poseidon had taught Nicolas well. When the time had come, Nicolas had been ready for the Sea Witch's practiced wiles and able to defend himself against them.

If only Chelsea might be as well prepared—

"Nikodemus, there is something I must tell you," Lysia said, abruptly laying her hand on his arm. "Something I have seen in the Window of the Oracle."

Nicolas felt a frisson of alarm. "Is this why you have been so silent?"

She nodded, and her eyes were heavy. "I have been trying to decide whether or not to tell you, but in the end, I feel I must."

A muscle tightened in Nicolas's jaw. He knew well the power of Lysia's gift, but he had never been the recipient of it before. "Has this something to do with Chelsea?"

"I'm afraid it has."

Afraid. So, there was to be misfortune in his future and it involved Chelsea. The gods had willed it. But did he really want to hear what it was to be?

Lysia took the decision out of his hands. "I see an accident," she said quietly. "A terrible accident that will bring you and Chelsea great pain. That which caused it cannot be avoided, and once events are set in motion, there will be no stopping it. But once it is under way, it will forever change the way things stand between you."

"For the better or the worse?"

Lysia shook her head. "I cannot see that far. This is all the Oracle showed me."

"Very well. Tell my father I shall come directly."

"Why? Where are you going?"

He saw the concern in her eyes, and his own softened. "Don't worry, Lysia, I'll be fine. Thank you for telling me."

Then he turned with the gracefulness of movement that was so much a part of him, and set off into the night.

He did not begin to ascend until he was well out of Lysia's sight.

The young woman stood at the edge of the beach and gazed out to the sea. The skirts of her long dress fluttered about her, and a wide-brimmed bonnet lay on the sand at her feet. A lacy white shawl was thrown over her shoulders, conceal- ing the bodice of the old-fashioned gown.

The sound of a splash caused her to turn and her eyes to brighten with anticipation, but when she saw that it was only a fish, she sighed and absently began to rub her shoulder. The look on her face was pensive, wistful.

Sometime later, she heard a voice calling to her. A man's voice. "I am here, Chelsea. I have returned. Come to me."

The woman's face brightened with joy, her excitement plain to see. Yes, I'm coming, beloved! *She ran toward the sound of his voice, not even, flinching as she hit the first of the waves.* I am coming. . . .

The water rose quickly to her thighs, and then her waist. Her lovely gown floated up around her, but she did not stop. He was waiting for her. After all this time, he had come back.

A large wave broke in front of her, knocking her off bal- ance.

The young woman staggered, struggling to regain her footing, but the current was too strong. It pulled her on until her feet no longer touched the seafloor. She began to be afraid. Help me, beloved . . . help me . . . !

But only silence came back from the icy depths, and when another wave rose from the darkness, the young woman's fear escalated into terror. She was being swept out to sea, carried like a will-o'-the-wisp, helpless to resist.

It wasn't supposed to be like this! It was supposed to be beautiful. He was supposed to be here. . . .

When black water closed over her head, the woman knew she'd made a terrible mistake. Invisible hands pulled at her clothes, trying to drag her into the depths. She was swimming blind in the emptiness of a great sea, her air nearly gone, her strength exhausted.

No, I want to live! *she cried feverishly.* Take me back, I want to live! I want to—

"Live!" Chelsea screamed the word as she shot up in bed, trapped in the aftermath of the dream. Her body trembled as though *she,* rather than the woman in her dream, had fought to escape the frigid waters.

But what had she seen? A woman calmly walking into the sea. A woman purposely intending to drown? Why would she do that, when she'd so obviously been waiting to meet a man? A man who'd finally come and who'd called to her in the sweetest voice imaginable.

But it was *her* name the man had called, Chelsea realized. *Hers!*

Another set of tremors wracked her body, and Chelsea closed her eyes. What were the dreams trying to tell her? Was there some kind of message to all this? Or had her subconscious merely imposed itself on the dream at the point where the man had begun to call out? Was that when the past and the present had merged?

Whatever the explanation, there was no way she was going back to sleep tonight. Chelsea flung back the covers and got out of bed. She wasn't going to risk getting caught in that terrifying nightmare again.

Dawn was already creeping over the horizon when she walked into the living room. Brilliant streaks of purple and rose splashed across the sky as though God had taken a paintbrush and swept it across a wide blue canvas. Far below, the waters of the bay were calm, dappled with gold that blended with the reflected hues of pink and magenta from the sky overhead.

Chelsea wearily leaned her forehead against the glass door. It was all so beautiful. She had always loved the sprawling vista of sea and sky. Why was it so different now? Why couldn't she banish the image of a cruel and vengeful sea? A sea that sought to destroy?

"Why are you haunting me like this?" Chelsea whispered. "Why did you betray me?" She dropped her eyes to the deck—and stared in disbelief.

A dark puddle of water shimmered in the light directly in front of the door. There were also two sets of footprints pressed into the sand. But whoever her late night caller had been, he or she hadn't come to the house the normal way. The first set of prints showed the movements of someone emerging *from* the bay and walking a straight line up to her house.

The second set showed that same person turning around and walking directly back in.

Nine

Chelsea walked into Jonathan Blaire's office at eight-fifteen the next morning and sat down in front of his desk. "Hi."

He looked at her in surprise. "I thought you were on vacation."

"I am, but I need to talk to you."

"Sure. Coffee?"

"Thanks. Cream, one sugar."

Jonathan buzzed his secretary and ordered a double skim latte and a regular. "So, what did you want to talk about?"

"Nicolas Demitry."

"Nicolas?" The director's smile broadened. "So you've fallen under his spell, too, have you? Well, I can't say I'm surprised. Most people do, once they see how brilliant his work is."

"It's not his work I want to talk to you about." Chelsea took a deep breath. "What can you tell me about the man himself, Jonathan, other than what I already know?"

"Probably not very much." The director leaned back in his chair. "Nicolas is an extremely private man."

"I know, but *you've* been a fan of his for years. You must know something about him the newspapers don't. Like where he was born."

"To tell you the truth, I've always assumed he was Greek, but he's never confirmed that. He speaks several languages fluently, so it's hard to tell which one's native."

"What about his home? If he's here for only part of the year, where does he spend the rest of it?"

"At any one of his many other homes. Nicolas travels extensively on research, and since he doesn't like staying at hotels, he usually buys a small piece of property, usually an island, in the area where he's based."

"He's *that* wealthy?"

Jonathan smiled. "Do you have any idea how much his paintings sell for, Chelsea?"

"None."

"They start in the high six figures."

"Are you *serious*?"

"As serious as a lawyer making out a bill. Nicolas does one painting, and one painting alone. No limited edition prints, no coffee table books, nothing. When he sells a piece, the buyer knows it's not going to show up anywhere else."

"But I thought he donated the bulk of his works to charity."

"He does, but he has to live on something, so every now and then he offers a piece for private sale. His last one started at three-quarters of a million."

Chelsea gasped. "Seven hundred and fifty *thousand* dollars for a painting of weird sea life? You've got to be joking."

"I never joke about that kind of money," Jonathan said. "Besides, why so surprised? From what I hear, *you* were the one staring at his painting long enough to make him come over and ask you what you thought.

"Thanks, Vivian," he said as his secretary brought in their coffees.

Chelsea decided she was better off not answering his question, and waited until the girl left before continuing. "You've seen several of the other paintings Nicolas has done, Jonathan. Are they all as depressing as *Poseidon's Sorrow*?"

He looked at her in astonishment. "You find *Poseidon's Sorrow* depressing?"

"Well, yes. Don't you?"

"Not at all. Haunting, maybe, and certainly thought-provoking, but not depressing. As far as I'm concerned, none of Nicolas's fantasy collection is."

"Fantasy collection?"

The director chuckled. "A phrase coined by one of his more ardent fans a few years ago. In the early nineties, Nicolas did a series of paintings that featured beautiful women as their central characters. All of the paintings were exceptional, but two of them were outstanding. The first portrayed a sea nymph seducing a sailor."

Chelsea frowned as she reached for her coffee. "Mermaids seducing sailors isn't exactly new. I'm sure other artists have painted that kind of thing."

"Perhaps, but I'll guarantee none of them ever captured the depth of emotion and sensual awareness in theirs that Nicolas did in his. The expression on the face of that sailor was . . . well, I've never seen such euphoria in my life. The man was on the verge of dying, yet you'd think he'd just been given the keys to the kingdom." Jonathan smiled ruefully. "Maybe I would have looked that way, too, if I'd thought I was going to spend eternity in the arms of that beautiful creature. Galatea was one of the most striking Nereids."

"The what?"

"Nereids." Jonathan sighed. "Don't you remember any of your Greek mythology?"

"Sorry. I never was much of a history buff."

"Obviously. The Nereids, commonly referred to as sea nymphs, were the daughters of Nereus, a sea god, and his wife, Doris, an Oceanid. There were fifty Nereids in all, and Galatea was one of the most beautiful. There's a poem by Hesiod that lists all of their names. Ever read it?"

Chelsea shook her head, but made a mental note to stop by the library on her way home.

"Anyway, Galatea's sister, Amphitrite, was one of the better-known Nereids. She eventually became a wife to Poseidon and bore him Triton, Rhode, and Benthesicyme. He also had several other wives, who between them bore him hundreds of children, but I've always believed that Amphitrite was the one he loved best."

"How do you know so much about this?"

"I make it my business to know." Jonathan took a sip of coffee, somehow managing to avoid smearing the rich, creamy froth all over his upper lip. "Besides, I've always enjoyed Greek mythology. But what I know doesn't hold a candle to what Nicolas does. He's like a walking encyclopedia. History as a whole seems to fascinate him. We once had an astonishing discussion about Napoleon. I've always prided myself on my knowledge of that period in French history, but Nicolas told me things I'd *never* heard before. You might like to keep that in mind if you ever decide to question his credibility. He is *exceptionally* well read."

Feeling there was little chance of that happening, Chelsea brought the conversation back to the subject of Nicolas's art. "You said he did two outstanding paintings. What was the other one?"

"Ah, now that was truly remarkable." Jonathan leaned back in his chair. "He called it *Passing Through the Shadow of Darkness.*"

"A biblical reference?"

"Not exactly. The painting was of a sea witch called Sephonia. Like Galatea, Sephonia was uncommonly beautiful, but there was malevolence to her beauty, a sense of evil lurking just below the surface. Nicolas communicated it beautifully. He painted her floating in a midnight blue sea directly in front of a door that led to a fantastic silver city. The first time I saw the painting, I thought she was guarding it."

"But she wasn't?"

"Oh, no. When I asked Nicolas about it, he told me that Sephonia was there to lure human souls away. To steal them in the final moments before death. Before they could reach, I suppose, what was in Nicolas's mind, a kind of heaven under the sea."

Chelsea shuddered. "Sounds a little twisted, if you ask me. Witches stealing souls. Heaven under the sea. He's back on the topic of death again."

Jonathan studied her. "These aren't the works of a madman, Chelsea, if that's what you're thinking. Nicolas is an incredibly gifted artist whose talents stretch far beyond those of a simple wildlife caricaturist. He doesn't just do whimsical paintings of mermaids and sea horses. His portraits of whales and porpoises could grace the pages of university textbooks. They're anatomically perfect, right down to the placement of the tiniest element. But I've always believed his true skill lies in his ability to go beyond the simple replication of life. He shows a remarkable reverence for the creatures he paints. You said yourself that his painting of Poseidon touched you. It's that ability to communicate emotion that sets him apart from the rest. It's almost as though he has a . . . spiritual link to the sea."

It wasn't what she wanted to hear. In fact, as Chelsea approached Nicolas's house a short while later, Jonathan's words were still ringing in her ears.

. . . *almost as though he has a spiritual link to the sea.* . . .

Nope, definitely *not* what she wanted to hear. She raised the brass knocker—whimsically shaped to resemble the head of a sea serpent—and brought it down three times, hard. If Nicolas was anywhere in the house, he'd hear her.

Within moments, he opened the door, looking like he'd just stepped out of the shower. His hair was still damp, and Chelsea could smell the wonderfully fresh scent that clung to him. He was dressed for the weather in brief white shorts, deck shoes, and no shirt.

Damn Elaine and her comments! Chelsea thought irritably. She was already starting to sweat—and it had nothing to do with the heat.

"Chelsea, this is a pleasant surprise," Nicolas said, opening the door. "What brings you all the way out here?"

Since she had no idea how to casually work up to what she wanted to say, Chelsea just blurted it out. "I have to talk to you. About last night."

One dark eyebrow rose. "Last night?"

"Or maybe I should say this morning. Very . . . early this morning."

She watched him carefully, looking for surprise, alarm, or anything in between. But not so much as an eyelash twitched. "Would you like to come in?" he asked.

And be alone in a house with you? She shook her head. "I'd rather stay here. This won't take long."

"Nevertheless, I don't like talking to people on my door-step."

Chelsea hesitated. Why *shouldn't* she go in? Nicolas might be a little off the wall artistically, but she didn't think he was dangerous. Squaring her shoulders, she walked past him into a spacious entrance hall. "I hope I'm not interrupting your work."

"Not at all. I'm a bit late getting started today." Nicolas let the screen door swing shut but left the inner door open. "Can I get you something to drink?" he asked as he turned and led the way down a paneled hallway.

Reluctantly, Chelsea followed him. "No thanks. I've already had two coffees and a donut this morning."

"Not exactly a healthy start."

She shrugged. "Some days need more of a kick start than others."

They walked into the kitchen and Chelsea glanced around, noting that while the room was immaculately clean, it was completely lacking in the human touches that made a place cozy and inviting. There was a large pine hutch against the far wall and an old fashioned wooden table and six chairs in the middle of the room. A braided rug in shades of blue and white was on the floor under the table, and wide wooden shutters covered the windows. The gleaming white stove looked as though it had never been used, and there wasn't a mark on the pristine white counters. It was a house where someone dwelled. Not where they lived.

"You said you wanted to see me," Nicolas said quietly. "About last night?"

Chelsea leaned back against the counter and tried to relax. Now that she was here, the words seemed to stick in her throat. Probably because in the plain light of day, her fears seemed a little ridiculous, even to her. "I came to see you for two reasons," she finally said. "You weren't here when I came by last night—"

"You came *here*?"

She saw the wariness in his eyes. "Yes. To return *Poseidon's Sorrow*. You must know I can't keep it."

He relaxed a little, the watchfulness easing. "Why not? I know how intrigued you were by it."

"Yes, but so were hundreds of other people, and you didn't give it to them."

The corners of his mouth lifted. "I didn't *give* it to you either. It's on loan, as I said in my note."

"But that doesn't make sense. Why would you do something like that?"

"I thought you might like to look at it in the familiar surroundings of your home. I was hoping that by doing so, you might come to feel more comfortable with it."

"But I've already told you, it doesn't matter how *I* feel about the painting!"

"It matters to me."

The brief answer stopped her in her tracks.

"Okay, let's be practical," she said, trying another approach. "What if someone breaks in and steals the painting? I don't have an alarm system. I don't even own a dog."

"Are many art thefts taking place in Milford-by-the-Bay?"

"There's always a first time," Chelsea said, ignoring the sarcasm. "And it's not only theft I'm worried about. What if my ceiling springs a leak? Or a . . . a pan of oil catches fire in the kitchen? The painting could suffer serious smoke damage!"

"Are you prone to accidents in the kitchen?"

"No, but I've never had a half-million-dollar painting hanging in my living room either. Who knows *what* I might suddenly become prone to?"

"You're overreacting."

"No, I'm not. I wouldn't be able to sleep knowing that painting was in my house, Nicolas."

"Do you really think I would have left it with you if I'd thought it would come to harm?"

"I don't know." Chelsea pushed herself away from the counter. "I honestly don't know."

Nicolas stayed where he was, but his eyes never left hers. "You said there were two reasons you wanted to see me. The first was to return *Poseidon's Sorrow*. What was the second?"

Chelsea looked at him, and against her will felt herself caught in the mesmerizing power of his eyes. "Someone paid me . . . a visit very early this morning."

"A visit?"

"I got up around five and went down to the living room. I was standing by the window when I noticed a puddle of water on the deck. Then I saw the footprints." Her voice sounded strained, even to her own ears. "There were two sets, one leading up from the water, the other leading back down."

"And you think *I* was your early morning visitor?"

"I don't know. But you do like to swim at night, and you're capable of covering the distance. You also know where I live."

"To coin your own phrase, so do a lot of other people."

"Yes, but they usually come by car. Look, this probably sounds a little crazy, but I know what I saw."

Nicolas watched her in silence for a moment. "Did you think to check the beach for footprints when you got back from Boston?" he asked quietly.

The question surprised her. She'd expected Nicolas to deny being anywhere near her house, not to put forward an eminently logical question. "No. I was too stunned at finding the painting in my living room to think about doing an all-points inspection."

"So it's possible the footprints were already there when you got home."

Chelsea thought the suggestion unlikely, but she couldn't dismiss it out of hand. "It's possible, but what about the water on the deck?"

"From what I remember, your deck's sheltered from the sun. Perhaps some kids were staring in your window earlier and left a puddle."

"Kids?" Again, Chelsea was tempted to argue, but she knew there wasn't much point. She couldn't say for sure that what Nicolas was suggesting was any more ridiculous than what she was.

"Okay, look, it really doesn't matter how the footprints got there. What matters is that I can't keep the painting. So I've brought it back. It's outside in my car."

Nicolas looked at her for a long time. So long, that Chelsea began to wonder if he'd forgotten what she'd said. His next words dispelled the impression.

"I really would like you to keep the painting for a few days, Chelsea. You and I both know it isn't going to come to any harm, and if it makes you feel any better, I'll come over next Saturday morning and pick it up myself. That's less than a week. Surely you can put up with a strange piece of art hanging in your living room for a few days."

"I'm not sure I can."

Nicolas only smiled.

Chelsea blinked and hastily looked away. Damn it, no man had a right to look that good.

"You still haven't told me why you left it," she muttered. "At least, not to my satisfaction."

"Let's just say your keeping the painting in your house would mean a great deal to me. I've never done this before, Chelsea, and I won't do it again. But because of who you are, I'm asking you to grant me this small favor."

As he'd been speaking, Nicolas had been walking toward her. Now he stood directly in front of her. His voice had dropped, and in spite of herself, Chelsea felt an unwilling surge of excitement. This man frightened her, but he fascinated her, too. He was like his painting: dark and mysterious, incredibly compelling. The smoldering flame she saw in his eyes startled her, as did her own reaction to it. There was *something* going on between them, even if she didn't know what it was.

"You haven't answered me, Chelsea," Nicolas murmured, raising his hand to brush his fingers against her cheek. "Is it to be yes, or no?"

Chelsea inhaled, caught off guard by the touch of his hand. She felt the coolness of his fingers on her skin; felt his thumb trace the line of her jaw, then follow the contours of her neck to her throat, a sweet, tingling caress. "I . . . don't know. . . ."

"Don't be afraid of me, Chelsea. Don't fight me." His voice was quiet, his eyes hypnotic. "You and I were meant to be together, but I won't force you. I'll give you all the time you need. I won't take you against your will."

Chelsea closed her eyes, lulled by the sound of his voice. He *must* be some kind of healer. She was starting to experience the same feeling of tranquillity she had at the gallery, and again when he'd touched her shoulder at the beach. But this time, it enveloped all of her. Even as the questions rolled around her mind, an incredible feeling of peace was suffusing her body, relaxing her. . . .

"I don't . . . understand what's happening to me. . . ."

"You will, in time." Nicolas's voice was low and soothing. "The dreams will tell you what you need to know. Listen to your dreams, Chelsea. Open your heart and don't be afraid, for they will remind you of what has passed between us."

The dreams. "How . . . do you know about my dreams?" Unsteadily, she opened her eyes. "Who *are* you?"

His burning gaze held her still. "Who do you think I am?"

Her eyes were fixed on his. "I'd like to think you're a . . . famous artist who paints bizarre pictures of the sea. A man who knows marine biology and who's as fit as the Bionic Man."

"But you think there's more?"

"I *know* there's more." She took a deep breath, fighting to shake off the lethargy. "You keep telling me about my dreams, about how much they upset me, yet I've never spoken a word to you about them. You make references to what's passed between us, but until a few weeks ago I'd never even *heard* of you."

"Perhaps it will come to you in time. But you'll have to look into the past. Into your heart."

Chelsea shook her head. "I don't know what you're talking about. What am I supposed to remember? We don't *have* a past!"

"Yes, we do. Perhaps this will help bring it back." Before Chelsea had time to react, Nicolas bent his head and pressed his mouth to the birthmark on her shoulder.

It was like being branded with a red-hot iron. She gasped, feeling the searing heat of his mouth against her skin. But what shocked her more was the sharp stab of desire that arced through her body. "Nicolas . . ."

The rest of her words were lost as he raised his head and brought his mouth down on hers.

Chelsea had been kissed before, but never like this. Never with such mind-numbing intensity. Her breath caught as his tongue traced the outline of her lips, dipping past them to sample the honeyed sweetness of her mouth. She felt the hard strength of his chest against hers, crushing her breasts, smelled the musky scent of his skin, and felt her legs begin to tremble.

"Hold me, Chelsea," he whispered against her lips, his voice hoarse. "Don't be afraid of me."

Helpless to resist, she touched him, and felt his bare skin hot beneath her hands. She ran her fingers up his arms in a series of slow, sensual movements, touching his shoulders and feeling the muscles tense. Chelsea didn't understand the depth of her response. All she wanted was to get close to him, as close as it was possible to be. His hands were cool against the fevered warmth of her skin. She shivered as he ran them down her arms, feathering them close to her body, his fingers resting just below her breasts, achingly close but not touching.

Think back, beloved, the voice in her mind said. *Think back, and open your mind. I won't hurt you. I would never hurt you. . . .*

Chelsea closed her eyes and let her mind drift away as his hands continued their exquisitely slow exploration. New sensations shimmered to life as he gently cupped the fullness of her breasts. She gasped, and heard a roaring in her ears as he caressed her with light, tantalizing strokes. She felt weightless; her body floating in the brilliance of an azure sea, her soft gasps swallowed by his mouth.

Yes, come to me, beloved. You know who I am. Come to me. . . .

The earth had no hold on her now. She soared above it, body and mind bathed by the light, her soul filled with sweet music—until suddenly, the brightness began to fade. A memory of something dark intruded, something sinister, and she plummeted back toward earth. The deep, glorious blue disappeared as blackness moved in, thick and oppressive. She was back in her nightmare, swimming blind in the emptiness of a great, dark sea, alone and terrified. "Nicolas!" she cried.

Stay with me, Chelsea, you're not alone. Take my hand. You will pass through the Darkness. . . .

Chelsea struggled to grasp the hand being extended to her, but the shadows were too deep. They closed in again, cutting her off. . . .

No! Let me go!

Immediately the assault on her senses stopped. The gloom receded and the mists began to clear. But from a distance, she heard Nicolas's voice, deep, strong, and resonant with emotion.

"I can't let you go, Chelsea. The promise given so long ago cannot be broken. You have no choice but to come to me." Then he added in a lower, huskier tone, *"I am your destiny."*

When Chelsea opened her eyes, Nicolas was standing a few feet away from her. His eyes were guarded, but his breathing was as unsteady as hers. "Now do you remember?"

Chelsea's breath came in quick, shallow bursts. "I don't remember anything! I didn't give you any promise."

"It wasn't you who gave me the promise, but it is you who must honor it. You can't run from me, Chelsea. You have no choice."

But she was already on her way to the door. "Of course I have a choice! As long as there's breath in my body, I have a choice! I don't know what you're trying to convince me of, but I know for a fact that we don't have any kind of a past." She hesitated, her fingers gripping the handle. "And right now, it doesn't look like we have much of a future either."

. . . the promise given so long ago cannot be broken . . . I am your destiny.

The words kept echoing in Chelsea's mind.

I am your destiny . . . I have waited for you . . . I am your destiny.

She paced back and forth in her living room, trying to figure out what it meant. But the more she thought about it, the less sense it made.

What had Nicolas been talking about? What was this *promise* he'd kept mentioning? She'd never promised him anything. She'd never even *seen* him before the night of the gallery opening.

And yet, if that was the case, how did she explain her startling reaction to his kiss? Nobody had ever made her feel that way before. Not her first boyfriend in high school, not the guy she'd gone steady with through college, not even Duncan Rycroft—and she'd been ready to marry him!

What was it about Nicolas that did this to her? Why was she so inexplicably drawn to him? It wasn't like her to think about a man the way she was thinking about him. And it certainly didn't explain why an intimate embrace had left her aching for more.

It wasn't you who gave me the promise, but it is you who must honor it.

What was that supposed to mean? If *she* hadn't given him this promise, then who—

Chelsea abruptly stopped pacing. *Dear God!* Was it possible—?

No! Things like that didn't happen, she told herself, shutting her mind to the possibility. They were living in the twenty-first century. Whatever bizarre tales her grandfather had told her about Rebecca Mallory were exactly that. Tales.

And yet, how could she ignore all the strange things that were happening to her? A terrifying encounter with something in the waters off the beach. A man's voice whispering in her head. Dreams about a young woman drowning—a young woman who had given an unknown man a promise!

In the attic an hour later, Chelsea sat on the floor surrounded by boxes. Boxes her mother had given her that might or might not contain what she needed to know. But what was she hoping to find? Proof that her grandfather hadn't been lying to her when he'd told her the story of Rebecca Mallory—or that he had? Proof that she and her great-great-grandmother hadn't shared a birthmark, or a love for the sea, or anything else that could possibly be tied into what was going on now?

Chelsea tore the lid off the last box and uncovered more mementos of the past: her grandmother's wedding dress, her own christening gown, photographs of her parents' wedding. Countless albums filled with pictures of holidays, of parties, and of children growing up. And there at the bottom, the one item she'd been looking for.

Rebecca Mallory's diary!

Hardly daring to breathe, Chelsea took the book from the

box. It was small and slim, nothing like the glossy journals today's teenagers used. The cover was plain, the word *Diary* neatly cross-stitched in pink embroidery thread on cream-colored fabric.

As Chelsea ran her fingers over the fabric, she thought about young Rebecca holding it in her hands. She thought about her forming the letters with needle and thread, and then about her opening it and recording the secrets of her life on its pages.

Holding her breath, Chelsea carefully opened the diary.

The pages were tissue thin, the edges beginning to curl and break, but for the first time, she saw her great-great-grandmother's handwriting. The penmanship was elegant, the script flowing and old-fashioned. But it was the entries themselves that captured Chelsea's attention. Because for those few minutes, it was almost as though she stepped back in history. As though she became . . . someone else.

> *November 24, 1863*
> *. . . the entire village turned up for church this*
> *morning, which was something of a surprise. But the*
> *vicar seemed pleased. He told everyone that a*
> *miracle had occurred. "God hath delivered His child*
> *from the tempest," he said, "and put her safe upon*
> *the shore." Mama cried all through the sermon.*
> *Even Papa seemed moved. They both thought my*
> *safe return from the sea was a miracle. Only I know*
> *what really happened. Only I know about the*
> *promise . . .*

The promise. Chelsea lifted her gaze from the page. So there *had* been a promise.

But what had it been, and who had the young Rebecca Mallory given it to?

Chelsea pored over the next set of entries. They were sporadic for the most part, relating to everyday events and occurrences in Rebecca's life. Then, there was a later entry, when her great-great-grandmother would have been thirty-two.

June 24, 1875
. . . I try to forget, but I cannot. After dinner tonight,
I went back down to the beach. Something told me
he might come, and I waited, hoping for him to see
me in my finery. Once, I even thought I heard him,
but it was only a fish jumping close to shore . . .

Chelsea stared at the words, disbelief etched on her face.
Just last night, she'd dreamed about a young woman standing
on the beach. A young woman who had been wearing a
pretty dress, and who'd said something about a fish jumping.
She, too, had been looking out to sea as though waiting for
someone.

Was it possible that the woman she'd been seeing in her
dreams was actually her great-great-grandmother?

But if it was, whom had she gone to meet? She'd been
married at the time, but it didn't sound like her husband,
Jeremiah, she'd been waiting for. Then who? A secret lover?

Chelsea picked up the diary again and carefully turned the
fragile pages. Again there were scattered entries, but nothing
more about the promise or the man to whom it might have
been given. Until the very last page. An entry made on the
night her great-great-grandmother had died.

An entry that slowly siphoned the color from Chelsea's
face.

November 21, 1926
. . . I fear this may be the last time I write. The
autumn winds blow colder this year. Or perhaps they
just seem to bite more deeply because I have less
stamina to face them. Whatever the case, the doctor
has told me my time is near. Already the pain is so
great that I pray for a swift release.

I leave these words for the one who follows, and
you will know who you are by the mark that you
bear. I pray you will have the courage to read these
words, for if you do not, your last days will be
fraught with fear and uncertainty.

I shall not try to explain what happened to me
that night in the sea, save to say that I did not

imagine the man who rescued me from it. There are those who say I'm crazy, and those who'll say I'm crazy in the years to come, but I alone know what happened that night.

It is true he spared my life when by rights he should have taken it. I do not know why he did this. I only know that in my fear, I begged for the life of my child, and in doing so, I gave him a promise. A promise I expected to keep every day of my life.

But now, as my life draws to a close, I realize it is not for me to fulfill the promise, but rather for someone who will follow. His gift was in giving me back my life. Not, sadly, in allowing me to share it with him.

Know, then, my child, that a day will come when he will return for you. He will bid the creatures of the sea precede him, for he is their master, and by their very presence, you will know of his arrival. What form he will take, I do not know. But he will call to you, and when he does, I wish you courage, for inasmuch as my life was spared fifty-one years ago, know that yours must now be forfeited in order to fulfill the promise I gave him. You are honor bound to do so, and I trust—nay, I pray—that you will grant this, my dying wish, and not see fit to hate me for the end I have inflicted upon you.

You will go to him by water. A sweeter death, I think, than any other. Many times I thought about walking into the sea, but it was only because he did not call that I did not give in to my desires. But I envy you, my child, that you should be the one so chosen. And I beg you, do not go in fear, for greater riches await you at his side than those to be found here. But know that once he calls, the promise must be kept. For this, truly, is your destiny.

Rebecca Lynn Mallory

Chelsea dropped the diary and stared at it as though it were evil incarnate. No wonder her mother had never talked about

Rebecca Mallory. The woman was obviously insane! Because if Chelsea believed, even for a moment, that what Rebecca had written in her diary was true, it meant that *she* was the one destined to fulfill her great-great-grandmother's promise.

. . . you will know who you are by the mark that you bear . . .

Chelsea shivered. There could be no question about that. It referred to the birthmark on her shoulder. The one she shared with her great-great-grandmother.

. . . For this, truly, is your destiny.

Rebecca had written those words almost a hundred years ago. Nicolas had said them to her earlier today. Coincidence—or something more?

No, it *had* to be a coincidence, Chelsea told herself, because the alternative was unthinkable. Nicolas Demitry couldn't possibly know anything about a man who'd saved the lives of Rebecca Mallory and her baby in the frigid waters off the coast of Ireland. He couldn't have been alive over a hundred and fifty years ago. And he couldn't possibly know anything about a promise her great-great-grandmother had given to a man from the sea all that time ago.

A promise Chelsea was now expected to fulfill by the willing sacrifice of her own life!

Ten

~

After suffering through several hours of anguished tossing and turning, Chelsea got up and shrugged on her robe. There was no point in trying to sleep. It wasn't the dreams that were keeping her awake now. It was fear. Fear of being caught up in something she didn't understand. Something terrifying. Something . . . unreal.

She stared through her window at the mist-glazed water and mulled over the words she'd read in Rebecca Mallory's diary.

. . . I shall not try to explain what happened to me in the sea that night, save to say that I did not imagine the man who rescued me from it. . . .

What did that mean? That her ancestor had been saved by a—what did Chelsea call him? A merman? Some kind of mythical sea god? Creatures like that didn't exist except on the pages of lurid fantasy novels or in Greek mythology.

Poseidon, god of the waves. Hades, lord of the underworld, and Zeus, ruler of the sky. Legends all, but in truth, nothing more than characters drawn from the pages of fiction. And yet, Rebecca Mallory must have *believed* in those characters. Believed in the existence of some kind of . . . super-

natural entity that had pulled her from the depths on the night
of that terrible storm.

But just because she'd believed it, did that necessarily
mean it had happened?

Chelsea pushed back tendrils of sweat-dampened hair.
What if her great-great-grandmother hadn't been swept overboard? What if she'd just imagined being rescued by some
handsome mythical creature? She had been pregnant with her
first child. Her hormones might have been raging out of control. She might have only *thought* all those things had happened to her. That was possible, wasn't it?

Chelsea sighed. It was possible, but it still didn't explain
how a young, pregnant woman could have survived such a
grueling ordeal when everyone else on that ship had been
lost.

Had there been another ship in the area? A small commercial trader, perhaps, or a fishing trawler? Had someone
set out in a boat and pulled Rebecca from the sea?

If they had, it couldn't have been easy. Chelsea knew how
dangerous deep-sea rescues were, and this was the twenty-
first century. There hadn't been any state-of-the-art helicop-
ters flying over the Atlantic in the late eighteen hundreds.
Besides, if Rebecca had been picked up by another boat, how
had her body come to be washed ashore only a few miles
from where she lived?

Chelsea wearily closed her eyes. It didn't make sense. In
fact, the more she questioned it, the more ridiculous it
seemed. But she couldn't rid her mind of the notion that
something very strange was going on.

Could there possibly be a connection between Nicolas Demitry and her great-great-grandmother?

Yeah, right. And fairies danced in the moonlight and
politicians were the most scrupulous men on earth. If she
believed that Nicolas Demitry was the man who'd appeared
to her great-great-grandmother, it meant he was nearly two
hundred years old—and if *that* didn't cry out for psychiatric
help, Chelsea didn't know what did!

Still, she couldn't deny that both Nicolas and Rebecca
Mallory had spoken of a promise, and that each of them had
indicated that someone other than Rebecca was destined to

fulfill it. Then there was that whole destiny issue. Rebecca had said it was the destiny of the one who bore the birthmark to fulfill the promise. By definition, destiny meant one's pre-ordained fate. Something fixed or established by divine decree. Something that was going to happen in the future.

Was Nicolas trying to tell her that something had happened in the past that was destined to make them more than just friends now?

Chelsea grabbed her car keys and a flashlight. Destiny be damned! She *had* to know who Nicolas Demitry was, and why he was having this effect on her life. She had to know if any of the bizarre writings in Rebecca Mallory's diary were true. She couldn't go on living like this.

She couldn't go on living her life in fear.

Nicolas didn't know what time it was—at least, not in terms of human measurement. The sea had its own concept of time. As he glided up through the silent depths, he knew only that he had spent a restless night on his bed of coral.

Would she come to see him today? Unlikely, he thought, remembering the way she had turned from him last night. He'd seen the fear in her eyes, glimpsed the turmoil and confusion in her heart. She had been trying to find answers to questions that had no answers.

Was he man or monster? Someone to be admired—or someone to be feared?

Nicolas had tried to share some of what he was with her, and for a moment, he thought he had succeeded. Chelsea had reached out to him, and during that link, he had tried to impart some of the beauty and joy he felt in his world, and of the love he knew could flourish between them.

But then, as always, she had caught a glimpse of the Darkness and everything had changed. The fragile bond of trust had shattered into a thousand pieces. Fear had replaced belief, just as it had in her dreams. Whatever affection she might have felt had been destroyed when he'd tried to tell her the truth, and she'd rejected him.

But she couldn't run forever, Nicolas reminded himself. Sooner or later she would have to listen to what he had to say. Poseidon was waiting for him to fulfill his obligation, to correct the imbalance he had created by sparing the lives of Rebecca Mallory and her child over a century ago. Nicolas just wished there was some easy way of telling Chelsea what she had to know. Some painless way of making her understand, because there really *was* no choice.

She would have to know it all, sooner or later.

There were no lights on at Nicolas's house, but this time Chelsea didn't care. It wasn't the house she was interested in. With flashlight in hand, she got out of the car and headed for the beach, looking for Nicolas's tracks.

It didn't take her long to find them. They were there, just as they had been before—a single line of footprints leading down to the water.

Chelsea bent closer to examine them. The imprint showed a human foot: narrow, with a high arch and long, well-shaped toes. But between the toes, the sand was slightly flattened, as though a thin membrane of skin had pressed it down. *Webbing?*

Chelsea straightened and peered across the water. It could, she supposed, be a defect of birth. She remembered once seeing pictures of a woman whose toes had grown together, and who'd had surgery to separate them. Perhaps Nicolas had been born with just such a flaw.

"Or a gift," Chelsea murmured, thinking of his ability to swim miles as easily as she walked across the street. But what about his complete lack of fear of the creatures in the sea?

What was she to make of a man who called his portrait of a mythical sea god realistic?

At sixty feet, Nikodemus began to detect the changes in the water all around him. Changes a mortal would never have sensed, but ones that he, with his body so closely attuned to the sea, couldn't help but notice. The smell of man-made products infiltrating the fragile ecosystem. The stench of chemicals and other wastes that had been dumped into the sea as though it were some kind of giant garbage repository. It made him thankful he lived at such incredible depths.

Depths not even man's most sophisticated diving and sonar apparatus were able to penetrate.

As he continued to ascend and darkness gave way to light, Nicolas noticed other, more pleasant changes taking place around him. He saw mighty humpbacks feeding on the rich soup of algae and plankton, slender finbacks and minkes winding their way through the silent depths. Higher still, a school of white-sided dolphins streaked by, performing their graceful dance to the accompaniment of pings and crackles. A group of them came toward him now, their gentle faces seeming to smile as they formed a circle around him, paying homage.

It was his father who had first hailed the dolphin as the sublime creature it was. Poseidon, who had awarded it the sea's highest honor, and placed an image of it among the stars, for it was the dolphin that had discovered the whereabouts of the lovely Amphitrite, the Nereid whom Poseidon wished to marry, after she fled to Mount Atlas in an attempt to protect her virginity.

With an answering grin, Nicolas sent the dolphins on their way, listening to their chorus of chirrups and squeaks as they resumed their games. Perhaps he should have followed his father's example and also chosen a dolphin to be his companion. He couldn't imagine Chelsea being terrified of the friendly creature with the laughing face, as she had been of the giant manta.

Would Rebecca Mallory have been afraid?

Nicolas smiled, perhaps a little sadly, as he thought about Chelsea's great-great-grandmother. What a remarkable woman she had been. She had demonstrated an amazing degree of courage and compassion on the night of that dreadful storm. She had asked for nothing but her child's life, willingly agreeing to forfeit her own if that's what it would take. Touched by that selfless act of love and devotion, Nicolas had abandoned logic and raised her from the depths, knowing even as he did that he was acting in direct contravention of his father's laws.

As expected, Poseidon had been furious. He had raised storms the likes of which no one had seen, making the seas impassable and causing more shipwrecks in those few short days than the world had ever known. Indeed, so great was his anger that Nicolas had been compelled to offer not one, but two promises as a sign of atonement. The first, that within a week of Rebecca's delivering her baby, he would bring her back into the sea. The second, that he would take her to wife.

Sadly, his father had not been appeased. Wanting only to punish Nicolas for disobeying him, Poseidon had refused to allow his son to take a life he had already spared, and had refused to accept as a daughter-in-law a woman who had been impregnated by a mortal male. Instead, he had ordered Nikodemus to wait for the next female child born to Rebecca Mallory.

Unfortunately, Rebecca hadn't had any more children. Believing it her duty to honor the promise she had given the man from the sea, she had not lain with her husband following the birth of her son, but had gone down to the seaside, spending long hours there, expecting that Nicolas would return to take her back to the depths.

He hadn't, of course. And as though to punish him further, the capricious Fates had sent only male children into the line. Boy after boy had been born to the descendants of Rebecca Mallory, and they, in turn, had married and sired more boys.

Still, Nicolas had waited, knowing that the time would come when he could make good on his promise. There was a pattern to the universe. An order. The gods could bend it if they wished, but they could not change it irrevocably. He knew a female child would eventually be born into the Mallory line, and he had waited for her, knowing that she would take Rebecca's place and become the woman he would marry.

Finally, she had. And her name was Chelsea.

Nicolas had known the moment of Chelsea's birth. His father had shown it to him in the Great Pool, and over the years, he had followed her progress, watching her as she'd grown from child to adolescent, and finally to young womanhood. He had been there when Chelsea had taken her first tentative steps into the sea. He had watched from a distance, smiling at her awkward attempts to use the clumsy apparatus mortals needed to exist under the sea. The heavy metal tanks filled with compressed air, the cumbersome black fins, and the strange-looking masks that allowed them to see. Even so, he had rejoiced that the woman who would be his wife was a creature of such beauty and passion, and that she found such pleasure in the wonders of the undersea world.

Would she think of him as kindly? Would she find in him a man to whom she could willingly commit her life? A man who was more than just a creature of mystery? Would she be able to look past her fears and learn to love him, the way he had come to know and to love her?

Would she make the transition to sea goddess willingly?

Not judging by the way she'd reacted last night, Nicolas thought sadly.

Ah, Chelsea, what passion you have within you. A passion so deeply felt, but so carefully restrained. I shall awaken that passion, beloved. Together we will explore the great seas, and you will discover what it is to truly love. . . .

At twenty-five feet below the surface, Nicolas closed his eyes and lost himself in the sweetness of his desires. . . .

Chelsea heard a rushing sound first, like that of a fast-flowing river. She turned toward the bay and aimed the beam of the flashlight out over the water—and felt stark, black fear twist around her heart.

The creature was back! She could see the giant ripples forming on the surface; the span between the outermost edges appeared to be at least sixty feet.

Her hands shook so badly she almost dropped the flashlight. Where was Nicolas? Was he even now swimming back to the house? Back into the monster's path?

The thought sent icy fingers crawling up Chelsea's spine. She couldn't let that happen. Whatever concerns she might have about Nicolas, she would never want to see him hurt.

She searched through the scrub, eventually finding a fair-sized stone, and advanced toward the water's edge. She felt a little like David about to face Goliath, but she had to try. Even if she just frightened it enough to make it go away—

Suddenly, Chelsea froze. The rock slipped from her hand as she gazed with disbelieving eyes toward the water. *A head was rising from the waves.* A human head, covered in dark, glossy hair, followed by a set of broad shoulders, then a muscular chest tapering to a slim waist.

A man was walking calmly out of the waters of Massachusetts Bay.

But it wasn't a man. In the breaking light of dawn, Chelsea saw its form, godlike and beautiful, breathtakingly masculine. She saw a flash of silver as the light from the flashlight fell upon its naked torso, glinting upon the thousands of tiny, iridescent—

"Scales!" The word emerged as a horrified whisper, her eyes widening in terror as she looked at the creature's face and realized who it was. "No! Oh please, *no!*"

Nicolas glanced up, the anguished cry snapping him from his trance. As soon as he did, he realized the magnitude of his mistake. He'd been so lost in his thoughts of Chelsea that he had forgotten to use his powers to test the safety of the beach, and to commence the transformation of his body. Now, as he glimpsed the horror on Chelsea's face, he knew how grievous that oversight was. "Chelsea!"

"What in God's name are you? Or maybe God has nothing to do with it!"

Nicolas flinched at the loathing in her voice. "Chelsea, please. Let me explain—"

"No! Get away from me! Stay *away!*"

She bolted for her car, wrenching open the door and flinging herself inside. She was already halfway out of the driveway when he caught up with her.

"Chelsea, wait!" He put his hands on the car and peered in at her. He could have torn the door from its hinges, but that would have served nothing. He would only have frightened her more. "Listen to me, I *beg* you!"

"Get away from me, or so help me, I'll run you down! Go back to the bottom of the sea where you belong!"

"Chelsea!"

Ignoring him, Chelsea rammed her foot down hard on the accelerator. She was beyond the reach of rational explanation. Throwing the gearshift forward, she tore down the road, hardly able to see through the tears that were streaming down her cheeks.

She had to get away. Away from that *thing* that threatened to drag her into the sea, because she knew that's what he was. Everything her great-great-grandmother had written was true.

Nicolas Demitry *was* the man Rebecca had given her promise to. As impossible as it seemed, he was the creature that had pulled her ancestor from the sea over a century ago.

And now he was after her! Chelsea could hear his voice over the frantic beating of her heart, calling to her to wait, pleading with her to listen. But she couldn't. Her mind refused to deal with the terror of what she'd just seen.

Nicolas, rising from the depths, his magnificent body shimmering silver. *Nicolas, an abomination of nature!*

Chelsea's sobs were torn from her throat as she flew down the dark stretch of road. She fumbled with the dashboard controls, trying to remember where the high beams were.

How could such a thing be? There were no such things as ghosts or monsters—or gods.

The night closed in around her, the blackness only adding to her disorientation. Even the air inside the car seemed thick and stagnant, but she wouldn't open the window. She couldn't let him get at her, because she bore the birthmark. *She* was the one destined to return to the sea with him.

She was the one who had to die!

The car hit a bump, and Chelsea winced as her head hit the ceiling. She was driving too fast. The thought registered dimly in some part of her brain, but her foot still held firm to the accelerator. Escape was her only thought now.

A sound—a movement beside the car—tore a scream from her throat. *Had he caught up with her?* Did he possess some kind of superhuman strength that allowed him to keep up with a speeding car?

Trees, rocks, scrubby outcroppings flew by with terrifying speed as Chelsea pressed the pedal down harder. All she could think about was Nicolas and his unholy quest.

Did she dare look back? What if he was only a few feet behind her? What would she do? What could *he* do? What other powers did he have?

A hundred arguments flew through Chelsea's head. *Look. Don't look! Look!* But in the end, she *had* to look. Whatever the risk, she had to know where Nicolas was.

She turned her head and cast one frightened look back over her shoulder. One quick look to tell her if she was safe.

One split-second glance that caused her to miss the bend in the road, and go hurtling toward the telephone pole. . . .

Nicolas was about fifty yards back when Chelsea's car left the road. He saw the nightmare unfold, and knew in his heart that *this* was the accident Lysianassa had foreseen; the disaster that would change everything. And as Lysia had predicted, there was nothing he could do to prevent it. In the sea he could travel at incredible speeds, but on land he was bound by the forces of gravity and the limitations of his body. He would never reach her in time.

He closed his eyes and willed his thoughts to reach her. *Chelsea, look out!*

From somewhere in her mind, Chelsea heard the sound of Nicolas's voice, but the warning came too late. As though moving in slow motion, she felt the rough pavement give way to uneven ground. She whirled around in time to see the road disappear and the telephone pole rush up to meet her. And just before impact, she realized she wasn't wearing her seat belt.

There was a horrific crash, followed by the sickening sound of metal twisting and wood splintering.

Chelsea's hands were torn from the wheel, her body thrown forward by the tremendous force of the impact. She heard glass shattering all around her, saw lights exploding, and felt pain worse than anything she'd ever imagined. Something warm and sticky was trickling down her face, running into her eyes and dripping down her cheeks. The mists of night began to close in, and the acrid smell of smoke stung her nostrils.

Seconds later, there was an explosion—and her world erupted into flame.

Chelsea knew she was going to die. Pinned in the mangled wreckage of the car, she could feel the intense heat of the flames searing her skin. The stench of burning upholstery and melting plastic filled her nostrils and made her eyes water.

The car that only moments before had been her means to safety had become a fiery coffin.

Suddenly, a figure loomed out of the darkness. The figure of a man, his body cloaked in a light so pure, so radiant, it was almost blinding.

Chelsea shut her eyes and turned her face away. She was dreaming. Either that, or she was dying.

"Take me," she whispered through lips that were cracked and bleeding. "Please . . . take me. . . ."

The angel did not speak, yet she heard his voice. It came to her in great rolling waves, washing over her like a healing balm.

Do not be afraid, Chelsea. I am here.

Then, in the space of a heartbeat, Chelsea heard water. Water raining down on the car, extinguishing the flames, the sound of it like the hissing of a thousand angry snakes. Seconds later, she *felt* water. It was running down her face, blending with the blood and washing it away. Water cool where the flames had burned, seeping in under what was left of her clothes, bathing her skin.

But the pain was still there, and Chelsea knew that help had come too late. No doctor on earth would be able to repair the damage the crash had wrought. And knowing there would be no tomorrow, she gave herself up to the comforting darkness where time ceased and pain did not exist. . . .

She was dreaming again. Drifting down through the indigo depths, surrounded by the endless silence of the sea. Her limbs were cushioned, yet nothing held her. Her eyes were closed, yet she could see all that was around her. And she was not alone.

Am I dead? she asked the presence beside her.

No, you only sleep.

Who are you?

I will take care of you.

What is your name?

I have been called many names.

Are you Death?

No.

Far below, Chelsea saw a sliver of white light emanating from the darkness. It grew in intensity until she could see nothing but the light, and strangely, she felt no fear. She felt . . . nothing.

Is this Death approaching?

It is life.

Will I remember this?

No.

Moments later, Chelsea saw them. Hundreds of figures garbed in magnificent robes. They were human in form, yet they were not human. They radiated light and color, and floated like silent beacons through a shimmering blue sea. And suddenly, she knew she had seen it all before.

I've been here . . . in the past. Long ago, when I was . . . someone else.

Yes.

Am I that . . . someone else now?

She is with you. Sleep, Chelsea.

As the voices rose in a heavenly choir, and light and color merged as though in the tunnel of a great kaleidoscope, the darkness faded and Chelsea was enveloped in a cocoon of deep, sapphire blue. Then, lulled by the voices and by the presence of the Radiant One beside her, she closed her eyes, and slept.

Part Two

THE AWAKENING

Eleven

Time ceased to have any meaning for Chelsea. Swathed in the darkness of her world, she knew only night. She was dimly aware of throbbing in different parts of her body, but she was unable to pinpoint where the pains were. When they became too intense, someone would come and give her something to send her back into the peaceful world of oblivion.

She did not dream. If she did, she had no recollection of the dreams upon waking.

She stayed that way for what seemed like a very long time.

Finally, after what might have been hours or days or even weeks, Chelsea floated up from her pain-induced darkness to the healing warmth of the sun. She felt it, as sweet as a breath of fresh air on her face, and like a withered flower seeking rain, she turned toward it, knowing instinctively that where there was warmth, there would be comfort and light.

It was a mistake. As soon as she moved, she felt pain. Deep, gut-wrenching pain that tore at her insides and left her gasping for air. "Help . . . me. . . ."

Was that husky rasp of sound her voice? She barely recognized it. Her jaw was stiff, her tongue swollen to twice its normal size in a mouth that was as dry as a sunbaked desert.

And there was a horrible, bitter taste in the back of her throat.

"Chelsea, can you hear me?"

She stiffened. It was a man's voice, refined, educated, slightly accented.

She turned her head to look at him, but she couldn't open her eyes. Something was holding them shut. And her arms were strapped down. *Dear God, what was happening to her?*

"Please don't try to move, my dear," the man said in a quiet, reassuring tone. "And don't try to speak. Nod your head if you can hear me, but use only the slightest of movements. Do you understand?"

Heart thundering, Chelsea stared in the direction of his voice, her breath coming in short, panicky bursts. *Where was she? How had she got here?*

"Do you understand what I'm saying, Chelsea?" he repeated gently.

Forgetting his warning, Chelsea jerked her head, only to gasp at the pain even that slight movement caused.

"Yes, you must be very careful," he told her in slow, precise words. "You have been in an accident. A very bad accident. But you're out of danger now. Do you understand?"

Chelsea swallowed, trying to fight down feelings of panic. *Bad accident . . . danger . . .*

"The reason you can't open your eyes is because they're bandaged," the man said gently. "I bound your wrists so you wouldn't be able to tear off the bandages before I could make you aware of the extent of your injuries. If you understand what I'm saying, nod your head, and I'll remove the straps."

Chelsea heard the voice but had trouble coming to grips with what it was saying. *She'd been in an accident? But how? And when? Where was she now, and how long had she been here? How serious were her injuries?*

Was she going to die?

"No, you're not going to die," the man said, making her wonder if she'd said the words aloud. "But you mustn't try to touch the bandages, especially those over your eyes. Do you understand?"

Bandages on her eyes. *Was she blind?*

Strangely enough, the man didn't answer that one. "Are you in pain?" he asked instead.

"Yes." Her answer was barely audible, another dry, throaty rasp.

"Then I'll give you something to ease it. My name is Asklepios, and I have been looking after you. When I am not here, someone else will be close by; you will never be alone. Do you understand, Chelsea? There will always be someone with you."

Chelsea felt tears well up in her eyes, only to be absorbed by the thick cotton pads covering them. She inclined her head as little as possible.

"Good. Now I've given you something to make you sleep. When you wake, the pain should be easing, but it is going to take time, Chelsea. A very long time. . . ."

Chelsea didn't hear the rest of what he said. As the drug took effect, she felt the curtain of darkness descend on her mind, and gently slipped back into the peaceful depths of nothingness.

Nicolas stood on the balcony that opened from his studio and gripped the railing hard. His head was bowed, his back bent as though he, not Atlas, was carrying the weight of the world on his shoulders. And why would he not? He had no one to blame for Chelsea's accident but himself.

He should *never* have breached the surface of the bay without first testing the safety of the beach. It was the first lesson he'd learned, and one of the most important rules of his life. Yet, lost in pleasurable thoughts of Chelsea, he had risen from the sea without giving a thought to who might be standing on the shore, and had allowed Chelsea to see what he was; a discovery that had sent her running from him in terror. Terror that had caused her to lose control of her car and crash it into a telephone pole.

Nicolas raised his face to the sky, anguish twisting it into a mask of pain. Would he ever forget the way Chelsea had looked at him as he'd emerged from the water? Would he ever forget the expression of horror and disbelief on her face when she'd glimpsed his underwater covering *before* it had changed back into the silken film of his human skin? She was eventually going to learn what he was, but he didn't want the first time she saw him to be like that.

Nicolas drew a long, shuddering breath. One thing he did know, he would never forget the sound of her screams. Chelsea should have died in that terrible crash. She *would* have, had he not called upon the forces of nature to help him save her life, for while it was true that her corporeal life would have to end before they could be together, he would never have wished it to be like that. He couldn't have stood by and watched her burn to death. He loved her too much to let her suffer such a horrible fate.

But there was a price to be paid for cheating Death, even for the son of a god.

She will recover, Nikodemus, a soft voice whispered in the air all around him. *This, too, I see. Your heart need not be so heavy.*

Nicolas turned his head and stared into the night sky. "I know, Lysianassa, but in saving her from the fire, I have taken away her choice."

She never had a choice, beloved, her voice drifted back to him. *It was for her to fulfill the legacy. Your saving her life now has only added to that obligation.*

Nicolas sighed as the whispers faded away. Lysia was right, of course. There was no question that Chelsea's debt to him had been compounded. If anything, he was fortunate that Poseidon himself had not risen from the depths to demand immediate reparation. Zeus certainly would have, and Nicolas knew that he would have been entirely within his rights. It was unpardonable for a god to interfere so flagrantly in the life of a mortal.

And yet that was exactly what he had done. He had spared not only the life of two of Chelsea's ancestors, but Chelsea's life as well, and there could be no question of what Poseidon would expect of him now.

He would be expected to make reparation. The Fates had inscribed the words in the annals of time. He had promises of his own to keep now.

The next time Chelsea awoke, the pain was easing. She took a few tentative breaths, afraid to breathe too deeply lest she aggravate her condition, but then breathed normally when she realized that the tightness in her chest was gone. There was still lingering tenderness in other parts of her body, but at least she could now move more easily. She was sitting up in bed, her back comfortably supported by pillows, her legs straight out in front of her. Her arms rested unbound at her sides, but she was still unable to see, so the bandages must still be in place over her eyes.

Somewhat encouraged, Chelsea moved her tongue around her mouth. It still felt like the inside of a dust bowl, but at least the swelling was gone. And she was thirsty. So terribly, terribly thirsty.

"Doctor . . . Asklepios?" she croaked.

No answer.

"Doctor—"

"He's not here right now, Chelsea. Can I get you some water?"

It was a different voice this time. A man's voice again, but deeper than the doctor's and without any trace of an accent. Cautiously, Chelsea inclined her head. "Thank you."

She heard water being poured into a glass, and without thinking, went to sit forward—only to collapse back against the pillows with a sharp gasp.

"Yes, you must try to remember not to move any more than is absolutely necessary," the man cautioned.

"Who . . . are you?" Chelsea asked, breathing through the pain.

"Someone who's here to help." She heard him approach the bed. "Open your mouth a little."

She did, and felt the smoothness of a glass straw inserted between her lips. Drawing on it slowly, she nearly groaned aloud as cool, refreshing water flowed into her mouth. Dear Lord, had plain old water ever tasted so good? She swirled it around her tongue, felt it wash over her gums, and then trickle down her throat. It hurt to swallow, but it was worth it, and Chelsea drank as much as she could. Surprisingly, it wasn't all that much.

"Thank . . . you." She opened her mouth so he could remove the straw. "How long have I been here?"

"A while."

"Is this a hospital?"

"No, you couldn't be moved that far. This is my house."

Couldn't be moved? "Why? What . . . happened to me?"

"You were in a very bad car accident."

Chelsea frowned under her bandages. Yes, she vaguely remembered the other doctor saying something about an accident, but she had no recollection of it happening. She couldn't remember the last time she'd even been in a car. In fact, she couldn't remember anything at all—

"I don't remember what happened to me," Chelsea said, fighting down a sudden wave of panic. "I don't remember anything."

"That's not surprising. You sustained severe injuries in the accident, Chelsea. Your car was on fire when I pulled you from it."

"Fire." She felt herself pale beneath the bandages. "You pulled me out of a burning car? Why don't I remember that? Surely I should be able to remember something so horrible."

"You will. The mind shuts out the pain while it deals with the healing. When the injuries heal, your memory will return."

Chelsea flicked the tip of her tongue over lips that felt dry, but no longer cracked. "Where's Dr. Asklepios?"

"He'll be back tonight."

"When will I be able to leave?"

His answer seemed a long time coming. "Not for a while yet, I'm afraid."

Chelsea wasn't sure if he'd put something in her water, or if it was just the effort of talking that was taking this toll. She felt a strange lethargy invading her limbs, numbing her mind and sending her back into the misty realms of that other world.

"Who . . . *are* you?" she asked, fighting to stay awake.

She felt the softest whisper of a breeze against her forehead, heard the sound of a door close, and then silence. The man was gone. The doctor was gone. She was alone in an alien world, surrounded by darkness.

Exhausted, Chelsea fell back into a deep sleep.

She was drifting down through water. The terror had passed, leaving in its place a calm acceptance of the inevitable. She did not struggle, nor was she afraid, because she knew that she was not alone.

"Are you God?" *she asked of the being beside her.*

"No."

"Are you a creature of the sea, like the fish and the whales?"

He laughed, and the sound was infinitely soft and melodious. "I am sometimes a creature of the sea, and sometimes of the land."

She frowned then, and looked at the darkness all around her. "Am I dead?"

"Are you afraid of dying?"

She hadn't expected the question. "I've never really thought about it before. The Church tells us there are wondrous glories awaiting us in heaven, but I didn't think I would be going there so soon." *She rested a hand protectively on her stomach.* "I thought I would live to see my child born and grow up."

He touched her face gently with the tips of his fingers. "No, Rebecca, you're not dead. But do you truly wish to go back? It is beautiful here beneath the sea."

Her face clouded. "I'm not afraid for myself, but what of my child? It hasn't had a chance to live, and I would do anything to give it that chance." *Her voice caught in sorrow.* "Anything."

He watched her for a moment, then said, "If I were to spare the life of your child, would you be willing to give me a promise?"

"You have such power as this?"

"I have, and I will use it to help you. But there will be a price, Rebecca. There must always be a price. . . ."

The dream ended there, and Chelsea slowly drifted up into consciousness.

What was she to make of all that? The man in her dream had spoken the name Rebecca. Was that *her* name? But why had she asked him if he was God? Had she thought she was dying? And what was that strange reference to his being a creature of the sea, like the whales and fishes?

As a breeze fresh with the tangy scent of the sea blew against her face, Chelsea forgot about the dream. It didn't seem important when compared to the other more serious concerns in her life—like the bandages that were covering her face.

Chelsea hadn't had the courage to touch the dressings before, but she wanted to now. She needed to know how bad her injuries really were. She took a deep breath and then lifted her hand to her head. There were two strips of gauze circling her head. One wrapped under her chin and over the top of her head, and the other circled it, holding in place two thick pads, one over each eye. Each strip of gauze felt about four inches wide.

Chelsea carefully touched her fingers to her cheeks. There was a plaster about two inches square on the left one, and the skin beneath it was puffy and sore. Her right cheek was bare, but it, too, was swollen, as was the area around her mouth.

Chelsea slowly lowered her hands. What did she look like under all those bandages? Had she been badly burned? Was she going to be horribly scarred for the rest of her life?

"I'm afraid you lost most of your hair in the accident," a man said quietly, "but your head and facial injuries were more a result of flying glass than of burns."

Chelsea started at the sound of the voice. It was the same voice she had heard the last time she'd woken up. The voice of the man who'd given her water. "Who's there?"

She heard the creak of a chair as he got up, then the sound of footsteps coming towards the bed. "My name is Nicolas."

Nicolas. Chelsea silently repeated the name. It meant nothing to her. "Are you a doctor?"

"No, I'm a friend."

"Is Dr. Asklepios here?"

"He will be here later this afternoon."

"I'd like to see him now."

"I'm afraid that's not possible."

For some reason, his refusal angered her. "Why not? I have a right to see him. If you won't bring him, I'll get out of this bed and—"

"And what?" Nicolas said in a voice that was neither hostile nor patronizing. "The minute you try to stand, you'll find out how weak you really are. And even if you could find your way to the door, where would you go?"

Chelsea fell into an uneasy silence. He was right, of course. She didn't know where she was, and even if she had, she was in no condition to make her way home. She didn't even *know* where she lived.

"What's wrong with me?" she whispered. "Why can't I remember who I am or what happened to me?"

"It's not unusual," he told her. "In fact, it often happens in cases of psychogenic amnesia."

"Psycho . . . ?"

"Psychogenic amnesia. It's a condition that allows you to access certain parts of your memory but not others," Nicolas explained in a kind voice. "Your entire memory hasn't been affected. Only sections of it."

Yes, that was true, Chelsea admitted. She could remember *parts* of her life. Scattered bits and pieces of her school days, images of her mother and father, distant relatives whose faces she knew but couldn't put names to, but there was nothing of her recent life. No memory of where she lived or who she worked for.

It was a frightening realization, and as Chelsea took a few deep breaths, the extent of the loss came home to her. "Will my memory return?"

"Eventually, but it's difficult to say when. It varies from person to person."

"That doesn't help *me* much."

"I'm sorry," Nicolas said, truly sounding as if he were. "I wish I could be more encouraging."

"What about Dr. Asklepios? Maybe he can tell me when it's likely to come back. Or some other doctor. It doesn't have to be him."

"I'm afraid it does. Right now you need highly specialized care, Chelsea," Nicolas told her. "The kind only Asklepios is able to dispense. But if it's any comfort at all, he is, without question, the best in his field."

"What field?" Chelsea asked, suddenly noticing that Nicolas didn't refer to the man as a doctor.

"Reconstructive surgery."

"Reconstructive?" Chelsea blanched. "You mean—"

She couldn't say the words, because she knew what he meant. She'd been in a horrible accident and lost her memory. She'd been trapped in a burning car and had required extensive cosmetic and restorative surgery to put her body back together. Now she was lying in bed, being looked after by somebody she'd never met and who wasn't a doctor. She'd lost all control of her life—and there wasn't a damn thing she could do about it.

"Please go away."

"Chelsea—"

"No, just . . . go away. I don't want to talk."

Chelsea heard the answering silence and never realized it could be so loud.

"I'll bring you something to eat."

"I don't want to eat."

"I know, but it's the only way you're going to get stronger."

"I won't do *anything* until I've seen the doctor."

"I'll try to get in touch with him." His voice was gentle but firm. "In the meantime, I *will* bring you something to eat."

And he did. A few minutes later he returned, and set something down on the edge of the bed. "I've brought you some clear soup."

Chelsea turned her head away. The thought of eating nauseated her.

"Is there anything I can get for you?" Nicolas asked gently. "Anything you need?"

"I need to know what's happened to me!" Chelsea cried in frustration.

She heard what sounded like a sigh. He moved around the room for a few minutes, but it wasn't long before Chelsea heard him leave. Only then, as the door closed behind him, did she finally give way to the tears that had been threatening ever since she'd awakened.

She was alone in a strange man's house, with no memory of who she was or how she'd gotten there. She couldn't have found her way home even if she'd been capable of getting out of bed, because she didn't know where she lived or how to get there. She didn't know what she did for a living, or how she'd come to know this man who seemed to be looking after her. It was all just a huge, black hole.

It was only then that Chelsea realized it wasn't anger or frustration she was feeling. It was fear.

Night settled on the house. At least, Chelsea *assumed* it was night. The air blowing through the window was cooler than it had been earlier in the day, and the familiar sounds of birds and insects were gone.

Dr. Asklepios finally came, but he didn't stay long. He told her she was getting better, but it was still too soon to move her, for fear of shock setting in as a result of what had happened. The problem was Chelsea still didn't *know* what had happened. She knew she'd been in a car accident, but she didn't know where she'd been going, or if anybody else had been hurt. She hoped Nicolas would have told her if someone had, but she couldn't be sure. He might not have wanted her to worry. Either way, she spent hours trying to put the pieces of the puzzle together, desperately seeking to remember what her life had been like before the crash.

Unfortunately, memories continued to hover like fleeting shadows at the edge of her mind, leaving the past an elusive mystery. She had no way of knowing what had caused an accident that had left her utterly helpless and possibly blind.

Blind.

Chelsea shuddered. Had she completely lost her sight? The bandages over her eyes prevented her from seeing now, but what would happen when the gauze was cut away? Would she still stare at the world through eyes that saw nothing?

"Nicolas?" she said tentatively.

"Yes?"

She turned in the direction of his voice. She never knew when he was in the room. She seldom heard him come or go. Sometimes she wondered if he waited until she slept before leaving or entering. "Did Dr. Asklepios say anything to you?"

"Only what he told you. That you're improving."

"Did he say anything about . . . my eyes?"

"He won't know until the bandages come off."

"Do you believe him?"

"I've never had any reason not to."

Until now, Chelsea thought irrationally. She fingered the blanket, dimly aware of the texture of the weave, and of how soft it was. She noticed a lot about texture these days. It was as though her hands were making up for her eyes. She touched everything: the slightly thickened edge of the blanket, the satiny smoothness of the sheets, the silky feel of her—

Chelsea frowned. "What am I wearing?"

"A nightgown," Nicolas told her. "One made of special fiber that won't irritate your skin. Asklepios brought it for you."

Chelsea nodded, and let her hands fall back to her sides. "I've never felt so helpless in my life. What if my memory doesn't come back? What if I'm still blind when the bandages come off?"

"The chances are good that your memory will return in time. As to the lack of sight, you may have to learn to deal with that."

"How does one deal with blindness?"

"By developing your other senses so that the necessity for sight diminishes in importance." Chelsea heard a light step, then jumped at the unexpected touch of his hand. Nicolas had never touched her before, but now, as he took her hand between his own, she was surprised at how reassuring it felt. It was comforting to feel the touch of another person. It made her feel less alone. Less isolated.

"For example," he said, "do you know that it is night?"

"Yes."

"How?"

Chelsea shrugged. "The birds aren't singing anymore."

"Good. Your sense of hearing tells you that. What else? What about the air?"

"It's cooler than it was." She breathed it in. "And muskier."

"That's right. Without the sun to warm it, the air cools and becomes heavy. The scent of the sea is stronger. See how easy it is?"

"I see how easy it is for *you*." Chelsea snatched her hand

back. "You don't have to rely on your senses to tell you where you are or what time of day it is."

"How do you know what I can do?" Nicolas said in a low voice. "You can't see me. You only know that I'm here."

"I know you can *see*," Chelsea said bitterly. "I know you can come and go as you please. That you're not restricted to a bed all day. I know you can remember what's happened in your life and who you are, but I can't!" Chelsea knew she was getting hysterical, but she couldn't help it. "I can't even remember an accident that nearly killed me! How do you think *that* makes me feel? Do you think I like the idea of having to walk with a cane, knowing that people will rush to get out of the way so I don't crash into them? Do you think that makes me happy?" The silence lengthened. "Nicolas, why won't you answer me?"

"Because there's nothing I can say that's going to make you feel any better," he told her. "Except to remind you that you're right. You *could* have died in that accident."

"Maybe it would have been better if I had." Chelsea's mouth narrowed. "At least then, I wouldn't be forced into being dependent on other people for the rest of my life."

"You'll be dependent only if you let yourself be."

"Really? Well from where I'm standing, the chances look pretty good." Her voice held a hard edge of cynicism. "If I'm burned as badly as you say, there's not much hope of my seeing again."

"No, but every now and then, miracles do occur. All it takes is faith."

Chelsea closed her eyes. "Sorry. I don't have much faith in miracles anymore. Now if you don't mind, I'd like to be alone."

Nicolas didn't say anything, but when Chelsea heard the soft click of the door, she knew that he had gone. She lay back against her pillows and stared blindly toward the ceiling, alone in a world more frightening than night could ever be. Because at least night was always greeted a bright new day.

Hers was a darkness that could go on forever.

Twelve

For a doctor, Asklepios had surprisingly little to say. And what he *did* say, he said to Nicolas—a habit Chelsea found extremely annoying.

"But he must have given you some idea as to when I could be moved," she insisted.

"He's afraid to rush you," Nicolas said in that same patient voice. "You could do yourself harm by trying to undertake things you're not ready for. You have to let your body heal."

"You would tell me if you thought I was ready to be moved, wouldn't you, Nicolas?"

"Of course. Why wouldn't I?"

Chelsea felt a prickling at the back of her neck. Had she just imagined the slight hesitation in his voice before he'd answered?

"I don't know," she said, deciding she must have. "You certainly don't have any reason for wanting to keep me here." She sighed, and plucked at the sheets. "Goodness knows, I must be getting on your nerves. And I can't imagine how you explain me to your girlfriends."

"I don't have girlfriends." She heard the amusement in his voice. "I'm too busy with my work."

"Really?" For the first time, Chelsea realized she didn't

know what he did. She'd been so caught up in her own problems that she hadn't spared a thought for his. "So what *do* you do?" she asked, genuinely interested.

"I paint."

"You mean as in houses?"

"No, as in pictures. I'm an artist."

"You're kidding. Are you any good?"

"Good enough to pay the bills."

"Wow, that's exciting." She paused for a moment. "Do you know what I do . . . or did, for a living?"

"Yes. You're an interior designer."

Funny, Chelsea had no recollection of working with fabrics or colors. "Was *I* any good?" she asked, hoping that wasn't why she couldn't remember.

"Good enough to pay the—"

"Nicolas!"

"All right, yes, you were *very* good," he said, laughing. "In fact, you were the senior designer in charge of a major project your company had just finished working on."

"Really?" Her voice grew excited. "Then I should call them. They'll be looking for me, wondering why I haven't shown up for work."

"No, they won't, because you'd just started a vacation," Nicolas informed her. "But you don't have to worry, Asklepios did call them."

"He did?"

"Yes. He told them you'd been in an accident and that you were recovering at a private facility."

"Oh. Well, I guess that's all right, then." Chelsea stared in the direction of his voice, suddenly feeling awkward. "So is anybody else looking for me? A devoted husband? A distraught boyfriend wondering if I've run off with the guy next door?"

Nicolas's hand closed gently over hers. "You're not married, and I don't think there was a boyfriend on the scene."

Chelsea sighed. She'd pretty much suspected that. She was sure she would have remembered somebody important like a husband or a significant other. "What about my family? Do they know about the accident?"

"I thought I'd talk to you before I told them," Nicolas said slowly. "You're not close to either your mother or father, and being that they're divorced—"

"My parents are divorced? When did that happen?" *And why did it seem so shocking?*

"I'm not sure. Your mother lives in Denver; your father, in Miami. You don't have any brothers or sisters."

"What about friends? I must have had some of those."

"You had dinner in Boston with a lady by the name of Elaine a few days before the accident, but I don't think you led an active social life."

Chelsea frowned, hoping she didn't look as apprehensive as she suddenly felt. "How well *did* you know me before the accident?"

"Not well," Nicolas admitted. "In fact, we'd only just met." He removed his hand, and Chelsea immediately felt its absence. "Sadly, you had the accident when you were driving away from here. Your car went off the road and hit a telephone pole."

And burst into flames. "And that's when you . . . pulled me out?" Chelsea said, only just managing to repress a shudder.

"Yes."

She was silent for a moment, picturing in her mind the mangled wreckage of a car. She saw fire licking up the sides of a telephone pole, destroying everything it touched. Then she saw herself trapped inside that car, wondering how or if she'd ever get out alive.

"How did you get me out without being burned yourself?"

"The impact of the crash had forced the driver's door open," he told her. "You were already halfway out when I got there. All I had to do was pull you the rest of the way."

He said it in such an offhand voice that Chelsea wondered if he made a habit of rescuing damsels in distress. "Then you really *did* save my life. What a terrifying thought. Not that you saved me," she added quickly. "Just that I came that close to dying." She lapsed into silence, thoughtfully biting her lip. "I don't know how or when, Nicolas, but one day I'll repay you. You have my word on that."

"Don't worry about it," Nicolas said, glad she couldn't see his face.

It wouldn't help her to know that the manner of repayment had already been set.

Nicolas worked on Chelsea's portrait most nights, alternating time spent on that with time spent on the commissions. Certainly there was no comparison in the pleasure he took in doing one over the other. When he was painting Chelsea, it was like she was right there with him. He could close his eyes and see her face, recalling every nuance of her complexion, every detail of her expression, and then transfer the images to canvas. And he missed nothing: the sparkle in her eyes, the quivering softness of her smile, the way the blush sat high on her cheekbone, just there, where he'd painted it. Even now, as he stood mixing the colors that would give life to Chelsea's hair, he felt the bond between them, tangible and strong. A bond that he had never felt for anyone before. . . .

"I can see why you've earned such a reputation in your world, Niko. Your likeness of her is remarkable."

Nicolas turned, shocked to see Lysianassa standing in the doorway. He had invited her to visit him here on numerous occasions, but this was the first time she'd taken him up on it. Knowing her well, however, he turned back to the canvas and said with studied indifference, "You think it a good likeness?"

"I think it a very good likeness, but you have no need of me to tell you that."

Lysianassa slowly walked toward the easel. She was wearing a short, belted tunic in the deep coral shade she loved, and had fastened her hair on top of her head with a beautiful comb made out of abalone. Her feet were bare, since it didn't matter if *he* saw the fine mist of webbing between her toes, and she wore a delicate gold chain around one ankle. The tiny gold shell she wore at her throat sparkled in the light of the halogen bulb overhead. "Do you not feel closed in here, Niko?" Lysia gazed around, her almond-shaped eyes bright with interest. "The room is so small. So confining."

Nicolas smiled as he carefully applied a golden brown wash to Chelsea's hair. "It feels that way only because you're used to the vastness of the ocean." He added a few streaks of light brown, blending it with the first color, then high-lighted it with streaks of gold. "Humans, on the other hand, find such enormity of space frightening. They're used to liv-ing in confined spaces, and they're comfortable in them."

"So it doesn't bother you."

"Sometimes," he confessed. "Other times, I find it useful, particularly when it comes to doing this. It forces me to con-centrate my thinking, and to bring it down small enough to focus on the detail in my work."

"An interesting concept," Lysia admitted, "but it still doesn't suit you. The smallness of the place, I mean." She walked around the room, placing her feet carefully upon the floorboards, looking down at them as though surprised by the feel of the wood. "Does such confinement suit Chelsea?"

Thinking of her house on the beach, with its wide expanse of windows all across the front, Nicolas shook his head. "No, given the choice, I think she would prefer bright, open spaces, too."

"Good. Then we have something in common." Lysianassa smiled. "Shall I wait for you, Nikodemus? Or will you come when you are ready?"

Nicolas stared at the canvas a moment longer, then put down his brush. "No. I've done all I'm going to for tonight." He reached for a cloth and wiped a dab of paint from his fingers. "Sometimes I get so caught up in this I'm not even aware of the passage of time."

Lysia glanced at the painting again. "Easy to do, I suppose, when one's work is a labor of love."

Nicolas smiled. He couldn't have said it better himself.

Chelsea awoke the next morning to the raucous sound of seagulls outside the window. She stirred, reluctant to leave the tranquillity of that other world, and wondered what day it was. She had no idea how long she'd been here. Neither Dr. Asklepios nor Nicolas seemed inclined to tell her, and though she knew she'd awakened to five mornings, how many more had she slept through—or been unconscious for—before that?

"Nicolas?"

When there was no answer, Chelsea frowned. Strange. He was always in the room when she woke up, which either meant she was awake earlier than usual or that Nicolas was late, either of which would be unusual.

And when did you start accepting the presence of a strange man in your bedroom every morning as being normal?

Chelsea slowly breathed out. Maybe when her *life* had stopped being normal. When an accident she couldn't remember had wiped out a life she couldn't recall, and pointed her in a direction she didn't want to go.

Well, she wasn't going to think about that now. Chelsea shifted uneasily beneath the sheets. She felt so confined in the bed. All she wanted was to splash some water on her face. She knew there was a bathroom close by because she'd heard Nicolas running water in it, but *how* close was it, and did she dare try to reach it by herself?

Carefully pushing back the covers, Chelsea inched her legs toward the edge of the mattress, stopping every few seconds to rest. By the time she'd raised herself to a sitting position, she was already damp with sweat, but she wasn't giving up. Gritting her teeth, she swung her legs over the side.

A wave of dizziness assailed her—and Chelsea took a moment to let her head clear. She supposed it was only natural after spending so much time lying down. She waited for the room to stop spinning, and then carefully put her feet on the floor. That felt strange, too. The soles of her feet were still tender, and they were puffy, as though she was retaining water.

Chelsea took a deep breath. This was turning out to be a lot harder than she'd expected. So hard, that she was almost tempted to fall back into bed, but the desire to get up was stronger.

She closed her eyes and, holding onto the headboard, slowly raised herself up.

It was too soon. Her knees buckled under the weight of her body. She started to fall, and instinctively grabbed for the headboard, wincing at the red-hot pain that burned down her left side. *"Nicolas!"*

The door opened, and he was beside her, catching her in his arms as she fell. "You're all right, Chelsea." His voice was close to her ear, his breath warm against her skin. "Rest your weight on me and take a few deep breaths. You'll be fine."

But she wasn't fine. She was hurting in a hundred different places, and she was breathing too fast. If she kept this up, she'd pass out. Either way, she was sure she was going to be sick. "Nicolas . . . help me . . ."

"Breathe, Chelsea," he said, his voice quiet but steady.

Chelsea did, clinging to his arms, hating to show this kind of weakness in front of him.

"It's all right," Nicolas said, his voice calm. "Just keep breathing. Concentrate on that and forget about everything else."

She forced herself to breathe, listening to the steady sound of her breath flowing in and out. She felt the comforting warmth of Nicolas's body, the strength of his arms around her, and his lips hovering dangerously near her ear. Dimly, she heard the sound of water, and then, seconds later, felt a fine, refreshing mist on her face, the tiny droplets cooling her cheeks and making her skin tingle.

Strangely enough, the nausea passed and the dizziness went away.

"Better?" Nicolas asked.

Chelsea nodded weakly. "What was that?"

"Just a drop of water. Are you all right now?"

"I think so." She ran her tongue over her lips, and tasted salt. *Seawater?*

"Why don't you use tap water, like everybody else?" Chelsea asked as he helped her back into bed.

"Because I'm not like everybody else." He tucked her in under the covers. "And the next time you feel like venturing out on your own, call me *before* you get out of bed, all right?"

"Yes, of course."

There was more amusement than annoyance in his voice, but Chelsea was too embarrassed to appreciate it. It wasn't until after Nicolas left that she realized what she'd been embarrassed about. It wasn't that he'd found her in a less than undignified state or that he'd felt it necessary to scold her for her behavior. It was the simple, unexpected joy of being held in his arms. The startling pleasure of his body pressed close to hers, and of his hands holding her, and his mouth close enough to hers to kiss.

Feelings that not only were sadly misplaced, but entirely inappropriate.

Two days later, Dr. Asklepios took the bandages off.

Chelsea sat up in bed, trying to quell her feelings of apprehension. What would she see when the pads came off? Would she have any clarity of sight at all, or would everything be blurry? Until now, she hadn't even realized how much she'd taken her sight for granted. She'd never truly appreciated the brilliance of a rainbow as it arced across the sky, or the brightness of a field of sunflowers basking in the sun. But she would from now on. In fact, she intended to do a lot of things differently in the future.

"Now, Chelsea, I want you to keep your eyes closed," Dr. Asklepios said. "Don't try to open them until I tell you to."

Chelsea held her breath as the doctor's fingers moved against her temple, the sound of the scissors loud as he snipped away the bandage. Finally, only the pads remained.

"Nicolas?" she whispered.

"I'm here, Chelsea."

She reached for his hand and felt the reassuring warmth of his fingers close around hers. In her alien world, he had become the one constant. The one person she could rely on.

"Ready?" Dr. Asklepios said.

At her tentative nod, he carefully removed the pads.

Chelsea felt the weight of them being lifted from her eyes, and held her breath.

"All right, open your eyes, Chelsea. Slowly," Dr. Asklepios cautioned. "Tell me what you see."

Hardly daring to breathe, Chelsea opened her eyes. Blinking, she glanced down at her hands.

"Well?" the doctor said.

Chelsea raised her head and turned in the direction of his voice. She tilted her head to look toward the ceiling, and then down and to her right. She closed her eyes and opened them again—and felt a wave of desolation so deep, so all-encompassing, that words couldn't even begin to describe it.

Because the one thing she'd wanted more than anything in the world was the one thing she had been denied.

"Nothing." Chelsea closed her eyes and felt tears roll down her cheeks. "I can't see you or Nicolas or anything in this room. All this time wearing bandages hasn't made a damn bit of difference. I am utterly and completely blind!"

An intense period of despair followed. Chelsea recognized it for what it was, but she couldn't pull herself out of it. The shock of finding out that she was blind pushed all other considerations to one side. Until the doctor had removed the bandages, she hadn't had to face the possibility that she might be blind for the rest of her life.

Now she had no choice.

Nicolas did his best to comfort her, but in her present state, there was nothing he could say that didn't sound trite or meaningless. *She* was the one who was blind, not him. Consequently, when she began to go through the motions of living, she did so with no particular joy or enthusiasm. She slept when she was tired and ate when she was told to. She cried when she was alone and made desultory conversation when she wasn't, but she didn't really live. She wondered if she'd ever truly live again.

"Chelsea, are you awake?" Nicolas asked a few evenings later.

She purposely kept her eyes closed. "Yes."

"I know there's not a lot I can say that's going to make this any easier—"

"There's nothing you can say, so I'd prefer you didn't try." Her voice was detached. "That way neither of us has to pretend that things aren't really as bad as they seem."

There was a brief silence. "The skin on your arms is looking better. I think that new cream Asklepios gave you is doing a wonderful job."

"Glad to hear it."

Another silence.

"Your hair's growing back."

"Great. Remind me to run to the hairdresser the first opportunity I get."

Chelsea flung the words at him, mindless of how they

sounded, wanting only to hurt him because he could see and she couldn't. But when she realized how selfish and ungrateful she was being, she bit her lip and wondered when she'd turned into this miserable, unfeeling woman even *she* didn't like.

"I'm sorry, Nicolas, you didn't deserve that. You've been a rock the whole time I've been here, and all I do is complain. You must be sick to death of having me around." Chelsea uttered a choked, desperate laugh. "And I don't care what you say, I must be putting a hell of a kink in your sex life."

"I'm an artist, remember? I don't *have* a sex life."

"No, that was me. *I'm* the thirty-something woman who doesn't have a husband or a boyfriend," Chelsea said dully. "The one who stepped out of her life and didn't cause a ripple in anybody else's. Except yours, of course. God knows, you must be getting so far behind in your work. You can't be painting when you're looking after me. Shouldn't you be off doing promotional tours or something?" she asked, wondering if some twisted part of her *needed* to know that she was intruding on his life.

"I don't do promotional tours. And believe me, I get plenty of painting done while you're asleep. I've always been something of a night owl. But I'll say one thing for you, you must be getting better."

"Oh?" Chelsea heard the creak of the chair as Nicolas stood up. "Why?"

"Because you've asked me more questions in the last half hour than you have in the last two weeks. Maybe it's time I got you something to do."

"That would be great." Chelsea made a sound of impatience as the door closed behind him. "Just make sure it comes in braille."

A young woman was lying on the beach. Her clothes were soaking wet, and her long hair was plastered flat against her head. Her cheeks were colorless, her lips tinged with the pale blue of approaching death. She was barely breathing.

As the sun began to rise, color slowly began to seep back into her cheeks. The alarming blue cast faded from her lips, replaced by a normal, healthy pink. As the sun's rays fell

full upon her, her translucent eyelids fluttered open, and she
raised herself to a sitting position.

She pushed back the hair from her face and stared out
toward the water. Then, slowly, she began to smile. . . .

Chelsea's blindness persisted, but there were definite gains
in other areas. For one thing, her memory was starting to
come back. She could recall parts of her life that had been
lost to her before, like the name of the company where she
was employed. She remembered she'd been working on
some kind of big project, though she couldn't recall what it
was. Unfortunately, she still had absolutely no recollection
of the accident or of the days leading up to it.

Nicolas had told her that she'd just started vacation, but
she couldn't remember having done anything special during
the first few days. She couldn't remember the dinner she'd
had with her girlfriend in Boston, or running into Nicolas in
the park. He'd told her they'd sat on a bench and talked, but
she had no recollection of having done so.

The strange part was not remembering somebody like Nicolas. The more time she spent with him, the harder it was
to believe they'd only been friends. He was so patient and
gentle, so forgiving of the emotional roller coaster she was
on. And he didn't care that she couldn't remember things.
He just kept encouraging her to try. He didn't even seem to
mind spending so much of his time with her, and she suddenly wondered what he'd done with his life before she'd
intruded into it.

"Nicolas, what do you like to do?" she asked him a few
days later. "Other than paint, I mean."

He'd been reading to her, as he did every night, but now
he stopped and said, "Any number of things."

"Like what?"

"Well, I like to read. I have an extensive library here, and
I'm always picking up books on my travels. Other times, I
write."

"What kind of things? Short stories? Novels?"

"No, usually just thoughts and feelings."

"Ah, a poet," Chelsea said, and heard him laugh.

"Nothing so profound, I'm afraid. More like a diary. I like

to jot down what I see going on in the world around me, or record the events that take place during my day."

"Does a lot go on in your day?"

"Sometimes. Other times, very little."

Chelsea moved her hand over the sheet. "Why don't you ever visit me at night? I don't go to sleep until quite late."

"I know, but I assume you have enough of me during the day. I remember a time when you weren't happy about my being here at all."

Chelsea grimaced. "I don't know *how* you put up with me right after the accident. I must have been such a pain."

His fingers folded around hers, warm and incredibly gentle. "It wasn't hard at all. That was a very frightening time for you. You had every right to be scared and suspicious."

Chelsea knew his words were meant to soothe, but it was the touch of his hand and the sound of his voice that were having the greatest effect on her. "So you don't go out in the evenings?"

There was a brief pause. "What makes you think I do?"

"I don't know. It gets so quiet. I don't hear you moving around, or the sound of a TV."

"You wouldn't hear a television because I don't own one. I have few electrical appliances or modern gadgets at all. I find them irritating."

"Well, I suppose if there's only yourself to please, you can do that," Chelsea admitted. "But don't you ever get bored? Or lonely?"

"Bored? Never. Lonely . . . ?" Nicolas released his grip on her hand and got up. "As an artist, I've grown used to my own company. Seclusion is an integral part of the creative process."

"But you must find yourself longing for the company of other people. You don't sound like you're very old."

His mouth lifted in a smile. "Older than you think. But I've never been one for socializing. I've always kept pretty much to myself."

As I've had to, Nicolas thought, knowing the risks involved in getting close to mortals. It was true he hadn't spent much time on land in the early centuries, when the world had been barbaric and the people who inhabited it, violent and uncivilized. But when sophistication had begun to work its way into the human psyche, he had finally ventured forth and established himself as a land dweller.

He had lived quietly, which had been easy to do in the simple times, and when he'd felt the desire or the need to move on, he'd done so with scarcely anyone the wiser that he had left. It was only during this last century, when technology and computers had made it so easy for the world to intrude into people's lives, that he'd had to start taking extra care. Yes, he had probably complicated matters by choosing to be an artist. He probably should have done something that would not have exposed him to the public eye, since by virtue of what he was, it was impossible that he would be anything *but* brilliant in his chosen field. But he had found expression for his thoughts in the form of visual art, capturing the existence of the sea world around him in the glorious images of his art.

Some had called him genius; others, a gifted painter with a penchant for the bizarre. Either way, he had established a somewhat unconventional lifestyle for himself, and for the moment that was fine. Living on the North American continent allowed artists a certain amount of eccentricity, but at the same time Nicolas knew he could only take it so far. He knew what would happen if anyone discovered what he was. He would be seen as an aberration, as much a creature of mystery as the legendary vampire. In fact, they both trod a tenuous path, bound by their limitations, shunned by mankind because of their differences. But at least Nicolas didn't require human blood to survive. He could exist on the proteins found in the sea, and on the fruits and vegetables so plentiful on land. He was not at risk of condemning another's soul to eternal hell.

And yet, was his love for Chelsea not as destructive as a vampire's kiss? Did his presence in her life now not foreshadow an end to the only kind of existence she'd ever known?

As to the loneliness, how could he tell her that the loneliness he felt was as a result of not being with her every hour of the day? How could he tell her that his life hadn't really begun until he'd heard her voice and looked into her eyes?

"I don't think I would have made a good artist," Chelsea said suddenly, her voice intruding into his thoughts. "I don't have your self-sufficiency. I've come to realize that, lying here day after day with only my thoughts, dull as they are, to occupy me."

Nicolas laughed, but the sound was filled with compassion. "Need I point out that you've taken some pretty hard knocks, Miss Porter?" he said, returning to her bedside. "It's only natural they'd be weighing heavily on your mind."

"I know, but it's more than that, Nicolas. I keep thinking I'd like to talk to somebody. Which is stupid, since other than you, I don't *remember* anybody."

There was a brief silence. "Am I such poor company?"

"Of course not. You're wonderful company. I don't know what I would have done without you. But you're my friend. You've already told me that's all we were to one another."

"So you're looking for someone who meant more to you?" he said. "A boyfriend, perhaps?"

"I . . . don't know," Chelsea said. "It doesn't sound like I had one. And yet, I keep thinking there *was* somebody. Somebody who was important in my life. Someone who—"

Chelsea went to say more, when she suddenly remembered the incident yesterday when she had collapsed into Nicolas's arms. She remembered the heady experience of being held in his embrace, and of his arms tightening around her. If she wasn't aware of him as a man, and if he was nothing more than friend, why did that memory stick so forcefully in her mind?

Chelsea heard the soft click of the door, and knew that Nicolas had gone. It was only in that brief, illuminating moment that she began to realize just how important his company had become.

Thirteen

In the shallow waters at the edge of the beach, Lysianassa stood and gazed up at the house. Nikodemus had been late several times this week, but she supposed that was only to be expected. Everything had changed since the devastating accident that had nearly claimed Chelsea Porter's life.

Lysianassa hadn't been there when Nikodemus had pulled Chelsea from the burning car, but she had heard about it from her father. Heard how he had commanded the waters to rise to extinguish the fire, and how, with his bare hands, he had torn the car apart and taken her from it. She knew that he had carried Chelsea's broken body into the depths, encasing her head in a bubble of air, and that he had called for Asklepios, the great healer, to come.

It was only after many hours, when Chelsea's fragile condition had stabilized, that Nikodemus had been able to return her to land and settle her in his house.

Asklepios had made several more visits to Chelsea in the world above, but had been forced to stop when Poseidon had learned of them. The omnipotent sea god had been furious at his son's deliberate intervention in the life of a mortal yet again, and he had refused to allow either his son or Asklepios to restore Chelsea's sight. That, Poseidon had said, Nikodemus must accept as punishment for his sins.

A night bird cried in the bushes, and Lysianassa jumped, still uneasy in this world above the sea. Not as uneasy, she admitted, as she would have been a few weeks ago. She had learned much about Nikodemus's world of late, and though she was reluctant to admit it, even to herself, she *was* finding mortals intriguing.

Now, for example, as darkness settled on the land, she knew they would be returning to their houses, where they would prepare food on things called stoves, and watch big black boxes called televisions, out of which people talked and music played. She knew this because she had peered into their windows at night, secure in the knowledge they couldn't see her, and had watched, and listened, and learned. But today, she had been very brave.

Today, for the first time, Lysianassa had donned mortal clothes and walked amongst them.

Truth be told, it had been an interesting experience. She had blended remarkably well into the colorful crowd strolling the streets. Some of the mortals had stared at her, particularly the males, but for the most part they had gone about their business, as though oblivious to her existence. And she had certainly seen some strange things. Young males with hair as long as hers, and whose bodies were covered with lines and patterns etched in dark blue. Females who sported gold and silver rings in their ears, and some through their nose, like the old bulls the farmers kept chained in their pens.

They had ranged in age from the very young to the very old, but they had all seemed to be having a good time. Most of them walked in pairs or in groups, some of them holding hands, many of them laughing amongst themselves. That had come as a surprise to Lysianassa. She hadn't expected mortals to laugh the way gods did. How could they, when their lives were so simple and their worlds so restricted?

Yet they did not seem unhappy, and she had to admit that, as a race, they were not unattractive. And they were bold, these mortal men. She had been startled when one particularly handsome youth had smiled at her in a way that had brought the color to her cheeks, and who had, by the act of blowing her kisses and clutching at his heart, made his thoughts and intentions perfectly clear. Strangely enough, the memory of it made her smile.

"Lysia, forgive me," Nikodemus said, coming down the path toward her. "I have kept you waiting again."

She turned bright eyes toward him, and her smile warmed even more. The sight of him always tugged at her heart, but she was getting better at dealing with it. She cared too much for their friendship to jeopardize it by grieving over something she couldn't have. He needed her to be strong, and because she loved him, that's what she would be. "That's all right, Niko. Actually, I've been enjoying the night air."

"Really?" He glanced at her quizzically. "I didn't think you were partial to air."

She waved her hand over the water, trailing stardust and moonbeams. "I find it is not as unpleasant as I'd expected."

"Careful, Lysia. You may find other things in the mortal world more to your liking than you expected."

Lysianassa sighed. There, had she not told herself Nikodemus would do this? His smugness was the reason she had been unwilling to share her thoughts and feelings with him in the first place.

"I have no need of your counsel, great prince. I am content with my life as it is."

He must have heard the warning in her voice, for he only smiled and started into the water.

"How is Chelsea coming along?" she asked, joining him.

"She is making gains in some areas, but she is still troubled by her lack of memory. And, of course, by her blindness."

"But why should that trouble her? Her sight will be returned once she crosses over."

He smiled enigmatically. "Yes, but *she* doesn't know that."

"Then why not tell her?" Lysia said. "It will help put her mind at rest."

"I doubt Chelsea would take comfort in the fact that she has to forfeit her life in order to get her sight back."

"Perhaps not, but she will have to be told sooner or later."

"Yes, but I wish to give her all the time as I can." Nikodemus stopped. "I can't force her to love me, Lysia, but I'm afraid that if she doesn't, the dangers will consume her."

"You mean the danger from Sephonia."

"Of course. Chelsea's mortal soul would be a great prize to her. Only the strongest are able to get past a sea witch; those who aren't afraid of dying, or who are possessed of the truest, deepest love for another. Sadly, Chelsea is neither."

Lysia shuddered. "I don't know why Poseidon allows Sephonia to remain. He should have banished her, as he did all the other witches and monsters."

"Perhaps, but Sephonia is too smart," Nikodemus said. "She panders to him. She uses her great beauty to charm him."

"But he cannot be blind to her evil. It may not affect him, but surely he knows how destructive she can be."

Nikodemus sighed. "On land, there are many such creatures. Insects that can strip a field of every blade of grass, and snakes whose venom kills in seconds. They live among the more peaceful creatures, and their presence is tolerated because they are part of the natural order. Good and evil have always existed side by side, Lysia. If you ever venture onto land, you will discover that some of the most evil mortals live right next to those who might be saints. The sea is no different."

Lysia sniffed. "I think Poseidon should *make* it different. Sephonia traps souls and then casts them aside, leaving them to dwell in a place that is neither of this world nor of the next. It isn't right that she be allowed to torment those who fall prey to her beauty, simply because they are unsuspecting of her evil."

"Nevertheless, she will remain a parasite outside the gates of the Kingdom, and there is nothing you or I can do about it."

"There is nothing *I* can do, but surely *you* have supremacy over her, Niko. She cannot touch you. Can you not use your powers to banish her?"

Nikodemus smiled. "I probably could, but I would not dare. I have already aroused my father's ire by interfering in the mortal world. I know better than to risk meddling in his!"

• • •

All right, so you can't see, Chelsea told herself the next morning. *Lots of people lose their sight, but they learn to overcome it. And there are worse things than being blind. At least you didn't die in that car accident. You still have all your limbs and the use of your other faculties. You have a lot to be thankful for.*

Then why didn't she believe it?

Chelsea shook her head, pushing away the negative thoughts. She *had* to believe it; she didn't have a choice. There was a chance her memory might return, but blindness was a fact of life. She was going to wake up every morning and stare into darkness.

The sooner she accepted that and got on with life, the better.

Besides, with Nicolas's patient teaching, she was already beginning to learn how to cope with her handicap. She knew how to recognize the different times of day simply by listening to the sound track nature provided, and she was utilizing her other senses more than ever before.

Unfortunately, the exercises she was doing to stimulate her mind did nothing to assuage the restlessness in her body. She was getting stronger by the day, and she wanted to start moving around, but she couldn't do that without Nicolas's permission. Which was why she never missed an opportunity to show him how well she was doing.

She could lift her arms and walk without difficulty, and she could even get to the bathroom by herself. That was one of the first things she'd asked Nicolas to acquaint her with. After all, the alternative had been far too embarrassing, especially given the way she'd come to feel about him.

Chelsea knew she owed Nicolas her life, but gratitude had nothing to do with the happiness she felt whenever he was near. Basic things, like the sound of his voice or the touch of his hand, had come to mean so much. They aroused emotions Chelsea had never thought to experience. It wasn't appreciation that made her quiver at the sound of his voice. It was something far simpler.

She was falling in love with him. He was her teacher and her guide, and she was learning from him in the way a child learned from a parent. But there was nothing childlike in the strength of her feelings for him. Her awareness of him was as a man, completely and without reserve. He made her feel alive, and in a way that had nothing to do with the stimulation of physical appearance—though she had to admit, she was very curious about that.

"What do you look like, Nicolas?" she asked him one afternoon.

He laughed. "Like any other man, I suppose."

"I don't believe you. You're nothing like any other man I've ever met."

"That's only because you don't *remember* any of the men you've met," he pointed out. "Besides, you don't know anything about me."

"Then help me to know you," Chelsea said eagerly. "Describe yourself to me. Paint me a picture."

"Paint you a picture?"

"Yes. You have such a wonderful way with words. When you speak, it's almost as though I see pictures in my mind. Paint me a picture. Help me see how you look."

Chelsea heard him come closer and felt the bed dip as he sat on the edge of it. "Perhaps I can do better than that. I will make you an artist."

Chelsea's brow furrowed. "An artist? How?"

"Do you trust me, Chelsea?"

"Of course."

"Good. Then you shall be the sculptor and I shall be your clay." Nicolas took her left hand in his and pressed her palm to his face. "Use your fingers to feel what you have created."

Chelsea felt her cheeks grow warm. It was the first time she'd ever touched him like this. "I'm not sure I can do this."

She started to pull away, but he caught her hand and held it.

"Yes, you can. Touch me, Chelsea. Feel my face. Let your hands do the work of your eyes, then let your imagination fill in the rest."

Chelsea bit her lip. She wanted to, but did she dare?

"Of course you can, I won't bite," he teased.

She laughed at the way he seemed to read her mind, and *because* she wanted to, she cautiously returned her left hand to his face. Raising her right one, she placed it against his cheek so that she could feel both sides at once. Then slowly, breathlessly, she began to explore.

His face was square—no, oval, she amended, running the flat of her palms over his cheeks and jaw. The texture of his skin was remarkably smooth, yet pliant, and he was clean-shaven. "I didn't think you had a beard."

"Disappointed?"

"No. I don't like the way they tickle."

"I'll keep that in mind."

Smiling, Chelsea let her hands drift upward, skirting the area around his mouth and finding well-defined cheekbones and a slim, beautifully shaped nose. She ran her fingers down either side, felt the nostrils flare, and then carried on up toward his eyes. Her touch was light as she moved them over the graceful arch of his brows. "What color are your eyes?"

"Like the blue of the sky on a summer day."

She ran the pads of her fingers along the silky strands of his eyebrows. When he closed his eyes, she felt the brush of long, curving lashes. "Gracious, you have long eyelashes."

"A trait inherited from my mother," he said, sounding far more at ease with this than she was.

Continuing, Chelsea discovered a wide forehead that curved slightly toward the hairline, and hair that was remarkably soft and wavy. "And your hair? What color is that?"

"As black as a night without stars."

Chelsea smiled. Trust an artist to wax poetic. Nicolas never just *told* her what color something was. He described it to her, making her see the images in her mind, and she had to admit it was effective.

She followed the waves down to his shoulders, then ran her fingers along his throat, feeling the muscles in his neck and the points of his collarbone. Satisfied she'd done a thorough exploration, she sat back. "Well, that was certainly an interesting experience."

"Ah, but you haven't finished," Nicolas said. "You haven't explored my mouth."

She held her breath. "I know it's there."

"But you can't describe it. And as a sculptress, only think

how sad your creation would look if you did not give it a suitable mouth through which to laugh or cry or express emotion."

His silky voice held a challenge, and even though Chelsea felt her heart begin to race, she rose to it. She put her hands back on his face and, starting at his nose, ran the tips of her fingers down, finding his mouth and slowly moving over it. She felt the ridge of his upper lip and traced it with her fingers, feeling the shape and the fullness of it, forming a picture of it in her mind. She did the same with his bottom lip, blushing when she felt his mouth pull into a smile.

Dear heaven, had she *ever* experienced anything so intimate before? Had she ever taken the time to really *learn* the contours of a man's face, or had she simply relied on her eyes to tell her what she needed to know? If she had, she'd certainly been missing a lot.

"Well?" he asked when she sat back again. "Can you see me now?"

Chelsea smiled as the images came together in her mind. "Yes, I can, and you're very handsome." She raised her fingers to brush them gently over his cheek again. "I can feel it."

Unable to stop himself, Nicolas reached up and caught her hand, surprising her by the quickness of his actions. He'd known that the touch of her hands would arouse feelings of desire in him, but he hadn't expected them to be this strong. Even now, tremors shook him, filling him with a burning need to reach out and touch her in return.

And he did. He caressed her fingers, watching her eyes widen as he circled his thumb over the sensitive skin on her wrist in a slow, seductive movement. He heard her soft gasp of pleasure as he pressed a kiss into her palm, felt her lean toward him, as though asking for more. And he wanted to do more. He wanted to lay her back against the pillows and kiss her until they both lost touch with the world around them. He wanted to discover the secret places on her body, the places she wanted to be touched, and to touch her until she cried out his name. He wanted to cover her with his body, and to feel her open to him, like a flower opening to the sun. He'd never wanted a woman the way he wanted Chelsea.

Never felt so drawn to anyone before. But why would he not be drawn to her? The bond between them was a powerful one. He could no more resist her than he could the lure of the sea. He had spent too many long, empty years alone waiting for her.

Waiting for Chelsea.

He was sorely tempted to share some of his thoughts with her. To let his own impressions slide into her mind. All he had to do was place his fingers in a triangle against her forehead and she would see all that he was, and all that he was feeling. But even as his hands hovered above her skin, he hesitated, remembering what Lysia had said.

Was Chelsea ready for this? She would have no way of understanding what she was seeing, and if he'd misjudged her feelings, she'd end up being frightened rather than fascinated. Did he want to risk undoing all the good he'd done? Did he want her to be afraid of him the way she'd been before?

Silently, he released her hand, and let his own fall back to his side.

"I'd better go."

"Is something wrong?"

He heard the quiver in her voice, and knew she was not unmoved by what had just taken place. As he gazed down at her, and saw the outline of her body beneath the sheet, Nicolas felt desire flare sharply to life again. He knew exactly how she looked, with and without clothes. Once Asklepios had stopped coming, it had been necessary that he change the seaweed poultices. It had been hard in the beginning, when he'd had to remove bits of blackened, fire-charred skin, and he had taken hours doing it so that he might not hurt her. But as radiant new skin had begun to grow and Chelsea had started to look once more like the beautiful woman she was, Nicolas had felt his strictly platonic thoughts change to more passionate ones.

Even so, he knew it was too soon to initiate any physical intimacies between them. There would be time enough when Chelsea was strong again. When she knew her own mind, and was ready to act on it.

"I think it's time we reintroduced you to your world, Chelsea Porter," he said instead. "Tomorrow, we eat breakfast downstairs. And if you feel up to it, we'll go for a walk along the beach. What would you say to that?"

Chelsea sucked in her breath. "You have no idea how much I'd like that!"

"Good. Tomorrow, we go outside," Nicolas said. "Tomorrow, you start living again."

Dressing proved to be a relatively simple matter. With the weather being so warm, there was no need for an excess of clothes. Nicolas provided her with a simple, dresslike garment that pulled on over her head and fell to just below her knees, with no sleeves or fastenings of any kind. It was incredibly soft and almost felt like she was wearing nothing at all.

"If you need my help putting it on, just call," Nicolas said. "I'll wait out here in the hall."

"I think I can manage," Chelsea said, grinning. "Besides, I'm so excited, I wouldn't care if I went down to the beach in my nightgown."

She heard his throaty chuckle. "You could. There's no one around to see you."

As soon as she was dressed, Chelsea stood up. She was careful not to move too quickly, still fearing a return of the dizziness that had plagued her so often during her first days on her feet, but thankfully, everything seemed fine today. As Nicolas said, it was just a matter of getting used to being mobile again.

Self-consciously, Chelsea lifted a hand to her head and felt the springy mass of curls. Her hair was growing back with amazing speed. Must be something in the food he was giving her. She ran her fingers through it, hoping she looked all right, and then took a deep breath. "Okay, Nicolas, I'm ready."

She heard the door open. When Nicolas didn't say anything, she laughed, a little nervously. "Is something wrong? Have I put it on backward?"

"Everything's fine," he said huskily. "I was just admiring the way you look in it."

Chelsea blushed at the caress in his voice. "What color is it?"

"Blue. As blue as the Mediterranean Sea. Ready to go?"

"Yes, but. . . ." She bit her lip, feeling foolish. "I'm . . . afraid."

"Afraid? Of what?"

"Of . . . going out there. Of finding out I can't cope with things as they are now."

He walked toward her, and his hands closed reassuringly on her shoulders. "You *can* cope, Chelsea. If I didn't think you were ready, I wouldn't be letting you do this. But there's nothing out there to harm you, and we're going to do this together, one step at a time."

Together. How comforting that word seemed, especially coming from Nicolas.

Chelsea felt his hand on her waist and smiled as she took her first tentative steps toward the door. Her first steps toward her new life.

"Now, when you get through the door, we're going to turn right," Nicolas said. "You'll walk about ten steps to the top of the stairs. Don't worry about your feet, you're not going to trip over anything."

Chelsea nodded as she counted the steps. On ten, Nicolas stopped and turned her toward the left. "Now you're at the top of the stairs. There are fifteen steps to the bottom."

"I'll fall!" Chelsea cried, clinging to him.

"No, you won't. I'm right here beside you, and you're going to take it very slowly. Ready?"

Chelsea bit her lip. Suddenly, the safety of the bed seemed like a haven, and for a moment, she was tempted to turn around and run back to it. But she couldn't do that. This wasn't about running away. It was about learning to deal with her problems and overcoming them. It was also the only way she was going to get anywhere on her own. "Ready."

Nicolas took her left hand and put it on the railing. She felt the warmth and smoothness of the polished wood beneath her fingers, and held fast to it. Her other hand gripped his arm.

"Now, one step down, and press your heel against the back of the stair. That's it," Nicolas said as they both started down.

"Now another step. Good. And another. That's it, Chelsea, you're already almost halfway down."

Chelsea felt elation bubbling in her chest. She was walking again! She was no longer confined to her bedroom. She felt the smoothness of the bare wood beneath the soles of her feet, and wanted to laugh out loud.

"All right, now at the bottom of the stairs, we're going to turn left," he told her. "The kitchen is that way."

"What's on the other side?"

"The living and dining rooms."

Chelsea sniffed the air. "Are we close to a door? I can smell the water."

"That's because it's all around us, but yes, if you walk straight ahead, you'll come to the deck, and then the beach farther on. But I don't think you're ready for that yet. We'll have some breakfast first."

Breakfast proved to be the most frustrating experience of all. Chelsea hadn't realized how much she'd taken the most basic things for granted, like buttering toast or pouring milk onto her cereal. More than once, tears of exasperation sprang to her eyes as even the simple act of pouring a cup of tea turned into a challenge.

"Ouch!" she cried, burning her fingers for the second time. "I swear I'm going to stick to water from now on."

"No, you're not. You're just going to get used to putting things in the same place," Nicolas chided gently. "For example, keep the handle of the teapot toward you and learn to put it so many inches from your plate. That way, it will always be there when you reach for it. And when you're pouring tea into your cup, keep your finger hooked over the edge so you'll know when to stop."

It was one lesson after another, but when she ended up putting too much sugar in her tea and pouring juice all over the table, Chelsea threw up her hands in despair. "It's no good. I'm useless. I'll never get used to being blind!"

With that, she burst into tears.

For once, Nicolas let her cry. He pulled her into his arms and held her, as though knowing she needed to vent her frustration. And sure enough, in a matter of minutes, Chelsea did start to feel better. But as her fears subsided, new sen-

sations began to creep in, not the least of which was an
awareness of Nicolas holding her, his strong arms cradling
her against his chest. She drew the scent of him into her soul
and felt the heat of his skin burn through the thin material
of her dress. She could hear his heart beating, strong and
steady in her ear, and was embarrassed to feel her body re-
spond.

Reluctantly, she pulled away. "Thank you. I'm . . . all right
now."

"Good." Nicolas's voice was strangely husky. He cleared
his throat and said, "Then I think it's time for that walk."

It was wonderful being outside again. Chelsea felt the gentle
warmth of the sun on her face, and carefully tilted her head
back to enjoy it. The air was fresh, and she felt new life and
energy filling her lungs. The breeze fluttered the fabric of
her dress, blowing it against her knees in a sensual caress.
She experienced the sounds all around her, not by listening
to them through her window but by standing here in the
middle of them. She heard the cries of the seabirds and the
rush of the waves, the distant clanging of a bell, and from
somewhere close by, the sound of wood knocking against a
rock.

"I want to go down to the sea, Nicolas," she told him
eagerly. "Take me down there, please."

With his help, she made it down the deck steps and across
the sand to the edge of the water. The sound of the surf was
louder now, the interval between the breakers easier to dis-
cern.

It felt strange to be walking outside, yet with no idea as
to where she was going. Chelsea kept expecting to stub her
toe or to trip over something, but Nicolas was always there,
ready to stop her before she did.

"All right, Chelsea, now the water's straight ahead of
you," he told her. "Fix a point in your mind and walk toward
it. And remember, I'm right behind you."

Chelsea nodded and began to walk: slowly, stiffly, her
arms stretched out at her side like a high-wire artist balanc-
ing. On the fifth step, her foot came down in water. Not

expecting it, she squealed and jumped back, the quick movement unbalancing her. "Nicolas!"

"It's all right, Chelsea, I've got you," Nicolas said, laughing. He caught her around the waist and gently drew her back against him. "I won't let you fall. I won't ever let you fall."

She felt the warmth of his chest against her back, felt the hardness of his thighs against hers, and nearly groaned as a quiver of heat shot through her, melting her bones. Her body went pliant, her curves softening to the contours of his. She had no desire to move, or to talk, or to breathe. She just wanted to stand there, surrounded by him, absorbing him. . . .

"I can't believe that . . . just the thought of walking in the surf is making me so excited." She knew her face was red, and hoped he wouldn't notice. "I wonder if I used to enjoy it this much before."

"You did at one time," Nicolas said. Making sure she was steady on her feet, he released her but didn't let her go. He took her hand, and with one arm around her waist, walked her into the water, stopping to give her time to get used to the chill. When she had, he took her a little farther out, but only until the water reached her knees.

"Oh, Nicolas, you don't know how good this feels," Chelsea whispered. "The sun, the water, the sand under my feet." *And you beside me, holding me and giving me strength.*

She smiled at her own foolishness, thankful that Nicolas couldn't read her mind.

Beside her, Nicolas smiled, too, thankful that he could.

Fourteen

They had been strolling for about ten minutes when Nicolas noticed the change in Chelsea's face. The tip of her nose was turning pink, but it was the total lack of color in her face that concerned him. "You're tired," he said, sweeping her up into his arms. "We've done too much."

"No, no, we haven't," Chelsea said, shaking her head. "It was wonderful. I loved every minute of it."

"But you're not used to it. This is the first time you've been outside since the accident. I should have known better than to let you walk so far."

Nicolas carried her back toward the house, furious with himself for not having taken better care of her. He should have seen the weariness creeping in, but he'd been so caught up in the joy of being with her that he'd lost all track of time.

The problem was, his desire for Chelsea was growing by the day. Even now, he felt his body hardening in response to her. At times, he was almost thankful for her disability. At least he didn't have to hide what was in his eyes or his heart. It wasn't just a physical awareness that made his time with Chelsea so special. It was having her beside him and being in the water with her. It was the joy of seeing her come alive again—until he saw her lying limp and pale in his arms, and felt the guilt and anger all over again.

She was mortal. Even at her best, she would never be able to match his endurance. He'd attempted too much this first time out. Asklepios had warned him to be careful.

He carried her back inside and took her upstairs to bed.

"Nicolas?" she murmured as he covered her with the blanket.

"Yes?"

"Thank you for taking me outside today. It was wonderful."

"I'm not sure Asklepios would be as pleased." Nicolas's voice was gruff as he bent over her. "He told me not to push you."

"You didn't push me, I pushed myself. Will you take me outside again tomorrow?"

He gently brushed the shining curls back from her face. "Of course, if that's what you want. I'm proud of you, Chelsea. You did very well today."

"Apart from the milk and the teapot."

Nicolas laughed. "To hell with the milk and the teapot. There are far more important things in life than making tea."

"What are you going to do now?"

He bent down and brushed his lips reverently against her temple, knowing that if he went anywhere near her mouth, he might never leave. "I'm going to pick up a few things from the store. We're running a little low on supplies. Sleep well, Chelsea. And remember, tomorrow's another day."

The aisles of the Bayside Market were relatively quiet, for which Nicolas was thankful. He'd come to accept that shopping was a necessary part of living on land, but he'd never learned to enjoy it. Most of the time he hired people to shop for him. That was the way he'd furnished his houses around the world. And since he required nothing in the way of mortal food, he never had to shop for groceries. Occasionally he'd buy art supplies, but that was only because he didn't trust other people to do it for him. Only he knew what types of brushes he wanted, and how they would feel in his hand.

But now that Chelsea was regaining her strength, there

were certain things he couldn't do without. Or, rather, that she couldn't. She needed the nourishment her own type of food provided. Fortunately, Nicolas had spent enough time on land to know what the various food types were, and though he adhered to the equivalent of a strict vegetarian diet, he knew that mortals required a mix of animal proteins and other products to adequately sustain their systems.

Chelsea had also expressed a desire for some perfume, and Nicolas intended to surprise her by bringing some home. But as he gazed at the wide assortment of bottles on the shelf, he shook his head in confusion. How did women ever choose from such a bewildering array?

"Excuse me, but . . . aren't you Nicolas Demitry?"

Nicolas turned and found himself looking at an older man whose tired blue eyes and lined face told Nicolas a great deal about his life. He looked like a businessman in beige slacks and a navy blue, long-sleeved shirt, though perhaps a somewhat disorganized one, judging by the smear of what appeared to be blue ink on his cheek. "Yes, I am."

"I thought so." The man put out his hand. "I'm Joe Turner, from Turner and Parsons. I saw you at the gallery opening, but didn't get a chance to say hello."

Cautious now, Nicolas returned the man's handshake. He knew the name Joe Turner. This was Chelsea's partner, the man who'd given her the time off. The man who would be expecting her to return to work in the very near future. "That's not surprising. It was a busy night."

"Yes, it was, but I heard what an incredible impact your painting made," Joe said. "It must be gratifying to generate that kind of excitement with your work."

"Thank you, but it's not so different from your own. You're to be commended for the splendid work you did on the gallery, Mr. Turner."

"Call me Joe," he said, smiling. "Actually, that was my partner's project. Chelsea Porter was the driving force behind the gallery. You spoke to her that night, I believe."

"Yes, I remember," Nicolas said quietly. "A charming and very talented lady."

"She is that," Joe agreed. His glance flicked to the bottles on the shelf they were standing beside. "Shopping for your wife?"

A man less experienced might have given something away, but Nicolas had spent too many years learning how to conceal his thoughts and emotions to betray anything now. He simply shook his head and smiled, recognizing the source of the man's curiosity. "I'm not married, but I have a friend staying with me who's feeling a little under the weather. I thought I'd get something to cheer her up."

"Yeah, I used to surprise my wife once in a while," Joe said, his eyes looking haunted for a moment. "Anyway, it was a pleasure meeting you, Mr. Demitry. Stop by the office sometime. I'm sure Chelsea would be glad to show you around."

Nicolas inclined his head. "Thank you, I might do that."

The older man moved off, and Nicolas took two bottles from the shelf and placed them in his cart. He knew he hadn't raised any suspicions on Joe Turner's part, but he wasn't entirely comfortable with the meeting either. Joe Turner was Chelsea's partner, a man she had a close working relationship with. And while Nicolas knew it wasn't an intimate relationship, there was a good chance they kept in touch outside work.

The problem was, Chelsea had been away over a month, and Joe Turner would be expecting her back at work soon. He might already have called her house, wondering where she was. The last thing Nicolas needed right now was someone starting to look for Chelsea.

Oblivious to the direction of Nicolas's thoughts, Joe finished his own shopping and then headed for his car. The four bags of groceries hardly held everything he needed, but it was a start. Man could live on junk food only so long, and he'd had his fill of potato chips, dry cereal, and take-out food.

Joe hadn't seen Patty since the day she'd told him she was leaving, but he was dealing with it. At some point, she'd come back and cleared out her things—and a few of his— before taking off for points unknown, but Joe didn't fool himself into believing he'd heard the last of her. Her lawyer's card had been left on the dining room table as a parting gift.

The realization that a month had gone by suddenly had Joe thinking about Chelsea, too. He'd said he'd call her, but he'd been so caught up in work, he'd forgotten. He spent most of his time at the office, often sleeping on the couch rather than going home, but he thought he'd left a message or two on her answering machine. He figured she would have called him back, just to see how he was doing. She'd seemed so concerned the day he'd told her about Patty. She cared about her friends, and Joe liked to think he was one.

Too bad she'd been so hurt by that Duncan Rycroft. What a smooth-talking playboy he'd turned out to be! Rycroft could charm the birds out of the trees when he put his mind to it. That was part of the reason Joe hadn't liked him. That and the fact that he'd had an ego the size of Texas. But he'd sure as hell bamboozled Chelsea. And when he'd walked out on her, and brought the walls of her world tumbling down around her ears, she'd turned into a workaholic, devoting all of her energies to her career.

Chelsea was an incredibly talented and creative interior designer, and Joe had enjoyed watching her come into her own. Offering her a minor partnership in the business hadn't had anything to do with getting an influx of cash. It had been about recognizing Chelsea's dedication. About giving her a sense of self-worth again. Whatever the title "partner" meant to her, it meant more to Joe to see her pride and self-confidence restored.

Maybe he'd swing by her place after work tonight to see how she was doing. He fully expected she was champing at the bit to get back to work, and had half expected to see her back last week. Maybe she was having a better time than she'd expected.

Hell, it was only fair that somebody should.

Chelsea slept well into the afternoon. When she finally opened her eyes, she didn't try to get up. She just lay against the pillows, reliving the events of the morning.

Her legs were sore from the unaccustomed exercise, but the pain was definitely worth it. It meant she was getting better. Stronger. And it had been so good to get outside again. To feel the warmth of the sun on her body, and the sea and the sand beneath her feet. Even breakfast had been an adventure.

Chelsea grimaced. Okay, so she hadn't done so well with that, but at least she'd tried. And Nicolas had been wonderful. So patient when it came to telling her what she needed to know, encouraging her when she failed and praising her when she did something right. What would she have done without him?

Chelsea's smile faded a little. She owed him so much. Not just for today, but for everything he'd done for her. He'd saved her life, for goodness' sake! How would she ever be able to repay him? All he seemed to want was for her to get better. It seemed so little to ask in return.

It wasn't long before she heard the sound of the bedroom door opening, and then detected the delicious aroma of food wafting in. "Mmm, is that dinner? It smells fantastic."

"I know it's earlier than you usually eat, but I thought I'd give you a treat after all your hard work this morning," Nicolas told her.

She heard him set the tray on the bedside table and suddenly wished she could see how she looked. Her hair must be a mess. She knew it was clean, but she'd been lying on it for hours and she wanted to look nice for him.

"Your hair looks lovely," Nicolas said. "In fact, I think it suits you better curly than straight."

Chelsea's head jerked up. "How did you know that?"

"What?"

"That I was wondering how my hair looked."

"I just assumed that's what was running through your mind. I could tell by the look on your face that you were concerned about something."

Chelsea felt her pulse quicken. "Have you ever been married, Nicolas?"

"No."

"Seriously involved?"

"No. Why?"

"Because for a man who doesn't have a girlfriend and who's never been married, you have amazing insight into what goes on inside a woman's head."

To her surprise, he just laughed. "I can assure you, any

experience I've gained is strictly secondhand. But I like to think my artistic sensibilities allow me to be more in touch with the feminine psyche than most men."

It was, Chelsea supposed, a logical answer, but she wasn't entirely convinced. In fact, she was beginning to wonder if Nicolas had been more seriously involved with a woman than he was letting on. There were so many times when he made some remark, some . . . astute observation that was a direct reflection of what she'd been thinking, it was almost uncanny.

Still, if he said he hadn't been involved with anyone, why shouldn't she believe him?

"So, what kind of culinary delight have you prepared for me tonight?" she asked.

"A kind of vegetable casserole."

Chelsea's mouth watered. "I can't believe how hungry I am. It must have been all that fresh air this morning. Are you eating with me?"

"No, I had something when I was out."

Chelsea picked up her utensils. She wasn't surprised. Nicolas always seemed to eat his meals before she did. She brought her fork down on the plate and connected with something firm.

"Cauliflower," Nicolas said obligingly.

"Oh good. I like cauliflower—I think." Chelsea cautiously guided the fork to her mouth. She'd already learned that stabbing herself in the lip was not a pleasant experience. Thankfully, this time she found her mouth first time—and realized she did like cauliflower. "Where were you born, Nicolas?"

There was a very brief hesitation. "What if I told you I was born at sea?"

"I'd say your mother was crazy for going on a cruise when she was that close to her time." Chelsea lowered her fork and speared something else. "Were you really born at sea?"

"Yes, which is why I find it hard to think of myself as being from any one place."

"But you must claim *some* country as your home."

"I do. Whatever country I'm in at the time," he said. "It's not really important that I'm from one place or another."

"Then you're an unusual man. Most people are very proud of their heritage."

"So am I."

"Then why don't you like to talk about it?"

"Because it isn't relevant to what I am now."

Chelsea picked up a piece of what turned out to be broccoli. "I still say you're an unusual man. And a lucky one, living so close to the water."

"You have a house on the beach, too."

For some reason, that surprised her. "I do?"

"Yes. I visited you there a few times."

"Really?" Chelsea sighed. "What I wouldn't give to be able to remember it. Or to see it again."

"You may very well do both," Nicolas said. "Your memory's coming back, and Asklepios didn't say the damage to your eyes was permanent."

"No, but I just have a bad feeling about this." Her voice was painfully matter-of-fact. "I might be more optimistic if I could see shapes or shadows, or even the faintest flicker of light, but there's absolutely nothing."

"What if I said I could make you see again, Chelsea?" he asked softly.

The question was so unexpected that Chelsea actually laughed. "I'd say you were many things, but a miracle worker isn't one of them. You're not even a doctor."

"Does a man have to be a doctor to perform miracles? Perhaps I know another way of making you see."

Suddenly, Chelsea heard the low rumble of thunder outside the house. "Is that a storm blowing up?"

She felt the bed rise as Nicolas stood. "I don't think so." There was a brief silence before he added, "Can I get you anything else? I may not have a chance to check in on you later."

Chelsea wondered why his voice suddenly sounded so remote. "Are you going out?"

"Yes, but you'll be fine."

Chelsea wasn't bothered at being left in the house, and she knew she *shouldn't* be concerned that Nicolas was going out. He'd told her he wasn't involved with anyone, and she had no reason to think he was lying to her. But surely the fact that he went out almost *every* night, and that he never told her where he went, must suggest the existence of *someone* significant in his life.

"Nicolas, we really should talk about my going home. I can't stay here indefinitely. I have to get on with my life, and you have to get on with yours."

"Why don't we talk about it tomorrow?" Nicolas suggested. "For now, I just want you to concentrate on getting better."

"But—"

"Rest, Chelsea. I'll see you in the morning."

After he left, Chelsea thought about what he'd said. What had Nicolas meant when he said he could make her see again? Did he know of a surgeon whose skills went beyond those of Dr. Asklepios? And why was he so reluctant to talk about her going home? She was sure she was taking up far more of his time than he was letting on. He must be missing his privacy. And yet he wasn't urging her to leave. If anything, he seemed anxious that she stay. Why?

For the same reasons Chelsea was reluctant to leave?

Joe heard the distant rumble of thunder as he walked into the office, but didn't bother checking the sky. This time of year, thunderstorms were common. Besides, his mind was already working out the details of the upcoming meeting with Peter Fitch.

"Joe?"

He looked up to see Chelsea's secretary standing before him. "Hi, Phyllis. What's up?"

"I thought you might like to handle this." She handed him a message. "Morris Kelton just called."

Joe strummed through his memory banks. "Oh, right, the Kelton Insurance Building. Sure, I'll give him a call. Chelsea can take over when she gets back Monday. Thanks."

"Speaking of Chelsea," Phyllis said as he went to walk away, "have you heard from her?"

"As a matter of fact, I haven't." He grinned. "She must be having a good vacation."

"Maybe."

Something in her voice had his smile fading. "What do you mean, maybe?"

"I don't know. I ran into Olivia Wainwright in town this morning. She told me Chelsea didn't show up for Crab Fest last weekend."

"Was she supposed to?"

"You bet. She volunteered to help out, and she purposely rescheduled things so she could be there," Phyllis told him. "Olivia said she left messages on Chelsea's answering machine a few days before the event, just to make sure everything was still on, but Chelsea didn't return any of them. She still hasn't."

"That's strange," Joe said. "Chelsea doesn't forget about things like that. And as far as I know, she's never missed a Crab Fest."

"Exactly. I know how much that commitment meant to her." The concern in Phyllis's voice was plain. "I'm sure if she'd changed her mind, she would have let Olivia know. I wondered if maybe she'd spoken to you and said she was going away for a while."

"No. The last time we spoke, she said she wasn't going anywhere. In fact, I remember Winnie Morrison telling me that Chelsea came in and bought a pile of groceries."

Phyllis shrugged. "Stocking up to go away doesn't make much sense to me."

No, it didn't, Joe thought as he walked into his office. Neither did the fact that Chelsea hadn't been in touch with Olivia. She might have a reason for not calling him, but she wouldn't ignore Olivia. Chelsea hardly ever backed out on commitments she made to people, and she *never* did so without telling them why.

Why was he suddenly starting to feel that things weren't as okay with Chelsea as he'd thought?

Nicolas moved through the water with the speed of a torpedo, a pinpoint of light in the subterranean darkness. He paid no attention to the sleek-bodied sharks swimming by him, prowling the depths for food. He was far more concerned with his father.

Poseidon had been angry tonight. Nicolas had heard it in

the distant rumble of thunder, and in the trembling of the sea when he had set foot in it. The water was like a conductor, channeling the energy of its god and sending it around the world. And the angrier Poseidon grew, the stronger the force became.

Does it surprise you that I would be angry?

The question drifted up to Nicolas from the depths, and brought him to an abrupt halt. He stood upright, as though his feet were planted on an invisible floor. Behind him, the manta hovered like a dark shadow. "No. But why should I not tell her I can restore her sight when you know that I can?"

Because I have forbidden you to do so, came the heated reply. *I have allowed you to spare the lives of three mortals, Nikodemus. I will not allow you to intervene again, even for something as trivial as this.*

"The loss of sight is hardly trivial to a mortal," Nicolas told his father in a hard voice. "And Chelsea is hurting. Can you not understand that in my love for her, I do not wish to see her suffer?"

I understand that, and a great deal more. But there is no need for her to suffer any longer. Bring her to us now, so that we may welcome her as your wife. You know she cannot go back.

Nicolas shook his head. "She is not ready. Her heart is not yet open to me, and if she were to try to cross over, she would not survive. She is not ready to face Sephonia."

Nicolas waited, hearing the emptiness of the sea all around him.

There must be no doubts on her part, or she will not pass safely through the Shadow of Darkness. But I am losing patience, Nikodemus.

"The day is coming when I shall make good on my promises, Father," Nicolas assured him quickly, "but only I will know when that day is here. All I'm asking for is a little more time."

The silence dragged on.

Very well, the voice boomed. *I will be patient a while longer, but do not do anything foolish. She bears the mark of the sea, and I would remind you of the terrible cost to yourself, should you attempt to remove it.*

Nicolas nodded. "I do not intend to remove the birthmark, nor do I intend to go back on the promise I gave you, Father. You have my word."

His commitment reaffirmed, Nicolas turned and, with a heavy heart, continued on the long journey into the abyss.

At quarter after six, Joe pulled his car into the driveway beside Chelsea's house and switched off the engine. For a few minutes, he just sat and admired the view. Boy, she had a nice spot here. He'd always regretted not buying waterfront property. Unfortunately, his first wife hadn't been partial to the seaside, so he'd bought a big, modern house in one of the new suburbs. And when he'd married Patty, she'd been happy to stay in the impressive house on Anchor Way.

Maybe it was time to get his own place, Joe thought, as he headed for Chelsea's back door. Maybe one of those new condos they were building out on Johnston Street, with views over the water.

When there was no answer to his knock, Joe strolled around to the front of the house, thinking Chelsea might be on the beach. When there was no sign of her there either, he climbed the deck stairs and tried the screen door. That was locked, too, and there were no lights on inside. Had she changed her mind and decided to go away?

Putting his hands against the glass, Joe peered into the dining room. Odd. All of the plants in the room were drooping, and there were yellow leaves all over the floor. Looked as though they hadn't been watered for days. He moved farther along the deck and glanced into the living room.

He saw the painting at once. It was hanging in the middle of the wall and directly in the path of the late afternoon sun. It sparkled and flashed as though its surface was studded with tiny gems and pieces of gold. But it wasn't the appearance of the painting that bothered him. There was something familiar about it. Something he'd talked about. . . .

Joe backed away from the window. Damn! Was it just a coincidence?

Heading back to his car, he rifled through the newspapers

and magazines that littered the backseat and finally pulled out a copy of *The Liberal Arts*. Opening it, he flipped to Laura Hopkins's article on the new gallery. He scanned the write-up, and found what he was looking for.

> *. . . the painting depicted the great sea god Poseidon, dressed in glowing raiment, seated on a rock surveying an old sailing ship, the newest addition to his kingdom. A brilliant work, filled with emotion and pathos, and painted in true Demitry style. . . .*

Joe let the magazine drop. Poseidon dressed in colorful robes and sitting on a rock at the bottom of the sea. It *had* to be the same painting. But if it was, what was it doing in Chelsea's living room? Nicolas Demitry didn't make prints, and there was no way the artist would have given her an original painting—unless she meant something to him.

Joe stared at the magazine as if he'd been smacked between the eyes with a baseball bat.

Chelsea and Nicolas Demitry? He sure hadn't seen that coming. But why would he? It wasn't like he and Chelsea had had much time to talk. Her leave had started a week after the gallery opened, and with Patty leaving, he'd been caught up in his own problems. He knew Chelsea had met the artist at the reception, and it was entirely possible they'd seen each other since. But if they *were* involved, why hadn't Demitry said something at the market when Joe mentioned Chelsea's name?

Perhaps he wanted to keep their relationship private. Or maybe Nicolas was no better than Duncan Rycroft, and was interested only in having an affair?

Joe got back into his car and tried to collect his thoughts. He could, of course, be barking up the wrong tree altogether. There might be a very good reason why a half-million-dollar painting was hanging on Chelsea's wall. Damned if he could think of what it was, though.

Acting purely on instinct, Joe pulled out his cell phone and dialed information. "Yeah, I'd like a number for Nicolas Demitry in Oyster Point."

His search turned up a dead end. The number was unlisted.

Joe tried to think of an alternative. He wasn't sure why, but something was niggling at his mind. There had to be some way of getting through to Demitry, but how? Who else would be likely to know the artist's number? The gallery! Of course, they'd have to have a listing of all the phone numbers in case they needed to get in touch with any of the artists about their work.

Reaching for the magazine, Joe scanned Laura's article again. Bingo! The gallery's phone number was listed at the end, along with the name of the public relations representative, Grace Thornton.

"Okay, Ms. Thornton," Joe murmured as he punched in the number. "Let's see if *you* can shed some light on the mystery rapidly gathering around Nicolas Demitry."

Fifteen

When Nicolas walked into Chelsea's bedroom the next morning, he was surprised to see her already up and dressed. He was even more surprised when, a few minutes later, she asked him if everything was all right.

"Of course everything's all right," he said. "Why would you ask?"

Chelsea shrugged. "I don't know. I just woke up with a feeling that something was wrong."

Nicolas took her hand and tucked it firmly into the crook of his arm. "Everything's fine. Really."

She nodded, but still looked unconvinced. "Did everything go all right after you left last night?"

"Yes. As a matter of fact, I went to see my father."

"Your father!"

Nicolas glanced at her. "Why would that surprise you?"

"Because you didn't tell me he lived so close by. I thought maybe you'd gone to see another—"

She broke off, and Nicolas smiled. "Another *woman*?"

Deep pink color suffused her cheeks. "Well, is that so surprising? Cooped up with me all the time, having to make my meals and look after me, it's not surprising you'd want to get out and let loose for a few hours."

"Believe me, Chelsea, that's not my style," Nicolas assured her, knowing the havoc that could result from a god *letting loose.* "Evenings are a time for the things that are important in my life."

"Like visiting family?"

"On occasion."

"Do you come from a large family?"

"Yes, but I don't see them often. We're spread pretty much all over the globe."

After helping Chelsea into her chair, Nicolas put the kettle on. A few minutes later, he made her tea and set it by her hand.

"Hey, that's cheating," she complained. "I'm supposed to be learning how to do these things for myself."

"I know, but I thought I'd spoil you today. Besides, the sooner you're finished, the sooner we can get outside and start your next lesson," he added, pouring cereal into a bowl and adding milk.

"My next lesson?" Chelsea turned in the direction of his voice. "What's that?"

"Learning to get around without my help."

Her breath caught. "Why? Are you going away?"

He laughed. "Not in the immediate future, but I thought it's something you'd want to be able to do."

Chelsea sat back in her chair, staring down at the table. "Maybe that's not the only thing we have to do. Maybe it's time we talked about my going home."

Nicolas drew a silent breath, felt a nerve jump in his jaw. "Asklepios said it's too soon."

"But why? I'm not bedridden anymore. Thanks to you, I can get around fine. Maybe I could arrange to have a nurse come and stay with me. I have to start picking up the pieces of my life, Nicolas," Chelsea said. "I know I won't be able to work, but there must be something I can do."

Nicolas didn't know what to say. He couldn't lose her. Not now, when they were growing so close. "Stay with me, Chelsea," he said, dropping to the floor beside her. "Stay with me until you're well enough to cope with life on your own."

"But that could be weeks, or even months! I can't possibly

impose on you for that long," she told him. "I have to get back to my old life."

"Why? Were you so much happier then than you are now?"

"Nicolas, I can't even make myself a cup of coffee, and you're asking me if I'm happier now than I was then?" she said, incredulous.

"There are lots of reasons why people are unhappy," Nicolas said. "Some of the time, they don't even know they're unhappy. It's easier to just go along and pretend everything's all right than face the fact that something's missing from their lives."

"Now you're starting to sound like a psychiatrist."

"No, just a student of human nature. It's become something of a hobby of mine." He hesitated for a moment. "What if you found out that you weren't happy, Chelsea? What would you say then?"

"I'd say it's not worth talking about, because I have no way of knowing."

"But if you found out that you weren't—?"

Chelsea laughed. "What are you going to do, Nicolas? Hypnotize me? Take me back in time? What are you, some kind of psychic?"

"No, but I do have certain abilities you're not aware of."

"Really. And what do your *abilities* tell you about me right now?" she challenged.

"That you're scared," Nicolas said softly. "That you're wondering what kind of abilities I have, and what I'm talking about. You're wondering whether or not you should get up from that chair and make a run for it."

The semi-mocking words sobered Chelsea. "I'd get a long way, wouldn't I? If I didn't fall flat on my face, I'd run into a wall. Not exactly a graceful exit."

"Then why *make* an exit? Why not just stay here until you've learned how to cope with life a little better?"

"Because I don't know that I'll *ever* be able to cope any better!" Chelsea cried in frustration. "Maybe a good fall down the stairs is exactly what I need. Maybe it would . . . shake everything back into place, the way the accident knocked it out."

"Maybe, but I'm going to do my best to make sure that doesn't happen. I don't want anything happening to you."

Chelsea thought about Nicolas's words long after he'd gone upstairs. Because there'd been something in his voice she hadn't heard before. Something that left her wondering whether it was a place of protection Nicolas was offering her—or confinement.

After breakfast, they headed for the beach. Chelsea, deciding that she had completely overreacted to Nicolas's comments during breakfast, promptly put them out of her mind. She was obviously being overly emotional. Nicolas was just concerned for her welfare. She had no doubt there were a hundred things he'd rather be doing than taking care of her, and she knew she ought to feel grateful for his concern, not suspicious of it. Thus, she threw herself into her lessons and refused to allow any kind of negative thoughts to affect their time together.

And it showed. Her balance started to improve, and though she was still walking slowly, it was with far more assurance than she had in the past. But when Nicolas suggested going for a swim, Chelsea balked.

"Why not?" he asked gently. "I thought you liked the water."

"I do, but I don't feel I'm ready to *swim* in it yet." Chelsea hung back. "There's a big difference between wading on the beach and going out into water deep enough to swim in."

"We won't go out that far, and I'll be right beside you."

But Chelsea held back, unable to get past some mental block. Had she suffered some kind of water-based trauma before the accident? Been frightened so badly, perhaps, that she was reluctant to venture into it now? She hadn't felt any of these apprehensions yesterday, but they were sure there today. Even now, she felt her pulse skitter as the water crept up over her knees, forcing her to lift her skirt so it didn't get wet. The water in the bay was rougher today, and she panicked as a wave pushed her slightly off balance. "Nicolas!"

"It's all right, Chelsea, I won't let you fall. Trust me."

His grip tightened on her arm, but Chelsea still felt uneasy. Why was he being so insistent that she swim today? Even

now, he was edging her into deeper water. And his voice
sounded different, as though it was important she did this.
Why?

Reluctantly, wanting to please him, she took another step
forward, feeling the water creep up her legs. Finally, it got
too high for her to hold her dress up. "Nicolas . . ."

"That's all right, Chelsea, let it go. It doesn't matter if you
get it wet."

The water was up to her waist now. Chelsea felt the movement of it, the backwash, pushing her back and then drawing
her forward. It was getting harder to keep her feet on the
sand, and she was growing more uncomfortable by the second.

She flinched as something ran across her foot. "What was
that?"

"Just a small crab," Nicolas said in a reassuring voice. "He
won't hurt you." But as if sensing her growing alarm, he
stopped walking and wrapped his arms around her waist,
anchoring her against the movement of the water. "Relax,
Chelsea." He rested his chin against her hair, his voice coming soft, like a whisper against her ear. "Feel the beauty of
the sea all around you. Feel her washing away your fears,
soothing your worries. She doesn't want anything from you.
She just wants to let you know she's here, and that she wel-
comes you."

They stood like that for a long time. And the longer they
did, the calmer Chelsea grew. She closed her eyes and let
herself enjoy the closeness of his body. He was like a rock,
never moving, even though the waves continued to wash
against them.

"There, you see? I told you there's nothing to be afraid
of. The sea won't harm you."

"I'm not afraid," Chelsea said, wanting to make him
happy. "Not as long as you're with me, holding me . . . like
this."

"I'll always hold you. For as long as you want me to.
Forever."

She caught her breath as Nicolas ran his thumb over her
mouth, the pad of it tracing the fullness of her bottom lip,
pulling it down. She closed her eyes and licked her lips,

tasting salt. Every nerve ending in her body was tingling with anticipation. His hand drifted to her ear and then to her jaw, following the curve of her neck in a soft, sensual caress. He nuzzled her hair, his breath warm on her scalp, Then, with an easy movement, he turned her to face him, all the while keeping one hand securely around her waist.

Chelsea sucked in her breath as he lowered his mouth to her throat, placing kisses where his fingers had just been, the intimacy of it bringing something to life deep within her. His lips brushed over her skin, but when his mouth found an acutely sensitive place on her left shoulder, Chelsea gasped. "Nicolas!"

He circled his tongue over the spot before pressing his mouth fully against it.

Chelsea moaned deep in her throat. There was no need for words. In her world of darkness, there was only touch. Even the motion of the waves, rhythmic and seductive, added to the sensual web Nicolas was weaving around her. And she wasn't the only one affected. In such an intimate embrace, there was no mistaking the evidence of Nicolas's arousal. But rather than being frightened by it, Chelsea felt exhilarated by his desire, feeling it stir even deeper, more urgent needs to life. She pressed her body against him, seeking more. Needing more. Until a wave broke over her shoulder, shattering the mood. "Nicolas!"

"It's all right, Chelsea, I have you." His voice was deep, husky with emotion. "You're safe. Nothing's going to happen."

But his assurances weren't enough this time. Something was warning her to go back.

"Nicolas, please! I don't . . . want to go out any farther."

He closed his eyes and held her against him, as torn by his need to possess her as he was by his need to keep her safe. By the gods, he wanted her! The ache in his loins was explosive, the blood surging through his body blinding him to all but his needs and desires. He wanted to make love to her right here, right now; to draw her into deep water and lose himself in the softness of her body. He'd been alone too long. Generations of emptiness were catching up with him, and he wanted nothing more than to drown his loneliness in the warmth of her heart, and in doing so, possess her very soul. He wanted to take them both somewhere they'd never been; to continue the seduction he'd so innocently started.

And yet, something stopped him. Every shred of decency screamed that it would be wrong to pursue this now. The panic in Chelsea's voice was rising with every step he took. How could he ignore that? How could he try to pretend she was ready for this when she so obviously wasn't? He couldn't force her to do this. If he did, he would be making a terrible mistake.

And so, steeling his mind against the pain in his lower body, Nicolas grimly turned around and took Chelsea back into shallow waters.

It wasn't easy. The sea fought to hold him. As though sensing his longing to bring the woman he loved home, it resisted every step he took, making his legs feel like lead weights. But he walked on regardless, thinking only of Chelsea and of how she must be feeling. Knowing that with every step closer to the beach, the less frightened she became. He could feel the tension draining from her limbs as the water grew shallow and she was able to stand without his help.

And that was when guilt slammed into him, striking him with the force of one of Zeus' thunderbolts. He had been wrong to try to force Chelsea into the sea. The time wasn't right. He might *have* to do it eventually, but not now. She was here with him, and that was all that mattered. As long as he could convince her to stay without making it sound like an order, everything would be fine.

He knew she was falling in love with him. It was there in her eyes, in her expression, in her touch. She might not have put a name to it yet, but it was there, blossoming in her soul like a delicate flower. And because he saw the beginnings of love, he would wait until Chelsea was ready to make the decision on her own. Poseidon had given him time, and Nicolas intended to use every last second to further his goal. By the time Chelsea crossed over, he wanted her to be his, body and soul. He didn't want there to be a single doubt in her mind. There couldn't be, or Sephonia would consume her. Chelsea had to be strong enough to make the transition.

For now, all he could do was love her and be patient,

because in the event she *did* regain her memory, he had to make sure that her reasons for staying with him were stronger than her reasons for wanting to go back.

After leaving the water, they walked along the beach for a while. Nicolas told her about the things he saw around them, his voice soothing as he painted pictures of the clear blue sky and of the area close to where they walked.

And later, when he pulled her into his arms and kissed her again, Chelsea lost herself in the intoxicating sweetness of his mouth. She listened with wonder as he whispered sweet, silly things into her hair. She heard his stifled groan as she touched him, the raggedness of his breath when she pressed closer to his body.

Chelsea thought about those things as she lay in bed that night, waiting for sleep to come. She remembered the way he'd held her in the water, and how the heavy, warm sensations had pooled in her abdomen and then spread like golden fire through her veins. She'd wanted him to make love to her right there on the beach. To lay her down and to love her in the way she needed to be loved. When she was with him, it was as though everything was all right with her world. She hardly noticed her absence of memory, and even her blindness struck her as being less than calamitous. Truly, he must be some kind of Svengali, Chelsea mused, to be able to free her so totally of her worries.

And yet, at other times, Nicolas *became* the source of her fears. She thought about his insistence on taking her into deep water, remembering how desperately she'd pleaded with him to take her back. She thought about the strange discussion they'd had at breakfast, when he'd asked her how happy she'd been in her past life. And she remembered him talking about having some kind of special abilities.

But what kind of abilities could he have that would allow her to see what had taken place in her life before the accident?

He hadn't brought the subject up again, but Chelsea hadn't forgotten it. *Was* he a psychic of some kind? Did he really have the ability to take people back into previous lives? Was that the nature of the gift he had spoken of?

If it was, why hadn't he already used it to bring back her awareness of her past?

Around her, the house was silent. Chelsea lay back against her pillows, wondering if Nicolas was in his studio painting, or if he'd gone out for the evening. Suddenly curious, she threw back the covers and got up.

Carefully making her way to the foot of the bed, she began counting the steps to the door. She walked with her arms in front of her, feeling for the wall, tentative as she made her way across the bare wooden floor. She had never attempted this before. Never tried to leave her room without Nicolas at her side.

Nor was she destined to tonight. When she found the bedroom door, she turned the handle but the door didn't open. Her fingers searched for a lock, but found nothing. And when she realized why, a cold shiver of fear ran up her spine.

The door *was* locked—from the outside.

The room was suffocatingly hot. Chelsea looked out over the heaving mass of people and wondered how they could all fit into this one tiny space. She heard the couple to her left cut up a woman on the other side of the hall, and a man on her right tell a lie about someone she worked with. But when she turned around to confront them, there was nobody there.

Puzzled, Chelsea walked into another room where everyone was standing around in pairs. Everyone except her. She was the only one there without a date or a companion. The only one alone.

Alone. The word conjured up a chasm of emptiness, a gaping black hole that swallowed emotions like happiness and contentment and left her struggling with despair and insecurity. She was successful, yet unhappy. She had no time for herself, because she didn't want time to remember how lonely she was. She had all the material things a person could want, but she didn't have love. She was unhappy and alone . . . so terribly, terribly alone.

"Alone . . ."

Chelsea breathed the word in her sleep, unaware of tears that trickled down her cheek.

Nicolas stared down at her as she lay in bed, his heart heavy. It hadn't taken much to bring back that part of her memory, and he'd brought it back, not so that she might see the images but so that she might experience the feelings of loneliness and despair. Perhaps selfishly, he wanted her to see and to remember how unhappy she had been before the accident had brought them together.

Knowing that she had, Nicolas quietly left the room. He didn't bother locking the door. There was no need. Chelsea would sleep peacefully for the remainder of the night. That thought, too, he had placed in her mind before removing his fingers and closing the triangle.

The next morning, Chelsea sat at the table in silence. She heard the sounds of Nicolas preparing breakfast, and listened to him moving about the kitchen and talking about what they would do that morning, but she couldn't find it in her heart to feel any enthusiasm for it.

"Why did you lock me in my bedroom last night, Nicolas?" she asked quietly.

There was a brief silence before he said, "I lock your door every night."

"Why? Are you afraid I'll get up and start wandering around the house?"

"The thought had occurred to me."

"But I haven't even been able to walk."

"That didn't stop you from getting out of bed the other morning."

Chelsea felt warmth steal into her cheeks. "That was out of necessity."

"Whatever the reason, you still got up and nearly did yourself an injury," Nicolas said patiently. "I couldn't risk you trying that in the middle of the night and falling down the stairs."

Irked by his lack of remorse—and by the sense his answers made—Chelsea sighed. "That still doesn't make it right. You didn't have to lock me in."

"You wouldn't have known you *were* locked in if you hadn't gotten up."

Outmaneuvered, Chelsea moved on. "How did you make me see my past?"

This time, his movements stilled. "How do you know I did?"

"Because I had a dream, but I know it wasn't really. I saw myself moving through crowds of people," she said slowly. "I knew it was some kind of business function, and I was there because of my job. I knew I was successful in terms of what I'd accomplished in my life, but I wasn't happy." She raised her head and turned in his direction. "You made me see that, didn't you? You did something to make me see what my life was like before the accident."

Silence stretched between them. At length, she heard Nicolas sigh. "Yes. I used a form of hypnosis to open a window in your mind. To prove you weren't as happy in your past life as you wanted to believe."

"Can you do it again?"

He must have heard the hope in her voice, because there was no hesitation this time. "No."

"But why not?" she demanded. "If you did it once, you could do it again. But this time, you could open up my whole mind, not just a small part of it. You could help me to remember my life! You could show me what happened before the accident."

"I could, but I'm not going to. There are some things you're better off *not* seeing."

"But that doesn't make sense," Chelsea snapped. "It's not like you'd be showing me anything that hasn't happened, and showing it to me now isn't going to change anything. I can't alter the past, but I can see it. It's all there on a subconscious level. You just have to take me there."

"Just because I showed you *part* of your past doesn't mean I *can* show you all of it," Nicolas said in a voice more distant than she'd ever heard.

She felt her hands begin to tremble. "Can't show me, or won't?"

"Chelsea—"

"No, I don't want excuses, Nicolas. I'm tired of being half

a person. I've accepted that I'm not going to be able to see again, but surely I have a right to know what's happened in my life! Last night you showed me it was possible to do that, and I don't give a damn *how* you did it. I just want you to do it again. I want my life back!" She stopped suddenly, and lifted her head. "Unless there's something you don't *want* me to remember."

A tense silence stretched between them, but it wasn't until Nicolas left the room without giving her an answer that Chelsea realized she'd been wrong. Something bad *had* happened to her before the accident. Something Nicolas knew but refused to talk to her about.

Something so bad he wasn't willing to risk letting her remember.

Sixteen

Nicolas went out that afternoon. He didn't say where he was going, or why. He only told her that he would be back before dinner.

"And don't try anything outlandish while I'm gone," he warned. "I don't want to come back and find you flat on the floor as a result of having overextended yourself."

"You won't," Chelsea said, though there was a noticeable edge to her voice. The argument that morning had strained things between them. They hadn't talked about it over breakfast, nor had Nicolas mentioned it when he'd taken her outside, but they'd both felt it. There had been no tender moments in the water today, no whispered words of endearment, and Chelsea regretted that. But damn it, it was her life, and she was entitled to know what had happened. Nicolas knew how to make her see it. Why was he so determined not to help her?

Chelsea took a deep breath. "Is it all right if I stay out here for a while?"

"Yes, but make sure you stay under the umbrella," he cautioned. "Your skin's too tender to withstand the full force of the sun. I don't need you back being treated for burns." The sound of a car horn startled them both. "That's my taxi," he said. "I'll be back as soon as I can."

Chelsea nodded, knowing he expected some kind of reply. Childishly, she felt like crossing her arms and refusing to say a word, but that kind of behavior hadn't gotten her anywhere when she'd been ten years old. She didn't figure it would get her anywhere now.

"I'll be fine, Nicolas," she said at last. "Don't worry, I'm not about to do anything stupid. I don't want to end up back in bed either."

"I know," he said, and she thought she heard a smile in his voice. "It's just that—well, about this morning—"

The taxi horn blared again, and Nicolas swore.

"Go," Chelsea said, aware that neither of them was ready for an emotional scene. "We'll talk about it when you get back."

"I'll hold you to that," he said, already on his way.

Chelsea heard the sound of his footsteps on the wooden deck, and then the roar of an engine as the cab pulled away. Nicolas was gone, and she was alone.

Strangely enough, the thought didn't alarm her as much as it would have a few days ago. Maybe because her emotions were in such a turmoil. She sat and drank her tea, listening to the sound of the waves and wondering what Nicolas had been about to say.

Had he been going to apologize? To say that he was sorry for upsetting her this morning, and perhaps to explain why he was reluctant to do what she asked? Or had he simply changed his mind and decided to tell her what she wanted to know?

"I don't think that's likely," a woman's voice said from somewhere close by.

Chelsea's teacup went flying. "What the—who's there?"

"I'm sorry. I didn't mean to startle you." The woman's voice was filled with contrition. "I hope you didn't burn yourself with any of that hot liquid."

Chelsea had no idea where the cup *or* the tea had landed, but obviously, it wasn't on her or her visitor. "I didn't, but no thanks to you."

"Oh, dear, now you're angry," the woman said. "I should

have realized you wouldn't have heard my approach, being as deep in thought as you were. But when I saw you sitting there all alone, I thought it would be a good time to come and say hello."

The voice had a wonderfully melodic quality to it, but Chelsea was too shocked by the fact that it had answered her unspoken question to appreciate it. "Why did you say you don't think it's likely?"

"Did I say that?"

"Yes. Just before I tossed my cup at you."

"You must be mistaken."

"I know what I heard."

"Do you?"

The woman's voice was so calm that Chelsea began to wonder. *Was* that what she'd heard? She'd been so sure, but the more she thought about it, the more she realized how unlikely that was. She hadn't spoken her question out loud, so the woman couldn't possibly have given her an answer— even one that might have made sense.

Feeling distinctly at a disadvantage, Chelsea said, "Should I know you?"

The question came out sharper than intended, but the woman didn't seem to take offense. "No. My name is Lysianassa."

It was a beautiful name, and one Chelsea had never heard before. "Do you live around here?"

"In a way. I often drop by and go swimming with Niko— with Nicolas, but it's actually you I came to see."

"Me?"

"Yes. I thought it was about time I met the woman Nicolas is in love with."

Chelsea drew a quick, sharp breath. She didn't know whether to be embarrassed, affronted, or just plain dumbfounded. "Nicolas isn't *in love* with me!"

"It's all right, you don't have to be embarrassed."

"B-but you've got it all wrong!" Chelsea stammered. "I was in a very bad car accident. Nicolas brought me here to recover. We're friends, that's all."

"Is that what he told you?"

"Yes." Something in the woman's voice made her hesitate. "Why? Has he told you something else?"

"Niko doesn't have to tell me. I know what he feels."

"Niko?"

"A childhood name," Lysianassa explained. "We've been friends for a very long time."

Chelsea stared in the direction of the woman's voice, doubts piling on top of doubts. Nicolas had assured her that there wasn't anyone special in his life, but Chelsea was beginning to wonder. She suddenly had a feeling there *was* a woman in Nicolas's life. *This* woman.

"You must be a very *special* friend to have stayed in touch with him so long," Chelsea said, hoping she didn't sound jealous. "He told me he's always been something of a nomad."

"We both are," Lysianassa told her. "We more or less grew up together, and we spent a lot of time traveling around the world. We still do, though not as much."

They'd *traveled* together? Chelsea's heart plummeted. That probably meant they'd *slept* together, too. But were they still sleeping together? "Are you . . . in love with Nicolas?" she blurted out.

"I was," Lysianassa admitted, "but Niko loves me like a sister, and always has. That didn't stop me from falling in love with him, of course, because he is an easy man to love. But I think you already know that, Chelsea Porter."

Chelsea felt her face burn. "I hardly think—"

"That it's my business to ask?" Lysia laughed softly. "No, it probably isn't. But I do have my reasons for asking."

"I really have no idea what to say," Chelsea said, completely out of her depth.

"I know, because you have no idea how deeply Nicolas loves you," Lysianassa said. "He would do anything for you. He proved that by saving your life."

"You know about that?"

"That, and a great deal more."

More confused than ever, Chelsea said, "Does Nicolas . . . talk to you about me?"

"Of course. There is no one else he can confide in. And there are times when he feels very confused."

"Tell me about it," Chelsea muttered. "Since the accident, being confused has become a way of *life*. I don't remember who I am or what I've done, and being blind severely limits the chances of seeing anything that might bring my memory back."

"I wouldn't worry about it," Lysianassa said. "It's only a matter of time before your sight and your memory are restored."

Chelsea sighed. "You can't know that."

"Ah, but I do." Lysianassa's voice was very gentle. "But above all, you must remember that you are Niko's future, Chelsea. You are the only one who has the power to save him."

"*Save* him? I can't even save myself! How am I supposed to save anybody else?"

"Because it's your love that will save him," Lysianassa whispered. "All you have to do is love Niko. Love him more than anything else in the world. Because to be loved *by* him is the greatest gift imaginable."

Chelsea listened in stunned silence. What was she supposed to say? A complete stranger was telling her that Nicolas loved her and needed saving—and that *she* was the one to do it? Who *was* this Lysianassa woman anyway?

She might have asked—had the telephone not started ringing in the kitchen. Talk about being saved by the bell!

"I should get that," Chelsea said, rising.

"No! Don't!"

Startled, Chelsea hesitated. "Why not? Do you know who it is?"

"It is a call you mustn't take. No good can come of it!"

This was getting stranger—and more alarming—by the minute. "Why? Who's on the phone, Lysianassa?"

"It is not for me to say."

"Then I'm going to have to answer it."

"Answer it if you must," the other woman said, "but I beg you to remember what I've told you! Only your love can save Nikodemus now!"

It was a few seconds before Chelsea realized that the woman had gone, and a few more before it registered that the phone had stopped ringing. She sat back in her chair in confusion.

What an extraordinary meeting—and what an extraordinary woman. But who was she, really? Nicolas's friend, or a great deal more?

There were so many questions rattling around in Chelsea's head that she hardly knew where to begin. Lysianassa had freely admitted to being in love with Nicolas, yet she'd told Chelsea that he wasn't in love with her. She'd claimed that Chelsea was the one he loved, and that she was the only one who could save him. But save him from what? He certainly hadn't struck her as a man who'd needed saving. Was there something he hadn't told her about himself?

Feeling like she'd had more than she could handle for one day, Chelsea got up and cautiously made her way inside. She wasn't feeling all that great. Her skin was burning and her head was pounding. On top of which, she kept getting sharp, stabbing pains behind her eyes. Either she'd stayed out longer than she should have or she'd reached her emotional saturation point.

Making her way to the kitchen, Chelsea stopped in the doorway, wincing as another pain hit. Then, the telephone rang again—and she froze.

Should she answer it? What if it was the same person calling back—the one Lysianassa hadn't wanted her talking to. There had been no mistaking the apprehension in her voice, but that didn't make much sense. How could she possibly have known who was calling? Besides, it might be an important call for Nicolas. Someone wanting to buy one of his pictures, or a member of his family trying to get in contact with him. Didn't she owe it to him to at least make an effort to find out who it was?

Deciding she did, Chelsea began searching for the phone. She had no idea where it was. All she could do was follow the sound of the rings. In the end, she almost knocked it off the counter. She fumbled for the receiver, hoping it wasn't too late. "Hello?"

Silence greeted her, and Chelsea thought the caller had hung up. "Hello?" she said again.

"Chelsea, is that you?" It was a man's voice, one she didn't recognize.

"Yes, this is Chelsea. Who's this?"

"Don't you recognize my voice? It's Joe."

Joe. Did she know a Joe? She must have, because he obviously knew her. "No, I'm sorry, I don't."

"Chelsea, are you all right?"

There was no mistaking the concern in his voice, and Chelsea wondered if he was more than just a friend. She went to answer, when another pain hit. "N-no, not really. I'm better than I was after the accident, but—"

"You've been in an accident? For God's sake, why didn't you call me?"

"I couldn't. I was . . . unconscious for a long time. But Dr. Asklepios did call my office."

"Who's Dr. Asklepios?"

"The physician who has been looking after me."

"I don't know who this Asklepios guy is, Chelsea, but nobody called."

Chelsea went ice cold. "That's impossible. Nicolas assured me that Dr. Asklepios had spoken to someone in the office."

"Then he's been lying to you. Chelsea, if you've been in an accident, why aren't you in a hospital? Come to think of it, why don't you just go home?"

Chelsea swallowed. "It's not that easy."

"Sure it's easy. Just get in your car and—"

"I can't drive," Chelsea blurted out. "I'm blind. And even if I could see, I don't remember where I live. I don't remember . . . much of anything."

"Jesus!" There was a very long silence. "Chelsea, I'm so sorry. I didn't know."

"How could you?" Chelsea's voice dropped away. "It happened in the accident. I have . . . no sight at all, and only fragments of memory. I didn't recognize your voice because I don't remember who you are."

"There's no need to apologize," he said after another lengthy pause. He was obviously trying to come to terms with the shocking news. "I'm just glad you're okay."

"I suppose I am," she admitted. "But what do you mean,

Dr. Asklepios didn't call? Nicolas told me he'd called my office and told them about the accident."

"Nobody called, Chelsea." Joe's voice was suddenly weary. "I would have known. You and I work together. You're my partner at Turner and Parsons."

She gasped. "I am?"

"Yes. Unfortunately, I've been pretty preoccupied the last few weeks, and haven't really tried to keep in touch."

Chelsea's grip tightened on the receiver. *Why had Nicolas lied to her?* "So Dr. Asklepios didn't call."

"Nobody called. I drove over to your house the other day, and it was obvious you hadn't been around. I thought maybe you'd changed your mind and decided to go away, until I started putting two and two together." There was a brief pause. "You don't have to answer this if you don't want to, Chelsea, but . . . have you been at Demitry's place the whole time?"

Demitry. Chelsea repeated that name, too. Nicolas . . . Demitry. The man who'd been looking after her. She pressed her fingers to her temples, feeling the start of another attack. "I think I must have. Apparently, I came here to talk to him about something. But when I was leaving, my car hit a telephone pole and burst into—" The pain struck deep, causing Chelsea to suck in her breath. "*Damn,* that hurts."

"Chelsea, are you all right?"

"I don't think so. I'm getting terrible pains in my head." She massaged her temple, wondering if Nicolas kept any aspirin in the kitchen. "They started a little while ago."

"Chelsea, I bumped into Demitry yesterday," Joe said. "He was picking up a few things in town. He told me he had a lady friend staying with him. I figured that was fine, the guy's entitled to a life, but when I went over to your house and saw his painting hanging on your living room wall, I started wondering if *you* were the girlfriend."

Chelsea concentrated on his voice, trying to focus on it rather than the pain. "What painting?"

"You know, the one Demitry had at the gallery opening. *Poseidon's Sorrow.*"

She smothered a cry as another pain sent her reeling. "I

don't . . . know what you're talking about." *God, this was hurting.* "I've never heard of *Poseidon's*—"

And then, Chelsea stopped; rocked by the image of *something* drifting into her brain. A memory of a painting, the image bizarre and surreal, followed by something dark and sinister hovering at the very edge of her subconscious. A memory of a footprint in the sand, of . . . ripples breaking the dark surface of the water. Of a man walking out of the sea, his body shimmering in the moonlight. A man covered in—

Oh, God, no! It wasn't . . . possible. It couldn't be possible!

"Chelsea, are you still there?" Joe shouted into the phone.

No, I'm not, Chelsea thought, fighting back hysteria. *This is happening to someone else. This can't possibly be happening to me—*

"Chelsea!"

She dropped her head forward as the images came tumbling back. The gaps in her life, the dark shadows, everything she hadn't been able to remember before. The horror of what Nicolas was. The reason he wouldn't—*couldn't*—let her leave.

"Oh, God!" Chelsea sobbed, pressing her hand to her mouth. "I . . . have to go!"

"Chelsea, wait! You can't—"

She hung up the phone, her hands shaking uncontrollably. She slid down the wall and collapsed in a heap on the floor. Her memory had come back. As though a door to the past had suddenly been thrown open, she could see all the details of her life. Her job as an interior designer. Her work on the gallery, the opening night gala. The first time she'd seen Nicolas.

Yes, she remembered it all now, but it was like looking at her life through a window. She remembered talking to Nicolas at the opening of the gallery, asking him about his painting, and wondering why it—and he—had such a powerful impact on her. In the days that followed, she remembered seeing him again, in her car, on the beach, in the middle of a busy city. She remembered the breathless feeling, the awareness of something developing between them. A tentative friendship, a budding relationship, a hope for more. . . .

Then, the tide had begun to turn. Chelsea remembered going home and finding *Poseidon's Sorrow* hanging on her wall. She remembered being totally confused, and driving out to Nicolas's house to find out why it was there, only to be confronted by more fear and uncertainty when he'd begun talking to her about a promise.

After that, Chelsea remembered reading her great-great-grandmother's diary. She remembered driving back to Nicolas's house, baffled by what she'd discovered, hoping to find answers. She remembered walking down to the beach and seeing the giant ripples forming on the water, just the way they had the night she'd been attacked by something in the water in front of her house.

And then she remembered Nicolas rising from the waves like a specter emerging from the mist. Nicolas, his body shimmering in the moonlight. Nicolas—*not mortal!*

Chelsea's head fell forward into her hands. Oh, God, it was all true. Everything her great-great-grandmother had written. As bizarre, as ridiculous, as *impossible* as it seemed, Nicolas *was* the man who'd saved Rebecca Mallory's life over a century ago. The one to whom she'd given her promise. And now, he'd come back for her.

That's why the accident had taken place. After seeing the horror of what Nicolas really was, she'd run away, flinging herself into her car and driving like a woman possessed, wanting only to put as much distance between them as possible. She'd taken her eyes off the road for a split second. A split second that had sent her crashing into a telephone pole and changed the course of her life.

She remembered the horrible pain of being trapped in the wreckage of her car. She'd cried out to God, and at the time, she'd thought God had answered her. She hadn't known that the man surrounded in a veil of blue light, with his arms raised as though in supplication, had been Nicolas. But she knew it now. Just as she knew that the great wall of water that had rained down on the car had been of his making, and that he had, with superhuman strength, torn apart the twisted metal and gently pulled her free.

Nicolas, the man who'd cared for her and fed her, bathed her and watched over her, hour upon hour, day after day.

The man who'd helped her get through the early days of her recovery, and who, with infinite patience, had taught her how to cope with her blindness and started her on the road to living again. Nicolas Demitry, the man she had fallen in love with.

The man who was, even now, waiting to take her with him into the sea.

Seventeen

Chelsea had no idea how long she sat huddled on the floor, too numb to move, too shocked to flee—because it wouldn't have mattered if she had run. *Nicolas wasn't human.* She couldn't elude him. She could run as far and as fast as she wanted, but he would always be there, waiting for her.

She closed her eyes and rested her head against the wall, trying to sort out the chaos of her emotions. Yesterday she'd been in love with the man. Today she didn't even know what he *was.* But did acceptance of one necessarily mean rejection of the other? Did everything between them change just because the line between fact and fantasy had suddenly blurred?

An image of Nicolas came to her, of his dark, wavy hair and incredibly deep, sea blue eyes. His was the most beautiful face Chelsea had ever seen. She'd thought that the first time she'd seen him at the gallery, and she still felt that way now. But where before she had seen only the physical aspect of his beauty, now she knew the beauty of his soul. She had experienced the depth of his compassion and the wisdom of his mind, qualities that had only added to her feelings of love and admiration.

Oh, yes, she loved him, Chelsea knew, because she had fallen in love with him as a stranger. She hadn't associated the gentle-voiced man with the frightening creature who had risen from the sea. Why would she? She'd had no memory of that other Nicolas when she regained consciousness. And she certainly hadn't been afraid of the man who had taken such devoted care of her; a man who'd sat by her bedside day after day and nursed her with the patience of a saint. A man whose simplest touch had sent her spirits soaring, and whose kiss had brought her frozen senses to life.

And yet, only moments ago, when she'd remembered what he was, it wasn't love that had come first and foremost into her heart, but fear. Fear of being faced with something she couldn't explain or understand.

Chelsea groaned as more images bombarded her. Memories of an afternoon in Boston when a chance encounter had led to a breaking down of barriers between them. Memories of Nicolas looking at her with sadness and regret as she'd told him about her mother, and how she hadn't wanted the child she'd given birth to. Then later, over dinner with Elaine, one simple question that had led Chelsea to the truth of her feelings, and to the acknowledgment, even then, that she had been falling in love with Nicolas Demitry.

Yet it wasn't love that had sent her tearing down the road the night she'd seen him rise from the water. It wasn't love that had caused her to glance over her shoulder to see if he was pursuing her. A chase that resulted in the terrible crash that should have killed her—and would have if it hadn't been for Nicolas's intervention. But it was love that had brought her back. Love that had healed her injuries and given her a reason to go on living.

But that didn't make any sense. Now that her memory had returned, and with it an awareness of what Nicolas was, Chelsea could no longer have any *expectation* of living. She was still the one destined to fulfill the promise—the one destined to die.

How could *anyone* equate the idea of being forced to sacrifice one's life with the concept of true love?

Nicolas wasn't sure why he suddenly felt a sense of deep foreboding. The meeting with Jonathan had gone well, and he had been on his way home when the feeling that something was wrong had struck. But was it real or just paranoia? Was it guilt rearing its ugly head over the way he had treated Chelsea this morning—or the Fates planning retribution?

Nicolas's mouth twisted. It might be both—and he deserved it. He'd hated seeing the look of suspicion and betrayal in Chelsea's eyes. She'd known he had the power to show her the past, yet he had purposely refused to use it. Was it any wonder she had been angry and hurt? He likely would have felt the same had their situations been reversed. But the truth was he'd been afraid to show her too much. Afraid that the fragile bond of trust they'd established wouldn't be able to withstand the pressures.

And that wasn't fair, he acknowledged grimly, to him or to Chelsea. He couldn't keep hiding the truth from her. At some point, he was going to have to tell her and hope she wouldn't hate him for not having revealed his secrets before.

Or was that was this was all about? Nicolas wondered grimly. Apprehension that it might already be too late?

Nicolas got his answer the minute he walked into the house. Chelsea was sitting at the kitchen table with her head down. Her cheeks were dry, but her eyes were red and puffy, evidence that she'd been crying, and crying hard. She raised her head when he entered, but from the look on her face, Nicolas knew that whatever she'd been crying about was directly related to him. "What's happened?" he asked quietly.

Her lips quivered, and for a moment, she didn't speak. Then, struggling to gather her composure, she took a deep breath and said in a low voice, "Once . . . before the accident, I asked you who you were. I asked you because I thought you were more than just . . . Nicolas Demitry, famous artist, marine biologist, and Bionic Man. But now I *know* you're more, and I want to know the rest of it." Her voice caught, and she closed her eyes. "I want to know who you really are, Nicolas. I *need* to know."

The silence in the room was deafening. Nicolas felt it sharply because he knew what it meant. The hour of reckoning had come. "Your memory's come back."

When she nodded, he didn't throw up his hands or let loose the force of his anger as other gods might have done.

Instead, he merely sighed and dropped his head, tasting the
bitterness of defeat. At that moment, he almost wished he
had been blind himself so that he wouldn't have had to see
the look of torment and grief on her face. "Has everything
come back?"

"Everything," Chelsea whispered. "Including . . . the night
of the accident."

The tremor in her voice spoke volumes, and Nicolas knew
his time had finally run out. "Then you're right, it's probably
best you do hear it all. You deserve to know the truth. Come
outside with me. I don't want to be shut indoors when I tell
you." He started toward the door, but hesitated when she
made no move to follow him. "Chelsea?"

"I won't go near the water," she said, shrinking back. "I
won't let you take me!"

Nicolas felt his hopelessness deepen to despair. "I'm not
going to drag you into the sea. There wouldn't be much
point." He walked to the screen door and opened it.

Eventually, Chelsea took a reluctant step forward, but her
movements were jerky and stiff. She came toward him
slowly, and only when she was at danger of walking into the
wall did he reach out to guide her. Otherwise he made no
move to touch her. Whatever closeness they'd shared over
the past few weeks was gone. They were right back where
they'd started.

Chelsea found her own way to the small wooden table and
chairs just outside the back door and carefully sat down.
Nicolas took a chair across from her. "Where would you like
me to begin?"

She clasped her hands together, as though hoping to disguise how badly they were shaking. "With Rebecca Mallory,
and with the p-promise she gave you."

Nicolas sat back. "How do you know it was she who gave
me the promise?"

"Because after I left here the night you . . . told me about
it, I went home and read her diary. I'd never read it before,
but something you said reminded me of something my grandfather once said, and I began to wonder if, bizarre as it
sounded, there might be some connection." She stopped and
tilted her head toward him. "But it wasn't bizarre, was it?

You *are* the one my great-great-grandmother gave her promise to."

Nicolas studied her in silence for a moment. As tempted as he was to deny it, he knew there was no point. He would gain nothing by lying to her now. "I found Rebecca Mallory in the middle of the Irish Sea," he said in a quiet voice. "She had been swept overboard during a violent storm. Not long after, the ship itself sank. Naturally, there was no hope for her, so I went to meet her, as is my way."

"Your . . . way?"

"Since the earliest of times, my father has held dominion over the sea. As his son, I've watched thousands of ships find their way to the bottom. Old masted sailing ships and huge ocean liners. Frigates and fishing trawlers, and the battleships of war. And when they do, we go to greet them."

Chelsea swallowed. *"We?"*

"Those who share an intimate association with the sea. Those who hail my father as their king."

She blanched. *"Their king?"*

"His name is known to you, as are those of his brothers and sisters."

"You don't mean—" She gulped. "You can't possibly mean—"

Nicolas drew a deep breath, knowing that what he was about to say would change things between them forever. "Poseidon isn't just a mythical character from Greek mythology, Chelsea. He does exist. And he *is* my father."

Nicolas knew that if Chelsea hadn't been sitting down, she would have fallen. Her eyes went wide, and by the time she found her voice, not a trace of color remained in her face. "You mean, you're the son of *Poseidon?*"

"*A* son," Nicolas corrected. "My father sired numerous offspring with several different wives. Polyphemus was the result of his mating with Thoosa, and Pegasus was his issue with Medusa, to name but two."

"Medusa!" Chelsea's eyes widened even further. "You mean . . . the woman with the *snakes* in her hair?"

"So you *do* know something of mythology."

"Well, of course, but I never believed for a minute that . . . that—"

"That the gods really did exist?" Nicolas smiled, sadness tracing the edges of his mouth. "Why would you? Most mortals don't believe in the existence of sorcerers or witches either."

Chelsea's lips parted in shock. "Are you saying they do?"

"Why not? *'There are more things in heaven and earth, Horatio, than are dreamt of in your philosophy,'* " Nicolas recited.

She blinked. "*Hamlet*?"

"Indeed. Shakespeare was credited with having a wonderful imagination, but if you take time to study his writings, you'll discover he had a particular fondness for ghosts and spirits. I admit it is one of the reasons I've always enjoyed his works. He would be pleased to know that his stories have survived and are being studied in the twenty-first century."

Chelsea stared at him, incredulous. "How old *are* you?" she whispered.

"How old is the sea?" Nicolas's eyes filled with an emotion Chelsea wouldn't have been able to identify if she had been able to seen it. "I've seen millennia come and go at my father's side."

"Then . . . you're immortal?"

"No. I will eventually die, but the time is so long in the span of human years that it would be enough to make me *seem* immortal."

She was clearly having trouble grasping the concept. "So your painting . . . *Poseidon's Sorrow*. It wasn't a figment of your imagination at all."

"No. None of my works are," Nicolas admitted. "I paint what I see. I paint . . . my world."

"This is unbelievable," Chelsea said. "I can't even begin to grasp . . . to understand—" She pressed her lips together and shook her head. "Listen to me. I can't even *say* how unbelievable I think this is."

"That's not surprising," Nicolas said, hoping to reassure her, wanting to take her in his arms. "I would venture to say that even the most open-minded of mortals would have trouble with the concept."

"You can say that again," Chelsea whispered. "So you really do live in the water?"

"Part of the time. The other part I spend on land. When I became a man, my father gave me the ability to do both. He asked only that I return to the sea each night so that I would not forget my roots."

"What is it like to live under the sea?"

"Peaceful," Nicolas said, amused by the note of wonder in her voice. "There are no harsh sounds or jarring noises. No cars or jets or machines of any kind. Just the natural silence of the sea, punctuated by the calls of the creatures who inhabit it."

"But don't you find it depressing to spend so much of your life in the dark?"

"You think it dark?"

"Well, any pictures I've seen of sunken ships or of men diving to the depths show a world that's black and gloomy."

"At the depths mortals can descend to, it *is* dark," Nicolas agreed. "But the place I'm talking about is far deeper than that. Depths to which man will never have the ability to go. A place where—" He broke off, knowing that words would never do justice to the magnificence of the Kingdom. "You would find it beautiful, I think."

"If I could see it," Chelsea said, almost sadly. "But with my eyes—"

"Your lack of sight is a reflection of your mortal life, Chelsea. When you reach the other side, your vision will be restored to better than it was before."

"When I reach the other side?" Her eyes froze on his face. "You mean, when I . . . die?"

"Yes. When you die and are reborn at my side, as my wife."

A soft gasp escaped her. "Your . . . wife?"

"Of course. What did you think this was about?" he asked gently. "Didn't you realize that when you read Rebecca's diary?"

She stared off in wonder. "No. I assumed that by dying I would be honoring the promise she gave you. But I didn't know that you . . . that I . . . that we—" She broke off, shaking her head. "Is such a thing even *possible*?"

"My father took many wives," Nicolas told her. "One of them, Cleito, was a mortal. She bore him ten sons, who became rulers of Atlantis." He stood up and walked toward the edge of the deck. "It is true, Poseidon did not approve of the manner in which I intervened in your ancestor's life, Chelsea. But neither could he refuse me the right to marry where I wished. And though I did not love her, I thought that by offering to marry Rebecca, I could make amends for what I had done. But it isn't the same with you." He turned back to look at her. "It isn't the same at all."

The raucous cry of a gull blended with the sounds of the waves crashing on the shore. It might have been a day like any other, the two of them just a man and a woman enjoying a quiet conversation on the beach. No one would guess it was actually a meeting between an immortal and the woman he had chosen to be his mate.

"The promise my great-great-grandmother gave you," Chelsea said at length. "How did that come to be?"

Nicolas returned his gaze toward the bay. "On the day I spared Rebecca's life—"

"You mean she wasn't *already* dead?"

"No. It isn't within my power to restore a life already taken, but your great-great-grandmother hadn't passed on. The temperature of the sea had slowed her bodily functions to a hypothermic state. That's why I was able to bring her back.

"But why *did* you?" Chelsea asked. "Others must have pleaded for their lives but were left to die. Why did you save her?"

"Because I saw something in her that was *worth* saving," Nicolas said, his voice dropping away. "You can't imagine the horrors I've seen, Chelsea. Death and destruction wrought by the cruelty of mankind, the demise of great civilizations through power and corruption, the destruction of a man's soul through avarice and greed. I've seen brave men go down with their ships and cowards cringing in corners, begging for their lives," Nicolas said in a hushed voice. "But, for all the bad, I've seen the good, too. I've watched the human spirit survive in the face of insurmountable odds, and seen tremendous acts of compassion committed by men and women of courage and conviction. Your great-great-grandmother was just such a person. Her soul was so pure that it shone from her like a white light. She knew she was going to die, and she was angry, not because *she* was going to perish, but because her unborn child was. She cried out to God, saying that she would gladly sacrifice her own life if He would spare the child's. And I suppose, hardened as I was to man's vices, I wanted to reward such selfless devotion."

"But there was a price," Chelsea whispered.

"Oh, yes. There is always a price for cheating Death. That's why I had to have Rebecca's promise that the next time I appeared to her, she would go with me."

"But you didn't go back for her. Why? She wrote in her diary that she waited for you."

"Yes, and on the day I saved her life, I fully expected to return," Nicolas admitted. "But Poseidon forbade it. He said I could not take a life I had already spared, and as punishment for my sins, I was made to wait over a hundred years for the next female child to be born."

Chelsea caught her breath. "But surely there were other girls born into the family before me."

"In fact, there were none. The Fates, having *also* decided to punish me for my disobedience, sent only male children into the line. They in turn, married and begot more sons." Nicolas sighed. "I began to think I was destined to be alone for eternity. And then, you came along."

Chelsea turned her head away, her jaw working. "Why did you . . . wait so long before coming for me?"

"Because I wanted you to experience life. In comparison to my age, you are an infant, Chelsea," Nicolas said tenderly. "What could we have had in common when you were ten, or twenty or even thirty years of age? You needed to know what it was to experience happiness and joy, as well as pain and disappointment. When your relationship with the man you loved ended, I watched your heart shrivel up and loneliness take the place of everything else in your life. I saw you channel all of your energy into your career."

"You saw that?" she asked incredulously.

"Of course. I've been watching you since the day you were born."

Her eyes widened. "How?"

"It does not matter how. Suffice it to say that I knew when you were happy and when you were not. And when I saw everything in your life begin to fall apart, I decided it was time to bring you to me." He stopped and took a deep breath. "I tried to call to you in a way that wouldn't frighten you, but in that, I failed. All I succeeded in doing was frightening you more."

"To call me?" Chelsea said, confused. "But how—oh, my God. *The dreams.*"

He nodded. "I put images of the past into your dreams. I tried to make you see me, and to make you understand my feelings for you."

"Then it was *your* voice I kept hearing," Chelsea said, as the pieces began to fall into place. "Your voice that kept telling me it was time. And our meeting at the gallery, that wasn't a coincidence at all. You *planned* it."

"Yes, because it was imperative that our first meeting be as comfortable and as natural for you as possible."

Chelsea tilted her head toward him. "But you had to have a reason for being there."

"That was easy. I simply contacted Jonathan Blaire and told him I had a new painting. We've kept in touch over the years, and I knew he would be happy to have something of mine to display. I also knew that if *Poseidon's Sorrow* was at the gallery, you and I would definitely have something to talk about."

"What if I'd just glanced at it and walked by?"

He shook his head. "There wasn't any chance of that happening. I knew exactly how it would affect you."

For the first time, Chelsea began to smile. "I suppose you also know what manner of beast attacked me in front of my house that night?"

"Of course. And he was not a beast, and it was not an attack." Nicolas smiled and reaching forward, formed his thumb and forefingers into a triangle over her forehead. "Close your eyes, Chelsea."

She did and, a moment later, gasped as an image took shape in her mind; an image of a huge, graceful creature with two huge wings flying through a brilliant turquoise sea. "Does such a creature truly exist?"

"He does. He travels with me wherever I go." Nicolas dropped his hands and the image disappeared. "His size makes him appear threatening, but you were never in any danger from him. In truth, he wanted to welcome you."

Remembering the way the water had churned and heaved around her, Chelsea just managed to repress a shudder. "Rebecca said that the creatures of sea would precede you, for you were their master."

"Yes. But knowing that the Guardian had frightened you so badly, I swam back to your house every night after that, hoping you'd find the courage to go back into the water. Alas, you never did."

"But if I had, would you really have . . ."

"Dragged you into the sea?" Nicolas shook his head. "It was never my intention to abduct you, Chelsea. It isn't now. If you come to me, it will have to be *because* you wish to."

"But from everything you've said, I don't *have* a choice," Chelsea said, uncertainty returning. "Rebecca Mallory gave you a promise, and I have to honor it. I bear the birthmark. And since I always will, you'll always know where I am."

"I'll always know where you are, Chelsea," Nicolas agreed, "but . . . you do have a choice."

A low rumble of thunder echoed across the sky. Chelsea looked up. "Is that another storm brewing?"

Nicolas also looked to the gathering clouds "No." He listened as another heavy peal of thunder rolled across the heavens. "It is Poseidon warning me that what I'm about to say will have its own particular consequences."

Chelsea gasped. "For me?"

"No." Nicolas drew a deep breath. "Your fate isn't a foregone conclusion, Chelsea. You *do* have a choice, and there's still time for you to make it."

Be still, Nikodemus! whispered Lysia's voice in his head. *Don't tell her!*

She must be told, Nicolas answered silently. *She must be allowed to choose.*

She cannot choose. If you allow her to, she will choose life, and the penalty for letting her go is too great.

Nevertheless, I will have her make her own decision.

Turning away from the sea, Nicolas pulled Chelsea to her

feet. "I love you, Chelsea. More than the sea, more than the air, more than the very sweetness of life itself. And now that you're here, it would be the easiest thing in the world for me to carry you down into the depths and make you succumb. You wouldn't even find it unpleasant. But I won't do that, because unless you come to me of your own free will, it won't mean anything."

Her eyes filled with tears. "You're letting me go?"

"I'm giving you the choice."

"But what will happen to you if I do?"

A brilliant flash of lightning split the sky, followed by a clap of thunder that shook the ground beneath them. Chelsea put her hands over her ears. "Nicolas, what would happen?"

Nikodemus, beware! His father's voice rang out. *Do not provoke me in this manner!*

Ignoring the warning, Nicolas said, "What happens to me isn't important!" He raised his voice to be heard over the howling of the wind. "Make your decision based on what your heart tells you, not on what your head does."

The sound of a voice startled them both. "Chelsea!" a man's voice rang out.

Chelsea gasped, and turned in the direction of the sound. "Joe?"

Nicolas followed her gaze, immediately recognizing the man from the supermarket. "You remember this man."

It wasn't a question, and Chelsea nodded. "Yes. He's my partner. Joe Turner. He . . . called here this morning after you left."

"You answered the telephone?"

Chelsea bit her lip. "I thought it might be important. Someone wanting to buy a painting, or your family trying to get in touch with you." She suddenly remembered the woman, Lysianassa, and was set to tell Nicolas about her when Joe's voice cut across her words. "Chelsea, are you all right?"

"Y-yes, I'm fine. What are you doing here?"

"I came to take you home." Joe turned and looked at Nicolas. "You should have told me she was here, Demitry. And you should have taken her to a hospital. You had no right lying to her."

"What are you talking about? Nicolas hasn't lied," Chelsea

interrupted fiercely. "I wasn't in any condition to be moved. Dr. Asklepios said—"

"Forget about Dr. Asklepios!" Joe said, angry now. "The man doesn't even exist."

Chelsea felt her face go white. "But that's impossible! He's been treating me since the accident. I was badly burned. Nicolas, tell him—"

"Yes, tell us, Mr. Demitry." Joe sent Nicolas a piercing glance. "Tell us about Dr. Asklepios. He's not listed with the AMA. In fact, he's not listed with any medical association anywhere."

"Asklepios is a private practitioner," Nicolas said tonelessly.

"Yeah? Well, he still needs a license, and according to the records, he doesn't have one."

"My family have been using his services for years."

At Chelsea's gasp, Joe turned to stare at her. "What's wrong?"

She couldn't speak. *My family have been using his services for years.* Which could only mean that Asklepios was also a—

"I think what Chelsea's trying to say," Nicolas put in quietly, "is that the man gave her exceptional care. You cannot begin to comprehend the extent of her injuries, Mr. Turner."

"Maybe not, but I can't ignore the fact that some kind of quack has been treating her either!"

"Asklepios isn't a quack!" Chelsea was stung into replying. She was still recovering from the shock of finding out that the man who'd treated her probably wasn't mortal, but she couldn't fault him for his level of care. "He's a good and caring doctor."

"There are lots of good and caring doctors, *all* of whom have licenses to practice medicine!" Joe retorted.

"I don't think there's any point in discussing this," Nicolas interrupted. "What matters is that Chelsea had excellent care at his hands."

"Excellent care? She should have been in a hospital! My God, she's blind!"

"Yes, but I would be *dead* if it weren't for Nicolas!" Chelsea cried.

The bluntness of her words seemed to take some of the wind out of Joe's sails. "And I'm grateful for it," he acknowledged huskily, "but that doesn't alter the fact that you've been treated by a man with questionable credentials, to say the least. That's why I'm taking you to Boston to see a *real* doctor. Unless Mr. Demitry has any objections."

Nicolas shook his head. He recognized a challenge when he heard it. Joe Turner was throwing down the proverbial gauntlet. Nicolas knew better than to pick it up.

"It's Chelsea's decision to make," was all he said. "She's weak, but she's well enough to leave."

Standing beside him, Chelsea felt as though her heart was being wrenched in two. How could she leave him? Her feelings of love notwithstanding, how could she just turn and walk away after everything he'd done for her? On the other hand, how could she stay, knowing what it would mean? Knowing that she had to die—

"Tell me there's some other way, Nicolas," she whispered. "I want to be with you, but I saw what the dark place was like. . . ."

"There is no other way, Chelsea," Nicolas said sadly. "The debt must be paid."

"Debt?" Joe interrupted. "What debt?"

Chelsea ignored him. "But you're giving me the choice to walk away. Who will pay the debt if I do?"

"That has nothing to do with you." Nicolas touched her face, a brief, fleeting caress. "Just know that I'll honor whatever decision you make."

Thunder exploded, booming like cannon fire around them. It shook the earth beneath their feet and rattled the windows of the house. In the space of a breath, the wind went from a gentle breeze to a raging gale, howling around their ears like a tortured soul.

"What the hell—?" Joe pulled his jacket over his head as the heavens opened and the sky began to cry angry tears. "Come on, Chelsea, let's get out of here. Leave Demitry to his fantasy world. Your life's in the real one."

Nicolas said nothing, but his eyes were intent upon Chelsea's face. "Chelsea?"

She couldn't do it. Chelsea was terrified by the thought of

walking into black, angry water. She kept remembering the nightmares, reliving the icy fingers of water reaching into her lungs, freezing her body and paralyzing her mind. She loved Nicolas, but she didn't want to die. She couldn't forget what it was like to drown.

"I . . . can't, Nicolas. I'm afraid!"

"Chelsea, come on!" Joe had to shout to be heard over the force of the storm. "We've got to get out of here! Now!"

"Nicolas," she sobbed, as Joe started to drag her away.

Nikodemus, this is your last chance! his father's voice boomed. *If you let her go now, be prepared to suffer the consequences!*

But Nicolas didn't try to stop her. He watched Joe Turner put her into his car, and then watched the car drive away, the image of Chelsea's tear-stained face gazing back at him burned into his heart. Only then did he finally acknowledge that it was over.

He sank to his knees in the sand, crippled with pain. There was a terrible roaring in his ears, a roaring that had nothing to do with the storm. *"Take me, Father!"* he cried, raising his arms to the sky and throwing back his head so that the rain slashed his face. "For inasmuch as I have broken my promise to you, so do I release Chelsea from hers. Take me, Father. I am yours to command."

As if in answer, a great black wave rose from the depths, a massive wall of water that soared hundreds of feet into the sky. It raced toward shore, gathering speed with every second, its tremendous height casting a shadow over the land. Then, as it hit the shallow slope of the beach, it began to fall toward earth, reaching forward like the grasping hand of a giant.

Nicolas saw it coming and fell facedown upon the sand.

Seconds later, it exploded around him. It hit the earth, sending thousands of tons of water crashing down with a force that would have shattered a mortal man. But it didn't break Nicolas. He welcomed its violence, feeling the sand disappear beneath him as the ground was cut away, as though God himself had taken a knife and cleaved the land in two.

Nicolas felt himself swept up in the curve of Poseidon's hand and carried back out to the depths, mindless of any pain, or discomfort, or anything other than the blackness of his thoughts.

Because nothing mattered anymore. Nothing mattered, now that Chelsea was gone.

Part Three

DESTINY

Eighteen

The doctor sat behind his mahogany desk and studied the file in his hands.

On the wall behind him, framed diplomas and certificates from some of the finest medical schools in the country attested to his skills as a surgeon. Steel-rimmed glasses, perched on the end of his nose, gave him a staid, professional appearance. But as he looked up from his notes to stare at the young woman seated before him, his face became a study in confusion. "And you're sure you've told me everything there is to tell, Miss Porter?"

Chelsea clenched her hands in her lap. "Yes."

"Well, I don't know how else to put this, so I may as well just say it straight out." He set the file on his desk and sat back in his chair. "According to my examination, you have been the recipient of some of the most remarkable plastic surgery known to man. The skin tests I did confirmed everything you told me. You did receive severe burns to ninety-five percent of your body. In fact, given the extent of the damage, you shouldn't be alive today."

Chelsea took the news in stride. "I wouldn't be, if it weren't for the skill of Dr. Asklepios."

"Ah yes, Dr. Asklepios." The doctor sighed. "I don't know

who attended you, Miss Porter, but it certainly wasn't anyone who's registered with the American Medical Association. Or any other medical association, for that matter. I found several practitioners with names that were similar, and I checked into the background of each and every one. I wanted to meet the man who could do this kind of work. Unfortunately, none of them knew anything about you."

"Maybe he's retired," Chelsea said, though she knew a team of researchers could check every database on earth and never find the ancient healer.

"Retired or not, he'd still be listed. Make no mistake, Miss Porter, what this man has done for you is nothing short of miraculous. I've never seen this type of skin grafting before. He's left absolutely no marks. No scars, no discoloration, no uneven skin tones. It's truly a shame you're not able to see how beautiful your skin looks."

Chelsea almost smiled. Obviously, Asklepios had learned his skill well over the centuries. She wished she'd had an opportunity to thank him.

"What about my eyes, Dr. Cole? Will I be able to see again?"

"I'm afraid that's something else I can't explain. I had an ophthalmologist look at your eyes, and he told me that you've definitely had surgery, but at such an advanced level that he was completely at a loss to explain it. He said he'd never seen this kind of work before." Dr. Cole leaned forward in his chair. "Are you sure you can't tell me anything about him, Miss Porter? Anything at all that would help us to find him? The man has an amazing gift. The world would benefit greatly by it."

"I'm sorry, but I was unconscious most of the time Dr. Asklepios was there. All I know is that he was a friend of Nicolas Demitry's."

"Nicolas Demitry." The doctor checked his notes. "That would be the man who pulled you from the burning car."

Chelsea swallowed. "Yes."

"Well, I wouldn't mind speaking to him as well. I don't know if anyone told you, Miss Porter, but I have a copy of the police report from your accident."

Chelsea felt a flicker of concern. "I didn't know a report had been filed."

"Mr. Turner instigated proceedings the day he brought you in. He told the police your car had hit a pole out on the Oyster Point road and then burst into flames. Accordingly, the police started checking. Strangely enough, they haven't found any trace of your car. Judging from the burn marks on what's left of the pole, it was nothing short of an inferno." The doctor sighed again. "It's a miracle *either* of you survived. I just wish we could find Mr. Demitry to ask him a few questions."

"He's not at his house?"

"No. The police haven't found any trace of him. But if he was anywhere near the beach when the tsunami hit—"

She stiffened with shock. "A tsunami hit Oyster Point?"

"That's what the authorities are saying. A regular storm wouldn't have had the power to take the end of the spit clear off. Strangely enough, it left the house standing. Never seen anything like it." The doctor paused. "Mr. Demitry was an artist, wasn't he?"

Chelsea blinked back tears. "Yes, a brilliant one. He painted pictures of the sea."

"That's right, now I remember. One of his paintings was on display at the new gallery. Quite bizarre, as I recall, but remarkable all the—Miss Porter, are you all right?"

"I'm . . . fine." Chelsea gripped the arms of her chair. "I just want to go home."

"Of course. Mr. Turner's waiting in the hall. I'm sorry to have upset you."

"No, it's all right. It's just difficult for me to talk about this."

"Of course. You've been through an incredible ordeal, though I think the worst of it's over. But if you don't mind, I'd like to keep an eye on you over the next few weeks, just to make sure nothing flares up again. My nurse will call you to set up the appointment."

"Yes. Thank you, Dr. Cole."

In the corridor outside, Joe was waiting for her. "So, what did he say? Is everything all right?"

"Everything's fine." Chelsea's voice quivered. "He said

it's a miracle I'm alive, but I already knew that. Whatever else you say, Nicolas and Dr. Asklepios *did* save my life."

"Yeah, well, I'd still like to know who the guy really was," Joe muttered, gently taking her arm. "You know I don't have any faith in all that weird herb and smelly root stuff. And what kind of name is Asklepios anyway?"

"I believe it has its origins in Greek mythology," Chelsea said, almost tempted to smile. "And there's nothing wrong with holistic medicine, Joe."

"To your way of thinking, maybe, but there's enough bona fide members of the medical community who say there's nothing *right* with it to make me wonder."

Chelsea rested her hand in the crook of her partner's arm. What was the point in arguing? Nothing she could say was going to change Joe's mind, and right now, she wasn't even sure she wanted to. *She* knew who had saved her life, and as far as she was concerned, that was all that really mattered.

It was a miracle. That's what the doctor told her. That she shouldn't be alive today.

Chelsea supposed that from a doctor's point of view, the comments were justified. But as she sat on her deck and listened to the sound of the waves, she knew that surviving the accident would never be the miracle in her eyes.

Falling in *love* with the son of a god, and being chosen to be his *wife,* now that was the miracle.

As Chelsea drank her coffee, she thought about everything that had happened to her. It didn't seem possible that so much *had* happened in such a brief period of time. Certainly, she'd never expected to find herself in love again after the emotional devastation wrought by Duncan Rycroft's departure.

And yet, what had she really *known* about love before Nicolas had come into her life? There was no question that what she felt for him made her feelings for Duncan pale by comparison. Perhaps because her love for Nicolas hadn't come easy. There had been so many emotional obstacles to overcome. She couldn't even say *when* she'd fallen in love with him, but she knew, on the day they'd stood together in the water and he had pulled her into his arms, that she had found a once-in-a-lifetime love. She'd never been kissed like that before. Never been shaken to the depths of her soul by the touch of a man's mouth on hers.

But then, how often was one fortunate enough to be kissed by a god?

The sound of a car arriving pulled her reluctantly out of her thoughts. "Hello? Anybody home?"

Chelsea cocked her head to one side. "Joe, that you?"

"Sure is. Feel like a visitor?"

"You bet. Come on round back."

Chelsea heard the sound of the big man walking along the deck, and a moment later, smelled the familiar scent of Old Spice as he bent to kiss her on the forehead. "Hey, kiddo. I brought you something."

Chelsea smelled the flowers long before he put them into her lap. "Oh, they smell so beautiful, Joe, thank you." She buried her face in the blooms, recognizing the scents of rose, freesia, and lavender. "What a nice thing to do!"

"I only got you the ones that smelled good," Joe said, sitting down in the chair beside her. "You know, this really is some place, Chelsea. It's got a fantastic vi . . . that is, it's so quiet out here."

Chelsea laughed. "I know it's a great view, Joe, that's why I bought it. I used to spend a lot of time sitting out here admiring it."

"Did the doctor say anything about your sight coming back?"

Chelsea ran her hands over the velvety petals. "He's reluctant to say. I guess the damage was pretty bad."

"Yeah, and I guess I owe Demitry an apology for blowing up at him like that," Joe conceded. "But I was so worried about you, I wasn't thinking straight. When I found out you'd been in an accident, well, I guess I just kinda lost it. But I know he saved your life, and I wish he'd stuck around to be thanked."

Chelsea felt a tightness at the back of her throat. "Are you sure he's gone?"

"Pretty much. Nobody's seen him for weeks. Course, a famous man like that probably has all kinds of demands of his time. Speaking of work, any chance of you coming back to work anytime soon? I sure could use another pair of hands, now that we've got Beckley Fitch as a client."

Chelsea smiled. It was a measure of the man that he even asked. "Tell you the truth, I was thinking it might be time for a career change. I don't expect there's much call for blind interior designers these days. Something about not being able to match the shades."

"Yeah, I guess that would be a challenge. Hell, I have trouble doing it with two *good* eyes. But that doesn't mean I don't want you back, Chelsea. I'm sure I can find some other way of putting your talents to use. Maybe I'll put you on the phones. Nobody can resist that sexy voice of yours."

Chelsea laughed, as he intended her to, but the words still brought a lump to her throat. "It's okay. You don't have to feel sorry for me.

Joe snorted. "You think I'm that kind of guy?"

"Yes, I do. Speaking of recoveries, how are *you* doing? We haven't had much time to talk about that."

Joe's voice was pragmatic. "I'm hanging in. The lawyers are dealing with it all now. In the meantime, I've put the house up for sale. Got my eye on a nice little condo on the beach. Figure it's about all I need. By the way, I spoke to a friend of yours the other day. Grace Thornton. She told me to give you her best."

Chelsea frowned. "How do you know Grace?"

"I called her to get Nicolas Demitry's number. Seems like a nice lady."

"She is." Chelsea flicked a glance in his direction. "Maybe you should call her yourself."

She heard him chuckle. "Talk about Phyllis being a match-maker."

"I just thought—"

"I know what you thought," he said good-naturedly. "You think Joe Turner's a lost cause and needs somebody to look after him."

Chelsea grinned. "Pretty much."

"Thanks for the vote of confidence. As for Miss Thornton, I may give her a call, but not right away. I need to get things settled in my own mind first." He sighed deeply. "It's time

I took a long, hard look at my life, Chelsea. Because if I *do* get involved with somebody, I don't want to screw it up again. I have to believe I've learned something by being married twice. But right now, work's all that's keeping me going. It's my salvation. You know what that's like. And frankly, I don't have anything to *give* to anybody. But I'm sure the time will come when I can."

"Yeah, but it's always nice to know there's somebody you can pick up the phone and talk to in the meantime," Chelsea said. "Other than me, that is."

Joe laughed. "You may have something there. Anyway, I've still got a bunch of things to work out, and on that note, I'm outta here. No, don't get up," he said as Chelsea went to do that. "Stay here and finish your coffee. And remember, if you ever feel the need for a dose of insanity, just pick up the phone and call me. I'll run you down to the office. Everybody's anxious to see you, especially Phyllis."

"Say hi to her for me, will you, Joe? And thanks again. For everything."

After he'd gone, Chelsea thought about what he'd said. She was lucky to have somebody like Joe looking out for her—both as a friend and as a business partner. She'd been so afraid he'd want to buy her out and bring in a more useful associate, but it didn't sound like that was what he was going to do. He wanted her to stay on as his partner, and he was going to find her a job she could do, which meant she could keep paying her mortgage and living her life. It seemed she'd escaped the jaws of death and come out scarred, but not lifeless, on the other side.

She prayed that Nicolas had been as fortunate.

On a private island in the Caribbean, Lysianassa walked through the rooms of the white house perched on the edge of the cliff, and tried to feel some sort of appreciation for the beauty all around her. She knew that, by mortal standards, the house was fabulous. The rooms were all bright and spacious, and most contained windows that gave view over the sea. The hand of a professional decorator had touched every room so that the furnishings, the paintings, even the draperies and rugs were of the highest quality and the most elegant style. But as Lysia walked through the off-white corridors, all she could think about was Nikodemus and the fact that he would never have the pleasure of walking through these rooms again.

That wretched mortal! Lysia fumed. *How could she have done this to him?* Thanks to her thoughtless behavior, she had condemned Niko to a life of isolation and loneliness. His father had forbidden him ever to walk on the land again. Even now, he was forced to wait for her at the base of the sea stairs, obliged to keep part of his body submerged.

If this was yet another example of love, Lysia decided that both of them were better off without it!

She moved swiftly through the house, looking for the items Nikodemus had asked her to collect. Most of them were displayed in elegant glass cabinets in the section of the house Niko called *the living room.* She found and took down the first one, an exquisite gold statuette of an Egyptian princess, her headdress studded with diamonds and pearls, and carefully wrapped it in the cloth he had given her. In the next cabinet, she found the bowl of swirled marble, and next to that, the beautiful silver chalice. All priceless objets d'art that meant something to him.

Nikodemus was waiting for her on the rocks far below. His eyes were closed, but she could see a smile on his face as she made her way down the stairs.

"Can you smell the flowers?" he asked. "I've always thought they were more fragrant here than anywhere else in the world."

"I find nothing beautiful about your world, Nikodemus," Lysia said with uncharacteristic bitterness. "Not after all the grief and unhappiness it has caused you."

He opened his eyes and looked at her. "It is not fair to hate the land because of my mistakes."

"*Your* mistakes? It is your *mortal* who made mistakes, not you!"

"On the contrary, Chelsea did nothing wrong. It was I who released her from her obligation."

"Only because she did not have the courage to die for you!"

"Only because she did not *love* me enough to die for me,"

Nicolas corrected her sadly. "And she cannot be blamed for that. I came into her life. She did not come looking for me."

"But it was for her to fulfill the promise!" Lysia insisted.

"Yes, but it was another woman's promise. Perhaps if we'd had more time. . . ." His words drifted into silence. "Anyway, it doesn't matter now. Without love, what good would her sacrifice have been?"

At the ache in his voice, Lysia's anger abruptly dissipated. "Oh, Nikodemus, what wouldn't I give to take this pain from you. It isn't fair that for all your good deeds, this should be your reward."

Nicolas picked up the silver chalice that had been given to him by an ancient king, and shook his head. "My reward is only what I have sown. I broke my father's laws and went back on my word. What should I expect *but* his condemnation?"

"And what of Chelsea's? You may not hold her responsible, but she's proven that she doesn't love you. Surely your love for her is not as strong as it once was?"

Nicolas sighed. " *'Love is not love which alters when it alteration finds,'* " he quoted softly. "Chelsea does love me, but rare indeed is the love that would make so great a sacrifice."

Lysia shook her head. " *'There is no fear in love, but perfect love casteth out fear.'* Those words, too, were written by mortals, Nikodemus. They appear in the Bible, and to me, they say most eloquently that there is no room for fear in a heart filled with love. At least, there shouldn't be." She looked at the items set out on the rocks. "I assume these all have special meaning for you?"

Nicolas nodded. "They're gifts that were given to me for no other reason than in the hopes of remembrance." He looked at the small golden statuette of the Egyptian princess and remembered the mighty pharaoh who had given it to him. "They will be my only link to what has gone before."

He sighed then, and looking up at the sky, watched the glorious spectacle of the sunset unfolding. But where in the past he had watched it from the heights of his balcony, now he was forced to gaze upon it from the level of the sea. Such was his punishment. He hadn't wanted to ask Lysia to go into his house, but he'd had no choice. It was necessary that he remove what few belongings mattered to him before others had a chance to do so. Because she was right. He would never set foot in those rooms again. He had risked everything for love, and he had lost.

Without another word, he smiled at Lysia and then slipped quietly back into the arms of the sea.

Nineteen

Chelsea stood where the sand met the water and gazed with sightless eyes toward the bay. It was just past one o'clock in the morning. Three weeks had passed since Nicolas had told her the truth. Three long weeks since the revelation that had taken him away from her side, and not once in all that time had she stopped thinking about him.

Did he ever think of her? She wished she had some way of knowing, but she didn't even know where he was. She didn't hear his voice anymore. Even the dreams had come to an end, and though she called to him every night, he never answered.

Lifting the edge of her nightgown, Chelsea took a step forward. The water felt soft on her skin, the waves warm as they washed over her feet. It wasn't the first time she had ventured into the bay, because she wasn't afraid anymore. She hadn't been ever since Nicolas had shown her an image of the huge manta, and she'd realized how stupid she had been. Now, when sleep eluded her, she often came down here, hoping for some sign that Nicolas was still in her life.

But as the days stretched into weeks and none came, Chelsea was forced to face facts.

Nicolas wasn't going to contact her. He had given up.

Chelsea dropped her head, letting her tears fall unheeded
into the bay. If she'd learned anything over the last three
weeks, it was that love changed you. It made you better than
you were before. It opened your eyes to things you'd never
seen before, and exposed your heart to emotions never before
experienced. It made you whole. Without it, there was just a
void, a terrible emptiness that nothing seemed to fill. Chelsea
hadn't realized just how much a part of her life Nicolas had
become until he hadn't been there anymore.

"Don't leave me in my darkness, Nicolas," she whispered,
sinking to her knees in the sand. "Nicolas, can you hear me?"

I hear you, Chelsea.

She gasped. "Nicolas!"

I'm here, beloved, I haven't left. I could never leave you.

The voice was in her head, but within minutes, Chelsea
heard the sound of water swirling around her. She struggled
to pierce the darkness with her mind. "Nicolas?" Holding her
breath, hardly daring to believe, she reached out her hand.
Seconds later, she uttered a soft cry as she felt the warmth
of his fingers curl around hers. *"Nicolas!"*

She didn't want to breathe. Didn't want to do anything
that might shatter the moment and take him away from her.
Because he *was* here. She could feel the warmth from his
body, and she moved toward him, like fire seeking fuel. "Oh,
Nicolas, I've missed you so much," she whispered, alternating between tears and laughter. She raised her hands to his
face, remembering the shape of it, seeing him in her mind
as clearly as though her eyes were open and looking at him.

"And I've missed you, beloved." His voice was as unsteady as hers. "I've heard you calling to me, but I told myself there was no point in returning." His hands cupped her
face and raised it to his, and she moaned softly as he kissed
her eyes, her nose, and then, finally, her lips.

They kissed in the way of lovers coming together, their
mouths alternately cool and hot, tongues deeply probing,
lightly touching. The flutter of breath against skin, the beating of one heart against another, as though trying to find a
way to beat in unison.

How could she ever have let him go, Chelsea wondered.
It was only now that she realized how desperately she had

missed him; how she'd longed for his touch through all the long, lonely nights. She had been searching for meaning in a life that suddenly had no meaning, for without Nicolas, she had no life.

Unable to see him, Chelsea resorted to using the skills he'd taught her. She traced the outline of his face with her hands, running her fingers into his hair, tangling them in the wet curls. She pressed her mouth to the strong column of his throat, sampling the salty flavor of his skin, while her hands traced the outline of his chest, feeling the muscles ripple and expand beneath her fingers.

"Chelsea!" Her name seemed torn from his lips.

Smiling, Chelsea put her mouth to his chest, until his hands tightened on her arms and a groan issued from deep in his throat. She marveled that she, a mere mortal, had the power to affect him in such a way.

But how much time did they have? A minute? An hour? Was he to be wrenched away from her again, leaving her to wallow in the loneliness of her life? Were they to be granted only these few, precious moments together? She needed him so much.

"Touch me, Nicolas," Chelsea whispered. "Make love to me. I want to have something to remember. Something to dream about when I'm lying in my bed without you."

As the winds began to blow, Nicolas laid her down in the shallows, the waves playing with her hair as they washed over her. Through the thin material of her nightgown, Chelsea felt the glorious nakedness of his body. She felt the smoothness and the strength of it, and abandoned herself to the mindless pleasure of his touch, catching her breath as the ache within her intensified.

But she was not the only one lost in the wonder of discovery. Pushing her back against the sand, Nicolas pressed tender kisses to her throat while his hands pursued their own sweet exploration. His hands moved up to cup her breasts, his thumbs brushing over her nipples, teasing them through the wet fabric of her nightgown, bringing them to life.

"I want to see you, Chelsea," he whispered. "All of you."

At her nod, he pulled her gown free, tossing it aside so that he could gaze down at her body. He reverently lowered his mouth to her breasts, licking seawater from first one and then the other, as his hand caressed the gentle curve of her waist; brushing over her hip before trailing across her smooth white thighs. His searching fingers moved lower, seeking the very heart of her femininity, and when he found it, she cried out his name. "Nicolas!"

Huskily, he murmured, "Beautiful. So beautiful, Chelsea. I never thought it possible. . . ." His voice drifted away as he caressed her with long, gentle strokes, feeling her unique moisture blending with the essence of the sea.

He took as much pleasure as he gave, though Chelsea wondered if anything could be sweeter than the touch of his hands. His caresses stoked the fire within, sending pleasurable shudders through her, until all she could see in her mind was the shimmer of stars in his eyes.

"Are you able to make love to me, Nicolas?" she asked in a whisper.

"My father made love to a mortal, so I assume it's possible. And I certainly couldn't turn away from you now, beloved." His voice was low, thrumming with emotion. "I've waited so long for you, Chelsea. Tonight, there is only you and I. But whatever else happens, remember that what I give you now will be my final gift."

Thinking he meant the gift of his body, Chelsea opened hers to him. She felt the heat of his body as he settled between her thighs, hot silk against cool satin, hard muscle against soft skin. She felt the swell of his arousal pressing against her thighs and moved to accommodate him, their legs intertwined in the water as she tucked herself into the contours of his body.

Then, rising up, Nicolas thrust forward, sheathing himself deeply, exquisitely, into the sweetness of her body.

Chelsea cried out, not in pain but in triumph. She welcomed his possession, needing to feel that he was a part of her. But at once he stilled, and she could hear his concern for her in his voice. "Did I hurt you, beloved?"

"You could never hurt me," she whispered. "You're a part of me now. Love me, Nicolas. Please, just love me."

And he did, slowly beginning to move, sinking himself into her body, feeling her muscles tighten and close around him. With every thrust, he felt the quivering heat of her, and let it fire his own passion. Her cries softened to a moan, but when he heard her breathing change, he increased the tempo, sensing that her passion was rising to meet his own. The softness of the sand cushioned them, salt water swirling around them, bathing them in the cool breath of the sea.

Finally, when he sensed her time was near, Nicolas pushed into her deeply—and in that split second, locked his mind with hers. He saw her world shatter into a thousand silver drops, felt the explosions that began deep within her body, heard his name whispered on her lips. A shuddering cry stopped the breath in her throat, and as tears of joy rolled down her cheeks, Nicolas experienced a depth of love and completeness that words could never describe. A love he felt with every breath, every heartbeat. And finally, knowing it was time, he gave in to the longing of centuries. Thrusting into her one last time, Nicolas cried out in triumph as his body shuddered with the power of his release.

This was not a gift he had given her. It was a gift they had shared. She was his now, body and soul, and no matter what else happened, he would always have the memory of this, their first and only coupling.

If nothing else, Nicolas knew he could content himself with that throughout the rest of time.

It wasn't until the following morning that Chelsea realized the true nature of Nicolas's gift. It hadn't been just the physical act of their joining. When the sun rose over the beach, she was there to see it, tears streaming down her face as she watched the fiery red sun change to gold as it began its slow, majestic climb into the sky.

Nicolas had given her the gift of her sight.

But it had not come without cost. As she raised her fingers to the place where the birthmark had been, she closed her eyes and wept.

Poseidon's Kiss was gone. Nicolas had given her the choice—and she had chosen life. He had removed his mark. She knew, without having to be told, that she would never see him again.

●　　●　　●

The doctor had no explanation for it. Reluctant to use the word *miracle* again, he suggested that Chelsea's initial blindness had been a result of shock-induced trauma, and said that now that she was settling back into her old life, her vision had returned.

He could come up with no other logical explanation.

Chelsea had thanked him and left his office, secure in the knowledge that she would not be going back. From there, she had driven her rented car to Nicolas's house.

Chelsea hadn't told anyone about the letter she'd found on a small pile of stones at the edge of the water. Nicolas must have left it for her after they'd made love. She had fallen asleep with him on the beach, but had awakened alone the next morning.

The letter had been there, waiting for her.

My darling Chelsea,

The fact you are reading this means I was able to give you my last gift, and for that, I am eternally grateful. The fact it also means that I will never see you again, causes me a depth of grief you cannot even begin to comprehend.

It is not my intention to impose any guilt on you, Chelsea, for I love you too much. But in allowing you to make your choice, I have broken a promise to my father and will not be returning to the land again. For this reason, and because the work of living goes on, there are certain practical matters which must be dealt with, and I would ask you to grant me this request in seeing to their completion.

I enclose a key to the front door of my house, and to the safe I keep upstairs. I have left certain documents there, along with instructions for the distribution of my artwork and effects. I hope you will look after this for me, as I will be unable to.

I love you, Chelsea. Please know that the precious gift you gave me—the gift of yourself—will stay with me forever. I hope that what I was able to give you in return will compensate for the fear and the pain I caused.

Do not fear to swim in the sea again. No creature will ever harm you. You have my promise.

Nicolas

Chelsea had read the letter over until it was crumpled and spotted with the paths of her tears. Even in his grief, Nicolas had thought of her first, blessing her with a gift far beyond anything of mortal value. But with the reading of his letter had come the clarity Chelsea had been seeking; the affirmation of her feelings, which had, at long last, allowed her to make her decision.

Her footsteps echoed on the wooden deck now as she walked to the front of Nicolas's house. Opening the door, she stepped inside, holding her breath as she walked into the kitchen. She looked at the table where she and Nicolas had sat together only a few weeks ago, and where she had listened to him tell her how to pour tea into a cup without burning herself.

She glanced at the telephone, remembering the call from Joe, and how it had triggered something and brought all of her memories back. She remembered Nicolas coming home, and his recounting of the most incredible tale she'd ever heard.

And then, through a haze of pain and tears, she remembered the devastating scene on the beach when he'd let her go, and when the terrifying forces of nature had closed in on him.

Was it really such a short time ago?

Not allowing herself to dwell on it, Chelsea headed for the stairs. She made her way to the second floor and paused at the doorway of what must have been her room, amazed at how small it was. When she had been trying to navigate her way around it, it had seemed huge.

There was the bed in which she'd first awakened, and the window through which she'd heard the sounds of the sea. And over there in the corner, the chair where Nicolas had sat and watched her. How strange it was to be here now without him.

Nicolas's bedroom was at the far end of the hall. It was sparsely furnished, containing only a single bed, a chest of drawers, and a small night table. Chelsea tried to imagine him in it, but couldn't. Perhaps because she knew he'd never slept here. Sometime around midnight, he had quietly slipped away, drawn back to the sea that was his true home.

And she thought he'd gone off to meet a woman.

Shaking her head, Chelsea closed the door and went up to the third floor. There was only one door here; holding her breath, she opened it—and saw Nicolas's world unfold around her. Here were his tools: his paints, his palettes, the brushes he used to create his masterpieces, all neatly laid out on a wooden table next to the window. And over there, an easel upon which stood a canvas, the picture turned away from her.

Chelsea closed her eyes. His presence was so strong she could almost feel him standing next to her. She was sure she could hear his laughter, rich and sensual, perhaps even the whisper of her name. In her mind's eye, she saw him, standing in front of the easel, his brow furrowed as he concentrated on getting the image just right.

She felt a wave of such intense longing that tears sprang to her eyes. "I love you, Nicolas," she whispered, feeling the emptiness, wondering if this pain was anything like what he had suffered the day he'd let her go. "I miss you so much."

The safe was against the far wall. Taking the key he had left for her, Chelsea opened it and withdrew three sealed envelopes. The paper was unlike anything she'd ever seen; each was neatly labeled with a name and an address on the front.

Clasping the bundle to her, she closed the safe and walked toward the window. Then, drawing a deep breath, Chelsea found and opened the one that was addressed to her.

Dearest Chelsea,

> *Around you are my works, some of which are finished, some of which are not. I give these to you to do*

with as you wish. Perhaps they will have more mean-
ing for you now that you know the truth of my life.

The house, the property, and everything I own I also
leave to you. A formal will is in the hands of a lawyer,
whose address and phone number follow. It will be
necessary for you to approach him, as he will have no
knowledge of my death. As I thought suicide the most
logical explanation, you will find a signed letter at-
testing to my intention to commit same in the appro-
priately marked envelope. Given what is generally
perceived to be "the instability of the artistic nature"
I doubt there will be many questions asked. Give it to
him and leave him to do his work. Needless to say, a
body will never be found.

I hope you will find joy and contentment in your life,
my darling. You have the capacity for great love, and
fortunate will be the man who awakens it in you.
Please burn the few personal letters I've given you.
They can only be a source of trouble if they are ever
discovered. I do not fear for myself, but I would hate
to see you so exposed.

I love you, Chelsea, and always will. I hope you will
keep the painting on the easel behind you. It was to
have been my wedding gift to you.

> *Yours for eternity,*
> *Nikodemus*

Chelsea wiped tears from her eyes and put down the letter.
Turning, she looked at the canvas on the easel—and then
burst into tears all over again.

It was a painting of her. She was wearing a long white
gown and a crown of shells on her head. Her hair was a riot
of curls, and on her face was the most incredible smile she
had ever seen. A smile of beauty and happiness. The smile
of a woman in love.

There were no lines of stress upon her face. No worries
or cares, no shadows beneath her eyes. They were clear and
untroubled, like those of a child. And that smile. Dear
heaven, the Mona Lisa's couldn't have been more tranquil.

Surely this was the image of a woman, captured and glorified by a man who had truly been in love with her.

Was this how she had looked in the weeks following the accident, Chelsea wondered. Or was this how Nicolas had seen her?

"That was how he saw you," a voice said softly from the doorway. "That is how he sees you still."

Startled, Chelsea turned—and knew, as soon as she did, that she was looking at the mysterious woman who had spoken to her on the beach. "Lysianassa!"

The ethereal creature smiled. "So, we see each other for the first time, Chelsea Porter."

"As you said we would." Chelsea stared at her in fascination, aware that she had never seen a more beautiful woman in her life. "I don't imagine you thought it would be like this, though."

"No." Lysianassa's eyes, shimmering with silver light, met Chelsea's with a boldness she found disconcerting. "I expected it to be in the sea after you had passed through the Shadow of Darkness. I did not think Nikodemus would have been willing to sacrifice so much to release you from your promise. But I should have known. His love for you was greater than his fear. Greater than anything."

Almost afraid to breath, Chelsea said, "What has he sacrificed? Tell me, I must know."

Lysianassa glanced at the painting on the easel. "This," she said simply. "The freedom to leave the sea and to walk on land. The right to see you."

Chelsea's heart turned over. "Is there no chance his . . . father will forgive him?"

The goddess's eyes flashed. "Are you afraid to say his name, mortal? Are you afraid to admit that the man who loved you is the son of Poseidon?"

"No! But it isn't easy to comprehend the nature of what he is," Chelsea said. "Of what *you* are. Or does being a goddess mean having a complete disregard for the feelings of those less mighty than yourself?"

Lysia's eyes narrowed. "So, there is spirit within you. Good. Perhaps Nikodemus did not choose as poorly as I thought."

Chelsea flushed, but said nothing.

"As for Poseidon," Lysianassa continued, "you should know that he does not forgive easily. He rules with an iron hand, and there are many who believe he has already been more than fair with Nikodemus."

"Nikodemus."

"His true name," Lysianassa told her. "Nicolas Demitry was the name he chose to use on land. Nikodemus was the name given to him by his father."

"And are you like him?" Chelsea asked softly. "A goddess of the sea?"

"I am a Nereid," Lysianassa said proudly. "My mother, daughter of Tethys and Oceanus, is a sea goddess. But even had I such powers as his, I could never *be* like Nikodemus. I do not have his compassion. He sacrificed himself for love, Chelsea Porter. He allowed you to withdraw from your ancestor's promise because you did not love him, and because he would not force you to submit. But in doing so, he broke a promise of his own and was drawn back into the sea." She glanced at the envelopes on the table. "That is what those letters are about. He bid me bring them here so that you could carry out his last wishes. The night he lay with you, and gave you back your sight, Poseidon forbade him ever to rise to the surface again."

Chelsea gasped. "You mean . . . he cannot even swim to the shore?"

Lysianassa shook her head. "He cannot so much as lift his head above the waves. He is being forced to stay within the depths of the Kingdom. Unless you go to him yourself, you will never see him again."

Primitive grief overwhelmed Chelsea, pain and guilt tearing at her heart like a jagged razor. "You must hate me for what I've done. Hate me for the misery I've caused him."

"I wanted to hate you." Lysianassa turned beautiful opalescent eyes toward her. "I wanted to scream your name from the highest peaks, and ask Hades to reach up his hand and drag you into the Underworld. I wanted you to suffer for the pain and anguish you've inflicted upon Nikodemus. But I could not. He would not have wished me to feel that way. His heart is too big."

Chelsea closed her eyes, sickened by what she had done. Nicolas had sacrificed so much for her, all in the name of love, yet never once had she told him what he'd wanted to hear. Never once had she said, "I love you."

Was it too late to say it now?

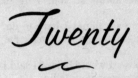

Twenty

Chelsea met with her lawyer, Beverly Hughes, the following afternoon. After advising her that she intended to take an extended vacation, Chelsea gave her a large manila envelope and asked her not to open it for ten days. She also gave her a key to her house.

"This seems a bit unusual, Chelsea," the lawyer said. "If you're only going on vacation, why the need for all this?"

Chelsea shrugged. "Just superstitious. It runs in the family."

Beverly shrugged. "If you say so. But are you sure you wouldn't like to leave the key with a friend or neighbor? They can water the plants and keep an eye on the place while you're gone." When Chelsea refused, the lawyer sighed. "Okay, I'll put all this into my files to be brought forward on—" She flipped her calendar. "—the fourth of September?"

"Sure," Chelsea said, knowing the date really didn't matter. She rose and held out her hand. "Thanks for all your help, Bev."

Chelsea left the lawyer's office and turned in the direction of Kensington Street. She had one more stop to make before heading home.

•   •   •

"What do you mean you're leaving?"

Joe glanced at the letter of resignation Chelsea had just given him, and shook his head in bewilderment. "You've got your memory back, your sight's returned, and you've got a wonderful future ahead of you. Why throw in the towel now?"

"Because there are things I have to do," Chelsea said. "I guess you could say the accident made me look at life a little differently."

"I don't suppose it would help if I said I really need you?"

"No, but I appreciate your telling me." Chelsea sat in front of Joe's cluttered desk, just the way she had two months ago when he'd told her to take some time off. Funny. That, too, seemed a lifetime ago. "Thanks for being such a great partner and friend, Joe. I don't know what I would have done without you. Your concern for me, and your giving me that leave of absence, was the best thing you could have done."

"Humph, I don't know about that," Joe grumbled. "Looks to me like it was the *worst* thing I could have done. For me, that is, since I'm losing you." He sighed heavily. "Are you sure I can't change your mind?"

"I'm sure. This is something I have to do."

Joe stared down at the letter in his hands, and sighed again. "There are about a hundred questions I'd like to ask right now, starting with where you're going and why I get the feeling there's a man behind all this." He glanced at her hopefully. "Is there?"

"Oh yes." Chelsea's smile widened. "A very special man."

"Nicolas Demitry?"

Chelsea felt her cheeks grow warm. "Yes, but please don't ask me anything more."

"I won't. If he makes you happy, that's all that really matters. But I want you to know that if things don't work out, you can always come back, Chelsea. There'll always be a job waiting for you." He got to his feet and pulled her into his arms. "I sure am going to miss you, Porter."

Chelsea hugged him back. She'd known this would be the hardest good-bye to say. In some ways, Joe felt like the only family she had. "I'll miss you too, Joe. Thanks . . . for everything. And whatever happens, *please* remember that I am happy."

She left his office before he had a chance to say anything more, and before she embarrassed herself by bursting into tears. Thank goodness Phyllis hadn't been there, Chelsea thought as she ran down the stairs toward her car. Saying good-bye to her secretary would definitely have pushed her over the edge.

Chelsea didn't make any other stops on the way home. Anything that needed to be said was in the letters she'd left with her lawyer. She just wanted to get on with it.

She'd been away from Nicolas long enough.

That night, Chelsea made the last of her preparations. She carefully packaged all of Nicolas's paintings and moved them into her attic, where they would remain until her lawyer gave Jonathan Blaire his letter. She'd already decided that Nicolas's works would hang in the gallery on permanent display, so that everyone could appreciate his genius.

As for *Poseidon's Sorrow,* she left it hanging on her living room wall. Jonathan would get it eventually, but for now, Chelsea wanted to leave it where it was. It was the painting that had started it all. It seemed only right that it should be one of the last things she saw before she went to her new life.

Finally, when everything was done, Chelsea went to her bedroom and started getting dressed. She'd found her grandmother's wedding dress in one of the boxes in the attic. It was very plain, little more than a long white shift with a wide border of lace at the neck and hem. It had long sleeves and fit close to the body—exactly what Chelsea wanted.

She pulled it on and carefully fastened the five tiny buttons at the neck. Glancing at herself in the mirror, she smiled, aware that in the old-fashioned gown, she could almost have *been* her grandmother. Her cheeks were pale, but otherwise, she felt relatively calm.

Amazing, really, considering what she was about to do.

At five minutes to midnight, Chelsea took one final walk around the house. Her gaze touched on all the things that had once meant so much to her: the furnishings, the accessories, everything she'd worked hard for and had felt so good about buying. But that's all they were to her now. Inanimate objects. The decorations of life.

Love was what mattered now, and with any luck, it would be out there waiting for her.

"Please be waiting for me, Nicolas," she whispered aloud.

At the first stroke of midnight, Chelsea stepped out on the deck and locked the door behind her. It was a beautiful night. A light breeze played across the surface of the bay, and the moon shone in a bright, clear sky. She cast her eyes upward to a million stars twinkling like tiny pinpoints of light.

Would there be stars where she was going? Would there be anything?

As she walked toward the waves, Chelsea tried not to be afraid. She knew she was doing the right thing. She loved Nicolas, and she wanted to be with him. This was the only way that was going to happen. She only prayed it wasn't too late.

She paused at the edge of the sand, turning to take one last look at her house and at all that was safe and familiar in her life. Then, saying a brief prayer, she closed her eyes, turned back to face the water, and started walking toward her future.

She comes, Nikodemus.

Poseidon's warning was unnecessary. Nicolas had known the exact moment of Chelsea's entry into the sea. He always did. He could hear the sound of her heart beating through the depths, letting him know she was alive and well, and he would take comfort from it. Such was the power of his love, and the strength of his connection to her.

But something was different tonight. There was determination in Chelsea's step. She wasn't staying in the shallows, or swimming parallel to shore. She was walking in a straight line out into the bay. But it wasn't until he heard her whispered plea that he realized what it meant.

"I must go to her, Father!" Nicolas cried. "Chelsea has changed her mind!"

Yes, but you are not to assist her. She must prove her love for you. You have already done all you can.

"But she will need my help!" Nicolas's voice was tight with emotion. "She cannot pass through the Shadow of Darkness alone. She must have a guide. Sephonia will be waiting for her."

Love must be her guide now, Nikodemus, Poseidon told him. *She must prove herself worthy of the sacrifices you have made for her.*

Nicolas clenched his fists by his side, anger and concern warring with logic and reason. There was nothing he could do. He was bound by his father's command, helpless to interfere. To go against those commands now would only do Chelsea harm. His father would brook no disobedience. He must wait here in the depths and pray that her love would get her through.

Be brave, beloved, he called through the darkness. *Be strong, Chelsea.*

Heart pounding, Chelsea walked into the surf. The roar of the water seemed loud in her ears, and the vastness of the ocean threatened to swallow her up.

She closed her eyes and thought of Nicolas. Nicolas, the man she loved, and with whom she would soon be reunited.

Chelsea . . .

She gasped. Was that his voice? It had sounded so weak, so terribly far away.

"Nicolas, I'm here," she cried. "I'm coming."

. . . be strong, Chelsea. . . .

His voice drifted away, leaving her alone again in the darkness.

"Nicolas?" Chelsea cried, waiting, praying to hear the sound of his voice again. "Nicolas!"

In the silence that followed, Chelsea knew she would have to be strong. She had taken too long to make her decision. Now, she must find the courage to do this without Nicolas's help. He would not be rising to the surface to guide her. She was going to find her way alone.

"No, not alone, Chelsea," Lysianassa said, emerging from the waves like a graceful white phantom.

Heart pounding, Chelsea turned to face her. "Lysianassa! What are you doing here?"

"I've come to help you." Silver mist swirled around her body, adding to the ghostly illusion. "The Guardian is waiting to show you the way. Together, we will help you pass through the Shadow of Darkness."

"Together?" Chelsea looked at her in surprise. "You mean . . . you're willing to help me reach Nicolas?"

"I am, now that I see what is in your heart. Nikodemus has been forbidden to intervene. I have not. And though my powers are not as great as his, I will do all I can. Are you ready?"

Chelsea knew it was her last chance to turn back. The last opportunity she would have to change her mind and go back to the safety of the land. And it wasn't too late. She could set aside the plans she'd made, and no one would be any the wiser. She could go back to her job, pick up the pieces of her life, and pretend that everything was all right.

But even as the thought drifted through her mind, Chelsea knew it was impossible. Nothing would ever be all right again, or could be the way it was. How could it be, when she had been blessed with the love of a god—of a man— like Nicolas Demitry?

"Yes, I'm ready," she said confidently.

Lysianassa nodded. "Then let it begin."

The water went very still, just as it had on that fateful night so long ago. Turning toward open water, Chelsea caught her breath as ripples formed on the water, indicating the presence of the mighty creature.

"Have courage, Chelsea," Lysianassa said. "The Guardian will take you into the depths, and I shall be waiting for you there, but you must be brave. What you will see tonight will be beyond the understanding of any mortal, and the path that lies before you is not an easy one. Temptation will be placed before you at the time of your greatest weakness, but you must find the strength to resist. I will do whatever I can, but even I am not immune to the terrible power of Sephonia."

"Sephonia?"

"The Sea Witch. All who reach the Kingdom must pass by her. And if the time comes when you must look for inner strength, think only of the one who loves you, and who waits for you on the other side." With that, Lysia slipped back into the water and disappeared.

Chelsea stared ahead of her. Temptation? Evil? Nicolas hadn't said anything about that when he'd talked about her joining him. But perhaps he hadn't needed to. Perhaps if she'd made the journey with him, he would have protected her from such things. Chelsea had no doubt that Nicolas's powers were greater than Lysianassa's.

But it was Lysianassa who had come to help her. Lysianassa who had managed to overcome her anger and to offer Chelsea a hand in friendship. Whether it was for her sake or Nicolas's wasn't really important. The Nereid's immediate concern seemed to be to help Chelsea reach the man she loved, and Chelsea would always be grateful to her for that.

Whether she was *able* to get there seemed to be the million-dollar question right now, but refusing to dwell on the dangers, Chelsea squared her shoulders and continued walking. Whatever the dangers, she would face them. Nicolas had suffered far greater misfortune than this.

The water deepened with every step. It inched up her thighs, crept up over her waist, and soaked her gown until it hung on her like a ghostly shroud. She tried not to cry out as a wave slapped against her chin, soaking the curls at the nape of her neck. Eventually, Chelsea's feet floated free of the seafloor, and she began to swim out to where the Guardian was waiting. The ripples came closer, then disappeared as the manta dropped down.

Chelsea felt the pressure wave again, but this time, she wasn't afraid. Instead, at the appropriate time, she took a last, deep breath of air, and then dived down, groping with her hands in the darkness for the curve of the manta's wing. Finally, she found it, and as her hands closed around it, the mighty creature began to move, taking her into the depths.

The crossing had begun.

Within seconds, Chelsea felt the pressure building in her ears. She swallowed to equalize it, then did it again and again as they dropped into the stygian darkness. They traveled at incredible speeds, seconds ticking by, each one taking her farther from all she'd ever know. They approached and passed the point of no return.

And still they descended.

Soon Chelsea felt her lungs begin to burn, a sure sign that her air was running out. She didn't know how deep they were when consciousness started to recede. She only knew that the pain had become a fire in her chest, and that the urge to panic was real now. Even though she knew what was happening, it didn't negate the fear. She'd never really thought about her mortality before. Never faced Death in the eye as she did now.

The water was icy cold and black. Chelsea couldn't feel her hands or her feet, and there was a pounding in her head as the terrifying darkness closed in. She fought to keep an image of Nicolas's face before her, praying he would be waiting for her, but there was no one. Nicolas wasn't here, nor was Lysianassa. She was alone in this terrible blackness. Alone . . . and terrified—

No, you are not alone, whispered a soft, beautiful voice. *I am with you, and I can take you back. Back to the light and the warmth, away from this terrible pain. Why do you wish to die? Come with me,* the voice whispered persuasively. *Leave this place of darkness while you can.*

Chelsea turned her head and saw a ghostly white figure hovering in the darkness beside her. But it wasn't Lysianassa. It was another woman of incredible beauty. Her face reminded Chelsea of an angel, and her skin was pale as foam, her eyes glowing like deep green emeralds. Starfish clung to her long blonde hair and glistening strands of pearls were wound throughout. Instead of legs, Chelsea saw the tail of a fish.

A mermaid?

Whatever she was, she held out her hand to Chelsea, her words growing even softer and more cajoling. *I can give you back your life, Chelsea. Come back to the surface with me. See even now, your pain lessening. . . .*

Strangely enough, as the mermaid drew closer, Chelsea *did* feel her pain begin to subside. The water was getting warmer, and even the tightness in her chest was easing. She was experiencing the most wonderful sense of euphoria. . . .

Yes, come. Reach out to me. Take my hand. . . .

Smiling, Chelsea took her hand from the creature's back. She began to reach out—

Chelsea, no! another voice cried. *You must resist! It is Sephonia's trickery!*

Chelsea struggled to understand, but her brain felt like it was wrapped in a fog. Someone slid between her and the mermaid, stopping her from reaching out. . . .

Chelsea, wake up! Do not let her cast her spell!

Chelsea's eyes fluttered open. That was Lysianassa's voice, but what was she saying? Something about . . . Sephonia?

Suddenly, the water all around her erupted in an explosion of bubbles. As the manta picked up speed, Chelsea looked back and saw two white figures, both female, locked in deadly combat. The mermaid was the bigger of the two, and in horror, Chelsea watched as she raised one slim white hand and struck hard at the throat of the other. She saw blood spurt from the challenger's throat, saw the two figures break apart—and then saw the mermaid turn and come after her.

Fear lanced through Chelsea's heart. *She* was now the mermaid's target, and Chelsea knew that she was evil. Her face was no longer that of an angel, but of a witch, her eyes burning like red-hot coals. She was closing the distance between them, and for the first time, Chelsea heard her horrible shrieks, and understood the danger she was in.

This was the evil Lysianassa had spoken of. The force that would try to keep her from Nicolas forever. Sephonia didn't want to take her to safety. She wanted her soul!

Chelsea closed her eyes. It wasn't supposed to end like this. She was supposed to be with Nicolas, but that wasn't going to happen. Even now, she could feel the witch's presence; feel the evil drawing near, and knew she was too weak to fight. She cried out in terror at the thought of what was to come, and in doing so, sacrificed the last of her air.

Her body spasmed once, and then sank onto the back of the Guardian. She didn't hear Sephonia's frustrated screams as the Sea Witch vanished into the abyss. As the gates of the Kingdom swung open, Chelsea's last conscious thought was that it had all been for naught.

She had passed through the Shadow of Darkness—and found nothing on the other side.

Twenty-one

Lysianassa knew the exact moment of Chelsea's passing. She felt it in her heart, sensed it in the deepest part of her being. She wished she could have been with Chelsea to ease the pain of her transition, but, weakened by her injuries, she could do nothing but lie helpless on the seafloor and watch the manta carry Chelsea safely through the gate of the Kingdom.

Sephonia hadn't won. Chelsea was with her beloved Nikodemus on the other side.

Too bad she hadn't fared as well, Lysianassa thought, as she tried to stem the flow of blood from her throat. The Sea Witch, furious at having been robbed of her intended victim, had fought a tremendous battle, lashing out at Lysianassa and opening a deep gash in her throat. But the altercation had lasted long enough to allow the Guardian to do its job.

She had given Chelsea the time she had needed to get away.

Lysianassa closed her eyes and lay back. Whatever happened now, she could rest peacefully, knowing she had done all that she could to bring happiness to Nikodemus's life. She had done what she had promised to do.

Lysianassa, open your eyes, child.

The voice was familiar, and Lysia looked up to see the face of the great healer smiling down at her. *Asklepios?*

She felt the gentle touch of his hands at her throat. *Your father sent me to care for you. He saw what you did, and he is very proud of you. We all are. You risked your life for a mortal's soul. She is now safe within the Kingdom.*

Lysia closed her eyes. *Then I am happy.*

But why did you help her? the great one asked. *I know how much you love Nikodemus. Had Chelsea died, he might have turned to you.*

Lysia gave him a sad smile. *I was not destined to sit at his side, Asklepios. Chelsea was, and once she realized how much she loved him, how could I turn my back on her? They have both suffered so much.*

The wise one nodded. *I am sure Nikodemus will be forever in your debt, but now we must get you back and see to your wounds.*

Then, to Lysia's astonishment, Nikodemus himself appeared, lifting her gently in his arms. *Rest easy, my valiant nymph.*

She gazed up at him, her joy tinged with bewilderment. *Niko . . . what are you doing here? You should be with Chelsea.*

I will rejoin her when she wakes, but it is thanks to you that she is safe. He smiled as he pressed his lips to her temple. *You made me very proud, Lysianassa.*

She smiled up at him wearily, suddenly feeling the effect of her wounds. *She proved her love for you Nikodemus. I couldn't let . . . Sephonia win.*

And for that, you will forever have a place in my heart, he told her. *And in my father's. You will be pleased to know that, even now, he is talking about banishing Sephonia to the Far Reaches. He saw what she did, and he is furious. But sleep, beautiful one. Sleep, knowing that all will be well when you wake, and that you, too, have experienced what it is to sacrifice in the name of love.*

Chelsea saw them through the shadows. Hundreds of them, perhaps thousands, rising through the depths, all in their magnificent raiment. From their lips, she heard the sound of mu-

sic sweeter than any earthly choir, and as the darkness
disappeared and a glorious brightness took its place, she
looked around and saw the wonders of the deep surrounding
her.

She saw the Guardian; the magnificent creature that had
brought her safely into the depths. She saw rainbows sweeping across a sky so blue it could have been poured from
melted sapphires, and the walls of the city rising up around
her, their gleaming towers made of silver and gold.

And she saw Nicolas. Nicolas, upon whose face was a look
of such joy and adoration that Chelsea felt sure the universe
must be able to see it.

I was so afraid I'd never see you again.

Chelsea gazed into his eyes and smiled. *I couldn't leave
you. When I realized how empty my life was, I had to come.
I love you, Nicolas. With all my heart.*

And I you, beloved. His eyes were tender as he bent to
kiss her. *For now and all time.*

Suddenly, Chelsea saw a circle of light that drew closer
and grew ever more radiant until it was nearly blinding. A
figure came into view; a figure standing in a magnificent gold
chariot drawn by white horses. His splendid robes flowed
around him, his hair and beard shimmering with silvery iridescence. His eyes were as blue as a sapphire's heart, and
on his face was a look of such compassion that it brought
tears to Chelsea's eyes.

As humbled as she had been upon entering the Kingdom,
she felt humbler still, in the presence of its king.

*So you have come at last, Chelsea Porter. We have waited
a long time.*

His powerful voice echoed through the depths. Chelsea
glanced at Nicolas, completely at a loss for words. Then,
seeing his encouraging smile, she turned back toward the
light. *Forgive me for . . . taking so long.*

The mighty god nodded his head. *It was necessary that
the decision to come be your own, for your love had to be
strong enough to withstand the ultimate test.*

Will you marry us, Father? Nicolas asked.

I will, but then I must send you both back.

Nicolas frowned. *Send us back? Why?*

Because there is the matter of your child.

Chelsea's hands went automatically to her stomach. *A . . . child?* She glanced at Nicolas in wonder. *Our child?*

For once, Nicolas was completely nonplussed. *What is there to consider, Father?*

The fact that she was conceived both on land and in water gives you the right to choose the place of her birth.

She? Chelsea said, her face alight with joy. *We have a daughter?*

You do. And because of her, my wedding gift to you both is the gift of life, the great god said. *The one you sacrificed to be with my son, Chelsea Porter, and the one you sacrificed, Nikodemus, to allow the woman you loved her freedom. Use your gifts well, my children.*

And then, in front of her eyes, Chelsea saw it all begin to change. The circle of light faded as the mighty Poseidon disappeared, and Nicolas receded into the distance. She was swept up in a vortex of color and sound and sent spinning away from the light.

She heard the sound of the waves in her ears, felt the touch of a hand on her shoulder—and then nothing more.

An impudent seagull wheeled overhead, its noisy cry signaling its presence as it combed the beach below for food. Chelsea stirred, rising from sleep, groaning at the tightness in her chest. She took a breath and drew air, not water, into her lungs. *She was . . . alive?*

"Come back to me, beloved," Nicolas whispered close to her ear.

Chelsea opened her eyes and saw him smiling down at her. She was lying in his lap, still wearing her grandmother's wedding gown. "Nicolas!" she said dreamily.

He bent his head and kissed her softly on the mouth. "You've been asleep a long time."

Asleep? Chelsea stared up at him in bewilderment. Had it all been a dream? It had seemed so real. She remembered walking into the sea, and Lysianassa appearing in the waves beside her. She remembered the Guardian carrying her down into the depths, and the temptation of Sephonia. She remembered the terrible pain as her lungs had filled with water.

"Nicolas, tell me I didn't imagine all that!" she said quickly.

"No, you *did* make the choice to be with me," he told her with a smile. "And everything you experienced was a result of that choice. But because of the strength of our love, we again have our life here together."

Chelsea blinked, not sure *what* to think. She rolled off his lap and slowly stood up. She looked at her fingers and toes, but saw no delicate band of webbing. "What about me? Am I . . . like you?"

"You will always be able to go where I go, beloved." Nicolas got to his feet and brushed the sand from the seat of his pants. "Whether you choose to is entirely up to you. As is the case—" he said, resting his hand on her stomach, "—with our daughter."

Chelsea's face glowed. "Then I didn't dream that either? We're really going to have a child?"

"Yes. One who'll grow up with the kingdom of the sea as her playground and, if she wishes it, the land above it as her home. A home with two people who love her very much."

Chelsea breathed a sigh of deep contentment as she went into his arms. "With two people who love *each other* very much, too," she whispered. "Because I do love you, Nikodemus."

"And I love you, Calida," he said, kissing her eyes, her chin, and then her lips. "Now, and for eternity."

"Calida?" she asked, looking bemused.

"It means 'most beautiful.' "

"Most beautiful." Suddenly, her smile faded. "Lysianassa! Oh, Nicolas, what happened? I saw her fighting with the Sea Witch. She took the most terrible blow. I saw the blood and watched her sink down—"

"Calm yourself, Chelsea. Lysianassa is fine," Nicolas assured her quickly. "It is true, she suffered a grievous injury at the hands of Sephonia, but Asklepios is tending her and she's going to be all right."

"Thank God!" Visibly shaken, Chelsea pressed her face into his shoulder. "It's only because of her that I reached you safely. She came and helped me. She warned me what would happen. And she came between us. If it wasn't for her, Sephonia would have—"

"I know." He pressed his fingers gently to her lips. "I saw all she did for you. All she did for us. And I've already thanked her and assured her that we would see her as soon as she is well enough. But now, we have to start making plans for the future."

"You mean, for the baby?"

"Actually, I was thinking of the step before that," Nicolas said, laughing as he pulled her into his arms. "Poseidon's powers may be recognized from one end of the universe to the other, but I doubt a judge in Boston would consider us legally married."

"I never thought about that," Chelsea said, loving the feel of his strong arms around her. "But you're right. For our daughter's sake, we should see to the proprieties. I'm going to enjoy telling Joe and my friend, Elaine, that we're getting married. Though I suppose I'm going to have to play down the part about you being a prince from a faraway kingdom."

"I would, if I were you." Nicolas chuckled as he kissed the top of her head. "It gets very complicated when you start trying to explain where the palace is!"

Author's Note

∼

Poseidon's Kiss is a work of fiction that draws heavily from Greek mythology, but it is not my intention to suggest that all of the characters in the book are taken from that period.

Zeus, Hestia, Hades, and Poseidon were, of course, four of the original Immortals, and Poseidon *was* a quarrelsome, unpredictable god who sired such unusual offspring as Polyphemus (the Cyclops) and Pegasus (the winged horse). He also sired Triton, Rhode, and Benthesicyme, as mentioned in the story. Nikodemus, however, was created purely from my own imagination, and to the best of my knowledge will not be found on the pages of history anywhere else.

Lysianassa, Amphitrite, and Galatea were written about in Hesiod's *Theogony,* Homer's *Iliad,* and, I'm sure, numerous other works of classical fiction. The Nereids were sea nymphs, the fifty daughters of Doris (an Oceanid) and Nereus (a sea god). They were all beautiful, and all said to be wise in deeds of perfection. Lysianassa, whom I have used as a character in this book, was referred to as "the redeeming mistress," and was known for possessing the gift of prophecy. Whatever other qualities she may possess, however, are strictly of my own making, and I apologize to historians knowledgeable in the field for any erroneous portrayals of her character.

Asklepios is also a recognized character from mythology, though I have likewise imbued him with traits that fit the story. The son of Apollo, Asklepios was the god of healing. He was felled by one of Zeus' thunderbolts, but some believed he achieved immortality as a result.

Nothing is more powerful than the magic of love...

The breathtaking

MAGICAL LOVE

series from Jove

MAGGIE SHAYNE

**"Maggie Shayne dazzles!
She's on her way to the stars."—Suzanne Forster**

*Three hundred years ago, the good citizens of
Sanctuary believed there was a Witch in their midst...*

ETERNITY

Her name was Raven St. James, a woman whose unearthly beauty and beguiling charms inspired rumors of Witchcraft. Only
one man tried to save her from the hangman's noose—Duncan,
the town minister, who thought it strange that anyone could
accuse this lovely and vibrant woman of anything wicked.
Stranger still was the fact that Raven was a Witch. And even
though she held the power to save herself, she could not
rescue Duncan—who died trying to help her...

___0-515-12407-9

INFINITY

For five centuries, Immortal High Witch Nicodimus has been suspended
in an eternity of darkness. His heart was stolen away in the ultimate
betrayal by his love, Arianna.

Now Arianna discovers a way to bring him back. But the power that
returns Nicodimus to her arms also summons an ancient enemy. To
fight this dark danger, they must confront the past—
and reclaim infinity...

___0-515-12610-1

**Available wherever books are sold or
to order call 1-800-788-6262**

SEDUCTION ROMANCE

*Prepare to be seduced...by the sexy
new romance series from Jove!*

Brand-new, full-length, one-night-stand-alone
novels featuring the most seductive heroes in the
history of love....

☐ **HEART OF A WARRIOR**
by Betty Davidson   0-515-13101-6

☐ **NIGHT SHADOW**
by Laura Renken   0-515-13155-5

☐ **TOUCHED BY FIRE**
by Kathleen O'Reilly   0-515-13240-3

☐ **DANGER'S PROMISE**
by Marliss Moon   0-515-13275-6

AVAILABLE WHEREVER BOOKS ARE SOLD OR
TO ORDER CALL:

1-800-788-6262